I0757580

LOVE & BULLETS

"**A Brutal Bunch of Heartbroken Saps** is a hell of a ride. Put on the Elvis tunes, or your best glittery suit, and enjoy Bill's escape from the boys in New York. He's trying to ditch his life of crime but it's pretty hard to do when you have a bunch of stolen money in your trunk and a band of people on your tail. Maybe a woman could save Bill's body and soul, and all that money? Whatever the outcome, Kolakowski's fabulous writing shines and the twists and turns will keep you reading to the very last page. A wonderful, entertaining read.
—**Jen Conley**, author of *Seven Ways to Get Rid of Harry*

"It's no surprise that Nick Kolakowski brought the heat with his latest novel **Main Bad Guy**. The surprise is that you won't know which landed harder: His stripped-down, hard-boiled prose, the explosive dialogue, or the wickedly insane and diabolical humor. Grab hold of this one with both hands and hold on tight."
—**Eryk Pruitt,** author of *Townies* and *What We Reckon*

# LOVE & BULLETS

## MEGABOMB EDITION

WRITTEN & REMASTERED BY

**NICK KOLAKOWSKI**

SHOTGUN HONEY
2021

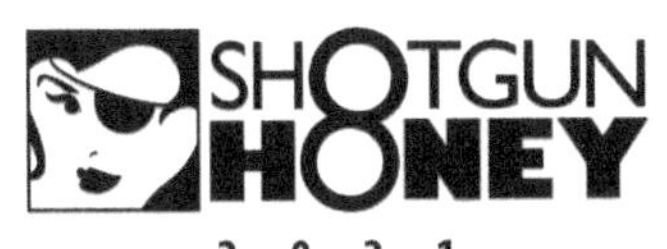

**ALSO BY NICK KOLAKOWSKI**

*A Brutal Bunch of Heartbroken Saps*
*Slaughterhouse Blues*
*Main Bad Guy*
*Boise Longpig Hunting Club*
*Rattlesnake Rodeo*
*Maxine Unleashes Doomsday*
*Absolute Unit*

*To G. (again and always)—*

# LOVE & BULLETS

## MEGABOMB EDITION

---

# A BRUTAL BUNCH OF HEARTBROKEN SAPS

# 1

**LISTEN.**

At some point, a poor sap will look at you and say, "This is the worst day of my life."

But as long as you have breath in your lungs to say those words, you're not having your worst day. You haven't even hit rock bottom, much less started to dig. You can still come back from a car wreck, or that terrifying shadow on your lung X-ray, or finding your wife in bed with the well-hung quarterback from the local high school. Sometimes all you need to solve your supposedly world-ending problems is time and care, or some cash, or a shovel and a couple of garbage bags.

If you see me coming, on the other hand, I guarantee you're having your worst day. Not to mention your last.

Let me show you how bad it can get. How deep the hole goes. And the next time your idiot friend says something about worst days, as the two of you stand there watching his house burn down with his pets and one-of-a-kind porn collection inside, you can tell him this story. It might even shut him up.

Let me tell you about Bill, my last client.

# 2

**BILL AWOKE, AS** one sometimes does, dangling upside-down over a pit, ankles wrapped in heavy chains, sweat stinging his eyes, head throbbing like a dying tooth. He heard a dog bark in the night, and the muted roar of what he guessed was the Interstate, but the only light came from a bare yellow bulb bolted to a corrugated metal shed far below.

Had he ever woken up in a more dangerous position? Bill racked his brain, recalling maybe five years ago when he'd opened his eyes to find both barrels of a 12-gauge shotgun staring back, the trembling weapon brandished by a cuckolded husband. (Only Bill's incredible gift for gab had gotten him out of that situation with his guts lead-free.) Or the time he dozed off behind the wheel and his car plowed into a ditch, the crunch of metal waking him up long enough for the steering wheel to whack him unconscious. He still had the scar on his chin from that one.

Even so, his current situation was a gold-medal contender for Crappiest Ever. His arms, twisted hard behind his back and bound at the wrists, tingled from lack of blood. They had secured the chain around his ankles with a jumbo padlock, hard to pick even if he had the tools, or could bend upwards enough to reach it.

He turned his head away from the bulb, letting his eyes adjust to the dark. Forty feet below, the pit bristled with huge shapes, hard angles; the faint moon glinted silver on the curve of a car windshield. If he fell down there, a piece of rusted-out machinery would turn him into a bit of raw meat on a shish-kabob.

"At least I still have my clothes on," he muttered into the breeze.

"Not for long," came a familiar voice, followed by a high-pitched squeal of laughter. The bartender. Of course. Bill shook his head like a Magic 8-Ball, hard, until memories of the recent past floated to the surface.

# 3

**WHAT DOES THREE** million dollars buy you?

A Ferrari for every day of the week.

A house so big, you would need a megaphone to yell across the living room, unless you lived in New York City or San Francisco, in which case that money might only buy you a luxurious closet in a building with a doorman.

A life of first-class airplane tickets, champagne by the bucketful, steaks carved from cattle massaged and pampered better than a trophy wife.

Freedom, in other words.

When Bill stole those millions from the Rockaway Mob, he thought it would buy him liberation so complete, it would eliminate every concern from his mind, forever. Instead he found himself gripped by a fear so pure, it soaked his shirt with a constant ooze of sweat.

The only thing standing between him and a gruesome death was his spectacularly anal-retentive escape plan. Any enforcer who kicked in the door of his apartment, ready to yank Bill's tongue through a new hole in his neck, would find empty rooms.

Bill's Lexus would stay parked on Ocean Avenue until the city towed it away. Not even his girlfriend had any idea he left.

Bill drove southwest in a secondhand lime-green convertible purchased for cash, with a couple of stolen identities in his wallet and a black canvas duffel bag stuffed with twenty-dollar bills in the trunk. The folding money would cover his expenses until he settled down in his new home in the tropics. The nest egg was safe in an online account.

For the first two days on the road he stopped for nothing except gas and energy drinks that tasted like robot piss. He traded his everyday uniform of expensive suits and designer shoes for a forgettable outfit of faded jeans and a gray t-shirt, although he kept his favorite pair of boots, calfskin leather and suede with tone-on-tone stitching. He had walked a lot of good miles in that thousand-dollar footwear, and he thought they might help him trod a few more.

He also refused to give up his favorite Piaget Altiplano, telling himself the watch would convert to currency if things went sideways on the trip self. It glimmered on his wrist as he drove, every tick of its second hand a blessing. For the first time in his rough life, he had a shot at hours, days, years of peace.

That is, if he lived through this little cross-country drive.

On the second night, finally needing to sleep for a few hours, he paid for a cheap motel room in cash and shoved a chair under the doorknob, caught some shuteye in the bathtub with his pearl-handled revolver within arm's reach.

Once he made it to Texas, he would link up with his contact, El Rey, who would escort him south to Galveston and put him on a fishing boat bound for the Caribbean. A crew down there would give him protection for a nominal fee, all pre-arranged.

On the evening of the third day, with the faint lights of Tulsa in his rearview mirror, Bill reviewed his mental checklist: arrive in Austin, strip the license plates from the car and dump it, and meet El Rey in a barbeque joint a block south of the convention center.

That was the plan, at least. His car had other ideas. As Bill accelerated to seventy, it began shimmying and bucking like a spooked horse, the dashboard dials swinging red. Cursing, slamming his fist against the steering wheel, Bill looked around for a place to turn off.

As if summoned by his panic, a billboard loomed out of the dark. "Eat this 72-OUNCE MONSTER in ONE HOUR," read the red words overlaying a truck-sized hunk of sizzling beef, "and it's FREE at SHARTLEY'S. Take Next Exit."

Roadside restaurants usually have garages nearby, Bill thought. If all the places are closed, I'll grab something to eat, hope the car cools down or whatever. I only need these wheels for another four hundred miles.

To his dismay, the bottom of the exit ramp offered a fat load of nothing. On his left stood a couple of crumbling farmhouses and a boarded-up box store. On his right, in the distance, the glowing speck of the restaurant. At least the car's rodeo leaps had settled down to a steel-rattling tremor.

As Bill eased the car toward the restaurant, his phone rang. That was odd: the device was a burner, purchased for cash in a drugstore near the Holland Tunnel, and the one person who knew the number also knew not to call for another few days. His throat tight, Bill answered: "Yo."

"Surprised?" asked a gravelly voice.

Bill swerved, almost barreling off the road.

"Bill, Bill, Bill." A chuckle like a meat grinder on a low setting. "You really thought you were going to get away with it, didn't you? Dear boy, you're not as slick as you think you are."

"What happened to Jimmy?" And the money Jimmy laundered for me, Bill almost asked.

"Gee, I don't know. He disappeared, I guess. Who knows if we'll hear from him again?"

Jimmy used to joke that one day he would end up swimming with the fishes, but the Rockaway Mob's favorite dumping ground was a weedy stretch of nothing that everybody called The Hole. If you were lucky, the cops found your body before the stray dogs did.

"Tell me why I'm not hanging up," Bill said.

"Pop's pretty wounded." A theatrical sigh. "You know how much it hurts him, you doing something like this? He's blinking something fierce. He put a lot of trust in you."

Just ahead, a red neon sign on a tall pole announced 'SHARTLEY'S.' Below the lettering, a bright yellow arrow pointed out a driveway. Bill turned into it. "I'm hurt that he's hurt," he said. "Maybe it'll help if he considers it a gift to me. For services rendered."

The rough voice broke into rougher laughter: "You think you still have the money? Champ, we got the money. And we got Jimmy, too."

"You're lying," Bill piloted the beast into the nearest parking spot and shut down the stuttering engine, his fingers so numb it took three tries to twist the ignition off.

"I'm not." That laughter again. "It was a big mess. Get ready."

"You won't find me," Bill said, thinking of his trunk with its duffel bag full of money, along with the pistol.

"You're wrong about that one," the voice said, and clicked off.

Bill stared through the windshield at the greasy temple of Shartley's, its neon trim staining the pavement bloody. Through the restaurant's steamed-up windows, he spied the elements of a true dive: the walls covered with battered license plates and beer signs, the booths full of heads-down truckers shoveling food. It looked like the perfect place for cool beer, which he needed in gallons at the moment.

"I'm so sorry, Jimmy," Bill said to the night, and exited the car. From the trunk he retrieved a linen jacket, which he slipped on before unzipping the side pocket of the duffel bag, removing the pistol. After checking the clip, he stuffed the weapon down the back of his jeans, the grip hidden by the edge of the jacket. If they corner you, he thought, save the last bullet for your brain. No way you let them tear you apart.

# 4

**I'VE ALWAYS HATED** the word "killer."

And don't get me started on "hitman."

A few months before we divorced, my now ex-wife asked how I could live with myself. How I could fire a bullet, or press a button, or toss a radio into a bathtub, and end somebody's existence.

If not me, I told her, then something else would have terminated those people: a heart attack, or cancer, or maybe a nice fiery car crash. I'm just the vessel, a way for the natural order of things to express itself. "I don't worry whether I'm a bad man," I added, "any more than a hurricane worries about the damage it causes."

I would have added a little something about the ultimate meaninglessness of existence, except I noticed she'd already fallen asleep. The story of our marriage, in one priceless interaction.

In those corny action movies that play on cable in the wee hours, the killers dress in black suits and carry violin cases heavy with rifle parts. I always preferred to look as messy and forgettable as possible when out on a job, meaning a standard uniform of faded baggy jeans, a flannel button-down over an old t-shirt with a funny but inoffensive slogan, and a pair of thick glasses.

I let my hair grow long, but not rocker-long: just a couple of scraggly inches to suggest a total lack of care.

"If you were interested at all in preserving our marriage," my wife said, toward the end, "you'd spend more time looking presentable. And would it kill you to work out a bit?"

I had spent the previous night in The Hole, dealing with one of my employer's accountants. The man wanted to live, but I had other ideas. Even after I pumped four bullets in his back, he kept crawling through the weeds, as if he had a chance of reaching the road at the end of the field. My fifth bullet won that race.

"Hey, I get exercise," I told her.

She rolled her eyes. "Yeah, right. You do reps with a vodka bottle, is how you exercise."

A week later, she left me. One of my colleagues joked about finishing her off ("How do hitmen get divorced?" he asked, slapping my back. "With a hacksaw!"), but I had no intention of finishing her existence on this miserable rock. What was the point? If she told the world what I did to make ends meet, she would need to explain how she lived with me for so many years without running to the police, and that would make every Thanksgiving really, really awkward for the rest of her life.

I took her departure hard. On a recent morning, while cleaning my guns in the garage, I shoved my newly reassembled .44-caliber revolver in my mouth, loaded, just to see how the barrel tasted as it rubbed against my palate. The gunmetal thick on my tongue, I felt a little tingle of fear in my gut, and that was good. It meant I wanted to live, rather than practice Russian Roulette after breakfast every morning.

As I pulled the pistol out of my mouth, my phone rang. I placed the weapon on the bench beside me and answered it. "Yeah?"

The voice was rocky as ten miles of dirt road: "You available for some tax work?"

"Not for another two months," I said.

"Sorry, wrong number." Click.

I put away my gun-cleaning kit and drove over to Long Island

City, at the edge of the East River, where the industrial yards and ratty Irish bars of my youth had given way to gleaming glass condos and overpriced gastro-hubs. I headed into the Pot O' Gold, the last true bit of scum on this particular toilet bowl, and found a seat across from The Dean, dressed as usual in one of his natty three-piece suits. On the table sat a large plate of shucked oysters, half of them already eaten. I had to hand it to the man: why bother trying to prove your courage in a shootout when you can order the shellfish in an establishment where the cockroaches are big enough to work an NFL defensive line?

"How goes it?" The Dean always sounded like he swallowed a wad of sandpaper every morning, his syllables rough yet velvety.

"Oh, you know, divorced, drinking too much, can't sleep. The usual."

The Dean was not in a joking mood. "Are you becoming a problem?"

"Just to myself," I said. "So what's next? Jimmy's settled."

His eyebrows arched. "Um, Bill's still drawing breath, when last I checked."

"I prefer if you used someone else for that one," I said, and meant it. I'd always admired Bill's disregard for keeping a low profile. You needed a pair of shiny brass ones to go out the door every morning and rip people off while dressed like a magazine model.

The Dean shrugged. "Jimmy tell you what they did?"

"All Jimmy said to me was 'no' and 'I don't want to die.' Like he had a choice. From what you told me before, I know they took some money."

"Oh, they did more than that." The Dean's face reddened. "The last time I met with dear Bill, he had the phenomenal cheek to pickpocket me, like some rube on the street. Specifically, he removed my black titanium credit card, the one with the infinite credit limit. And do you know what he did with that credit card, before taking millions from us?"

"Blew it on hookers who take plastic?"

The Dean paused to slurp down a new oyster, his eyes blazing with rage. "Worse. He donated a hundred thousand dollars online to an organization that helps children with cancer. He knows how much I hate moral quandaries, despite my chosen profession. It's not exactly the sort of sum you can take back, at least without looking like a total scumbag."

"So what did you do?"

"What do you think? I took the money back. Sent the organization a very nice note. Blamed it on the accountant, which is true, in a certain way." Another oyster down the hatch. "But our friend Bill wasn't done yet, no sir. Having donated to cure childhood cancer in our lifetimes, he further abused my poor, suffering credit card by taking Jimmy to lunch at the Caviar Room in Midtown, where they ordered a Balthazar of Château Margaux 2009 for the low, low price of fifty thousand dollars, along with their three-hundred-dollar meals."

"There were a lot of French words in there I didn't understand."

"Château Margaux is a very expensive bottle of red wine, you idiot. Try to keep up."

Although I refused to take crap from just about anyone on the street, I always made an exception for my employer, in light of the enormous amount of money he paid me every few weeks. Not that the cash stopped me from spending a few lovely moments imagining an alligator tearing The Dean apart limb from well-tailored limb.

Turning my head, I flagged the joint's lone waiter, a sad sack of middle-aged flesh named Ivan. I needed my morning alcohol something fierce. "So he took your card, and then…"

"Their very satisfying meal completed, they proceeded across the street to one of our banks, to try and screw us thoroughly." The Dean sighed. "Jimmy could access too many accounts. If the banker hadn't called me right after they left, the money would have been on a round-the-world laundering tour, never to be seen again. Pop is so pissed, we had to give him a shot so he'd calm down."

"Speaking of shots, I need a beer," I told the waiter, who had drifted into our orbit.

"Kinda beer?" Ivan asked.

"Guinness, if you haven't already watered down the keg too much." Once he lurched away, I returned my attention to The Dean, offering up the obvious: "Bill's probably out of the country by now. He's too smart to stick around."

"He was dumb enough to trust in Jimmy's so-called intelligence. We already have two people on his trail, but I haven't heard from them in two days." He shrugged, as if losing a pair of trained assassins was a daily occurrence. Maybe it was, in his life. "So now I send you in. You're my backup. And I expect you to make Bill regret what he did."

"If it's an out-of-town job, I'll need more money."

The Dean smiled wide, exposing his perfect teeth as he went for the kill: "Of course. You need a great divorce attorney, no?"

A day later I found myself on the road, halfway between Who Knows and Who Cares, listening to my ex-wife's Cat Power albums and trying not to cry as I thought about our best moments, like the time she overcame her weak stomach to help me dissolve a mob informant in a bathtub full of acid. Go ahead, call me a wimp: I can kill you thirteen different ways with a penknife.

# 5

**TWO PINTS OF** cheap beer and a shot of engine-cleaner whiskey into his night, Bill found himself less mordant than earlier. The bartender had something to do with his newfound cheer. Raven-haired and dark-eyed, dressed for tips in a pair of tight jeans and a sleeveless shirt, she managed to give as good as she got from the lousy drunks crowding the bar. It was a pleasure to watch her work.

Bill figured the bartender had a lot more patience than he did. If working here meant having to listen to the same annoying pop-country songs on the jukebox over and over and over again, he would have burned the place to the ground a long time ago.

"You're sure patriotic around here," Bill told the bartender, after she finished helping a blind-drunk customer find his dentures on the sticky floor. He pointed to the red, white, and blue paper bunting draped around every window, along with the giant papier-mâché head of George Washington gazing sternly from atop the liquor shelves.

"The Fourth's coming up, we always do a big party," she said. "As if people need an excuse to get smashed. Just look at Gareth over there, the guy I just helped? He's a billion years old, won't buy teeth that fit his mouth, but he'll blow each Social Security check on that bottom-shelf shit."

"Speaking of getting smashed and bottom-shelf shit," he said, tapping the side of his empty pint glass. "You got something better than Bud?"

"Who'd ever want to drink anything other than Bud?" Her innocent look would have made a preacher think grubby thoughts. "Isn't it the best thing ever?"

"You're confusing it with pretty much anything else." A sane part of his brain told him to order a plate of fries or the infamous steak, to absorb some of the alcohol, but Bill ignored it. After that phone call with his former boss, the prospect of food made him feel nauseous.

"I'll check the fridge, see what we have." She grinned and stuck out a hand. "I'm Casey, by the way."

"Rick." They shook. He noticed the way her eyes lingered on his timepiece.

"Nice watch," she said, and winked, in a way that let him know she wasn't someone bowled over by flashiness. He tipped an imaginary hat to her, and she sauntered away.

As he waited for his beer, Bill ran through sums in his head. The duffel bag in the trunk held fifty thousand in twenties and fifties. He had another eighty-two dollars in his wallet. That was enough for a fresh start somewhere, right? On some islands, you could live like a king for thirty bucks a day.

Casey returned with a fresh pint. "Miller Genuine Draft," she said. "Not quite what the doctor ordered, I suspect, but you'll have to drink it anyway."

He took a sip. "I think I'll live."

"So, Rick, you sticking around or passing through?"

He shrugged. "Passing." Provided the car actually starts up, he thought. Don't ask about a garage nearby. Don't advertise your engine trouble unless you have to.

"Heading west?"

He shrugged again.

She pouted a bit. "You're a mysterious man."

"Mystery's an asset in my business."

"What business is that?"

"That's the point, I can't tell you."

"Or you'd have to kill me?"

"That's too high a penalty. I was thinking a good Dutch Rub or something."

Her head jerked back. "Are you some kind of pervert?"

He squinted at her. "What?"

Her voice rose. "What the hell is a Dutch Rub?"

"How old are you?"

She took a step back, horrified. "Are you trying to figure out if I'm *legal*?"

"No, a Dutch Rub, it's a thing, like you take your knuckles, rub them on the top of someone's head, like." He mimed it. "It's an older phrase. Maybe people don't use it as much anymore."

She met his eyes, a slow smile parting her lips. "I know what a Dutch Rub is. I'm just messing with you a little."

He sipped his beer. "You're good at it, but I'm still not telling you what I do. Why ruin a good mystery?"

Her smile widened. "I know all the cops around here. I should let them run your name, Rick, see if you got some outstanding warrants."

Bill had an excellent poker face. "All you need to know is I try to be good, and I've never done anything bad without a really solid reason. Most of the time, I'm a well-behaved boy."

"Well, that's no fun. Anyway, back to my point, if you're staying any length of time, I was going to recommend our fine hotel in this wonderful little town."

"How fine?" Bill glanced down the bar, noticing a couple of locals giving him a hard stare, probably wondering why he wore a decent linen jacket in a bar where the dress code leaned toward faded jeans and baseball caps.

"You won't have to fight the bugs for the bed," Casey said.

He laughed. "Sounds good enough."

"They also have those old vibration things, you know, you put in a quarter and the bed shakes."

"The Magic Fingers."

"Hey, yeah," she winked. "Seems you know something about those."

"I grew up in a motel."

"No crap?"

"Oh yeah. My mom cleaned rooms." If you want to educate a kid fast in the underbelly of the world, set him loose in a twenty-room motel on the Texas-Louisiana border: a new movie of human depravation every night, courtesy of a traveling cast of losers and lunatics. Bill's key lesson from his childhood: never be poor, if you can avoid it.

"Sounds rough."

"Yeah." He wanted to say something more. Having a conversation with a real human being, no matter where it went, made him feel warm and tingly after the past few days of brutal tension. Except the moment he opened his mouth to tell a crummy-hotel joke, a glass shattered at the end of the bar, and they turned to see old Gareth sink his fake teeth into another drunk's neck.

Casey spun on her heel, waving an arm toward the door, where a hulk in a black hooded sweatshirt sat on a small stool that seemed ready to break under his weight. With a shout loud enough to quake the floorboards, the hulk stood and marched for the bar, the crowd scrambling to clear a lane.

The bouncer gripped Gareth's shoulders, and the geezer responded by trying to bite one of his shovel-sized hands. The bouncer's fist rocketed forward, plowing into Gareth's nose with enough force to knock the old drunk clean out of his untied sneakers, which would remain beside the bar for the rest of the evening. Gareth's teeth flew across the room, almost smacking the head of George Washington, who looked nonplussed.

The crowd broke into applause as the bouncer carried Gareth, toothless and shoeless, out the front door. If the old man whacked his head on the doorframe on the way out, well, that was the price you paid for starting a fight in this joint.

Casey tossed a dishtowel to the drunk with the bleeding neck and headed back toward Bill, who had downed his pint. "Big guy," he said.

"That's Rex," she said. "He's my half-brother. Different mom."

"Seems like a good guy to have your back."

"Yeah, helps keep the flies off." She plunked a fresh beer in front of him. "Where you from?"

"Philadelphia."

"Where you headed?"

He shrugged, smirking this time.

"Traveling with anyone?"

He shook his head. "Not yet. Picking up a friend in Austin tomorrow night."

Everything seemed a little too blurred around the edges. Maybe it was the days of driving finally catching up to him, or the alcohol hitting him harder than usual. On a normal night, Bill could down enough beers and hard liquor to stun an adult bull. How odd that a couple of pints made his vision blur so badly.

"You okay, champ?" she asked, smiling sweetly.

His jaw felt a few tons too heavy, dragging his head onto the bar. Casey kept staring at him, her eyes twinkling. He wanted to speak, to tell her that he was finally ready to order food, take a run at the giant steak. Before he could muster the strength to say the words, blackness descended like a curtain.

# 6

**I WASN'T GETTING** any respect from these chumps.

If the billboard advertised seventy-two ounces of steak for free, provided you ate it all in under an hour, I wanted my seventy-two ounces of steak for free, because I had cleaned my plate in fifty-eight minutes and thirty seconds.

"No, you took over an hour, man," said the pimply waiter in the 'SHARTLEY'S' t-shirt. Something in his voice reminded me of the unctuous little midget who had served me divorce papers, and it took every ounce of my self-control to loosen my white-knuckle grip on my fork, which (pro tip) can serve as an excellent close-range weapon in a pinch.

"Fifty-eight minutes," I countered, through a mouth still half-full with slaughterhouse bits. Have you ever eaten four and a half pounds of meat in that amount of time? The family in the next booth kept glancing at me with dawning horror, frightened by the noises of my *enjoyment*, for which I make no apologies: I had a mission to consume some calories, and failure is never an option.

"Sorry, sir," he said, trying to take my empty plate.

I placed a hand on his arm and squeezed—gently, but he still felt it. "What happened to the customer is always right?"

"Not in this town." He offered the saddest little shrug.

I glanced toward the other side of the establishment. Bill had downed only a couple of beers since settling in, and yet his chin hovered maybe two inches off the bar, his eyes locked with laser-like precision on the bartender's chest. Lightweight. The bartender didn't seem to mind the drunken attention, which I found a little odd. Maybe they do things a little differently in the Midwest.

The waiter tried to get away, so I squeezed my hand harder, feeling his bones grate. "Fifty-eight minutes," I told him. "Besides, it sucked. Tasted like shoe leather."

"What did you expect?" the kid whined. His thrashing threatened to disturb the other diners, so I let him go. Besides, it was almost time to go to work. Once he disappeared into the kitchen, I stood and fished in my wallet for five dollars—the exact price of my drink with tax, no tip included—and tossed it on the table before heading for the bar.

Bill knew my face, but with his brain teetering on the edge of system shutdown, he probably wouldn't put up a fight as I escorted him from the building. By morning, I would have his noggin in a cardboard box full of dry ice, tucked safely in the backseat of my car.

From thirty feet away, I watched as Bill's cheek slowly came to rest on the sticky bar. His eyes fluttered closed. Perfect. Everything was going smoothly, for once.

The bouncer ruined it.

A calloused hand the size of a dinner platter thumped on my chest, hard enough to leave a bruise. I looked up at a mountain of a man. "We have a situation," he told me, in a surprisingly high-pitched voice.

"Fifty-eight minutes," I told him. "And I should get a medal for choking down that crap. It was an existential horror."

"Waiter says different," the bouncer said, nodding toward the kid, who stood beside the kitchen doors with a stricken look that suggested he was two seconds away from soiling his tighty whities.

"Punk's a liar," I said, a little louder now. "Or is that the scam you pull here? Claim nobody beats the meat?"

The bouncer looked confused, to put it mildly, and I took the opportunity to remove his hand and step out the front door. No point anymore in grabbing Bill. Too many potential witnesses at the bar had turned to watch the brewing fight, their eyes bright with anticipation. The bouncer let me go, figuring it would prove easier to deal with me outside. Big mistake, as the kids say.

I made it ten feet into the parking lot before the bouncer slapped a hand on my shoulder. As I pivoted around, grabbing his wrist, I thought about my ex-wife telling me I needed to exercise more, that I was losing it. *I don't think so*, I thought as I twisted that wrist, torquing the bouncer's absurdly muscled arm behind his back.

The bouncer mewled and dropped to one knee. I stepped back a little, in case he wanted to risk his elbow by trying to kick my feet out from under me. Instead he kept still, gasping from the pain. It felt good, hearing that sound. I needed victories these days, even small ones.

I turned to the waiter, who had stepped outside with the bouncer, probably excited to watch my mauling. "Fifty-eight minutes," I said. "What am I, a parrot?"

"What?" the waiter said.

"Because you keep making me repeat myself."

"Fifty-eight minutes," he said.

"So what's the problem?" I asked.

His jaw twitched. "What?"

I twisted the bouncer's arm to within a millimeter of snapping like a wet wishbone. "Why are you giving me issues?"

"No reason," he said. "You're not being very nice."

"Have you ever contemplated the size of the universe, kid?" I asked. "Terms like 'nice,' or 'bad,' or 'good,' none of those things mean anything in the grand scheme. It's all just molecules." That philosophical lesson imparted, I leaned toward the bouncer. "If I let you go, we going to have a problem?"

Sweat pouring down his bald forehead, veins popping in his neck, the bouncer growled: "I'm going to kill you."

With my free hand, I reached down to my ankle, drew the small pistol I always kept in a holster there, and pressed the barrel into the top of his head. "Try again," I offered. *"Répétez, s'il vous plait."*

The bouncer said nothing.

"Exactly," I said, and released his arm, taking three steps backwards with the pistol held out in front of me, in case his balls convinced his brain to do something stupid.

The bouncer was clearly in survival mode. He stood, flexing his insulted arm, and offered a look of sullen rage before retreating back toward the restaurant, the waiter scampering in his wake like a kicked lapdog.

I needed to leave before someone called the cops, or the bouncer screwed up some courage and decided to come out here with a gun. On the way to my car, I glanced through the restaurant's windows and saw that Bill had disappeared from the bar. I wondered if someone had dragged him into the bathroom, in anticipation of his stomach hitting the eject button, or if they had tossed him out back.

I started the car and motored behind the restaurant, my headlights illuminating a pair of dumpsters and an irritated busboy trying to smoke a cigarette in peace. Instead of returning to the main road, I took the access lane that led to the parking lot of the shuttered strip-mall next door, wheeled around so I faced the restaurant, and shut off the engine. Sooner or later Bill would emerge, and we would get to work. I had all night, if it came to that.

# 7

**WHEN BILL STARTED** out in the game, he operated on the assumption that nobody would ever understand his trip, so why bother trying to explain himself? As a young hustler, he spent nearly all of his time listening, because people love to talk. If you listen long enough, you can understand how someone thinks, and their life becomes an open book written in 40-point font.

On a long-ago Monday night in an everything-neon sports bar, Bill scanned the crowd and decided on his mark, a guy in a lime-green polo shirt glued to the football game on one of the establishment's many big-screen televisions. All the mark's details added up: The washer-softened tips of the man's shirt collar, the timepiece a passable imitation of a more expensive brand, the soft cheeks indifferently shaved. As Bill knew too well, there is nobody on this planet more vulnerable than a broke man who aspires to luxury.

Bill's own desires ran to sleek black sedans and Japanese whiskey, first-class seats and prime weed. That meant Bill, like any fine young predator, lived through periods of glorious wax followed by humiliating wane. He liked to think that pattern gave him insight into people's hopes and fears.

"So I was laid off a few months ago," Bill said, midway into the conversation he started with George, the mark, by yelling about the unfairness of the game on the screen. That was a safe opening gambit. It seemed as if every other month the economy hit some sort of speed bump, and if the mark hadn't lost a job, he or she knew someone who had.

"That sucks," George replied, less effusive than his puppyish face might have led Bill to expect.

"I know, right? And the bitch of it is, no severance." Bill snorted at the unfairness of it all. "Something in some line of the contract, coming back to bite me in the ass when it really hurts, excuse my French."

"That's all right." Mister Empathy shrugged and sipped his beer, attention slipping. Bill needed to take things to the next level.

"Is it? Good. Because you strike me as a man who likes to tell it as it is." Bill leaned in. "Anyway, it was a little tough there, for a while."

As expected, George grew a little suspicious of where this conversation was headed. He tipped backward a few inches, arms crossed over his chest, squinting in a way that clearly broadcast his thinking: is this punk about to hit me up for cash?

And Bill flipped the script: "Then I stumbled on this thing—no, that's a lie: a friend set me up with it—so I got no money worries, knock on wood." He tapped the bar four times. "Anyway, you got a bet on the game?" He pointed his beer bottle at the screen, where a few oversized monsters in neon spandex were busy breaking the quarterback's ribs over the right to the little brown ball. "I don't think New York's going to make it."

That triggered it: George started speaking at length. If nothing else, he was one of those sports fans who will talk forever about percentages and points and whether a torn tendon will deny a team the chance at a championship. He countered Bill's opinion with such an extensive rundown of the Giants' history that Bill felt his eyelids drooping.

After twenty minutes of babbling about rosters and injuries,

George mercifully switched topics: "How did you get back on your feet?"

"Pull out your phone," Bill said. No matter how desperate and broke their lives, people never discard their small slab of touchable glass. He noted with some relief that George's device was the right make and model.

Bill told George to open the phone's Web browser and type in a certain address, summoning the Website of a small spirits distillery in the great state of Kentucky. He then prompted George to tap on a link near the bottom of the screen, which directed the browser to a list of establishments across the United States that offered the distillery's high-class whiskey. "I convince bars to carry this company's liquor," Bill said. "It's so easy. There's a demand for premium, small-batch stuff, and they give me a pretty good cut."

When George tapped that link, it opened up a pipeline between his phone and a laptop two thousand miles away, the latter controlled by an acne-riddled social disaster named Brian Kennedy, who paused his virtual-warfare game long enough to hit a few buttons and start pumping every byte of George's personal data to a special server.

George, blissfully unaware of the theft, sat there as Bill walked him through every step of the program, from commissions to the types of bars most receptive to Kentucky's finest export. Since Bill's job was to keep the Web browser active for as long as possible, he directed George to tap on link after link. George didn't seem to buy the whole concept of whiskey commissions, but that was okay: the charade was almost over.

"Hey, this is cool. You have a card?" George asked, his voice flat.

Bill most certainly did, complete with the distillery's logo in one corner. "Here you go," he said, flicking one from his shirt pocket.

"I'll look into it," George said, which meant he would never call any of the numbers listed below the logo, which fed into an unchecked voicemail box. The distillery never existed, of course, beyond the Web.

"Sure thing." Like any good shark, Bill's attention had already shifted to richer seas: the fine lady nursing a vodka-and-something at the far end of the bar. She had arrived an hour ago with a roundish gentleman in a sweatshirt and baseball cap, their body language telegraphing first date headed rapidly toward disaster. After a drink, the date had checked his phone and hurried away, leaving her alone.

Bill scanned the curl of blue tattoo peeking from the edge of her t-shirt sleeve, the gaudy boots with chunky heels, and thought: bohemian, brilliant, bored by anyone who couldn't keep up with the conversation. Fortunately, Bill saw himself as someone who specialized in intellectual types.

"I know that lady down the bar. Would you excuse me a moment?" Bill asked. George answered with a distracted grunt, his attention already drifting back to the television.

Bill clapped him on the shoulder and, grabbing his shoulder bag, headed off at a confident clip for his new target. Her head was tilted away from him, her eyes focused on her phone-screen bubbling with green and blue text messages. Probably picking over the smoking remains of her date with her friends, he guessed. Her distraction worked in Bill's favor, allowing him to reach into his bag and extract a dog-eared paperback, its spine cracked by multiple readings: Haruki Marakami's "The Wind-Up Bird Chronicle."

He dropped the book beside her stool, the noise of its impact drowned out by the football games blaring at full blast, and tapped her on the shoulder. When she looked around—her eyes blue as her tattoo, electric—he pointed at his feet and smiled.

"Excuse me," he asked. "Did you drop this?"

She laughed. "Does that one work often?"

Bill took a step back. "I don't know what you're talking about," he said, off-balance for a moment. "You mean that's not your book?"

She shook her head. "By the way, nice job you pulled on that dude over there."

He almost walked out. She could have been a cop, or some sort of white-hat hacker eager to take him down. Witnessing his slick trip detonated below the waterline, with one sentence, stunned him into silence.

"Listen," she said, reading his mind. "I know you're thinking 'police,' but I'm not police. You don't have to take my word for it." She reached into her tight designer jeans, slipped out a small card that she passed across the beer-sticky table. "There's a number on that card. Give it a call, if you want to take your hustle to the next level. Trust me, somebody actually checks the messages."

"What's your name?" he asked.

"Fiona," she said, and smiled at him, showing teeth. "I'll make you so much money it's ridiculous. You'll never have to rip off another aging frat-boy again."

# 8

**DANGLING HIGH IN** the air, Bill took slow breaths as he brushed his fingers over his wrists, feeling toothed plastic: plastic restraints, and not the heavy-duty riot cuffs that cops liked to use. At least he had that going for him. The bastards who hung him here had taken his watch and wallet, and under normal circumstances that would have sent him into a spasm of boiling-hot rage. Except rage wouldn't help him escape, would it?

Instead he focused on taking six deep breaths a minute, while he reviewed everything he needed to do next.

From a young age, Bill had been obsessed with escape artists. While the other kids in his school burned their waking hours on video games, Bill taught himself to pick a pair of fur-lined handcuffs his mom discovered in one of her motel rooms. Within a few weeks, Bill could pop those cuffs in three seconds with a twisted paperclip. That goal accomplished, he graduated to jiggling open car doors with a coat hanger, which opened up a world of opportunities for fun and profit.

As an adult, for purely professional reasons, he never lost that interest in slick methods of escape. So he knew that plastic cuffs had one glaring vulnerability.

Bill rotated his forearms until the cuffs stretched taut between his wrists. Hopefully the locking mechanism was at the right angle. They had done him a favor by taking his jacket, because the fabric would have blunted some of the force he needed to apply. Lifting his arms away from his body, straining every muscle in his shoulders, he brought his wrists down hard on his tailbone.

No luck.

He did it again.

Nothing. Damn it.

"What are you doing up there?" Casey asked. "Whacking off?"

"You wish."

A click, followed by a flashlight beam in his face, making him squint. "You better let me go," he said into the glare, because begging was never his style.

At the blurry edges of the light, Casey tilted her head, curious. "Why?"

"Um, because I'll kick your ass?"

She laughed. "You want bravery, it comes just before 'bullshit' in the dictionary." The flashlight clicked off, Casey evidently satisfied by the state of his tie-down.

Bill gave it three minutes by the count in his head before he resumed slamming his taut wrists against his backside. This time it worked. The plastic, subjected to the right amount of lateral force and velocity, snapped. His arms dropped down.

Task completed, he counted off another minute, listening for any movement from Casey. Had she heard the cuffs snap? Based on the crunch of gravel, she lurked directly beneath him. He heard a faint creak that might have been her derrière settling into a chair, and decided it was time to move (stealthily, old boy, stealthily) to stage two of his great escape.

This next part would require a higher level of physical effort. Clenching his abdominals, Bill strained to curl his body so his head was level with his torso, but after a few seconds his muscles quivered like gelatin and he sagged down again. His skull throbbed. Whatever they had slipped into his drink, it produced far worse than your garden-variety hangover.

As he hung there, getting his breath back, his eyes adjusted a little more to the darkness. He could see that he hung from a gantry, a tall steel frame designed to hoist very heavy things like shipping containers. The shackles that bound his ankles connected to a thicker chain, itself wound through an enormous pulley attached to the gantry's crossbar. Shifting his gaze down, he found the dim shade of Casey in a folding chair beside the gantry's right pillar, the faint cherry of a cigarette flaring beside her head. That little bit of light would destroy her night vision, which was fine with Bill. She had no idea he snapped the riot cuffs…

"That's a neat trick," she called up.

"What?" he said.

"Snapping the riot cuffs."

"How about you let me down, so you can put another pair on?"

"How about I take some target practice with your pistol here?" A silver flicker as she waved his gun over her head.

"Not very sporting," he said, in his cheesiest British accent. Swinging his arms back and forth a little made his body sway like a pendulum, the chain creaking softly. If she left for a few minutes, he could swing harder, his momentum carrying him to a gantry pillar, and…

Then what?

He had no key for the padlock binding his ankles, and no tools to pick it. And if you slip free of the chain, he thought, you'll still have to face your favorite bartender taking shots at you from the ground, while you try to inch your way down a gantry not built for climbing. I'm so screwed.

"What do you want?" he yelled down to her.

"We already got the money from your trunk," she said. "We bet you got more where that came from. You give it up, we'll let you go."

Yeah, right. Casey and her partners in crime, whoever they were, would kill him the second he handed anything over.

Not that he had anything left to give. "How do I know you'll let me go?"

She sounded offended. "You calling me a liar? Somebody driving around with that much money in cash probably doesn't want the cops finding out about it, I'm guessing. We know you won't report it. Why wouldn't we let you go?"

"Let me make you a counteroffer," Bill said, summoning up every spare ounce of toughness into his voice. "You let me walk, with my money, and maybe the people I work for won't feed you to the dogs while you're still alive."

"Who do you work for?"

"Some very bad people who're going to miss that money."

"Yeah? If that's true, why didn't you have security?"

"Ever heard of keeping a low profile? That's how couriers roll."

"I don't believe you," she said, sounding a little unsure.

"Whatever," he said. "You've bitten off way more than you can chew. Those dogs will swallow you right down, though." He swiveled his knees, rotating his body on the chain, so he could scan the night beyond the junkyard. From deep in the murk came a white flash, which grew over the course of a few seconds into a pair of headlights cutting past the black shapes of trees. "Somebody's coming," he announced.

"What?" Casey stood and walked to the chain-link fence that bound the property.

"Maybe those are the cops," Bill said.

"Oh, those aren't the cops."

The headlights ate up the yards, rocketing straight for them. "Maybe they're friends of mine," Bill said, wanting to scare Casey—except he was probably right. The idea froze his guts solid.

**9**

**THE FOUR-ODD POUNDS** of red meat in my stomach pressed against my spine like a bowling ball every time I slammed the gas pedal. That wasn't a complaint, mind you. It felt good to ingest a huge load of fat and salt, even if it meant my colon would end up fighting a real Battle of the Bulge in a few hours.

Instead of killing myself by jamming a pistol in my mouth and painting the ceiling with my brains, maybe I could do it at a more stately pace, by eating myself to death.

From my surveillance post beside the shuttered strip mall, I watched as the bartender's truck pulled up behind the restaurant. The kitchen door popped open, its antiseptic light framing the unmistakable silhouette of my friend the bouncer. Hopping out of the truck, the bartender helped the bouncer lift something heavy into the backseat. The bouncer headed back inside, and she drove away. Headlights off, I followed.

The two-lane took us parallel to the Interstate, into a dark backcountry of tombstone cottages and the occasional gas station. There was nobody else on the road, so I let her lead a full quarter-mile. We had gone five miles when my phone, nestled in its slot on the dashboard, rang its merry little tune.

I swiped the device alive and hit the speaker button. "Yeah?" I asked.

"Status?" The Dean's unmistakable voice inquired.

"You wouldn't believe me if I told you."

The truck turned left on an unmarked turnoff, bouncing down a narrow road through the woods. I slowed a little before following.

"Do tell," The Dean offered.

"Your boy's been kidnapped by other parties."

Stunned silence. "What do you mean?"

"Your boy stopped in a honky-tonk bar for a drink, and the locals nabbed him. He's in some bartender's truck, probably being taken to some chainsaw cannibal's lair. Hopefully they have the good grace to kill him before they eat him, you know what I mean?"

I grinned, picturing the confusion on the other end of the line. Whatever you think about gangsters, at heart they're businessmen, not much different from anyone who puts on suit every morning and heads into an office. Sure, they might prefer settling disputes with a couple of bullets and a barrel of gasoline as opposed to a passive-aggressive email, but they still expect business to run in predictable ways.

"Whatever happens, I don't care," the voice said, "so long as you follow the contours of the agreement. Is that understood?"

"Sure," I said. "Who doesn't want a severed head of their enemy under the Christmas tree? Look, I know you really loved that Peckinpah movie, but trust me on this one: with the ice, you have, like, a day before the smell gets unbearable."

"Your mouth is going to get you in trouble one of these days," he offered. "Any sign of my other hunters?"

"Nope. When it comes to Bill-whacking, it's just me and the voices who live in my head. Doesn't that make you feel so confident?"

"If you do see them, and they're following through on their mission," he hissed, "you are not to engage, understood?"

"Okay, mom." I shot back. "Got to go." I disconnected the call. The trees hemming the lane fell away, revealing hilly grassland lit gray by the moon. I tapped the brakes to give myself even more distance from the truck, which slowed as it approached what looked like an industrial zone, its headlights glinting off a chain-link fence.

I yanked my wheel hard to the right, sending my car off the road and into the tall grass. Shutting off the engine, I climbed out and opened the trunk, where I kept one of my favorite toys hidden beneath a plastic sheet. Ten years ago, I might have parked and crawled a few hundred yards through the grass to reach the target, dirtying my clothes and forcing me to get a little too personal with any creepy-crawly that decided my pant-leg looked like a pretty good place to spend the night. Now I could take to the sky like Superman. A tiny, slow Superman that ran on batteries.

If you think drones are something used only by the U.S. military to vaporize cave-dwelling terrorists and the goats they love (you have to feel a little sorry for the goats; they didn't sign up for that shit), you are sorely mistaken. It takes three clicks and fifteen seconds to purchase a top-of-the-line quad-copter from your friendly online retailer. After my personal air force arrived on my doorstep in a big cardboard box, I shelled out a couple hundred bucks to an overeager Russian kid in Brighton Beach to wire an aftermarket goodie to its frame.

After clicking the drone on, I used the app on my phone to send it aloft and west, toward the distant fence. Its camera broadcast real-time video to my screen in luminescent shades of night-vision green.

Beyond the fence, a huge gantry loomed above a pit filled with junked cars. I saw Bill's body floating in the air beneath the gantry's crossbar, suspended by a long chain, and the bright smudge of the bartender pacing the edge of the hole. Despite the drone's small size, its motor was loud as a buzzsaw at close range, so I kept it a hundred feet overhead. Even from this altitude, watching Bill struggle to break free was pure comedy gold.

A loud roar behind me. I ducked behind my sedan, drawing the pistol from my ankle holster, as a pair of headlights sliced through the woods. The car nearly airborne as it hit rocks and ruts at seventy-five, barreling straight for the industrial zone. I glanced over my trunk in time to see a familiar face at the wheel, her face hard with some high-octane mix of determination and fear. Or maybe it was embarrassment, given how her little jalopy was a particularly obnoxious shade of yellow: the kind of wheels you drive only when you can't rent or carjack anything else.

# 10

**AS THE CAR** barreled down the road, Casey stepped to the fence, stuck the barrel of the pistol through it, and fired seven times. Bill knew that handguns sucked at hitting moving targets over long distances, but Casey seemed professional in how she spaced out her shots, breathing and re-centering between each one.

The car kept coming. Bill took the opportunity to twist his legs back and forth, making the chain sway in an ever-wider arc.

Casey tried firing an eighth time and the hammer clicked on an empty chamber. Tossing the pistol aside, she sprinted along the edge of the fence, pulling the glowing rectangle of a phone from the back of her jeans. She disappeared into the dark without sparing him so much as a second glance.

Bill's swinging carried him up, up until his outstretched fingers scraped the edge of the gantry's right pillar. On the next circuit, he managed to wrap his hands around the metal and hold on, his lower back howling in agony. If he managed to get out of this alive, he would need one hell of a chiropractor to knock his spine back into place.

The car smashed through the fence, skewing right at the last moment to avoid the pit. Its front bumper stopped a foot from the gantry's base, a snarl of chain-link under its tires, and the driver's door swung open, a shield for the driver who ducked out low behind it, pistol-barrel atop the open windowsill.

In the reflected glow of the headlights, Bill recognized the curve of the driver's head, the hair. He stayed very quiet and still, wondering what would happen next. Surely she'd seen him, right? Of all the people affiliated with the Rockaway Mob, why would they send her?

"I see you," Fiona said, peering over the door.

Bill said nothing. Redo the equation, he thought. Considering how we broke up, why *wouldn't* the Rockaway Mob send her to chop my head off?

"What are you, mute?" She glanced up at him.

"Hi," he said.

"What're you doing up there?"

"Oh, just hanging around."

"I ought to shoot you just for that," she said, flicking her pistol toward him.

"The lady went that way," he said, jabbing his chin. "Why don't you chase her?"

"The one who strung you up?"

"Uh, yeah."

"Kinky."

"Do not even start. You here to kill me?"

She shrugged. "Those are my orders."

"At least get me down from here, so I can die on my feet," he said.

"Or you can try to escape, right? Let me clear first," she stood and ran for the cover of the gantry. A few yards away stood a pair of crumpled shipping containers, and she darted there next, pistol leveled at the night beyond the pit.

"There should be a control panel or something," Bill offered. "This thing is on a winch."

"What did I say about letting me clear?" Fiona circled behind the containers before returning to circuit the pit, taking her time, being careful—Bill starting to think she was screwing with him, letting him dangle, just like old times. When she returned, she stuffed her pistol into her waistband, opened a box attached to the gantry's left pillar and threw a lever.

With a low whine, the motorized pulley began to creep along the crossbar, yanking Bill with it. Once he passed over the crumbling edge of the pit, Fiona pulled another lever. He descended to the ground, swinging like a meat pendulum.

When Bill's outstretched hands brushed *terra firma*, Fiona cut the motor and stepped toward him, picking up with one hand a monster pair of bolt-cutters that someone had abandoned beside the pit. Still upside-down, he scooped a handful of dust, readying to toss it in her eyes.

Fiona was too smart for that trap. Rattlesnake-quick, she leapt forward, her free hand flashing metal, a handcuff snapping hard against his left wrist. No flimsy plastic riot cuffs for this lady. Before he could do so much as yelp, she had not only locked his left wrist to the right, but jerked his arms behind his back. The sand went down his sleeve.

"Not again," Bill snarled.

With Bill trussed like the world's ugliest holiday turkey for the second time that night, Fiona went to work on the chain around the padlock. "My orders were to bring you back to New York, your head packed in dry ice," she said. "I got the box and the ice in the trunk, and a hacksaw."

"Lovely."

"Then I thought: if I kill you, I'll have deprived the world of your endless wit." She paused to squeeze the bolt-cutters, and the chain snapped. His freed legs hit the ground in a cloud of dust.

"I like where your head's at." Bill said, deadpan, as she gripped him by the handcuffs and pulled him upright. Figuring if he knocked her off her feet, he could find the handcuff key and escape in her car, Bill tried for a sweeping kick—only to have Fiona block his leg with her own, before slamming her heel into his ankle.

Bill crashed to the dirt, Fiona's knee in his back, the cold muzzle of her gun jammed hard against his neck.

"You remember that night in Newark?" she asked. "By the stadium?"

He nodded.

"You want the same thing?"

He shook his head.

"Then stop pretending you can fight."

The darkness made it hard to read her face. His thoughts collided like a pair of out-of-control trailer-trucks on a highway, leaving confused wreckage all the way down the median. Fiona the loyal soldier, double-crossing Pop? Fiona the hardcore killer, who maybe still had feelings for him? The uncertainty made his aching head throb harder.

She hoisted Bill to his feet again, braced him as he shook the tingling from his legs. Below the rough chorus of insects, he heard a faint buzzing. "What's that sound?" he asked.

She shrugged. "Maybe the electrical box. Let's try and focus here, sweetie: what weirdness have you gotten sucked into?"

"I was hoping you'd know better than I would," he said, stepping toward the pit beneath the gantry. It seemed bottomless, its rough throat stuffed with at least a dozen cars he could see, along with chunks of concrete and rebar, an old fridge, wrecked engine bits. What the hell was this place?

"Come on," she said, hustling him toward her yellow jalopy, which Bill recognized as a model with zero pickup under the hood, a fact that could lead to real problems before the night was out. From the direction that Casey had run, he saw a blaze of headlights cresting a hill: three vehicles, powered by roaring engines, charging hard for them.

# 11

**I'D ALWAYS APPRECIATED** Fiona's style: tough, disciplined, with a wildness that came out at odd moments, like when she decided to ram that fence with her car. The bartender fled across the fields, and I sent the drone to follow her progress, my finger hovering over the digital button on my phone screen that would deploy the little goodie screwed to the drone's underside.

I kept glancing between the drone-view on my phone and the industrial zone, where the headlights of Fiona's car illuminated Bill descending from the gantry, still alive. Call me crazy, but usually you kill someone before they have any chance to escape or kill you in return. Next Fiona helped Bill to his feet, which was weirder.

When The Dean talked about sending two guns after Bill, he neglected to drop Fiona's name. I wondered whether her partner was still alive. Probably not. Although I'm not the sharpest knife in the drawer, I know an elaborate double-cross when I see one.

On my phone, I saw the bartender stop and wave her lit phone over her head. In the distance, the bright blooms of three SUVs angled toward her. Hey, it was a party now. I brought the drone around in a wide arc, lowered its altitude by fifty feet, and sent it buzzing after the vehicles as they headed for Fiona and Bill.

No matter what happened, I was going to need Bill's head.

What has two thumbs and will need to make alimony payments? This guy.

# 12

**"GET IN THE** car," Fiona said.

"What happened to your Mustang?"

"Crashed it. Long story. Get in."

"What's this delightful color supposed to be, Baby Shit Yellow? Maybe I'm better off on foot." Bill glanced away from the inbound headlights, toward the inviting darkness on the other side of the pit, and realized that was a stupid idea. How far could he run before these new vehicles caught him? Twenty yards? Forty?

Half-crouched behind her open driver's door, Fiona clicked the hammer back on her pistol. "They'll make you squeal like a pig."

"Then get these cuffs off me. I can help."

She rolled her eyes. "You're not exactly a great shot, dear."

"That's not what you used to say." Figuring she was too distracted by the incoming cars to swat him in the back of the head, Bill squatted down, placed his fists on the dirt, and, with a few painful contortions, worked his cuffed arms from behind to front. Standing again, he opened the rear door of the car and ducked inside, figuring that he could increase his life expectancy from five minutes to maybe a couple hours if he stuck close to Fiona. Through the windshield, he saw a pair of headlights break away from the main grouping and drift right, disappearing behind a small hill.

Fiona leveled the pistol at the closest truck and fired off a clip, ducked to reload. The side mirror beside her head dissolved in a spray of metal and safety glass, followed a quarter-second later by the commanding boom of a high-velocity rifle.

The lead truck arrived at the fence and skewed broadside, revealing a mud-splattered Sheriff's logo on its door. An amplified voice bellowed: *"You're under arrest."*

"Oh bullshit." Diving behind the wheel, Fiona twisted the key and slammed the gas, rocketing the car backwards. Just to raise the difficulty level of the escape, she poked her left arm out the window, firing the pistol in the direction of the Sheriff's truck. Another rifle-boom, and the windshield cracked into a spongy mess, Fiona cursing as she shook glass-bits from her hair.

"This is not my night," Bill offered from the backseat, peeking up in time to see the second truck ram the fence to their left, crumpling it.

"Shut up," Fiona suggested. "That bag at your feet. Give me a clip."

Bill opened the Louis Vuitton bag in the footwell, found a pair of ammo clips nestled beside her cute purple wallet and a dog-eared copy of Anaïs Nin, and handed them over. He watched with no small appreciation as Fiona, one hand never leaving the wheel, popped out the pistol's empty clip, stuffed the weapon grip-up between her thighs, slammed a fresh magazine home, and cocked it.

Turning back to the bag, Bill rooted for a handcuff key or even a paperclip, finding nothing. Damn.

With the car outside the fence, Fiona twisted the wheel into a reverse power-slide, pistol out the window and firing again at the two trucks as she shifted into drive, foot on the gas and headed down the dirt road. Bill upright in the backseat wondering about that third truck, where was the third truck, as something gray flickered in the side window closest his head.

The third truck, headlights off, barreled out of the black to smash head-on into the yellow car's flank, Bill's world shattering in a screech of metal.

# 13

**YOU DON'T JUST** wake up one day and decide to rip off the Rockaway Mob, not unless you have a death wish. Bill had no such thing. If you put a gun to his head (and a lot of people would end up doing just that) he might have blamed his actions on that ultimate cliché, his nature. Or as he once said to Fiona: once a hustler, always a hustler.

Soon after Fiona brought him onboard, a couple of scary gentlemen escorted Bill into a sleek silver car and drove him down to Bay Ridge, where enormous houses enjoyed sweeping views of the strait between Brooklyn and Staten Island. They parked in front of a Tudor Revival mansion with an awe-inspiring lawn, and gestured for Bill to head inside alone.

The Dean, dressed in a three-piece pinstripe suit in midnight blue, met him in a foyer the size of an aircraft hangar. "Illuminate me with your wit," he said in greeting.

"What?" Bill's head swiveled from the crystal chandeliers, to the Picasso drawing framed on the wall, to the Persian rug thick enough to tickle his ankles.

"Tell me something funny, hopefully a little weird. Astound me with your creativity."

"Um, everybody you kill on Christmas has to serve you in the afterlife."

The Dean chortled. It sounded like a truck engine trying to turn over on a cold day. "Nicely odd," he said. "I appreciate the effort. Everybody else in our little organization, they just want to talk numbers and beefs. They have no *joie de vivre*, you understand me?"

Bill shrugged.

"Excellent. I want you to meet Pop."

They headed upstairs, to a cavernous bedchamber retrofitted as a brightly white hospital room, every angle draped in clear plastic and filled with beeping equipment. A pair of nurses, heads together, whispered in the corner. In the center of the space, in a bed larger than Bill's apartment, lay a skeletal man wired into a respirator.

"Say hello," The Dean ordered.

Bill stared at the shriveled body in its thick blue robe, the thin chest heaving with every pulse of the machines, the left eye covered with a cotton patch. The right eye, green and bright as an emerald, blinked rapidly.

"You're being rude," The Dean said, tapping Bill on the shoulder. "Say hi."

"Hi?" Bill offered.

"Good. He blinked 'hi' back," The Dean said. "Pop, this is Bill. He's an expert in manipulating people and computer systems in order to earn us significant revenue. I feel he'll be a real asset."

A minute of frantic blinking from the man in the bed.

"What did he say?" Bill asked.

"He said, in Morse, 'I don't care what he does, so long as we kill those inbred fuckers down in Brighton like we planned.' He is a very focused individual, Pop."

The Rockaway Mob was not your usual crew of goons. They were smart and accomplished men—real-estate developers, hedge-fund managers, and a certain dapper academic—who had joined forces after Hurricane Sandy raked the city's waterfronts to tatters. At first they rebuilt houses with shoddy materials, took kickbacks from the contractors, and laundered the cash through their existing businesses.

The scheme worked well for everyone, until a few ripped-off chumps threatened to talk to the police. Instead of deploying an army of lawyers to meet this new threat, the Rockaway Mob hired some top-shelf muscle whose idea of conflict mediation was a blowtorch and a pair of tongs. By the time the cops found the first bodies in the marshland behind the airport, the Mob had already diversified into protection, murder-for-hire, arson, and anything else that paid cash and resulted in bloodshed. They had looked into the abyss and found the view pretty fine.

Pop was the key element in the Mob's decision to crank its violence dial to 11. Some people said he had learned his trade among hardcore Boston crews; others claimed he was the head of a Sicilian *cosca* hiding out in America. If you believed one set of stories, a bullet had paralyzed everything except his right eye; one night over drinks, The Dean suggested a jilted woman had driven a knife into Pop's skull. The only thing the Mob needed to know was that Pop would lend his army of very bad people to your cause, so long as you coughed up a quarter of your revenues.

For his part, Bill did his best to avoid the heavy stuff. He ran insurance scams and quiet info-hacks, with a little sports book to keep his ear to the street. His former partner in crime, Brian, had wrapped a Porsche around a tree, an ending that made a few cops regain their faith in karma while leaving Bill depressed. Brian, in accordance with his last wishes, was buried with a bottle of Jim Beam in his hand, headphones over his ears blasting GG Allin as they lowered the coffin into the hard Michigan soil.

After that, Bill found himself mired in low-grade depression. He spent most of his days at a corner table at the Sea Shack, a little seafood restaurant on Rockaway Beach Boulevard, a ragtag strip of Chinese restaurants and liquor stores near the oceanfront. The servers knew to keep the calamari and coffee coming all day.

"It's not exactly caviar and Cristal every day of the week,"

Bill told Fiona around that time. "But we're making thoroughly decent cash."

"It's nice to know a girl could always do worse," she replied, smacking him lightly on the cheek.

Earning screw-you money for the first time in his life, Bill bought the first of several really nice timepieces, and a collection of bespoke suits. He would drive into Manhattan and sit with his chosen tailor in a cubbyhole of an office off Madison Avenue, watching the man's calloused hands at work. The tailor bemoaned his dying art, how no teenagers wanted to spend sixteen hours a day in a hot and windowless shop, learning to build the perfect two-piece. Bill chose the same ultra-fine wool as his tailor's other clients, the titans of industry and the late-night talk show hosts, because it cost three thousand dollars a yard. None of the new duds quieted the storms building in his head, although he did look fantastic in the mirror every morning.

On weekends, he and Fiona drifted through Chelsea warehouses filled with odd and colorful artworks, underground clubs off cobblestone streets, hole-in-the-wall restaurants where the chef killed an octopus live at your table. On Sunday mornings in her apartment, as he gazed into the white sun streaming through the skylight above her bed, the same thought kept surfacing: *I made it, but at what cost?*

But if Bill had to point to the moment that everything finally curdled, it was the morning the shabby guy walked into the Shack.

With his stained khakis and wide-brimmed hat, the man blended into the eatery's usual clientele of sunburned hipsters and tourists about as well as a pit-bull in a nursery school. He stank of trash left in the sun, and yet something about his bearing—the squared shoulders, the regal tilt of his chin—stopped the waiters from blocking his path as he walked across the restaurant to Bill's table.

Leaning back against the wall, Bill slipped a hand into the left pocket of the suit jacket he always wore, cocked the hammer of the silver .22 he hid there. Without a word, the shabby guy took a seat across from Bill, who spied the brownish-red bandana peeking out from under the crown of the hat. Bill had spent enough time around head wounds to know drying blood when he saw it.

"You know who I am?" the man asked.

Bill usually expected that question with some anger behind it, punctuated by a fist rocketing at someone's head, but this dude only sounded tired and a little sad.

"No," Bill said.

The man glanced at Bill's pocket. "You can put that away. I'm not here to do you harm."

"That's great." Bill's hand stayed on the pistol. "Now what's your name?"

"The Ghost of Christmas Past," the man said, and grinned, exposing some less-than-sterling dental work. "I was a short-con wizard, just like you."

Bill shrugged, playing it cool, wondering if this was the weirdest undercover cop in the history of mankind. "I have no idea who you're talking about."

"I even sat in that seat." The Ghost chuckled. "You think the mad professor set you up here because of the food? The whole kitchen is on his payroll."

"Tell me something I don't know."

The Ghost sighed. "Nothing, I guess." He leaned back in his chair, scanning the crowd, and something in his distant gaze reminded Bill of a kid staring at fish through aquarium glass. "I was just going to the beach, figured I'd stop by and see some old haunts. What's your plan?"

"Huh?"

"You know, for life. Or when you were a little boy, did you always dream you'd be sitting in a beachside bar somewhere, thinking about the best ways to take money from idiots?"

"I don't remember," Bill said, and that was true. Who cared about childhood dreams, anyway?

"Then I'm the Ghost of Christmas friggin' Future, too," the Ghost said. "And I'm here to tell you there's no big score at the end of it all." His eyes hardened into small stones. "You think you're too smart, too handsome, too polished to do anything but make it big. Except it doesn't work like that. I was smarter and better-looking than you, and I still ended up in a gutter. So get out of here. Do anything else."

"I'm going to take issue with the 'handsome' part," Bill said, trying to ignore his skin crawling into gooseflesh. "Why don't you get out of my face?"

"Go ahead, don't listen," the Ghost replied. "Just you see." He stood and left, never looking back, leaving no sign of his presence except for a single drop of dark blood on the far side of the table. When the waitress, arriving with a fresh coffee pot, drew a rag from her apron to wipe it away, Bill stopped her with a raised hand. The sight of that black spot made his stomach churn, and yet he couldn't stop looking at it.

There were no lifeguards on Rockaway Beach after Labor Day, and precious few swimmers. The best anyone could figure, the shabby guy waded into the surf until the current lifted his feet off the ocean floor. The cops found his body washed up two miles away. The tabloids reported no suicide note, which made sense to Bill, who knew the corpse was the message: there was no retirement from their line of work.

A month later, Bill started ripping off his bosses. Just a little bit at first, no more than ten dollars here, a hundred dollars there. He knew that they knew about it, and he knew they considered it acceptable for employees to skim off a little bit of cream every month. When the time came, Bill felt only the slightest hesitation about asking Jimmy to help him take a lot more. His escape strategy was flawless, right?

If you want God to laugh, tell her your plans.

# 14

**YET AGAIN, BILL** woke up in chains.

He was never, ever going to get used to this.

Although his arms and legs ached, nothing felt broken. Leaving his eyes closed, Bill explored the space with his ears and nose. He smelled damp and mold, heavy over the faint odor of old shit. He heard water dripping, the faint rumble of a truck, someone else breathing softly.

He cracked his eyelids slightly and saw cracked concrete walls, windowless, and a steel door. The room lit by a bare bulb overhead. Clearly not anyone's living space, unless they had a North Korean army interrogator for a personal decorator.

On his left, Fiona sat chained to a sturdy metal chair, staring at him with sun-boiling fury. She seemed okay, aside from a few scratches on her head and the beginnings of a nasty bruise on her neck. "You know what I said earlier, about not killing you?" she said sweetly.

He opened his eyes wide. "I remember."

Her eyes narrowed. "I'm seriously rethinking that," she snarled.

"I'm sure. Let's just focus on getting out of this alive, okay?" Bill evaluated their restraints. Fiona's chair was bolted to the concrete. They had bound her arms to the back of the chair with duct tape, and handcuffed her wrists. More tape fixed her shins to the chair's front legs. Meanwhile his friend the bartender must have told someone about his escapist skills, because they had mummified his legs, arms, and torso in what felt like fifty pounds of stainless-steel chain, held in place by two padlocks.

Bill flexed his muscles, feeling for any slack in chains, finding none. "By the way," he said, trying to leaven the mood. "How did you know I was heading south?"

"You remember like six months ago, we were in bed one morning, just sort of lounging around, and we got to talking about how we'd disappear if we had to?"

"Oh no."

Fiona's lips twitched as she struggled not to grin. "You said you'd drive to Texas, hook up with El Rey, head for some island, pay some scary group of people to watch your back. I was just following your footwork. On a scale of zero to ten, with ten being 'hardest to find,' like harder than Osama bin Laden, finding you was like…"

"Don't say it."

She flashed her teeth. "Negative two."

"Shut up." His cheeks flushed red. "Were you alone?"

"They sent Watanabe along with me. Things got a little weird, let's say. He didn't make it. My Mustang didn't make it, either, which is why I was driving that turd-mobile. Only thing with wheels I could steal at that moment."

"Why did things get weird?"

Fiona swerved the conversation into a new lane: "Here's a tip, sweetie. If you're running for your life, don't do it in a flashy old convertible. The second I saw it, outside that motel a couple nights ago, I knew I was on the right track."

"That car had some serious class. They don't make them like that anymore. But how did you find me tonight?"

Fiona nodded toward his feet. "I put a tracker in your booth-eel. GPS, good for a couple miles out."

Bill frowned. "When?"

"Um, months ago." Fiona looked away. "Sorry, I get paranoid."

"Wait, what?"

Was Fiona blushing a little? "You're a good-looking guy."

"You put a tracker in my favorite boots because you thought I was *cheating* on you?" Bill thinking it wasn't the worst idea, actually, to put a little leash on him. He was an awful flirt, and sometimes the sight of a nice pair of legs almost overrode the fear of what his badass girlfriend would do to him if she found out he was conducting the midnight meat train with anyone other than her. "How dare you?"

"Can we not bang out our relationship right now? Because I bet they can hear us." Fiona raised her voice: "Why don't they just come in and talk?"

Bill expected the door to crash in.

Nothing happened.

Looking down, Bill noted a drain in the center of the room, covered with a rusty grate. Something white and small had lodged in it. With a shudder, he realized it was a broken tooth.

Fiona puffed her cheeks, blew a strand of hair from her eyes.

Bill swallowed and shook his head. The fear that had seized him in New York, filling his head with images of blood and pain, returned with claws. Fighting to keep his voice steady, he said: "Where'd you learn that crazy reloading thing in the car?"

"You remember Rob King?"

"I met him once or twice, yeah. Did some heavy stuff, right?"

"He was an Army Ranger, before extenuating circumstances put him in our industry. He upped my game with all sorts of gun-fu, how to load a pistol one-handed, stuff like that. He said you don't always have the benefit of two working arms in a gunfight."

"You ever sleep with him?"

"Really? That's the first thing you ask? Really?"

Fighting kept the fear back. It felt good. "Maybe I should ask if you were cheating."

"I'm not indulging that crap."

"You got anything better to do?"

She snorted. "Every time you unleash one of your trademark snappy comments while looking at me with those puppy-dog eyes, I want to punch you in the mouth."

"You always did want more passion," he said, baiting her.

She rolled her eyes. "Nice to see that you're acting like a martyr right up to the very end."

"Oh, come on. You kept setting me up to fail. Like with the radiator thing."

"Not something I shouldn't have had to ask for."

"Those sort of things you need to ask for."

"If we were truly compatible, I wouldn't have to."

"Did Rob do the radiator thing?"

"No, he did the bathroom sink thing. It's a variation on the radiator thing, not that you'd know much about that."

A loud click from overhead, and a voice boomed loud enough to startle them: *"What is wrong with you people?"*

Fiona snarled back, her cheeks flushed, the sight of which made Bill's nether regions stir. Memories of that sunlit bedroom, knotted grinding. Nice to know the fear of imminent death couldn't stifle that part of him.

The door creaked open, revealing a man as tough and brown and thin as a stick of beef jerky. His gray hair combed back in a shiny helmet. The armpits of his tan Sheriff's uniform slick with sweat. In his right hand, a white plastic box with a handle, the kind you use to store lures and fishing tackle.

Setting the box on the floor, he closed the door and studied them for a long moment. "I'm Sheriff Bob Parkins," he said, chuckling, "and you're in some deep doo-doo."

Fiona smirked. "Do we not say 'shit' around here?"

"Not if we can help it." Parkins shook his head slowly, as if appalled by the very idea. "We're wholesome folk. Simple, straightforward people. Which is why we don't appreciate when a couple of yahoos come in, shoot up the place."

"Last I recall," Bill offered, "the shooting started only after you kidnapped me, dude. Plus you stole my watch." He nodded at the Sheriff's left wrist, loaded down with peerless Swiss engineering. *I'm going to get that back,* Bill thought, *even if it means I have to chop off your hand to get it.*

The anger coursing through his blood felt fucking fantastic.

"Don't mention kidnapping, dear," Fiona stage-whispered back. "Remember, he's wholesome."

Bill showed Fiona his fangs, sensing more of their old banter coming back, the way they could verbally destroy a random moron in a matter of minutes.

Ignoring Bill's little speech, Parkins knelt and worked the clasps of the box at his feet. "You want to come into my town, stir up trouble, and then just walk out of here?" he said. "I don't think so. There's a penalty for everything, kids. That's how the world works."

Bill did not like the looks of that box. Neither did Fiona. Her jaw tightening, she said: "This is some sort of off-the-books thing, isn't it? This doesn't look like a police station. You didn't process us. If you had, we'd have a lawyer shouting for our release before you could down your fourth donut of the day."

She was right. Bill hadn't heard any noises from the corridor when Parkins opened the door, none of the hustle and bustle that filled an ordinary police station. Where were they?

Closing the box, Parkins stood with a skinning knife in his right hand. "All you need to know," he said, "is that I'm the law around here."

At the sight of the knife, Bill's stomach dropped like a busted elevator. He had never been tortured before, had never seen anyone tortured. Torture was a thing that existed in whispered stories over pints, or movies where the torturers built elaborate devices out of razor wire and motors. Parkins didn't seem like the engineering type. He was a guy who liked to get to the point, so to speak.

"Our friends are coming for us," Fiona said. "And if we're hurt in any way, they're going to do horrible things to you. I'm talking things that would make a medieval executioner lose his lunch. If you let us go, maybe we'll leave you alone."

"What makes you so sure your friends know you're here?" Parkins asked.

Fiona hesitated, and Bill wondered if she had come alone. "You see, there's this amazing invention called a phone," she said. "And every so often, I use this amazing invention to talk to people who might be a long, long distance…"

Shifting the knife to his left hand, Parkins slapped Fiona hard across the face. Maybe the Sheriff expected her to scream, or shed a tear. Fiona only smiled. "You're going to pay for that," she said. "Big time."

Bill expected the Sheriff to hit her again. Instead the man stepped back, waving his hand in the air. "I didn't like doing that," he said. "We're not animals here. But you pushed me, threatening me about your friends. You think we haven't made folks disappear before? You think we're amateurs at this?"

"I know you're not," Fiona said. "Back at that junkyard or whatever it was? I saw inside those shipping containers. You've taken a lot of stuff from people."

"Just tell us what you want," Bill said, hoping to distract Parkins. The blade in his hand promised nothing good.

Parkins seemed only too happy to change subjects. As he talked, he began to play with the knife, running its edge along his tanned wrist. "You come to town acting all suspicious, with a lot of money in your trunk," he told Bill. "I think you got a lot more where that came from, and I think you're going to give it to me."

"You're going to kill us anyway," Fiona said. "So go screw yourself. You might have some crazy idea that you'll torture us beforehand, but trust me, that's not going to work out so well, either."

"Yeah?" Parkins cocked his head like a curious rooster. "Why's that?"

She nodded toward her shoulder. "Pull my shirt back."

Parkins yanked her shirt away from her collarbone, revealing a tangle of ragged scars.

"I was stabbed four times there," Fiona said. "I lost a lot of blood. The only reason I'm still alive is because Bill here got me to the hospital just in time. Now reach down and pull my shirt away from my waist."

Parkins did so, revealing a pair of purplish scars just above her hip.

"Those are two bullet-holes, from something else," Fiona said. "They had to take out some bits of me. Sometimes it hurts, and sometimes I shit too fast. Otherwise I'm all good."

Parkins placed his free hand lightly atop her head, like a psychic trying to get a reading. It might have been the icy light from overhead, but Bill thought the man looked a little pale.

"The thing about pain," Parkins said, running his fingers through her hair, "is there's no bottom to it. Sure, you've taken some lickings. We all have. You want a contest, I can pull up my shirt, show you some of my greatest hits. Just because you didn't break before, doesn't mean you won't break when I start working on you."

"I thought you were an upstanding guy," Fiona snarled, twisting her head to lock eyes with him. If looks could kill, the cop's head would have erupted in a geyser of bright red gore.

"Oh, I am," Parkins sounded positively cheerful. "I'd never torture a citizen. Scum like you, though, that's something different. The way I see it, once you start behaving like a criminal, you sort of lose your human rights, okay?" His hand clenched, yanking her hair by the roots. "So let's talk cash: How much you two got, and how you're going to give it to me."

# 15

**I WATCHED AS** dark figures tossed Bill and Fiona like sacks of potatoes into the backseat of one of the trucks. It started up and headed west, trailed by the second truck. The third stayed behind, its two occupants poking through the wreck of Fiona's godforsaken yellow crapmobile.

After they retrieved the purse and pistol from the backseat, one of them turned on the motor—it coughed and bucked like a rodeo horse ready for the glue factory—and drove the car at walking speed through the hole in the fence. As the front bumper edged toward the junk-pit, he climbed out again, tossing the vehicle a middle-finger salute as it tipped over the edge. From across the fields, I heard the crunch of metal and glass.

With that task completed, the driver joined his friend for a cigarette at the truck. I hovered the drone overhead, zooming the camera for a better view of their faces. Hardy Midwestern stock: blonde beards, square faces. Each had a badge on his chest and a regulation sidearm on his waist.

Cops charging in like cowboy cavalry to break up everybody's fun? I had seen that a million times. Except these boys had neglected to read Bill and Fiona their rights, and dumping a suspect's car in a pit is not official procedure. My spidey-sense tingled something fierce. I needed to get out of here as quietly as possible, regroup, and figure out where they took my people.

Just as I swiveled my thumb on my screen, to guide the drone back to my car, one of the cops looked up. Probably wondering about that buzzing noise.

I love it when a situation goes totally dumpster-fire.

The other man, head tilted to follow the first one's pointing finger, drew his pistol. Well, I couldn't let that aggression stand. Tapping my screen, I aimed the 9mm semiautomatic that my engineering friend had affixed to the underside of the drone. My little goodie.

You know those science-fiction movies where the ruthlessly efficient robot guns down human beings with pinpoint accuracy? If you fear something like that coming true one day, you can rest easy for at least a few more decades. Trying to put a bullet in a moving target from a flying drone is sort of like trying to perform brain surgery with a pipe wrench and a screwdriver, after someone covers up your left eye: frustrating, inaccurate, and very, very messy.

My first five bullets not only missed the two men by a country mile, but the recoil sent the drone tumbling in random directions with every shot. Pistols raised, the men fired. Despite their inability to see a slate-gray drone against a pitch-black sky, one of their rounds grazed a rotor. My robo-vision suddenly pitched diagonal, the controls goofy. Good thing I misspent my youth playing video games, because otherwise I would have lost control of my machine and plowed it into the dirt.

My next shot hit one of the two men in the neck, and he fell. That damn recoil kicked the drone upwards again—something to tell the kid in Brighton, so he could build me a better version 2.0. The other man crouched behind the truck's front bumper to reload, which did him no good, as I limped the drone around on its three surviving rotors and put a bullet neatly in his back.

Did I kill him? No, that would have made my life far too easy. By the time I landed the drone and walked over to the truck, he had managed to crawl around to the driver's side. I grabbed his hand before he could claw the door open and gently eased it back to the grass. Next I took his phone and gun. While he groaned on the ground, I searched the truck, finding two bags of fast food in the front console and a bit of weirdness in the backseat.

"What the hell is this?" I asked, holding up the bundle of gleaming fabric.

The man had regained a little of his strength. "An Elvis costume."

I unfolded the rhinestone-studded lycra and held it against my body, evaluating. It could fit. "Dare I ask?"

"Second job, man. Weddings, birthday parties. Fourth of July coming up, everybody wants the King." His smirk revealed bloody teeth.

"So let me get this straight. You're cops, and you got what I'm guessing is some sort of kidnapping gig on the side. And you still need money."

He sighed and leaned back, wincing at the pain. "Nothing pays good around here, dude. You gonna kill me?"

Draping the costume over my arm, I drew my pistol, ready to move onto the next phase of my evening. The man squeezed his eyes shut, awaiting the bullet. And yet. My finger refused to apply that last half-pound of pressure. My eyes burned, and I felt wetness on my cheek.

What in the fresh hell was this?

You are a miniscule speck of carbon in an enormous and unfeeling universe, I thought. You know that feelings are a rooster illusion, a trick of electricity that everybody calls a 'mind.' You have no reason to start tearing up like a little girl at a teen idol concert. Pull the trigger.

My finger remained frozen.

The man opened his eyes and squinted at me, confused.

My pocket buzzed. Anxious for a distraction, I pulled out my phone and checked the screen, expecting yet another incoming call from The Dean, that worrywart. Instead I saw ten digits burned forever in my heart. My hand trembled. My forehead prickling with sweat.

After a long pause, I swiped the call to voicemail. I knew I was in no shape to answer it now. She would leave a message. Or even call back. Please, call back.

"Look, man," said the guy on the ground.

I looked down. "What?"

"If you're going to shoot me, shoot me."

That was surprising. Most people, you know, beg for their lives. "What?"

He shook his head, suddenly angry. "The waiting. It's worse."

Yes, what a good point. The waiting was worse, wasn't it? Life itself was a process of waiting, waiting, waiting for something that never arrived, at least not for most of us. Even the pleasures of chicken-fried steaks and everything-meat pizza and oily breads could only do much in the face of that void.

"I can see that," I agreed.

He opened his eyes. "So what are we doing here?"

It came to me in a golden rush. "To be loved."

"Huh?"

"It doesn't matter if it's an illusion or not. It transcends that." I lowered the pistol. "Hold on. I need to return a call."

I raised my phone, tapped the voicemail icon, and placed the device to my ear. Ready to hear my ex-wife explain how wrong she was, that she needed me back in her life. That we could start again.

Instead I heard a series of clicks, a muffled curse, someone coughing, a car honking. And then her lovely voice: "Wait, is this on?"

My ex-wife had butt-dialed me.

I am not proud of what happened next, although I suppose I stayed true to character: I raised the pistol, and the man on the ground merged with the infinite. From alive to dead in approximately one-quarter of a second, leaving me to stare at my smoking firearm, a little surprised at what I'd done.

And whoops, I'd forgotten to ask him where his little buddies had taken Bill and Fiona. Or why they'd kidnapped Bill in the first place.

Although I had precious little clue about the plot, I did discover one thing: the dead man had remarkable taste in fabrics. The costume felt smooth, luxurious in my hands. Whether or not he just wore the outfit for the money, it must have been a real pleasure to slip on, along with that Elvis persona: strong and confident and ready to hump the world. Yes, that sounded like a pretty good mentality right about now.

The rear pocket of the dead man's jeans lit up like a firefly's ass, accompanied by the auto-tuned caterwaul of stadium country. I pulled out his phone, shrugged, and answered it with a soft grunt.

"Yo, dude, where are you?" The voice panicked, loud.

I grunted.

"Well, you better get your behind down to the ranch. Parkins is pissier than grandma's bed."

I mumbled through parted lips, hoping I sounded a bit like the dead man: "Where?"

"His ranch, idiot." A long pause. "Where are you?"

I hung up. Flicking through the phone's contacts, I found the address for one Roy Parkins. The map app suggested it was ten minutes away. If those trucks had headed there, it meant I had very little time before the locals returned to check on their friends.

Eight minutes later I was back on the main road in my own car. The Elvis suit fit snug as a sock, and by sweeping back my unwashed mane, I managed a passable Duck's Ass hairdo. In honor of the King I stuffed my mouth full of burgers and fries from the dead cops' truck.

My phone rang again. "Yeah?"

"Status?" The Dean asked.

"You didn't tell me you'd sent Fiona after Bill. What a brilliant move."

"I sent Fiona and Watanabe. Did you see Watanabe?"

"I have some bad news," I said, grinning. "There's just Fiona, and she freed Bill."

I heard a sharp intake of breath.

"Then they both got kidnapped," I continued. "In Bill's case, kidnapped again. By the locals. Again. Who might still end up eating both of them. It's very trippy. What's your favorite Elvis song, man?"

"What?" For the first time ever, The Dean sounded on the verge of underpants-soiling terror. "Elvis?"

"'Playing for Keeps,' that's mine," I said. "I don't even know what I'm doing, but the power of the King is guiding me through."

The Dean paused for another deep inhale, and then he began to speak. What started as a trickle of profanity quickly swelled into a river of hilariously arcane threats. By the time he was finished with me, The Dean promised, I would beg for a time machine so I could travel back forty years, find my pregnant mother, and kick her in the stomach, in order to spare my future self all the pain he planned on inflicting on my sorry ass. Two minutes into his non-stop screaming, I began to wonder whether all the stress over Bill had finally snapped his mind like a dry twig.

"You got a gift for gab, buddy," I told him, and hung up the phone. Chewing down the last greasy bites of fast food, I let my mind drift onto the topic of love. Sure, it might be an illusion, designed by our lizard brains to keep us from killing each other before we can reproduce, but it always feels so worth it in the moment. Too bad it didn't work out for me.

# 16

**OH FUCK, BILL** thought.

Oh fuck, my *finger*.

Oh fuck, my finger *chopped off.*

Parkins had yanked Bill's left hand from the mass of chains. Bill tried making a fist but Parkins smacked the back of his hand with the knife-handle until the fingers splayed open. As Bill thrashed, Parkins grabbed the index finger and brought the blade down hard on the second knuckle. The steel was sharp but it took some sawing to split the bone.

Blood drizzled on the concrete floor. For a moment Bill felt nothing. Then the pain hit like a bolt of white fire that sizzled up his arm to his neck, destroying all strength and thought in its path. Bill screamed. Over the roaring in his head, he heard Fiona yelling at Parkins, promising to hack off his balls.

"You got nine more," Parkins announced, "The next little piggy better tell me where the money is." Ignoring Fiona's threats, he wiped the knife on his pant-leg and loped across the room, relaxed as a man on a Sunday fishing trip. From the tackle-box he retrieved a mini chef's torch, the kind that restaurants use to set fire to crème brûlée, before returning to Bill's seat.

Bill's screams subsided to a low moan. Some semblance of thought returned: Oh fuck. My finger. Fuckity-fuck-fuck-fuck. Why haven't I passed out yet?

Parkins ignited the torch.

The pain was different this time, an ache that faded to numbness as the nerves in Bill's finger charred and died. When the torch shut off, Bill's stump was charred black. Bill slumped, pale and sweaty, wheezing through clenched teeth.

"Smell reminds me of bacon," Parkins said.

"You sick bastard," Fiona snarled.

Bill swallowed back his vomit. I'm not going to die down here, he thought. And if the worst happens, I'll make damn sure I use my last breath to laugh in this miserable pissant's face. Just keep him talking. He'll make a mistake.

"There's a lot more money," Bill said. "We'll give it to you." Locking eyes with Fiona, he tried to send her a telepathic signal: I'm buying time here. "I just need a laptop with wireless. Something that can connect to the Internet."

"Or you could just tell me the login and password," Parkins replied. "We don't got wireless at the ranch."

Fiona read Bill's cues, interrupted: "So what will you do with all your ill-gotten gains? Party on a beach somewhere?"

Parkins chuckled and wiped his forehead. "I know it sounds crazy, and you won't believe me, but we put this money back into the community."

"Aw, shucks," Bill snorted, "that's so heartwarming." His hand pulsed with agony but he felt a little stronger, more in control of his gut. I'd rip out this prick's throat for half a painkiller, he thought. Just give me a chance.

"Lots of departments do it," Parkins said, his cheeks reddening. "Civil asset forfeiture, it's a thing, look it up. We think you look like trash, we pull you over for a busted taillight, we're taking your cash, your car, whatever else you earned the wrong way. Been going on for years, all of it legal."

Bill heard of cops taking money from drug busts and spending it on everything from swanky offices to new vehicles. Nor did the law need to find Joe Q. Public guilty in order to requisition his brand new car, because good old-fashioned probable cause was often enough to seal the deal. Sure, you could hire a lawyer to fight the case, but how many people have the money to unleash a legal pit bull?

"I have to hand it to you, cop." Fiona shook her head. "I've seen some pretty hardcore scams in my time, but you're taking this to a whole new level."

Parkins swung around, his face moist under the bright light, almost shouting: "You seen our community out there?"

Fiona drew back. "Drove through it."

"It's dead," Parkins said. "Died when the factory went away, then came back a little bit when Walmart put up a store, then died all over again when Walmart decided to pull out. You think the Feds will help us? Don't make me laugh. You think the state cares about us? Yeah, right. We got to help ourselves."

"That doesn't make this right," Bill said. The sight of his severed digit, curled like a pale tadpole on the concrete, gave him the serious heebie-jeebies. "And would you mind picking up my finger…"

"I'm okay with cops," Fiona chimed in, "so long as they stay honest. While I can't say I like to see them coming, I understand what they're doing. But once a cop gets a taste of the money, they become worse than regular criminals. Like, extra-super amoral. It's just depressing."

Parkins laughed. "A couple of criminals telling me what's right. My family's lived here a century. A century. You ever fought to keep your home? To help your friends keep their homes? That's what's right."

"I'll make you a deal. If you pick up my finger, and let her go," Bill said, nodding toward Fiona, "I'll give you the password. But not before I verify she's out, okay? With the finger, you can do whatever. Not sure they can reattach that at this point."

"I might deal with you," Parkins said, the lie in his eyes. Before he could say anything else, the metal door behind him crashed open, and Casey charged in, followed by that enormous bouncer, Rex. Bill noted how all three townies had the same high cheekbones and bright blue eyes. The family that slays together, stays together.

"We got a big problem," Casey said.

"Get out," Parkins shot back. "We're not done in here."

"They got friends," Rex said. "We're missing some guys."

Casey drew a pistol from the waistband of her jeans, checked the clip with shaking hands. "I told you," she said. "We shouldn't have brought them here."

"Kiddo, come with me. Rex, stay here. Take another finger if they act up." Parkins winked and left the room, Casey trailing in his wake. The bouncer closed the door and stood in front of it, hands clasped at his waist, giving Bill a look that promised much cutting indeed.

Bill opened his mouth, ready to make a pithy comment about steroid abuse, when the door exploded inwards.

# 17

**PEOPLE GIVE ELVIS** crap for gaining too much weight and letting those pills get the better of him. If you ask me, though, I think the King produced some of his finest music during his later years, when the burdens of life tempered that youthful exuberance. It takes a lot of soul to sing something like "Burning Love" and not sound like a self-conscious fool, especially if you're doing so in a rhinestone-studded leisure suit.

Not that age stopped old Elvis from ripping out a classic tune, if he felt like it. When he blasted "Hound Dog" as his second-to-last song at his final concert, he had the crowd on its feet, energized by that old-time magic. Watch the footage, and you'll see. Sometimes you need to rip the joint in half.

I could relate, and not just because of this beautiful costume. Although I loved my drones, this current situation required the firepower equivalent of a blood-pumping guitar solo. Too bad I had neglected to bring an arsenal with me to Oklahoma.

Wondering where I could pick up some heavy artillery, I followed the main road to a turnoff marked by a single lamp on a tall pole. A half-mile down a narrower lane, headlights off,

I passed a cattle gate and the distant glow of what looked like a compound.

"You have reached your destination," announced the phone in my hand.

"Sure, if I want to get shot," I replied, driving another mile down the road, until the fence on my left gave way to a dim wall of twisted trees and tall grass. Easing the vehicle onto the shoulder, I cut the engine and climbed out.

With the drone damaged beyond easy repair, I would need to do this next part on foot. Infiltrating hostile territory in a bright white outfit, a pair of mismatched pistols strapped to my hips, probably wasn't a recommended tactic in the Seal Team Six handbook, but I felt the shielding strength of rock 'n' roll in my blood, a high purer than cocaine.

The hike through the woods, ending with a hard slog up the hill behind the compound, left me out of breath, the costume sticky and cold with sweat. If I survived the night, adopting a serious cardio routine would dominate my to-do list from now on. From this height I could see a ranch house, long and narrow, with a glassed-in porch on its western side. Next to it stood a barn, so old and ramshackle it looked like a pile of timber, and a windowless brick cube the size of a garage. Four trucks were parked beside the cube, surrounded by a black cluster of men.

I listened for dogs, hearing no barking. I scanned for patrols, seeing nothing. I crept down the hill in a wide arc that ended in the deeper shadow of the barn, beside a narrow door. Close enough to hear the faint murmur of conversation, punctuated by a deep laugh. Using the sound as cover, I tried the knob, and the door opened smoothly onto darkness.

I stepped inside, easing the door shut behind me, and felt around until my thumb hit a light switch. A row of fluorescents flickered to life overhead. I spun around in awe.

As the King once said: Sweet Baby Jesus.

When I stepped back outside, I had a long metal tube in my arms. Its curved side featured a pictogram of a little stick figure pulling at the end of the tube, which I did, sliding out an inner section to double its length. Following the directions, I flicked up a little tab at one end, hefted the weapon onto my shoulder, and figured out where to send its explosive bit of good cheer.

Once upon a time, I knew a woman up in Idaho who ran a smuggling operation. She bought one of these toys online and gave it to her right-hand man, in case a deal ever went Peckinpah on them. Her guy was a real weirdo, wore a rubber gorilla mask on the job. Not the sort of dude you want around high explosives, which he proved by using the hardware on a fast-food joint when they got his drive-through order wrong.

This really happened, I swear. Look it up online.

After she told me that story, I realized that Monkey Man had the right idea, although he lost points on the execution (so to speak): if you need to wipe out everybody in the vicinity, you can't go wrong with something designed to take out a tank.

Rocket launcher on my shoulder, I aimed at the brick building, and the men between the vehicles.

# 18

**THE EXPLOSION HURLED** two-hundred-fifty pounds of bouncer across the room like a rubber ball. Smoke boiled through the shattered doorway. Working his jaw to ease his screeching eardrums, Bill heard the muted pops of gunshots from outside. Some rescuer here to save the day, or take his head back to New York in a bag. Either way, Bill did not consider himself in a good place. Bracing his feet, he strained against the chair, as if the blast had magically loosened the chains.

A figure stepped through the haze, gleaming white. Bill thinking this must be some weirdass pain-dream, Elvis Presley coming for him in a spangly jumpsuit, assault rifle in each hand.

Rex stood on quaking legs, blood dribbling down his bald head, eyes wide at the sight of the Once and Future King.

"Good to see ya, champ," Elvis said, and blasted the man full of holes, the shots achingly loud in the tight space.

*There goes my hearing again,* Bill groaned.

Elvis pivoted on his heel, pointing one of the smoking rifles at Bill's chest. Staring down that barrel deep as infinity, Bill realized he knew the man in the costume, from his life in New York.

"We've met," Fiona said, as if reading Bill's thoughts. "You're that guy."

"I am that guy," Elvis said, keeping the rifle steady as he swiveled his head in her direction. "Can I ask you something, little lady?" He had that famous Presley sneer down pat.

"Only if you promise to never refer to me as 'little lady.'"

"You had a mission to kill Bill here."

Fiona nodded.

"And yet Bill ain't killed. Color me confused."

"It's corny."

"My mood right now is unconventional. Try me."

Fiona sighed. "I love him, okay?"

"Why you acting all ashamed of it?" Bill asked. Maybe ten seconds away from death, and his mind had the nerve to spin up the highlight reel from their relationship, the sweet and awkward things that you cringed at remembering once it was all over. Like the time he had rushed her to the hospital after someone had pumped a bullet in her gut, and the car radio started blaring some awful Nirvana imitation, and she sank her teeth into his hand because he refused to change the station.

"You really love him?" Elvis asked, his rifles drooping.

"I do." Fiona locked gazes with Bill, her eyes sweet as honey. "I really do. If you have to kill us over it, so be it."

Elvis sniffled, and they looked up to see his bright blue eyes brimming with tears. Snot dribbled from his nose. His chin quavered. "Don't mind me," he blubbered, wiping his face with a dusty sleeve. "I'm going through a weird time."

The jukebox of Bill's memory rang cherries. "You punch tickets for The Dean," he told Elvis. That explained the man's presence in Flyspeck, Oklahoma. But the outfit? The mawkish tears?

"That's right," Elvis said. "And right now…"

The rifles dipped lower, pointing at the concrete.

"Right now, I'm thinking to myself: 'Screw it.'" Bending to one knee, Elvis placed the rifles on the floor. Standing again, he reached behind his back, drew a small knife, and commenced to sawing the duct tape that bound Fiona's arms to the chair. "I killed a bunch of men outside. A lot more of them went into the trees. Probably calling in backup. They'll wait a little bit, I bet, see what we do."

"The whole town's in on it," Bill said.

Freed except for her handcuffs, Fiona opened the tackle box that Parkins had left on the floor, scooping a handful of small keys from the top tray. Tried a few until she found the one that unlocked the cuffs. "So we got the makings of a nice little Alamo here," she said. "Any brilliant ideas so we don't end up like Davey Crockett?"

"No brilliant ones," Elvis said, picking his rifles back up. "Just a lot of shooting."

Fiona walked over to Bill and tested keys until she unlocked the padlocks, helped him unwind the chains from around his aching arms. Fresh blood flowing into his hands ignited every pain circuit in his burnt stump, making him grit his teeth as he stood and looked down. At least the flame had cauterized all the cut vessels in his finger.

Meanwhile the severed digit seemed so lonely on the concrete. He bent and slipped it into the pocket of his jeans. Maybe I'll make a talisman out of the bone, he mused. Like those dried bits of saints you see in Italian churches, all done up in gold.

*You're hysterical*, a harsh voice in his head whispered. *Get your shit together.*

Ten-four, major.

"But if we make it out of here alive," Elvis said, "you crazy kids got to promise me something."

"What's that?" Fiona asked.

"You go to Vegas, you find that Elvis chapel, and you get married."

"If that's what she wants, who am I to argue?" Bill knelt to feel up Rex's bullet-riddled corpse, finding nothing of value. "I'm a lucky guy."

"Can we snap back to reality here?" Fiona said. "We need weapons."

"I know just the place." Elvis grinned and, holding the rifles aloft, executed one of the King's signature hip-thrusts toward the door. "Follow me."

# 19

**"I SNUCK IN** here before, grabbed that rocket. Only one, alas," Elvis said, pacing the aisles of the barn, running his hands along rack after rack of shotguns and rifles and pistols and weirder things, machetes and tribal blades and antique firearms. Reaching the rear wall, he stopped to appreciate a compact lump of steel and lacquered wood. "You recognize that?"

Bill paused from sorting through bins to check out the hardware. "Some kind of shotgun?"

"It's a shotgun on steroids, also known as the TP-82. The cosmonauts used to carry them into orbit. Triple barrels, plus there's a hidden machete." It also had a hinge above the action, which Elvis broke open to show them the empty barrels. "Looks like 12 gauge ammo up top, maybe 7.62 rifle below. See if there's any on the shelf over there."

"I'm looking for bandages."

"You're going to be looking at my boot up your ass."

"Well, if you put it like that." Bill did as ordered, rooting through boxes of ammunition with his good hand until he discovered the right gauges. "That seems like a really stupid thing to take on a space station. You fire it, hit a wall, all your air leaves through the hole, right?"

"It wasn't for the space station," Elvis said, taking the ammo from him. "Once you landed back on the tundra, it was so you could hunt or fend off bears or whatever until help came." Loading all three barrels, snapping the weapon closed, he gripped the canvas cover of the collapsible stock and pulled it off, revealing a wicked blade. "As impressed as I am, I have to admit, it's sort of overkill. Which is exactly what this situation calls for." With that, he handed the weapon to Bill.

"Where you think that Sheriff seized it from?" Bill asked, holding the hardware with the respect it deserved.

"Maybe some Russian driving through," Fiona said from the next aisle, as she picked through plastic bins filled with tangles of necklaces and bracelets, stacks of loose paper, piles of sad and dusty toys, heavy tools starting to rust, chunky cameras with cracked cases. "Back at that junkyard, those shipping containers, they were full of stuff like this. Purses, backpacks. It's like, decades of stuff."

"And not a single bulletproof vest," Elvis said. "You notice that? Whoever heard of an armory without vests?"

"They're probably wearing them out there," Bill said.

"Comforting thought," Fiona said. "How about you and your fancy-ass gun find something to cover up that hand of yours?"

Instead of resuming the hunt for medical supplies, Bill walked to the wall and peered between the slats, checking for movement in the woods beyond the ranch. His lizard brain could feel them out there, waiting for their moment. That rocket had transformed every truck outside into flaming pyres of steel and gasoline, and some people into corpses, none of them Parkins or Casey. How many more men could the Sheriff call?

Too many, whatever the number. A whole army of bastards.

Beyond the far trees, a finger of pale flame arched toward the sky and burst. A half-second later, they heard the boom.

"Fireworks?" Fiona asked.

"Someone's setting them off in town," Elvis said. "Probably to cover any ruckus we're making here. These townies ain't dumb. Bill, I'd get away from that wall, in case one of them sees ya."

Bill returned to the shelves, sorting through bins until he found one stuffed with medical supplies, including an elastic bandage and a handful of butterfly clips. Sure, he did a piss-poor job of wrapping his damaged hand, especially with the TP-82 tucked in his armpit, but the idea of asking Elvis or Fiona for help made him cringe: they seemed a little intense about loading up on guns.

The bins also held a pharmacy's worth of prescription bottles, not to mention whiskey and vodka. He washed down a couple of Tylenol-3 with a swig of fifteen-year-old single malt. A last drink for the condemned.

"By the way," he asked Elvis. "How did you track me down?"

"It was easy. The Dean called El Rey, offered him a ton of money to give you up. El Rey mentioned your route down." Elvis shrugged. "Once I felt I was close, I had The Dean give you a call. You realize we can track phones, right?"

"He's dense sometimes," Fiona said, walking over to Bill. "But don't hold that against him. I'm impressed he could open a childproof cap, given his missing finger."

"I got mad skills," Bill said, taking a deep breath as she stepped close. Beneath the stink of dust and gunfire on her clothes, he caught a whiff of her familiar scent: sugary rose.

"You should have told me you were going," she said, lowering her voice. "Did you think I wouldn't come along?"

"I wasn't sure. I'm sorry."

"I know we've been snarly lately, but you shouldn't have doubted." She smacked him on the shoulder. "That's what you get."

He winced. "I felt that in my hand."

She hit him again, harder. "Nut up, baby."

"I sincerely hate to interrupt this lovefest," Elvis called. He appeared at the end of the aisle, holding a beautiful silver six-shooter with a pearl grip. "Those guys outside, I bet most did time in Iraq, Afghanistan, other sandboxes. You a better fighter than some pissed-off Jihadi looking for a good deal on afterlife virgins? Because if not, we ought to talk about plans for getting off the property."

More fireworks boomed, close enough to quake the dirt beneath their feet.

"We're going to head to wherever you parked your car," Fiona told Elvis. "But we got to tax these people first." Walking over to the far side of the barn, she pulled a pair of empty duffel bags from a low shelf and zipped both open. "I'm surprised you eagle-eyed killers didn't notice, but there's giant bundles of cash over yonder, wrapped up. That's why they haven't attacked us yet: they're probably worried it'll go up in flames."

They joined her in stuffing the bags full of bills. The idea of carrying heavy loads of cash through a gunbattle seemed about as appealing to Bill as firewalking in a suit soaked in gasoline. On the other hand, several pounds of tightly packed currency would also serve as the world's most expensive body armor.

Bill hefted a duffel bag onto his back, his spine scrunching like a rusty accordion. It was an open question whether his sudden dizziness was due to the bag's padded strap cutting off the blood-flow to his chest, or the pills and liquor kicking into higher gear.

Elvis cracked open the side door an inch, peered out. "We'll run for that big house first. Give us a little cover while we plan our next step. My car's a mile down the road. Too far to reach, unless we cut their numbers down."

Stopping by the explosives aisle, Fiona plucked two grenades and a loop of fishing wire from a rack. "Before we get this party started, can I ask you something?"

"Sure thing, my hunka burning love."

"Why are you doing this, really?"

"Because us three, we're a brutal bunch of heartbroken saps," Elvis said, working the words like a song lyric. "And we need all the help we can get."

# 20

**BILL TRIED THE** back door of the house. Unlocked. He swooped in low and fast, expecting to face Parkins and a brigade of irate gunmen, surprised to find only Casey on a couch in the front room, pistol loose between her thighs, her cheeks streaked with mascara-gritty tears.

Casey regarded Bill with zombie eyes as he snatched away her pistol. "You killed my brother?" she asked.

"I didn't, no. Anyone else here?" Heavy thumps behind him as Elvis and Fiona dropped their heavy bags of cash and split off, to clear the rest of the house room by room. Bill took the opportunity to let his own duffel slip off his shoulder and crash to the floor.

Casey refused to answer, until Bill pointed his cosmonaut shotgun at her. "No one," she enunciated carefully, as if to a child. "They're waiting to kill you outside."

"I don't blame them. This place gives me the creeps." The décor was old-time hunting shack: dark wood paneling, cheap furniture frayed at the edges, the walls lined with framed photographs and a forest of yellowing antlers. Weak light seeped from antique lamps. It smelled of stale tobacco and refried beans.

"You're telling me," Casey said. "This is where I grew up. You're looking a little unsteady there, buddy. You really think you got me covered?"

With a recently severed finger, holding anything steady with two hands is an exercise in pain management. Bill had to clench the muscles in his forearms to hold the barrel steady. "Shotgun this big, I got the whole room covered," he said. "So why are you here?"

She shrugged. "I was supposed to ambush you. Then I decided I'm very tired of all this."

Bill swallowed hard and asked the only question that really mattered: "Why me?"

"Your watch." Casey said. "You come to our town, wearing that? Might as well wear a sign saying, 'I got money. Rob me.'"

"You rob a lot of people."

"My Dad does. Since before I was born. String 'em up, strip 'em down, feed 'em to the pigs. Bury the cars. I don't think we even need the money anymore. Now it's like, a habit." She laughed and shook her head. "Don't tell me you don't understand. Second I saw you, I knew you were a criminal."

"Unlike your messed-up family, I'm actually trying to change." Bill lowered the shotgun. "Want to hear a joke?"

"I got a choice?"

"There was no money." He made a point of laughing, even though he felt no glee whatsoever. "They stole it from me, before I got to town. I just kept telling you there was, so you wouldn't kill me."

"Well, that sucks," she said, with zero feeling.

"I know, right? I liked you. I'm not sure I could hurt you, and that's okay. Because you're going to leave now, and if you come back, my girlfriend here will blow your head off."

Fiona had entered the room, shutting off every light in her path. "Kitchen door," she told Casey. "Guy in the Elvis suit will lock it behind you." Before she turned off the lamp beside the couch, Bill glanced at the nearest photograph on the wall: a portrait of the Sheriff on a wide lawn, smiling, his arms draped over younger versions of Casey and Rex. And looming in the background, the Parkins family abode: four bedrooms, two baths, basement, barn, and a torture chamber for out-of-town guests.

They heard Casey leave. A moment later, Elvis ghosted into the room, tucked low. "You're gonna want to duck," he said.

They ducked. Glass shattered, wood popped, and a small pair of antlers crashed to the floor. Someone firing from outside. "Porch," Fiona said, scrambling through the doorway to their right.

The wraparound porch was enclosed by a wall of single-pane windows in serious need of caulking and cleaning. Ratty couches, wooden chairs, and musty boxes of junk lined the windows, creating a waist-high barrier that would probably block a rifle bullet about as well as a piece of tissue paper. Bill knelt behind the arm of one of the couches, figuring its wooden frame would give him a bit more cover.

Another pane shattered, followed by a series of hollow bangs as the bullet exhausted its energy on pots and pans in the kitchen.

"Where did you wire it?" Elvis asked Fiona.

"Right underneath," she said.

Edging his head above the couch, Bill peered through the smeared glass at the distant ghost of the propane tank in the yard, between the house and the barn. A shadow whisked in front of it, so quick it might have been an illusion. Bill thought he heard someone muttering out in the dark. Or maybe it was just the house creaking around them.

"Well, nothing's happening," Elvis said. "I bet they found it. These guys aren't idiots."

"I figured they'd find it." Fiona rolled her eyes. "I figured they figured we're smart enough to set up some booby traps. So I took precautions."

Elvis grinned. "What sort of precautions?"

The propane tank exploded in a flash of white light and a skull-busting bang so intense it flopped Bill onto the floor. The windows rattled in their frames. When he looked up, a greasy fireball had risen over the yard. In its flickering orange glow, he saw the black lumps of bodies scattered on the grass.

"Second grenade," Fiona yelled. "Goes off if the line goes slack."

"Slick," Elvis yelled back, a note of admiration in his voice.

What was left of the windows shattered as a fresh round of bullets passed through, chewing up the wall behind them. A symphony of shattering and banging as the furniture inside the house blew apart. As he dove for the floorboards, Bill glimpsed the night beyond the yard lit up with muzzle flashes.

"Don't be cruel," Elvis hollered, laughing.

The air smoked. Lying on the floor, Fiona poked her pistol over the nearest windowsill and fired off an entire clip blind, ducking her arm back down before a fresh bullet-storm chewed away the sill. Slithering on her back to a different position, she reloaded, stuck the pistol through the window again, and fired, spacing her shots. More return fire from the yard, and she screamed, so loudly Bill thought for a moment that she'd been hit.

Winking at him, Fiona let the scream fade to a loud moan that softened to a liquid gurgle, before lapsing into silence. She crossed her eyes and let her tongue flip out of her mouth.

"Get in the kitchen," Elvis sang at Bill, "and make me some pie."

"What?"

"Whoever's left is going to try and flank us, if they're not moving that way already," Fiona said, resuming a serious expression. "You, back there, funky shotgun, try and stop them."

Bill crawled back into the house, doing his best in the dimness to steer around the sprays of broken glass and splintered wood. Every time his hand brushed the floor, his busted hand screamed bloody murder. Sweeping the TP-82 in front of him like the world's deadliest mop, he made a hard left for the kitchen, trying to will his ears to stop ringing. If he ever had kids, it would make a hilarious story. *How did you lose your hearing, Daddy?* Well, kid, I was in a firefight in some backwoods hellhole...

His arm bumped against something sharp and rough: a magnificent six-point buck rack, hurled to the floor by bullets. He tossed it skittering into the darkness ahead of him. Powering through the kitchen doorway, he took cover against the flank of the fridge, the one object big enough to block any bullets flying through the back door.

From the front of the house, he heard glass shatter, a single shot that sounded as loud as a cannon, a grunt. Fiona murmured something, and Elvis responded with a soft chuckle. Another thunderous bang, and Elvis cursed. Bill wondered if the situation had gone from bad to worse.

# **21**



**OKAY, THIS WAS** bad.

Fiona's little trick with the propane tank had killed five guys, maybe more, but I didn't have time to count up all the arms and legs scattered everywhere. Even if my righteous rocket rampage had killed another four or five, we still faced a lot of heavily armed and highly irate townies in the treeline. Based on the amount of gunfire they had already poured into the house, they had ammunition to spare.

One of those dudes must have brought out a .50-caliber rifle, because a hole the size of a dinner plate exploded in the wall behind us, showering the living room beyond with bits of wood and plaster. A second shot tore through the musty couch on my left, filling the air with blackened stuffing. Sooner or later those massive bullets would find us, and the coroner would need a spatula to scrape what was left into a plastic baggie.

So I made a decision.

"Stay here," I told Fiona, loading the last clip into my pistol, and crawled for the living room.

"Where the hell are you going?" she asked, eyes fixed on the yard.

"Doing a little flanking of my own," I said, and left it at that.

The real Elvis died on the toilet, his heart popping like a sad balloon as he strained to squeeze out a final nugget.

Not much of a death for a King.

"Don't worry, Presley," I said. "We're getting a do-over." Rising to a low crouch, I sprinted out the front door. The scattered flames from the explosion had died down, but not before smearing the night with gray smoke. I trusted that would add a little more cover as I ran for the smoldering remains of the propane tank.

At the edge of the wreckage, I stumbled across a relatively intact body in a uniform. The tin star on the chest said Deputy. Before the explosion had removed most of his head and his right hand, the officer had toted a modified M16 with a single-shot grenade launcher fitted underneath the barrel. I popped the clip free, eyeballed the ammo count. Full load, which was great, but it was the promise of a grenade that really gave me a stiffie.

Rifle clutched to my chest, I rose up for a better view, trusting that the blackened metal would provide me a little cover. Someone must have seen me. I heard a rustling from the trees, followed by a low click, and figured I had maybe a second before another bullet-storm swept over the yard.

Sighting over my barrel, I fired the grenade at the barn. It punched through the thin wooden wall, a white flash pulsing between the slats as it detonated. I hit the grass before the fire cooked off the racks of spare ammunition and loads of flammable goods inside. The sudden heat baked the skin of my face, rendered the jumpsuit hot and slick as a piece of plastic left in an oven.

But my stupid plan worked. As that rush of nuclear air swept over me, I rose to my knees in time to see a crowd of armed men running from the forest and across the lawn, trying to escape the rain of flaming wood and consumer crap. I counted ten, all with long-guns pointed roughly in my direction. My shiny costume must have reflected the inferno like a beacon, but that was okay. My big moment.

I was about to kill a lot of folks, and not for money.

This time, I was doing it for the most sacred thing in the universe: love.

"Burning love," I said, and opened a little fire of my own.

I filled the two closest men with enough lead to transform them into paperweights. As they jerked and fell, the other eight lifted their rifles and began to fire as they advanced. A bullet snapped past my cheek close enough to take a bit of my earlobe with it. Another snatched a chunk of hair. I ducked behind the propane tank, my left knee almost squishing into the broiled remains of a man I hadn't noticed in the shadows. A stubby assault weapon clutched between his ashy fingers.

When I rose up again, I had a weapon in each hand, like a bandit in a cheesy Western film, and I was laughing my head off, because the whole thing was so ridiculous. This life was a joke, and it had taken me until now to realize it. My rifles laughed with me, and the men on the other side of the propane tank crumpled over with mirth. It took every muscle in my arms to keep the barrels steady as I stepped into the middle of the lawn and extended message of laughter to the treeline, aiming low to wipe out any frisky lurkers.

I was really enjoying myself when my spine snapped in half.

# 22

**ANOTHER EXPLOSION RIPPED** the world in two.

The kitchen doorway framed the living room blazing orange. Before Bill could so much as gasp, an invisible fist punched him in the chest, sending him to his knees. The house groaned around him, the tile shuddering beneath his feet, plates and glasses rattling in the cabinets above his head.

That lunatic hitman must have blown up the barn.

Sucking air, Bill stumbled to his feet and stepped toward the doorway. His mind blaring Fiona's name like an alarm. Before he could take a second step, the back door crashed open, framing a hulking silhouette against deeper blackness.

Moving on instinct, Bill spun and fired off the TP-82. The figure disappeared, blown out into the night by the hail of buckshot. The recoil kicked Bill's shoulder like a mule on meth, his arm howling in pain. He had one shell left, plus the 7.62 in the third barrel.

Another figure darted through the door, ducking left into the narrow space between the sink and the wall. Bill took cover behind the edge of the fridge, waiting for his moment. He wasn't much of a warrior, not like Fiona, but he could still bring the hammer down on anyone threatening his life. Show them how it's done, he thought, and spun away from the fridge, ready to fire his second round.

The flash came from three feet away, just below the level of the sink. A bullet shredded Bill's jeans, leaving a trail of fresh hurt along his hip. Bill yelled, his arms jerking upward, and his own fire went wild, tearing a chunk out of the doorjamb.

"I get you, you little runt?" Parkins himself, crouched in the darkness.

Falling back against the steel flank of the fridge, Bill thumbed the selector on his firearm, switching to the 7.62. Warmth trickled down his leg, cooling as it soaked into the denim. His knees trembling, heart hammering, vision tightening to a black tunnel. From behind him came a distant gunshot, followed by a yelp.

"Surrender now, I don't make you taste your nuts before you die," Parkins yelled. "Best offer you're gonna get at this point."

*This time, just try to not totally fuck up.* With that self-encouragement, Bill leapt away from the fridge, weapon leveled, ready to rocket lead into Parkins—only for his world to burst red. He dropped facedown to the floor, spine rubbery, every nerve in his jaw sizzling. The Sheriff looming tall, pistol held butt-first like a club, the grip shiny with Bill's blood.

"Didn't see that coming, did you?" Parkins said, kicking away the TP-82. "This old man got the drop on you, boy."

Bill rolled on the tile, hands scrambling after his weapon, fingers scraping the rough canvas edge of the stock with the machete hidden inside. His face felt cracked. You're too damn slow, his mind wailed at him. You'll never make it.

"I coulda shot you just now," Parkins said, spinning the pistol around like an old-time gunslinger. "But I wanted to see the life go out of your eyes." Aiming at Bill's forehead, he took a step back.

And slipped.

On Bill's severed finger.

As Parkins crashed against the kitchen wall, Bill's frantic brain mashed the pieces together: the Sheriff's bullet, splitting

Bill's jeans, had also torn a hole in the pocket, freeing that mangled bit of flesh and bone to flop on the tile, right in the path of a size-11 cop boot. Parkins rebounded with his limbs flopping, his pistol flailing wild.

The adrenaline coursing through Bill's veins made it seem like he had all the time in the world to find the TP-82, raise it, slip his finger around the trigger, aim, and pump the 7.62 slug into the Sheriff's side. The force of the shot drove Parkins against the wall again, leaving a blood butterfly on the cracked paint.

Parkins fell to the floor at Bill's feet.

It might have been a few seconds or a couple of years, but eventually Bill sensed Fiona in the kitchen doorway. She held a smoking pistol in her hand. Aside from new scratches on her face and hands, probably from flying glass, she looked fine. "You okay?" she asked.

"I'm trying to think of a joke about my amputated finger." Rising to his knees, Bill found the Sheriff's left wrist, slid the sleeve back, and retrieved his precious watch. "But I'm stumped."

"The good news is, you haven't lost your crappy sense of humor." Fiona frowned. "The bad news is, well, how much do you care about our new friend?"

# 23

**THROUGH THE SHATTERED** frame of the porch windows, Bill saw the roof of the burning barn collapse in a geyser of sparks. The smoke and heat made his eyes water and his nostrils sting. As he stepped outside, trailing Fiona, he saw the fresh bodies scattered across the property. It looked like the aftermath of a small war, which wasn't that far from the truth, come to think of it.

Bill wondered whether someone in authority would ever show up to process the scene, or if the town would cover it up like everything else. We'll make a phone call once we're back on the road, he decided. All these missing folks over the years, their families deserve some sort of peace.

Elvis lay in the middle of the yard, a spent-shell halo gleaming around his head, his pristine white outfit stained crimson. "What happened?" Bill asked, kneeling beside him.

Elvis rolled his eyes and smirked: isn't it obvious?

Stupid question, Bill almost said. Except it wasn't, because he couldn't see any wounds, which meant Elvis had taken a bullet in the back. Had he tried to run away? Who shot him?

"For what it's worth," Fiona said, walking over to one of the duffel bags of cash on the floor, "I'm sorry." Hoisting it onto her shoulder with a grunt, she headed for the road beyond the house.

Elvis hooked a bloody finger over Bill's thumb. Bill squeezed back. "Thank you for not killing me," he said.

Elvis shrugged.

"I think this is the worst day of my life," Bill added.

Elvis started to laugh, pink froth bubbling out the corner of his mouth. Paused long enough to suck in a little breath, said: "You... don't have..."

Bill stooped close. "What was that?"

"The... least... fucking..."

"What?"

"...clue."

Elvis closed his eyes with a smile, his first genuine one in years.

# 24

**FIONA JAMMED THE** pistol into the back of El Rey's neck and thumbed the hammer. "Hey, Rey," she said. "We need to have a little bit of a clarification session."

# 25

**STRIDING ONTO THE** hotel's pristine swath of private shorefront, Bill performed some fancy footwork to prevent a herd of sunburned German tourists from trampling him beneath their brightly colored sandals. It was dusk, and only the suicidal risked standing between the guests and the newly opened bar on the beach.

The five-star hotel, with its elegant meals and endless drinks, made Bill feel like a fattened calf. After a few days of sitting in the perfectly manicured gardens, gazing over the mangroves while smoking fine cigars, he started wandering through Puerto Plata, the town on the other side of the barbed wire that ringed the resort area. It was a world of battered cars farting diesel smoke, packs of stray dogs rooting through the gutters, curbside vendors hawking pineapple and phone cards. The night beyond the wire moved with its own fast rhythm, the roadside shacks pulsing with music, the churches bright and humming with worshippers, the people sitting on the curbs wary as kicked dogs.

If I knew more Spanish, Bill mused, I could probably set up a nice little hustle here. But he could never join this brand of street chaos, not completely. From now on, Bill was a man of means, sitting in the back of the restaurant in his cool linen suit. The idea made him worry about softening too much, like an ice cream left in the tropical sun.

Soon after arriving, he had driven south to Santiago, the car jostling over unpaved roads, buzzing motorbikes passing him on the left and right, fields of crushed sugar cane blurring past. In the city, his new contact had taken him to a dinner of grilled goat at a four-star place high in the hills, protected from afar by guards with pump-action shotguns. Their table on the porch had an excellent view of the glittering streets below.

Once the waiters cleared the dessert plates, his contact, who called himself Joaquin, reached into his jacket and pulled out an elegant leather cigar case, opened it to remove a pair of fat Cohibas, and handed one over.

Bill smelled the cigar. "Cuban. That's sacrilege around here."

Joaquin shrugged as he placed a box of wooden matches in the center of the table. "Tradition is for the small-minded."

"Couldn't agree with you more," Bill said, lighting up. "So let's fast-forward to the actual you-know-what."

"You were good at what you did," Joaquin said. "Back in the States. Made your people a lot of money."

"Yes."

Joaquin nodded. "The gentlemen I represent, they have use of your talents. It is a very international crew: Russians, a couple of Brits, Israelis. You would be the first American."

"If I want the job, what do I need to do?"

"You have the job already." Joaquin studied the tension in Bill's face for a long moment, his eyebrows slightly raised. "We have no tryouts, or meetings, unless we are sure of someone. It will be hard work, but we will make a lot of money."

"What if I'm not sure? I mean, I'm willing to do a couple free-lance jobs here and there, but I consider my ass retired. I'm trying to hurt fewer people these days."

Joaquin shook his head. "It was you who reached out to us, before you left New York. Offered us money to help shelter you from your people. You came down to Texas, had some trouble along the way. You must have known all along what we'd want. We have a problem with uncertainty, if you catch my meaning."

"El Rey sold me out."

"El Rey refunded your fee. He said your girlfriend was very persuasive." Joaquin laughed. "That was your deal with El Rey, the middleman. I am talking about your deal with us."

Bill decided to play out this thread a little. "I'm all for making money," he offered.

"Good. Before we begin, one small matter to address," Joaquin took a sip of coffee, building the suspense. "We will need to spend a lot of money, go through a lot of trouble to keep you safe from your former associates. You will not need to pay the full amount of your protection, but we expect you to contribute to your upkeep."

"How much am I expected to contribute?"

"Thirty percent of your current holdings, plus a tax every month."

"No negotiation?"

Joaquin shook his head. "It is not our way. We also hold the option to increase this fee, should it become necessary. Do the work, and I do not foresee any rise in costs."

Once a hustler, Bill thought, always a hustler. "And if I say 'no,' something bad happens, right? To me and my girlfriend."

"I cannot say. You have a lot of enemies." Joaquin blew a tight smoke-ring before placing the half-finished cigar in the giant ashtray between them. "We can continue this dialogue about your concerns at another time. There is a project with a tight deadline, and we need you to start work. I will have more information by Monday."

For a wild moment, Bill considered picking up the ashtray and bringing it down on Joaquin's head. But what good would that do? He would only find himself on the run again, in a new country. Instead of capping an otherwise excellent dinner with a bloody burst of homicide, he turned away and puffed on his cigar, making a point to keep staring at the distant city as Joaquin silently stood and left the restaurant.

This is your punishment, Bill thought.

Did you really think you'd get away with it?

There is no retirement, not for people like you.

Back at the hotel, standing on the beach as the evening rain sprinkled down, Bill let his memory drift to that distant afternoon when the shabby man told him to shed his wicked life. He thought about the friends and colleagues who had placed the pistol to their skull and said why not, who had perished in stupid car smash-ups and druggy stupors and at the hands of psychopaths, their bodies left to dissolve in backwoods loam. The rain came down and Bill said to himself: Considering all that I've done, I have no right to be happy.

No, you're wrong, another voice said.

You've survived this long. You can make it through this, too. You'll play them like a violin. And maybe then, finally, you'll be safe.

Fiona walked out of the hotel and stood beside him, looking out at the emerald ocean under the darkening sky. "What are you thinking about?" she asked.

He grinned at her. "All the trouble I'm going to cause."

She slapped him on the back of the head, playfully. "You pretentious jackass. Let's get you a drink."

# GOOD DEATHS ALL AROUND

# 1

**JAMES DYZEK PUSHED** a thin blade through the Wehrmacht lieutenant's eye-socket until the brainpan cracked and the man trembled and went still. Everybody knew the war was ending and that anyone taken prisoner today would walk away free in a month or two and so James took the time to kill every Nazi he met. He had watched too many friends die to leave any of the enemy alive in good conscience.

Four decades later James would read a history book that described Americans in those last days of the European War as tired of killing. No such folks existed in his platoon. They bayoneted every Nazi they saw, raided every house they passed, pocketed every coin or trinket they could find. Once he tied a screaming German lady to the hood of his jeep, thinking it would make even a Nazi hesitate before taking a shot, only to change his mind after a sniper pumped two bullets into her spine. He carried a pearl-handled pistol like his idol George S. Patton but preferred the knife for close work. Years later he would use the same blade to cut meat at the neighborhood barbeques he hosted at his home in Queens and nothing about that fact struck him as odd or sacrilegious.

James pulled the blade from the German's eye-socket and wiped the brains on the grass. He shook some of the splatter off his boots. That evening he soaped his pits and crotch and submitted to the icy field shower, the blood on his skin mixing with the mud. After showering, he made sure the small bag retrieved from the lieutenant's pocket was safely tucked away in his pack.

In his old age James would view the War as the finest time of his life.

Later he would challenge his sons to push-up contests, laughing every time the kids collapsed while he pumped on and on and on. Later he would leave his respectable house in the middle of the night and drive to the unrespectable parts of town and throw a burning bottle through a random window and speed away as the flames licked the black sky. Later he would inherit his father's bar and preside over endless nights of wild debauchery.

# 2

**JAMES'S FATHER OPENED** the bar near Union Square in 1938 and spent forty years collecting coins and crumpled dollars from half of New York City in exchange for glasses of foamy beer and whiskey shots. James's father kept an oversized American flag pinned to the wall beside the front door, and liked to proclaim to anyone who would listen—and they all listened, thinking he might pour them a free drink—that his bar functioned as the world's last true democracy: that anyone, whether a greengrocer or a tailor from the Garment District or a Wall Street trader, could slap down a quarter for a boilermaker and take a seat on one of the chipped stools and voice an opinion.

When James came back from Europe he would spend his afternoons sitting beneath the flag, listening to the dried-out old men talk about horrors they witnessed in the First World War. He understood that they wanted to relate to him. In those years James worked for a butcher off Cooper Square and walked around the neighborhood in his bloody apron, and when he sat beneath the flag it was usually with a couple handfuls of peanuts, which he would shell and eat while nodding at those recollections of Belleau Wood and Blanc Mont Ridge and Hamel and the Second Battle of the Marne, mud and gangrene and artillery.

Before he met his wife and moved to Queens, James would use the bar's dingy closet of a bathroom to shave in the mornings, and oftentimes sleep atop the bar. He wanted to stay close to the valuables he had brought back from Germany, which he kept in a locked steel box on the bottom shelf of his father's safe in the back room. When his father started asking too many questions about the box, James hid it beneath the floorboards.

**3**

**AFTER HIS FATHER** lost his mind, James had to shave him twice a week. His father's skin had gone slack with age and James needed to pinch him beneath the jaw in order to smooth his cheeks enough for the razor. His father's pupils staring into him the whole time, deep and merciless as black holes. Although his father could still dress himself, sometimes James would come over to the house and find the old man sitting in his own piss, his thighs red and raw.

The woman paid to watch his father was good at preventing him from leaving the stove on, or tumbling down the stairs, or torturing the cat, but sometimes he fought when she tried to change him, and she would call James, who always spent the drive to his father's house yelling about how much time and money this all cost him, this refusal to die. Yet every time he came through the door with his fists balled and his face twisted in anger, his father adopted a look of such childlike contrition that it sent guilt slamming like a nail through James's guts, and he wasted hours doing the laundry, the dishes, and all the other chores his father would never notice.

That guilt never lasted. His father wandered around the house looking for his long-dead brother, or pissed into bottles that he left in the fridge. His father placed the radio in the stove and turned on the heat. On those bad days James would contemplate his famous knife, and whether the time has come for a long drive, just the two of them, into the forests upstate. James had killed a couple dozen men in Europe but ending your father's life is something else, even if your father has a head of broken clockwork.

One winter afternoon, on the woman's day off, James came over with groceries and found his father stiff and dead on the couch, and that was okay, it was better than shipping the old man off to a hospital to wind down his last months under the bored watch of nurses. James put the paper sacks on the table and sat on the couch and held his father's cold hand, rubbing his thumb over skin translucent as parchment. Outside the snow dissolved the world in white.

# 4

**AFTER HIS FATHER** died, James refused to change much about the bar, besides replacing the long maple stick beneath the register with a baseball bat. Every morning he opened the rear door to the dogs skulking in the alley and fed them organ meat donated by his old friends in the butcher business. When a health inspector tried to lecture him about the presence of canines in an establishment serving food and drink, James made a great show of taking the baseball bat from behind the bar and thwacking its barrel into his palm until the man left.

James quit drinking the day he inherited the bar, preferring to nurse a soda water while the men around him downed gallons of beer and harder stuff. To anyone who asked, James said he had no intention of slurping away his margins. He let undercover cops rub shoulders with the butchers and salesmen and artists, because he believed in law and order and the city around them roughened by the day. His sons were cowards and so he made them run drinks and break up fights in order to toughen them up for a hard world.

No matter how often people suggested he update the furniture, or at least vacuum the floor, James left the interior untouched. Portraits of John Brown and Theodore Roosevelt glowered from ornate frames above the liquor shelves, and the rococo mirror beside the bathroom door miraculously survived every brawl. Before he opened the bar to the day's drinkers, James would always head into the back room and unscrew the three floorboards nearest the north wall and peek into the space beneath, where that battered metal box contained his riches from overseas.

His retirement, as he thought of it.

His *treasure*.

# ACT II

## SLAUGHTERHOUSE BLUES

# 1

**KEEP JABBERING ABOUT** the Dusty Brothers Memorial Stripper Pole, Fiona muttered under her breath, and I swear I'll paint the walls of this bar with your guts.

The man across the table from her, John Dusty, raised his sun-reddened hands to mime how the local strip club's only pole had torn free of its bolts after too many years of vigorous use. His thick fingers flicked the air as he described how much "humanitarian aid" he delivered the next morning, in the form of a shopping bag stuffed with American dollars. That generous assistance helped put the hard-working employees of the Pussy Cat Disco back on their glittery five-inch heels within two days. "I even had the manufacturer make a little plaque for the new pole," he laughed. "It reads: 'In gratitude of all you've done, love, John and Don Dusty.'"

Fiona's hand drifted beneath the hem of her loose linen shirt, skimming the checkered grip of the automatic strapped to her hip. John was a mountainous dude, his frayed black tank-top barely holding back an avalanche of flesh, but a bullet has a nice way of reducing everyone to the same level.

A half-second on the draw and pull, she mused. Then, peace and quiet, once the bystanders stopped screaming.

So quick, so easy.

But ending her jackass client's existence would have meant dealing with the local cops, not to mention returning to Managua without a payday. Chewing the inside of her cheek, Fiona settled back in her seat and wondered when the waitress would deliver their food. Beside her, John's reed-thin brother Don sipped his lukewarm beer and stared at her chest with an intensity that suggested he was trying to gauge her cup size.

God, she hated these two.

Good thing they always paid in cash, half in advance.

John plowed onward: "In fact, this one little señorita, she's so overcome with happiness that she shows up at the factory a couple days later, offering to give me a lap dance right there in the office, and I…"

"I got a question," Fiona interrupted.

"Can I finish?" John frowned.

"In a sec," she said. "Before your ego gets too inflated and you float right off the face of the earth, I want to talk business. It was a long drive up. Why am I here?"

John fired an artillery round of a glare at Don, who shuddered in response. "Bro, she's right," Don said. "It's getting late."

"Late for you, maybe." Slugging down the last of his beer, John slammed down the glass hard enough to startle the nearby barflies. "Not for me, though. Since we gifted the pole, the club's always open."

The waitress arrived, bearing two steaming platters of grilled goat mixed with vegetables and rice. The bartender on her heels held three full pints of beer to his chest. The glorious smell of food roasting in well-seasoned iron made Fiona's stomach rumble. The one silver lining of driving through the Nicaraguan highlands to Estelí was the opportunity to eat at El Porrón, a bar that, like the neighborhood around it, offered some treasures behind its rough exterior.

Without waiting for either brother to make a move, Fiona

popped a sizzling-hot shred of goat in her mouth, washing it down with a mouthful of beer. "Business," she said. "It was a rough trip, and I want to get some shut-eye."

Don scanned the establishment for anyone within earshot. The three scruffy amigos on the far side of the bar cared more about their respective glasses than a conversation at the corner table. "We're being blackmailed," he said. "They want money we don't have, or they'll burn the factory down."

"The factory's concrete," Fiona said. "You got guards, fences."

John snorted and shook his head. "Someone torches the tobacco we got curing, the storerooms, we're out a couple years of stock. And sure, we could hire even more guards, but who knows if that'll work? Maybe it's an inside job."

"Other firms hear about our troubles, they'll make a play for our most skilled rollers, our back-office guys," Don added. "There are eight big cigar companies in town, including us. Competition's too tight for any disruption, you get me?"

"Loud and clear," Fiona said. "Any idea who's doing the blackmailing?"

"We got suspects." John shoveled down goat.

"All seven rivals," Don laughed.

"You're not paying me enough to start a war." Fiona slid a hand to her hip, drawing their eyes to the outline of her pistol. "I'm here to mop up a problem, spritz with cleanser, leave everything all shiny. That means you give me real leads, okay? What you got?"

Don frowned and crossed his arms. "Last night, someone throws a Molotov cocktail over the fence, hits that mural we had painted last summer. You know the one I'm talking about?"

Fiona sighed. A decade ago, these brothers, in the throes of a shared midlife crisis, started their foray into cigar-making with money from their small liquor-distribution business. They had built their factory a kilometer outside of Estelí, and filled it with two hundred employees who spent six days a week rolling dark Nicaraguan and Honduran tobacco leaves into cancer-sticks that sold for two hundred dollars a box. It was a sweet living, and a nice success story, but Fiona always winced when she took the curve near their property and saw a three-story-tall swimsuit model looming above the trees, a porno leer on her face as she brandished a pair of pink Uzis.

The brothers could afford to grow up a little.

Good thing they always paid in cash, half in advance.

"She's seen it," John said, reading her face. "Anyway, mural's wrecked, but we figured it's just someone wilding out. Until early this morning, when this kid shows up on a motorbike at the gate."

"You know the kid?" Fiona asked.

John shook his head. "Kept his helmet on the whole time, guard said. Visor down. Kid says get together five hundred thousand cash, that's U.S. dollars, be ready to deliver it by tomorrow at noon, or the whole place goes up in flames."

"Guard try to stop him?"

"Sure. And when he did, the kid pulled out some dinky pistol, shot him in the leg, drove off. Our nurse pulled out the bullet, guard's fine. We called you right after. We're taking this as a serious threat."

"You call the cops?"

Don shook his head. "You know the cops won't do crap."

That was good. The fewer *Policía Nacional* involved here, the better. "Where's the drop-off?"

"They haven't given us details. Said get the money together, wait for the call." John downed his pint in a single gulp, wiped the foam from his lips, and snapped his fingers at the bartender. "Whoever it is, we're not paying. We just don't have the liquidity. So we need you to grab whoever shows up, follow the trail from there."

"You know the deal: three thousand a day," Fiona said. "Minimum five days, plus expenses."

"Oh, come on." Don rolled his eyes. "How much money have we given you over the past couple months? We deserve a friends and family discount, or something."

"You're not friends, and you're not family. That's my rate." She scooped up a fresh load of animal protein and chewed it slowly, letting the silence build.

From his hip pocket, John pulled out one of his signature cigars, tore off the tip with his teeth, and spat a glistening nub of tobacco on the floor. Don slipped a butane lighter from his pocket and torched his brother's smoke.

"Fine," John said, exhaling a long white plume. "Fifteen grand to save half a million, not so bad, right?"

"It's good math," Fiona agreed, wrinkling her nose at the stench of burning tobacco. "And I get half up front, as always."

Another long pause from the brothers, mostly for theater's sake, before Don reached into the bag at his feet and slapped a padded envelope the size of a brick on the table. Fiona nodded her thanks and slipped it into her own bag.

"Where you staying?" John asked. "Need a room anywhere?"

"I'm right around the corner," Fiona said. That was a lie. A healthy sense of paranoia had kept her upright and breathing far longer than anyone expected, especially herself. "Don't worry about me, guys."

"So as I was saying about this little señorita…" John shifting gears again, as the waiter brought him a fresh pint.

Fiona tuned him out, vaguely hoping his beer contained a generous load of spit, courtesy of the bartender. Her seat offered a view of the bar's front door, open to the night. She heard the mosquito whine of an approaching car, a click, and an amplified voice hollering in Spanish: one of the propaganda vehicles that circled these neighborhoods at all hours, pumping out slogans at ear-bursting volume. Headlights brightened the crumbling curb beyond the door, driving away a bony dog.

"By the way, at this point I can recognize half these chicks just by their tattoos…'"

As it passed the bar, the car backfired, loud as a shotgun blast. John yipped and dove for the floor, hitting hard enough to rattle every plate and chair in the room. His flailing arm smacked the legs of Don's chair, and then both brothers were down, roaring in surprise and pain.

Fiona bit a knuckle to stop her laughter. "Nervous much, boys?" she asked sweetly.

Don't humiliate them, murmured the saner voice in her head. You need the money. Without it, you and Bill are dead.

# 2

**BILL KNEW THE** bastards were following him.

Maybe he should have dressed a little less conspicuously, but the white seersucker suit had called to him as he rifled through his luggage that morning. Paired with a straw hat, a cornflower-blue dress shirt, and a natty bow-tie, he looked every inch the Hemingway character as he exited the five-star Meliá Cohíba, a block away from the crumbling splendor of the Malecón, the road that separates Havana from the sea. Weeks of dressing like a stereotypical tourist, in t-shirts and baggy shorts, had sickened his soul.

He hungered for a decent meal, a difficult thing to find in the state-run hotels, where the employees swiped the best stuff behind the scenes. Those stolen morsels often found their way to the *paladars*, or the small restaurants that Cubans ran out of their homes. A concierge had recommended a good one a half-kilometer from the Cohíba, claiming the family there served the best coffee in Havana, provided you were copacetic with drinking it beside a coop that housed an irate rooster.

Crossing the Malecón to the crumbling sea-wall, he paused to reach into his jacket and extract a flat alligator-skin case. Inside sat a trio of Dusty Brothers cigars. Yesterday morning Fiona had left for their factory in Nicaragua, to solve some sort of problem. Bill had never met the guys himself, but he knew they paid her a lot of money to do their dirty work, and always sent her home with a fresh box of smokes. Cupping a lit match in his hands, he torched the smallest of the cigars. The smell and the smoke he could take or leave, but the nicotine really helped him think.

Truth be told, he needed a few days away from his girlfriend. If you think relationships are hard, try maintaining one while on the run from some of the worst people alive. Sure, Bill drank when stressed out, and sometimes let his mouth run a little—that didn't give Fiona the right to throw things at his head, or tell him over and over again to get his crap together.

He missed the days when they would lie in bed until eleven, find something sugary to eat, and spend the afternoon listening to music while Fiona cleaned her guns. Nothing big or fancy: just living life. During the worst night of their escape, chained in a redneck psycho's basement, Bill had clung to those memories the way someone religious might grip a crucifix. But even in Havana, their old routine failed to return; they were too wired, counting and recounting their cash, jumpy at the sound of footfalls and loud voices.

Returning the case to his pocket, Bill noticed the man and woman standing fifty yards further down the Malecón. They were dressed like the vacationing Europeans who filled this section of the city: linen shirts, khaki pants for him and a knee-length red skirt for her, their faces hidden by sunglasses and wide-brim straw hats.

Something about the couple set Bill's inner alarm wailing. Maybe it was how they kept glancing his way. Or how their hands stayed in their pockets.

Bill breathed smoke and strode with purpose in the opposite direction. At this hour of morning, swarms of kids dashed along the low wall to his left, breaking around the old men sunning themselves on the concrete. A few stopped their frantic activity long enough to ask Bill for a peso; he waved them off. Another quick look over his shoulder confirmed the worst: the couple was following him, fast. From twenty yards away, he could see the man was hulking as a football player, the woman small and lithe.

What did they want?

When you make a living by ripping folks off, the list of those who want you dead becomes very, very long after a few decades.

Top of the Kill Bill list: the crew in the Dominican Republic who had offered Bill protection after he ran out on his old employers, the Rockaway Mob. After a few weeks, Bill and Fiona had decided the "security" came at too high a price, and took their leave. Maybe he shouldn't have left with a big chunk of the crew's money.

Competing for the number-one spot on that same list: the Rockaway Mob. A group of scary dudes back in New York City who wrecked things better than a herd of bulls in an antique shop. It was fun when the bulls were on your side, and you wanted that antique shop stomped flat, but it was far less entertaining when those horns thirsted for your blood. Maybe he shouldn't have left with a big chunk of their money, either.

And if you excluded those two fine groups, you still had thirty-odd years of rubes itching for a shot at Bill's head. Hell, for all he knew, his fifth-grade teacher had signed away part of her retirement savings to a hit team as retribution for Bill stealing her car back in the day.

"I should've been an accountant," Bill sighed.

It was suicidal to stay in the open. He waited for a break in traffic and trotted across the Malecón again at Calle 19, skirting the elegant hulk of the Hotel Nacional. On the opposite curb he stopped and turned, cigar clenched between his lips, waiting to see what the couple did next. He was reasonably certain neither one carried a pistol. When you arrived at José Martí Airport, just outside of Havana, the customs agents ran your bags and bodies through metal detectors. The regime's paranoia made it almost impossible to buy a gun on the street.

But knives were pretty easy to find.

The couple stopped across from Bill as the Malecón swelled

anew with Russian-made taxis and ancient Fords. Their sunglasses and hats mostly hid their features, aside from sharp jawlines. The woman had slashed her mouth with a deep red lipstick that made it look like a wound.

Just as quickly as it appeared, the traffic began to slacken again. A beautiful battleship of a '57 Chevy, all fins and polished chrome, slid to a stop in front of Bill. The young driver craned his head toward the open passenger window, asking if señor needed a ride somewhere for cheap.

Yes, señor most definitely needed a ride, price no object.

Opening the heavy rear door, Bill slid into the backseat. *"Vamos!"* The Chevy heaved onto the road, its joints creaking as it picked up speed. Bill stuck his hand out the window and offered the disappearing couple a proud middle finger.

The driver asked him slowly: *"¿Adónde quieres ir?"*

Bill settled into his seat, puffing his cigar. His nerves demanded something a little stronger than *paladar* coffee. In halting Spanish, he told the man to take him to El Floridita, one of the most notable drinking-holes in town, where the bartenders could whip him up one or three world-class daiquiris. As the Chevy squeezed through avenues clogged with antique cruisers, the fear struck Bill hard as a bullet:

Of course they hadn't chased him. Morning on the Malecón meant too many witnesses and cops, in a country that doubled as a jail.

They were testing his perimeter, seeing how he reacted.

And they knew where he was staying.

**3**

**FIONA SPENT THE** night in her usual Estelí haunt, a small apartment above a coffin store in Barrio Villa Esperanza, on the city's eastern edge. The luxurious accommodations included a bare mattress on a low wooden platform, a small desk teetering on a splintered leg, and a window that opened onto the next-door neighbor's roof. She paid the coffin store's owner fifty bucks a night to stay up there, and in return for that princely sum he asked no questions. He also allowed her to park her rental jeep a few blocks away, in a garage he owned.

"One change from last time," the owner told her in Spanish, after unlocking the apartment door and ushering her inside. "Do not use the shower."

"Why?" Fiona peeked into the tiled shower stall. "Does it bite?"

"Heater's broken. The wires, it's a mess."

As with more than a few bathrooms in this part of the world, the shower-head included a built-in heating element. Cold water from the pipes flowed over a hot, insulated coil inside the unit before jetting out the nozzle at a piss-warm temperature. Stepping into the stall, Fiona saw a deep crack in the shower-head's plastic shell. If that wasn't worrisome enough, the electrical cord that snaked from the back of the unit to a hole in the ceiling looked a little frayed.

"Zap," Fiona said.

The man nodded. "Zap."

"Guess I'm not cleaning up."

Once she settled in, she powered up her phone and tried Bill. Eight rings before it cut to voicemail. A minute later she tried again. Still no answer. She tried to squelch the fright prickling her belly. He's probably asleep, she told herself. Passed out drunk, like he did every time she left.

Or maybe he's not picking up because he's still mad at you, a nasty little voice whispered. You keep saying he's too soft for this fugitive thing, but maybe you're too hard, too quick with the gun. You shot that man in Oklahoma when he tried to help you—

*He was a killer. Shut up.*

Or maybe Bill's dead. Maybe someone finally came up behind him on the street and put a bullet in his skull, or a knife between his ribs, and you weren't there to save him—

"Shut up," she whispered to the empty room.

After sending Bill a text, she forced herself to go to sleep. If she had to worry, she preferred to do so on a full night's rest.

The owner had provided two thin pillows and a stack of blankets. After piling most of the bedding into a human-shaped form on the bed, she retired to the bathroom, where she spread one of the blankets on the floor of the shower stall and curled up there, her pistol and phone in easy reach. Without air conditioning, the night was humid and still. Sweat trickled from her skin as she slept fitfully, dreaming of dead Bill afloat in the middle of the ocean, the jacket of his fabulous suit billowing in the current.

When she woke up, her phone displayed no new voicemails or texts. Her worry sprouted claws and fangs, ripped at her insides. She did a hundred push-ups to exhaust it, dressed in a t-shirt and jeans, and headed outside for a cup of coffee.

Following a hefty dose of caffeine, along with a jumbo bottle of water to replenish her sweat reservoir, Fiona drove across town to meet with one of her old contacts, easing the jeep through narrow streets teeming with kids kicking soccer balls, whining dirt-bikes, factory workers stuffed in rattletrap sedans, dogs nosing through rubble in search of scraps. The bright stucco walls still scarred from a civil war decades in the past. She took a left down a dirt alley, followed by a hard right into an open garage, parking beside a rusty pickup missing its wheels.

Shutting off the engine, Fiona climbed out of the jeep and unlocked the rear hatch. A door opened in the back of the garage, framing an old man in khakis and a starched white shirt: Ortiz. She noted his bare feet, the skin toughened to callus, three toes missing thanks to a Sandinista torture session.

After giving her a fierce hug, Ortiz reached into the bed of the pickup and whipped back an oily tarp, unveiling a very special payload.

"Will this do?" he asked, smiling because he already knew her answer.

"Yes, it most certainly will," she replied, reaching into her back pocket for a fat wad of American dollars.

"How is your father?"

"He's good," she said, handing over the cash. "Enjoying retirement, smoking too damn much. He sends his love."

"When you speak to him again, please tell him that Luis still enjoys the chickens. He will understand." Ortiz chuckled softly.

"Sure thing." I don't even want to know what that's in reference to, she thought. Two old wolves making in-jokes about the bad old days in Black Ops, when her Dear Old Dad helped plant more than a few bodies in the hills around here.

On the return trip to the apartment she tried Bill twice. No answer. She was tempted to drop everything and drive back to Managua, catch the first flight to Havana. But the Dusty brothers had paid her half in advance, and that meant seeing the job through.

In her apartment again, after changing into a loose linen shirt, she armed herself. A handful of plastic riot-cuffs went in the left back pocket of her jeans, along with an extra pistol magazine in her right. She checked the spring release on the push dagger nested in her oversized belt buckle. With those tasks complete, she stripped down and rebuilt her pistol—a regular habit before every mission, and one that served her well.

Before leaving, Fiona undertook one final task. Sure, she could have rented a room practically anywhere in town, but this one offered another advantage over a hotel. The push dagger slipped neatly into a crack between the floorboards in one corner of the main room. A little tug, and a trapdoor sprung open on a hinge, exposing a crawl-space. Another artifact of the civil war. She slipped her bag into the hole and lowered the hinge again.

Separating from the money gave her a jolt of anxiety, but the hidey-hole was the safest place for it until she returned. Back in the jeep, she phoned Bill. Still nothing. She needed to finish this job as fast as possible and leave.

It was a pleasant drive out to the Dusty Brothers' cigar factory, a low red building on a hill overlooking the muddy churn of the Rio Estelí. On the approach, the bikini mural flickered into view through the trees, its bottom half scorched to ash, the model's smile blackened. The two guards at the gate waved her through without a word, and she parked beyond the glittering rows of workers' bicycles.

Don appeared in a doorway, dressed in a t-shirt with the Captain America shield on it, puffing on a stubby cigar. "You're a little early," he said, barely meeting her eyes. Probably embarrassed after last night. Nobody likes falling on their ass in a public place.

"I like to shake things up," she said, noting how his hands quaked.

"Want some coffee? We got time to kill."

"Sure."

The interior of the factory was raw industrial space. Don escorted her through the rolling room, sunlit by tall windows covered with steel mesh. At rows of wooden desks, rollers smoothed out tobacco leaves on thick boards before trimming the edges with their curved *chaveta* blades. The clacking of steel blended into a backbeat to the Latin pop pounding from the speakers bolted to the walls.

Fiona watched a nearby worker expertly stuff a tight handful of filler leaves into a wooden mold. The wrapper leaf went over that molded bundle, followed by a small cap held in place with vegetable paste. Floor inspectors walked between the rows, examining finished cigars in the wooden bins atop the desks. Fiona knew from previous visits that the cigars would end up in boxes in the *escaparates*, cool chambers deep inside the factory, where they would age for months. That is, unless someone lit the place on fire.

They climbed a flight of concrete stairs to the lounge. A pair of coffee-makers hummed on a table at the far end, beside a pair of plush leather couches that had seen better days. Along the longest wall gleamed a spray-painted canvas, cartoon soldiers firing bolts of light at a purple tentacled monster. Large windows overlooked the rolling room.

"Where's John?" Fiona asked, as Don plucked two empty cups from the stack beside the machines and went to work.

"Out," Don said. "He'll be back in a bit."

"He traveling with any security?"

Don shook his head. "No. You know how he is. Thinks he's got the biggest nuts in the jungle. When we were kids, our father made fun of his weight all the time, made us do push-ups. So now he compensates."

Fiona plopped on the couch, angling herself so she could keep an eye on the stairs and the large television bolted to the far wall, the latter turned to a cable news channel flashing images of a very familiar scene. "Trying to compensate is a good way to get killed. Any evil blackmailers call yet?"

"Nope. I figure they'll wait until noon, right? That was the deadline."

"Maybe. Or they might ring earlier, try and keep us on our toes." On the muted screen, the blackened remains of a large barn smoked beside a farmhouse. The image cut to what looked like an industrial pit, surrounded by forensic specialists in white jumpsuits. Fiona felt around the couch cushions for the remote, interested in what the newscaster might have to say about the small town where she and Bill almost lost their lives.

Before her hands touched anything other than scuffed leather, Don spun around with two cups of coffee in his trembling hands. "I don't know," he said, frowning as he tried to avoid spilling hot liquid everywhere. "We're not exactly pros at all this, okay? That's what we pay you for."

"Yeah, yeah." Fiona stood and liberated her coffee from his shaky grip. "When they do phone us, you're coming with me, okay?"

Don paled. "Why? We're not giving them any money."

On the television, the camera zoomed in close on a handsome FBI agent's face. Although Fiona considered her lip-reading skills subpar, she could tell when his mouth formed the words 'suspects,' 'fugitives,' and 'New York.' Wonderful. "Because they'll be suspicious if one of the famous Dusty brothers doesn't show up," she said. "I want them thinking they still got the advantage. Don't worry, I'll keep you safe. And one other thing: we're taking my car."

"Why?"

"I like how it handles. It does off-road really well, if we need it to."

"Okay."

"You got a big bag with a zipper, one you don't care about?" Fiona knew from personal experience that a half-million dollars in hundred-dollar bills weighed somewhere in the neighborhood of thirty pounds. There was a good chance that whoever arranged this blackmailing knew the right weight, too.

"Why are you rushing me?" Based on his tone, Don had decided to substitute dread for anger. "We got like three hours before they call…"

A phone beside the coffee-makers buzzed, jolting Don hard enough to spatter coffee on his hands. Fiona checked her watch, sensing it was showtime.

# 4

**BILL HAD HIS** passport, his hotel key-card, and a hundred in Cuban pesos. The money would last him hardly any time at all on the street, unless he started pickpocketing tourists. There was also the Piaget Altiplano ticking on his wrist, but he would never part with his favorite timepiece. Not after all the blood and thunder he had endured to keep it.

Tucked in the cool, dark womb of El Floridita, he downed his third daiquiri and reviewed his options. The blonde lady beside him, dressed in denim shorts and a t-shirt with the Cuban flag on it, seemed like a convenient target: her leather bag hung from the back of her seat, unzipped.

At this early hour, only a few tourists occupied the round red tables along the wall. The crimson-vested bartender—distracted, tired, or maybe hungover—ran a rag along the lacquered shelf behind the bar. Nobody glanced at Bill as he leaned toward the bag, spying a folded wad of pesos and the shiny edge of a phone just inside the opening. Perfect. Go for the cash first.

Gesturing to the bartender for another drink, he pulled out his wallet—and promptly dropped it on the floor. Leaning over to retrieve it, he let his forearm brush the bag, his fingers darting inside. As he straightened, the pesos disappeared into his cupped palm.

The blonde lady, fixated on the life-size statue of Hemingway leaning on the far end of the bar, appeared none the wiser. Hells bells, Bill thought. I guess I haven't lost my skills after all. After transferring the stolen money to his jacket pocket, he turned to his freshened daiquiri and puzzled over his crisis.

He couldn't go back to the hotel right now. The lobby of the Meliá Cohíba offered visitors a wide selection of couches and chairs, most with excellent views of the doors, front desk, and elevators. The creepy couple, in their fashion-forward tourist gear, could haunt there forever without anyone bothering them.

And who's to say they didn't have his room number already? They could wait for a maid to open the door and walk in as if they belonged there, ambush Bill whenever he entered.

With a little more money, he could take a chance on the airport, buy a flight to somewhere less heavy. That would mean abandoning everything in his room: the suits, the cash, his phone, Fiona's luggage…

Fiona.

He pictured his phone tucked in his bag beside the bed, ringing nonstop, his girlfriend panicking on the other end. Why hadn't he brought it with him, or at least checked for messages before walking out the door? He knew the answer: their last fight had left him in a mood.

When the blonde lady turned to him, he tensed, ready for the accusation. Instead she smiled, flashing rows of perfect teeth, and his guts unclenched a little. She was young, maybe early twenties, her unlined face suggesting a lifetime of only trivial worries.

"Hey," she said, slurring a little. "I'm Marnie."

"Steve." He made no move to shake her hand.

Marnie leaned into him. "Where you from, Steve?"

He placed her accent in the Midwest somewhere, the vowels flat as Kansas. "Arkansas. How about you?"

She dodged the question. "We're here on educational

exchange. Part of a graduate program thing." Her voice dipped to a confidential timbre. "I know they say it's dangerous to leave the group, because of crime? But I had to get a drink. Our professor's been driving us just that crazy."

"Sounds like you're having a heck of a morning."

She laughed. "Could be worse, I guess. Can I ask you something weird?"

"Sure."

She nodded at the statue. "That's Ernest Hemingway, right?"

"Uh, yeah." Bill jabbed a finger at the wall behind the bronze figure. "See that photo above his head, to the left a bit? That's Hemingway and Castro. He used to live down here. As a kid I used to read all his stuff, loved it. Even 'To Have and Have Not,' although I think I'm the only one who does. Have you read it?"

"No, he's too macho for my taste." Her face scrunched, in the way of drunk people trying to concentrate on reality, and she gestured at Bill's raised hand. "I'm sorry, I shouldn't ask, but how did you lose…"

He turned his wrist, giving her a better view of the index finger, which ended in a scarred stump at the second knuckle. "A crooked cop chopped it off because I wouldn't tell him where the money was."

"You're kidding."

"Nope." He wiggled the stump. "Don't worry, though. Once I broke free, I shot him."

Her smile died. "No, tell me you're kidding."

"Nope. I got the drop on him because he slipped on my severed finger. I'm in Cuba because I'm a wanted man back in the States."

Her hands flattened on the bar, her legs stiffening. She was about to leave, and that was a problem, because he needed her phone if he wanted to stay alive. Working every ounce of warmth he could into a broad grin, he said: "Got you."

Marnie's lips twitched upwards. "Really?"

"Yeah. Severed in a car accident. No big deal. I mean, it was a big deal at the time, don't get me wrong, but I'm sort of used to it now."

She relaxed into her seat. "You're weird."

He saluted her with his glass. "What'd you expect in a bar at this hour?"

"No, not weird in a bad way. Just different." She skimmed a strand of hair away from her face. "So you're a tourist? You here alone?"

Bill took the opportunity to bend closer, his hand on the back of her chair. He could smell the rum and lime on her breath. "I'm on a Hemingway tour. Told you I was a fan, remember? We see his house, pet the cats, all that jazz."

"Petting the cats sounds macho." She gestured at her empty glass. "I think I need another drink. I can't face the idea of heading back to the hotel quite yet."

"I'll get it." Bill's hand disappeared into his jacket.

"Thanks." Marnie stood, slinging her bag onto her shoulder. "And I have to hit the loo. Be right back."

Once she disappeared around the corner, Bill leaned back in his seat, flexing his fingers like a pianist after a long concert. Always a little paranoid about his health, he wondered if the ache in his bones was the first sign of arthritis. Her stolen phone sat heavy in his jacket pocket, beside her cash.

*You're slick, boy! Still got it!*

Slipping another few pesos onto the bar, he stood and headed for the door, his feet only a little unsteady. You want another sign you're ancient? When you can't down copious amounts of alcohol with no ill effects. I got to retire, he thought.

The bright Havana sun smacked him full in the face. Pausing at the curb to allow a few bright junkers to cruise past, he pulled out Marnie's phone and flicked the power button. The device ran an older version of Android he could crack, provided he had enough time. Pocketing it again, he crossed the road, intending to disappear into Havana's grungy Chinatown for a few hours.

Marnie shouted behind him.

So much for being slick. She must have wanted to check her Facebook in the bathroom, or something.

Bill forced himself to walk at a normal pace. *Find a cab, get the hell out of here.* A half-block away, a pair of teenagers tucked beneath the open hood of a cherry-red Ford, banging on the engine with a wrench wrapped in tape. When one of them paused and turned around, Bill caught his eye and raised his hands to grip an invisible wheel.

The kid started to nod, only to jolt upright and tap his friend's shoulder. They slammed the hood and ducked into the car, which squealed away from the curb fast enough to leave a black comma of burnt rubber behind.

That was odd. Who around here turned down a chance at cold, hard cash?

Bill risked a glance behind him.

Oh.

A cop stood in front of the bar, a hand on his sidearm. Marnie gripped his elbow while spinning a tale of deception and thievery in what sounded like pitch-perfect Spanish. The cop asked a question, and she waved an arm at Bill.

Shit.

While dressing that morning, Bill had selected a pair of Berluti calfskin loafers, hand-stitched and sleek and totally unfit for running. The slick soles squeaked on the pavement as he sprinted through the crowds, praying that the law would hesitate at the prospect of tackling a tourist long enough to give him even the most pathetic head-start. His beautiful hat flew off, disappearing into a gap between two parked cars. In the reflection of a startled bystander's sunglasses he saw the distorted shape of the policeman in pursuit, firearm free of its holster, Marnie hard on his heels. Ankles already screaming in pain, Bill tried to accelerate, his panicked breath loud in his ears.

# 5

**THE CALLER TOLD** them to drive into the hills, take a certain road to a clearing. Fiona and Don piled into the jeep and headed off, saying nothing as the bright colors and chipped concrete of town gave way to grassy slopes, barbed-wire fences, and the occasional brick house. Along the dusty shoulder of the road, workers walked in single file, waving whenever Fiona tooted the horn.

"What'd you put in there?" Don said, nodding at the soiled duffel bag in the backseat.

"About twenty pounds of tobacco, but don't worry, no leaves, just the little bits. I asked the sweepers to give me the scraps."

Don laughed. "A couple years back, we tried taking those scraps, making cigarettes out of them. They sold, but not enough. You can't fight Big Tobacco."

"You know what's a good rule for life?" Fiona said. "Don't fight groups dedicated to killing millions of people."

"That's hilarious." Don fumbled beneath his shirt and drew a silver .32-caliber pistol from his waistband, waving it at the ceiling like a bandit on a drunken rampage. "By the way, I brought this. You know, just in case. Better safe than sorry."

Fiona resisted the urge to snatch the pistol out of his hand and toss it out the window. Mostly because the road had transitioned into a series of dusty switchbacks, and she needed to focus on steering. "Wonderful," she said through gritted teeth. "You have a gun. You ever shoot that before, champ?"

"I'll have you know our father taught us to shoot. I'm pretty good. No expert marksman, but I can sure hit a target."

"Do me a favor: put that away before you blow your balls off," she snapped.

Don let his pistol sag between his knees. "Fine."

"Now do me a second favor: pull out your phone, and check how many ways we can get back to town other than on this road."

"I think this is the only way. Trust me, I've lived here for years."

"I want to see what Google says."

With a shrug, Don slipped the pistol into his jeans and pulled his phone from his pocket. After tapping and pinching the screen, he frowned. "I told you, it's just this one."

She took her eyes off the road long enough to look at the screen. "Crap."

"Doesn't mean there's not another way back down, dirt or something, but it's not showing up on here. As far as Google's concerned, this road is it."

"We'll have to make the best of things." Her thoughts drifted to that news clip of the barn in flames, and the FBI agent talking about fugitives. How do you make the best of things when everybody in the world wants a piece of you?

"I think we're close." Don pointed through the windshield. Straight ahead, the road terminated in a tangle of rocks and greenery. The cliff to their right offered a panoramic view of Estelí's ragged grid of red roofs, softened by the morning haze. On their left, through a gap in the scrawny trees, a narrow dirt lane led into a glade stippled in shadow.

"I guess so," Fiona said, turning down the lane. After five yards she slammed on the brakes.

"What? What's wrong?" Flailing Don scrambled for his waistband, head thrashing as he tried to locate the threat.

"Nothing yet," Fiona said, throwing the jeep into reverse. "Just setting us up." One hand on the wheel, she executed a deft three-point turn that left the vehicle angled toward the road. In the rearview mirror, she saw a shirtless boy in a muddy dirt-bike helmet step into the clearing, the fractured sunlight through the trees flashing off something metallic in his hand.

"Don?" Fiona said, shutting off the engine.

"Yeah?"

"I want you to take a breath and hold it."

Don let his head flop forward, inhaling through his nose.

"Good," Fiona said. "Now exhale slowly. Count to ten in your head as you do it."

Don obeyed. When the last of the air left his lungs, he inhaled again and asked: "Why am I doing this?"

"Feeling relaxed?"

He grinned. "A little, sure?"

Fiona gripped her door handle. "Good. There's a kid with a gun right behind us, and I don't want you losing your shit like a little girl."

Don lost his shit like a little girl. While he flailed in his seat, Fiona opened the rear hatch of the jeep and fetched the duffel bag. The jungle air wrapped her head like a sauna towel, her forehead instantly beaded with sweat.

The kid stopped in the middle of the glade, cheap pistol loose in his grip, finger off the trigger. Fiona decided to meet him there, tall grass slapping against her calves. She made a big show of wrestling with the bag's weight. She wanted the kid to take it and hold it close.

When she came within fifteen feet, the kid raised a hand, palm out. She stopped and asked: *"Habla inglés?"*

The kid shook his head and pointed over his shoulder at the forest, where a second man emerged from the trees: white, older, his gray hair shorn in a tight crew cut, his arm muscles bulging like stones in a leather bag. He wore a black bullet-resistant vest over a gray t-shirt, and jeans. A black .45 automatic dangled in the holster on his hip.

"Oh crap," Fiona said, her pistol drawn and raised before the second word left her mouth.

Crew Cut lifted his arms and smiled, seemingly unconcerned about the prospect of a bullet in his brain. "Been a long time, dear. When's the last time I saw you? That night in Newark, the thing with the pen?"

Her weapon aimed at his forehead, Fiona considered taking the shot. Quarter-second for the pull, then shift to the kid if he tried to draw down. After that, hit the dirt and crawl back to the jeep, in case other shooters lurked in the woods. Through the trees she glimpsed—or imagined she glimpsed—the white flank and tinted windows of a large SUV, although the light out here played tricks.

The dry click of a pistol-hammer behind her. She risked a look back. Don stood beside the jeep, his .32 aimed squarely at her back. His cheeks bloodless, the pistol wavering only a little.

"Your luck's run out." Crew Cut mock-apologetic as he crept for her. "But did you really expect any different? From the very beginning, you must have known how this would end."

"There was no blackmail, was there?" Fiona, you idiot.

Crew Cut shook his head. "The Dean had a great idea: set up a fake job, lure you out."

"I'm sorry, Fiona," Don called out, his voice quaking.

"I'm going to chop your balls off," Fiona yelled over her shoulder. "You and your brother."

The kid gestured for the duffel bag, and with a shrug Fiona tossed it at his feet. He hefted the strap onto his shoulder, the bag angled toward Crew Cut. Good.

"Bill's not with me," Fiona said.

"Oh, I know," Crew Cut said. "He's in Havana. We have two people on him now."

And Bill's not much of a fighter, whispered that nasty voice in Fiona's head. Sure, he can take care of himself, but not against two killers. Not in a place where we don't have friends.

Crew Cut began to lower his arms. The kid, standing near him, fumbled one-handed with the bag's zipper. Something clanked.

Fiona chuckled. "Good thing I believed this was blackmail."

His hands level with his ribs—low enough to make a play for his holster—Crew Cut smirked at her, probably expecting a joke. "Yeah? Why's that?"

A hard tug, and the bag unzipped.

Fiona squeezed her eyes shut.

The blackness inside her eyelids exploded nuclear red. The bang smacked her eardrums hard as fists, dropping her to one knee.

Over the apocalyptic ringing in her ears, she heard a high-pitched scream. She opened her eyes again. The world was a squirmy purple octopus. She blinked her overloaded retinas clear. The kid danced shrieking for the trees, the skin on his right side black with ash, bits of flaming bag and tobacco scorching his helmet. Crew Cut stumbled in the other direction, hands pressed to his ears, mouth open in a silent howl.

Fiona took the opportunity to lift her pistol and fire one, two, three times, aiming for the head-shot but hitting Crew Cut center-mass as he swiveled, a pink spray as a bullet found meat. He dropped out of sight. Without pausing, she spun to the jeep, ready to put a bullet in Don before he put one in her.

Don had already dropped his pistol. Over her gunsights Fiona had a prime angle on his skinny ass as he ripped open his passenger door. Her next bullet, aimed at his knees, only skimmed his left hip, shredding the leg of his jeans. Yelping Don plowed headfirst into the glove compartment before flopping out of the vehicle and onto the grass, thrashing as he clutched his bleeding nose with both hands.

Fiona scrambled to him and leveled her smoking pistol an inch from his forehead. Her ears had settled enough to hear him gurgling in pain. "Flash-bangs," she yelled. "Friend gave 'em to me."

Don howled something that might have been *"what"* or *"shit."* His pulped nose made it hard to tell.

"Come on." She shoved him hard against the side of the jeep, reaching into the back pocket of her jeans for the riot cuffs. It was hard to lasso his wrists while holding the gun, but she had some experience. With his hands bound at the waist, and his nose freely pouring red, she pushed him into the passenger seat.

As she slammed the passenger door, the jeep's back window exploded in a glittering spray of safety glass. She ducked and spun, glimpsing Crew Cut's head as he dove beneath the grass. Pacing off her shots, she retreated around the front of the jeep, using its bulk as a shield, until she reached the driver's door and yanked it open. Sliding into the seat like a normal person would have made a nice target of her silhouetted head, so she flopped inside on her stomach, stabbed the key in the ignition, shifted into drive, and pressed down the gas pedal with her hand.

The windshield coughed glass, two small holes appearing above the steering wheel. Don yelped. The jeep rolled slowly down the dirt lane, picking up speed as gas and gravity did their work, and she tucked her legs onto the seat. The open driver's door banged against a small tree, slamming it shut against her heels. She risked peeking over the dashboard, gripping the wheel in both hands as she did so.

*"I'b sobby,"* Don blubbered, his chin a mess of blood and drool. *"Sobby, tho sobby."*

"Better duck," Fiona said. The rearview mirror framed Crew Cut in a classic two-handed shooter's stance, his shoulder above the black vest soaked red, not that the damage spoiled the steadiness of his aim.

Don's head flopped forward, speckling the dashboard with blood from his nose, as Crew Cut's next shot hit something in the jeep's rear that responded with a loud boom. The wheel turned traitor, burning her palms, and she tried to steer into the slide as best she could, but the jeep was too close to the edge of the cliff.

They went over.

Through the windshield she saw sky, trees, sky again.

Fiona's stomach dropped.

Don shrieked.

The jeep skidded broadside down the slope, its wheels

spinning great plumes of dirt and rocks, branches slapping the windshield. Fiona tried to control the descent, steer away from the larger boulders, only to have the vehicle tilt hard on two wheels, inches from toppling over. Don screeched in harmony with crumpling steel. Through the trees she saw a flash, maybe sun on glass, and they crashed through a screen of thorny shrubs into the shanty.

The jeep plowed through the first shack clean, wooden boards bouncing off the cracking windshield, boom, chickens flapping scared in her path, a plastic barrel crushed beneath her wheels as the bumper missed a rusty stove by inches, boom, an instant of sunlight before they plowed into the next house down the hill, a loose lump of clothing smacking the hood making her think oh God she hit someone maybe a child but it was only laundry thank God, the jeep demolishing a mattress in an explosion of springs and stuffing before smashing through a tin wall, boom, bouncing off a flat boulder hard enough to send her throat hard against the seat belt, choking, blood trickling down her face as she slammed against the steering wheel, the ceiling, the window that broke under the force of her elbow sending a fresh jolt of pain up her arm but she could still grip the wheel not that it did much good as the jeep ruined yet another shanty-house a chicken splattering the crumpled hood leaving a dark fan of blood some poor family's livelihood, shit, bouncing off a log and airborne weightless about to vomit—

The jeep crashed onto a paved road, engine grinding, headlights shattered, the paint scratched away, the hood peeled like the lid of a used can.

Good thing I used that fake name with the rental agency, Fiona thought, otherwise I might be in some real trouble here. That was before she spied, through the gummy mess of the broken windshield, something that made her erupt into hysterics: a tattered bra, with faded flowers on its cups, wrapped around the top of the jeep's antenna like the flag of a lunatic pirate.

Someone hollered above them, and her laughter died. Halfway

up the hill, an older woman stood on the wooden platform that had once been her house, unleashing a torrent of curses.

Fiona ran shaking hands over her body for wounds. A few cuts on her hands and forehead, a deeper gash on her wrist, otherwise nothing serious. Lodged between her thighs, a severed chicken head glared at her.

"Sorry, little dude," she said, and the chicken head blinked.

Beside her, Don clutched his leg and wept softly.

"Don." Fiona searched the trashed interior for her pistol, finding it wedged between her seat and the middle console. Prying the weapon free, she engaged the safety and slipped it back in her holster. Even if Crew Cut had a car handy in that glade, she doubted he felt suicidal enough to drive down the cliff after them, and taking the switchbacks would require a few minutes.

Don looked at her, his cheeks wet with sweat and tears, his lips a tight white line.

"You told me once you chartered planes," she asked, trying to keep her voice level as her stomach lurched. "Can you get one? Like right now?"

He moaned deep in his throat, and she felt an absurd pity for him. Then she remembered his betrayal, and the feeling passed. Leaning across the seats, she pinched his ear and bent it toward her. "Earth to Don," she whispered. "Come in, Don."

He sniffed as his brain returned from its interstellar journey. *"Yeb,"* he said, before pausing to swallow. His breath whistling through his damaged nose, he tried to enunciate more clearly: "Managua. The airport. We *hab* our share of it, pay maintenance, but we *habn't uthed* it in a long time. Cost-cutting…"

"Spare me. We're going there, after we make a stop." Fiona fed some gas to the engine, which responded by whining louder. The wheels inched forward. With a little luck, they might make it to Estelí, although luck was in short supply lately.

Don rubbed his bound wrists together and said: "Doctor."

"How about a Cuban doctor?" Fiona said, pushing their deathtrap vehicle faster. "I hear they're the best."

Don shut his eyes as Fiona navigated the broken jeep toward

town. She prayed no cop would pull them over. Her dream image returned, of Bill floating in the dark ocean, his skin food for fish. She tried to send him a psychic message across time and distance: I'm coming, baby. Don't do anything too stupid until I get there.

In the skewed rearview mirror, a white SUV bounced into view, spraying dust as it took the curve hard.

6

**ONLY THE DUMBEST** of luck saved Bill in his flight from the cop. At the first intersection, in defiance of gravity and his aging muscles, he vaulted over the hood of a pink Ford sedan. The driver, startled by the body flying past, accidentally stomped on the gas—and plowed into the officer pursuing Bill. Three tons of antique Detroit steel sent the poor bastard flying into the air.

Marnie stopped in her tracks and screamed.

Bill kept running, the meaty hard drive in his skull cycling up memories of a hundred chases through the streets of New York: times he dodged, times he chased. What worked, or left him broken and covered in blood. In this case, the penalty for failure was prison in a country with precious little concept of the words 'due process.'

A few blocks later, with no pursuers in sight, Bill slowed his stride and ducked into a dusty gift store. The brown husk of a proprietor regarded him with suspicion as he paused near a wooden shelf stacked with neatly folded t-shirts. Bill bent down, his hands on his knees, concentrating on deep breaths. When he stood again, he pulled the wad of bills out of his pocket, and the proprietor softened a bit.

Yes, the t-shirt he bought featured the glowering face of Ernesto 'Che' Guevara. Bill often wondered how the world's hippest guerilla revolutionary would have felt about all the capitalist dollars earned on his image over the years. He also purchased shorts with the Cuban flag stitched on the left leg, another existential puzzle of commercialism and branding that he would need to work out over several glasses of something high-proof. A new baseball cap and a pair of rubber sandals completed the disguise; his watch, far too expensive to wear on his exposed wrist without drawing attention, went into his pocket along with his passport and hotel key-card.

His lungs still burning from the run, Bill walked the narrow streets a few blocks east of El Capitolio. Bystanders kept glancing at the beautiful suit and shirt balled under his arm, his nice shoes dangling from his hand. You're going to have to do something about the clothes, he told himself. They're attracting too much attention in a place where nobody earns anything.

In the three weeks that Bill and Fiona had stayed in Havana, neither had wandered into this part of town. The elegant facades and curving archways reminded him a little of Paris, although decades of sea air and neglect had sanded away the detailing and color. Everything was peeling and crumbling, ghostly in the tropical sunlight. The residents on the rusted balconies regarded him coolly as he passed.

At the end of one street, he found an apartment building reduced to a shell, its walls choked with vines. He ducked through the open doorway and climbed over piles of rubble until he stood in the bright and roofless center of the space. Setting the suit on a flat chunk of brickwork, he pulled out his borrowed phone and powered it up. A solid four bars of signal. Good.

The Android operating system is the most popular in the world, with good reason: any manufacturer can load it onto their devices without paying a fee to Google, which developed it. Dozens of types of phones run Android, and the carriers that connect those devices to the world often fail to update the software on a regular basis. No matter how smart the people who created it, older operating systems have flaws, some of which Bill had memorized in the course of his hustling life.

Holding down the phone's power and volume buttons forced a reset. When the screen revived, a message box asked if Bill wanted to activate 'Recovery Mode.' More button-pushes, and a few screens later, he had the option of deleting all of Marnie's data. "I'm sorry," he told his drinking buddy in absentia, and fried her precious info.

The phone, now cleansed, rebooted. As it ran in setup mode, Bill held his breath, praying that it would start up without too many complications. A cheerful Welcome screen bloomed to life and asked for his Google ID, which he gratefully provided. The home-screen appeared, followed by a message bubble from Fiona: "Bill?"

According to the time-stamp, she had sent the text last night. Was she still angry? Or just worried?

"In trouble," he texted back. "They found us."

Hitting send, he slipped the phone into his pocket, retrieved his bundle of clothes, and exited the ruin. Up the street, a group of kids jumped and splashed in the spray from a burst pipe, yelling with such joy it made Bill smile despite his worries.

He headed for his hotel, plotting a path through the neighborhoods that would swing him wide of El Floridita. Every so often, he noted a police car cruising in the distance, usually a Peugeot 106 with white detailing that made it easy to pick out amidst the browns and grays of the crumbling buildings. He was on the lookout for a specific kind of bystander, and found him in the shadow of a Stalinist apartment tower, a five-story concrete cube enlivened by an aquamarine paint-job badly in need of a touch-up. Or rather, the man found him.

"Cigars? Good price."

Bill turned, sizing up his questioner: scrawny, dressed in an old shirt and a loose pair of slacks that, like the buildings around him, had seen much better days. He had a scraggly beard that would have done the Fathers of the Revolution proud, and a faded baseball cap. Best of all, he was roughly Bill's height.

*"Habla inglés?"* Bill asked.

The man waggled his hand. "A little, *si.*"

I'm having all the luck today, Bill thought. "No cigars," he said, and flashed a tight roll of pesos. "I have a job, though. *Dinero, si?*"

The man stepped back. "*Si?*"

"Quick job," Bill said. "How do you say that, *rápido*?"

An hour later, the wind had picked up, hurling massive waves against the seawall of the Malecón. Heavy spray doused the walkway and the road. The gutters had a hard time swallowing down that water, and cars surfed through the deepening puddles with suicidal sangfroid, sometimes skidding out of control. The waves also cleared away the pedestrians, and thus any witnesses.

Fiona had texted him back. "Things went wrong here," she wrote. "Heading your way."

Whenever Fiona, the master of understatement, said that things had gone wrong, that probably meant a stack of dead bodies and a couple of buildings on fire.

"I think it's Rockaway," he texted back.

"Yes. Ran into old friend," she wrote. "Still after us."

Time to run again, Bill thought. Where should we go this time? Where *can* we go, with the money we have left? Despite his reputation as a spendthrift, Bill would curb his splurging if forced to do so; but even then, their savings would only last a few more months. Living as a fugitive meant burning cash on everything from safe houses to ammunition, with precious little opportunity to stop in any one place and earn more.

A few blocks from the Meliá Cohíba, a secondary road paralleled the Malecón, lined on either side with tall apartment buildings. It could have been Miami, if you squinted a little. With the wind had come clouds, darkening the sky to a premature dusk. The cars that deviated onto this road to avoid the waves had their headlights on.

In the dimmer light, the man in the white suit glimmered like a specter. He ambled down that side road, hands in his pockets, a baseball cap tucked low on his forehead. At the intersection he angled left, toward the rear of the hotel. You could probably see him from the lobby, if you sat on a couch with a good view through the windows.

Two blocks behind the man wearing his suit, Bill ducked from parked car to parked car, shadow to shadow, his calfskin loafers still in hand. Even if he lost his beautiful seersucker, which was looking damn likely at this juncture, at least he had saved his shoes. When his hustler friend disappeared behind the hotel, Bill accelerated, keeping his eyes locked on the front driveway. A doorman bent to speak through the open window of a cab idling at the curb, but otherwise the world was empty.

Then, the couple.

They drifted out of the black doorway of the Meliá Cohíba like ghosts, shoulder to shoulder. They wore the same clothes as when Bill had spotted them on the Malecón, their hands still deep in their pockets. They took a left at the bottom of the drive-way and floated toward the rear of the building. Bill hoped his new friend had taken his advice and started running once he passed the hotel, but maybe things had gotten lost in translation.

Once the couple disappeared from view, Bill trotted across the intersection and into the lobby, offering the doorman a quick nod as he did so. Tourists clustered around the couches and chairs, along with a crew of giant men in sunglasses and cargo pants. Their t-shirts bore the logo of a popular film franchise in which a group of beautiful people traveled around the world racing expensive cars and robbing banks. Bill remembered that the government had shut down portions of the Malecón for two days so that a pair of Ferraris could engage in a simulated chase across a couple miles of crumbling infrastructure.

"Freedom," Bill announced to nobody as he ducked into the elevator, slipping his key-card into the slot that would gain him access to the higher floors. Despite the full lobby, he was alone in here. Only when the doors slid shut did he exhale, loudly, and lean against the softly vibrating wall of the car. He felt like he could sleep for a week.

Pulling out his phone, he texted: "Hotel not safe."

No response. Was she on a plane? Still in Nicaragua? He hadn't felt this scared since Oklahoma, when he lost his finger. It was the sort of dread that grew in your stomach until it was a heavy mass that threatened to drag you down to the floor. You could squeeze your hands into fists and breathe deep to keep your nerves under control, and maybe that would help for a few minutes, but Bill knew the only real solution was to escape the threat as soon as possible.

The doors hissed open, the car bobbing in that disconcerting way of elevators in need of new parts. Ducking his head into the hallway, he checked in both directions before stepping out. Their room was two doors to the right, the black plastic 'Por Favor, No Molestar' sign still on the knob.

It felt like a century since he'd left. His duffel lay open on the bed, piled high with clothes. Stripping off his obnoxious t-shirt and shorts, he wiped himself down with a towel still moist from his morning shower. The sprint in his expensive shoes had left his feet reddened, two toenails cracked and bleeding. He bandaged the wounds as best he could from Fiona's small medical kit on the sink and returned to the bedroom to dress.

He chose a blue button-down from the closet and paired it with a summer wool suit, gray, his favorite. His passport went in his right pants pocket, his cash and cards in the left, a last Bolivar cigar inside his jacket. Slipping his watch back onto his left wrist made him feel complete.

The loss of his white seersucker reduced his luggage by roughly a third, making it easy to stuff the rest of his underwear, designer jeans, and shirts into the duffel. His phone buzzed: a message from Fiona: "Inbound this eve. Meet at spot?"

Instead of replying, Bill opened the closet and retrieved Fiona's canvas overnighter. His lady had mastered the art of traveling light, mostly because she refused to wear anything other than jeans and a rotating collection of t-shirts. Shouldering both bags, he walked across the room, testing the heft and balance. It felt awkward, clumsy.

The phone hummed again: "Forget bags. Just take what matters."

"Baby, you know me too well," he said to the empty room.

He had no intention of giving up his duffel, a buffalo-leather number he had picked up in Nassau the day after they escaped their hosts in the Dominican Republic, or any of his remaining clothes. *I'll just tell her my bag had more room, and that's why I had to abandon hers. Besides, didn't she want to buy a new one, anyway?*

Finding a loose thread on the bottom of Fiona's bag, he yanked. The seam split, revealing a secret space between the inner and outer walls. Cash tumbled onto the bed, along with a fresh set of credit cards and Fiona's spare passport.

Tossing those goodies atop his clothes, he tapped out a message on his phone, telling Fiona where to meet. After hitting the Send key, he paused, transfixed by the image of her emerging from the misty jungle like an avenging goddess, her eyes blazing hellfire through a dirt-crusted face, her skin speckled and smeared with mud and gunpowder. Ready to hurt someone. Especially someone who neglected to provide her with fresh underwear.

Before he zipped his bag closed, he slipped in a pair of her panties and a clean t-shirt.

*It's the little things that keep a relationship alive.*

Onto the next task: exiting the building with his throat and balls intact. Had the gruesome twosome returned to the lobby, or were they still pursuing his suit across Havana? He hoped that hustler had given them the slip. Either way, he needed to take a service exit—after he armed himself appropriately.

Wrapping the Che t-shirt around his fist, he entered the bathroom.

# 7

**FIONA AND CREW** Cut went way back.

Crew Cut had always told her that his name was William Bonney, but Fiona saw right through that bullcrap. His haircut, his orderliness, and the way he moved suggested a military background, so Crew Cut fit as well as any other name that Fiona could have given him. She did believe his stories about serving in Iraq as a contractor, banging it out with insurgents on dusty streets and rooftops, but only because she had seen him in action on more than one job. He was dangerous.

And he was right behind her.

In its crippled state, her jeep had a hard time accelerating. Steam whisped from the crumpled hood, and the wheel shuddered in her hands. In the passenger seat, Don groaned every time the vehicle hit a bump, his nose swollen to clownish dimensions.

The white SUV lurked twenty feet behind her, trapped in place by a rattling red jalopy that looked worse for wear than her jeep, if you could believe it. Through the SUV's windshield, she saw Crew Cut hunched over the wheel. No way to tell how much damage her bullet had done to his shoulder.

Fiona stuck an arm out her window and offered him a hearty thumbs-up. After the punishing ride down the hill, even that simple gesture sent bolts of pain shooting into her chest. Nothing felt broken, and she had none of the chills or shakes that came with internal bleeding, but her skin would probably look like a purple blanket come morning.

Crew Cut responded with a middle finger. So much for civility.

"How you feeling?" Fiona asked Don.

Don wheezed something about his face ruined forever.

"Think of all the chicks you'll pick up with the scars," Fiona said. Ahead of them loomed a school bus painted in swirls of bright color, its roof loaded with bags. She eased the jeep into the oncoming lane, judging traffic, and decided it was time to make her move. Provided, of course, that her wheezing, coughing, shuddering, *dying* engine held out long enough.

Fiona floored it. The jeep's choked snarl rose to a high-pitched shriek, its frame shimmying. A truck loomed in her shattered windshield, its horn blaring. She veered back into her own lane, in front of the bus, with only a few feet to spare.

With that daredevil maneuver, she increased her lead over the white SUV by a hundred yards. A quick right sent her off the main road and onto a side-street, a cloud of dust marking her path like a flag. The yellow front of the coffin store appeared, the owner's daughter sitting in its open doorway.

The white SUV screeched through the intersection, almost hitting two dirt-bikes, and braked at the head of the dirt alley that ran behind the coffin shop, blocking in the battered jeep parked beside the rear door. Crew Cut scuttled out low, pistol in his left hand, his right shoulder moist and red above his vest. His forehead slick, his cheeks pale, but his eyes clear and cold.

Keeping low, Crew Cut angled around the jeep. Empty seats, keys in the ignition, a chicken head in the footwell. He hissed. He turned to the door that led into the coffin shop.

The first floor was dim. He crouched in the doorway while his vision adjusted, then swept through the only room, lined on either side with cheap coffins on wooden platforms. The open front door framed the girl on the steps, who twisted around to watch him. He raised a hand for her to stay quiet, wincing at the pain flaring up his shoulder.

Crew Cut reached for the lid of the nearest coffin, ready to play whack-a-mole, when something thumped overhead. It sounded like a heavy footstep.

Offering the girl a tight smile, he moved left, where a narrow stairway led to the second floor. He took the risers slow, ready for Fiona to try something, his whole world reduced to the view over his barrel. She was a tricky one, that lady. Not so great when it came to picking men, but a damn virtuoso with a Kalashnikov.

At the top of the stairs, he faced a closed wooden door. Taking a deep breath, he drove a foot into the knob, shattering it, and ducked into the next room. His pistol swept over a few pieces of cheap furniture, an empty floor, an unmade bed.

He tiptoed to the window. The adjoining rooftop was flat and empty. Over his pounding heartbeat, and the hum of cars below, he noticed another sound: the steady patter of a shower on low. It came from behind the only other door in the room.

Crew Cut hesitated. Who turned on the shower in the middle of a chase? Or had Fiona hid downstairs, leaving him to blunder like some idiot into a stranger's apartment?

Instead of wasting time thinking over this dilemma, Crew Cut put two bullets into the bathroom door, just in case that bitch was waiting behind it. Sly boys stay alive, as he always liked to say. The door drifted open, framing a red-tiled bathroom with a shower stall in one corner. The shower spat water onto a small pile of cracked tile and grouting left by his bullets.

He entered the bathroom. No bodies in a corner, no blood, no signs of a gun or broken glass or any of the other things you shed when you're injured after driving a car off a cliff.

From behind him came the click of wood on wood.

What felt like a sledgehammer hit him between the shoulder blades. He heard the dry crack of a gunshot. His knees sagged, dipping him headfirst into the shower stall.

What happens when electrified water meets flesh?

Nothing good.

Fiona slid from the crawl-space beneath the floorboards, smoking pistol in hand, in time to see Crew Cut trembling and twitching against the drain, the water swirling pink from the wound in his shoulder. His boots hammered a hard beat against the tiles.

There was no way that plan should have worked. She knew Crew Cut was the kind of killer who took his time, swept each room before moving onto the next. That bought her a full minute to turn on the shower, pry up the floorboards, and tuck beneath. It was a half-assed plan, but she was too injured to face him in the open and live.

Fiona sighted the pistol on his head.

Her hands began to shake. As if the electricity had somehow shot out of the shower stall and across the floor and into her body through the soles of her shoes.

She braced her gun wrist with her other hand.

*Just a case of nerves or something.*

A low growl in her throat, her jaw tightening.

Her finger steadied on the trigger.

The next bullet finished things.

Shivering Don flinched like a vampire at dawn when she raised the lid of the coffin where she had placed him before running upstairs. "Time to go, Lazarus," she said, her ears still ringing from gunfire, the comforting weight of the money-bag on her shoulder.

On the way to the jeep, she handed a thousand dollars to the owner's daughter. It made her feel a little better about leaving a body behind. Crew Cut wouldn't have to travel far for his coffin.

**8**

**FIONA HARBORED A** deep hatred of flying. Turbulence, no matter how slight, always drove her into a feral panic. Over the years she had read dozens of articles proclaiming the safety of air travel, and the infinitesimal chances of dying in a wreck, and yet the roar of plane engines still made her lizard brain queue up an inflight mind-movie of exploding fuselages and bodies.

*Ever think you'll win the lottery?* Bill once asked her during takeoff, as she clutched his fingers hard enough to make him wince.

*No*, she replied. *It's an idiot tax.*

*So why do you think you'll die in a crash?* Bill smiled. *It's even higher odds.*

She had leaned over and kissed his cheek, more for his benefit than hers. Those mind-movies continued to play: fireballs, screaming, death.

Before leaving Estelí, Fiona and Don stopped at the cigar factory. Don's house, a two-story block of rough concrete and big windows, stood at the far edge of the parking lot, beyond a high fence. It took him forever to find his keys and passport. They traded up the wrecked jeep for Don's aging BMW, which stank of old tobacco and feet.

Fiona put Don behind the wheel for the trip to Managua. They said almost nothing to each other, although she sensed him relaxing a little more with each passing mile. She prayed to whatever God watched over killers and outlaws that his talk about a plane would result in something other than an old Cessna stuck together with duct tape and baling wire.

They made a single stop on the way, so Fiona could strip down the pistol and toss the parts over a bridge railing. She had purchased the weapon in Managua and kept it hidden in a storage locker between trips, but it had outlived its usefulness.

"You stay calm the rest of this trip," she told Don as they approached the airport, "and you'll get through this, okay? Act up, or say the wrong thing to someone, and this gets messier than it needs to be."

Don nodded and wiped at the snot leaking from his busted nose.

At the private-jet terminal, Don filled out the appropriate paperwork while Fiona helped herself to a steaming cup of coffee from the urn on a nearby table. There were no other passengers in the small lounge, no awkward glances or questions about her bruised arms and cut face. She hoped this ride was smoother than going commercial. How often did millionaires die in plane crashes?

Their gleaming white jet came with a pair of pilots in uniforms and aviator glasses, standing on the tarmac with their hands behind their backs. "Passports?" one asked as Fiona and Don approached.

Fiona handed over her best fake one, followed by Don's real deal. The senior pilot gave their documents a perfunctory read before glancing at the bag slung under Fiona's arm. She thought he might ask her to open it up. Instead he grinned and said: "How much does that weigh?"

"I'm sorry?"

The pilot raised a hand in apology. "Sorry, weak joke. We

have to determine weight before we fly, but that bag is fine." She could sense him evaluating their galaxy of scrapes and bruises.

"Oh." Silly rabbit, bag searches are for the peons who line up for a flying cattle-car. She felt naked without a firearm, but there was always the knife in her belt.

"This is swank," Fiona said, once the pilots entered the cockpit and closed the door behind them. Although the plane cabin was tight quarters, the leather seats along the port side were plush, and the small galley across from the bathroom offered a variety of snacks. A small screen embedded in the bulkhead flickered to life, displaying a digital map of Nicaragua and the surrounding countries, with a little plane icon representing their location.

"We *ged—get*—twelve hours a month." When he spoke slowly, and took care to enunciate every syllable, he sounded almost normal. "Too expensive, but my brother insists that we keep it." Don buckled himself into a seat and sighed. "Medkit, *pleath*."

"Where?"

"Galley."

The bottom drawer of the galley held a white plastic box with a red cross on the lid. Fiona handed it over before resuming her search for food. The cabinets yielded crackers and cookies, but no bags of barbeque chips, her personal favorite. She craved the comfort of salt and fat, a little reward for her aching body.

The intercom clicked to life. "Take your seats, please," the pilot said.

Fiona grabbed a small box of animal crackers and a bag of whole walnuts, along with a silver nutcracker from a drawer, before taking her seat nearest the door. The engines cycled to a throaty rumble, the cabin swaying gently as the plane eased forward. Fiona felt her pulse accelerate, her palms already slick with sweat.

Don smiled. "Hate flying?"

Fiona nodded.

The smile widened. "Scared?"

Tearing open the bag in her lap, she held up a walnut. "Want to swallow this whole for me?"

Don leaned back in his seat, smile trembling at the edges.

"Keep looking at me like that," she said, "and we'll try to do the whole bag, so help me God. Just cram them down there one by one. Trust me, it's two hours in the air, we'll have time."

Don lowered his gaze to the floor. Fiona eased into the cushions and cracked her first nut, chewing down its smoky deliciousness as the plane bounced off the runway. It took every ounce of her self-control to sit there and chew, denying Don even a flicker of fear. The plane felt like it took off vertically, dropping her stomach like an elevator with its cable cut.

After a few minutes, the plane leveled off, and Fiona's stomach crawled to its proper position. Don opened the medical kit and fished out a bottle of pain pills, dry-swallowing three. "That man—the one you, uh, shot—he offered a lot of money," Don said, sniffing. "When you're in a hole, any amount looks good. I'm sorry."

"Is that a tear I see?" Fiona asked.

Don turned his face to the window.

"Usually when people aim a gun at me, I kill them." Fiona bared her teeth. "You're still here, so that's a start. Good thing I remembered you had a plane."

"Said I was *thorry*, damnit, sorry."

"Help me get my boyfriend back, fly me somewhere safe, and we'll call it even, okay?"

Don's lip quavered.

"What?" Fiona asked.

Don shook his head.

Fiona raised her eyebrows. "Don, use your words."

Snot dripped from Don's bruised fruit of a nose. He wiped it on his sleeve, swallowed, and said: "We only paid you half."

"That's right."

"You want to earn the rest? Plus a lot more?"

Fiona cracked another nut, swiping the shell fragments from her lap onto the carpet. She had never been a fan of littering, but dirtying up a private jet felt downright luxurious. "Sure," she said.

"Then we go to New York. After Cuba. I know where there's money. A lot of it."

"Why don't you get it yourself?" She had no intention of explaining how New York was permanently off-limits to her and Bill.

"It's in a weird place," he said. "I'd need help. Folks who know how to break into things."

"How much money are we talking?"

He shrugged. "Millions. Enough to solve our debts. And yours."

Fiona stared at the passing clouds, the infinity of cold space beyond the aircraft's thin metal skin. In the window's reflection she glimpsed the pink swirl of Crew Cut's blood disappearing down the drain. That was a righteous kill, she thought. So why did my hands shake? Why did I have such a hard time pulling the trigger?

*Maybe a part of you doesn't want to kill anymore.*

Maybe, but what choice do I have? This is my life. This is what I do best.

"Tell me more," she said. "But if you're lying to me, God help you." After all the misery he had dumped on her head, it was fun watching Don squirm nervously in his seat.

**9**

**ON THE FAR** side of Canal de Entrada, the narrow mouth of the Port of Havana, stands the Castillo De Los Tres Reyes Del Morro, a mouthful of a name for an imposing stone hulk of a fortress. Originally designed to protect the harbor from raids, it now serves as a tourist destination. A few hundred yards further down the shore stands La Cabaña, a crumbling line of fortifications that dates back three centuries; the one and only Che Guevara, hero of the Revolution and eternal t-shirt icon, once used the place for tribunals and executions.

A lot of blood had dripped into the soil here over the years.

Bill hoped not to add to it.

In the decades since Fidel's takeover of the island, La Cabaña had become a museum. The grassy fields behind the stone walls hosted a shining line of antique equipment: wheeled artillery pieces, a MiG jet fighter, and huge missiles still looking ready to deliver the pain to the *Norteamericanos*.

Whenever Bill wanted to clear his head, he liked taking a cab to this side of the harbor, where he would spend hours walking along the fortifications, hoping to hear the answer to his problems on the breeze whispering along the bay. The answers never came, but the view was spectacular.

Speaking of views, the area around La Cabaña offered clear lines of sight and multiple exits. He and Fiona had agreed on this spot a long time ago, in case they were apart when the proverbial cow-patty smacked the fan.

Bill stood near the MiG, smoking a cigar, his duffel bag at his feet. The threatening storm had moved further offshore, leaving the skies clear in time for evening. Above the stone ridge of the fortress, the darkness descended like a slow curtain. Soon the guards would start clearing the park. He hoped Fiona, who had texted him from the airport, would make it in time.

To his right, a narrow road led to Che's House, which the state had converted into a memorial. Bill puffed and worried. Had his new assassin friends seen him leave the hotel? He had taken a cab to Chinatown, where he hailed a second cab to take him across the bay to La Cabaña. Hopefully his spycraft was good enough.

Two figures appeared at the far end of the road, their features hidden by dusk and distance.

Bill dropped the nub of the cigar into the dust, crushed it cold. His fear was a small match burning in his stomach.

The amber sunlight arcing through the trees gleamed on what was unmistakably Fiona's hair, and intense relief snuffed out his fear. She had a canvas duffel bag over her shoulder, her left hand on the strap. Her right hand gripped the shoulder of a thin, gray man Bill had never seen before.

Slinging his bag onto his shoulder, Bill trotted down the road, meeting them halfway. "Excuse me," he said. "I'm a little lost. Can you give me directions?"

Fiona's lips tightened into a bloodless line. "Not the time for jokes, sweetie."

At least she had called him sweetie.

"Sorry," he said, nodding toward the man. "Who's this?"

"Bill, meet Don," Fiona said. "My cigar-factory client? Decided to sell us out to our old friends in the Rockaways."

"Surprised you're still alive," Bill told him, gesturing at his purple nose and bruised cheeks.

Fiona's hand shifted from Don's shoulder to the back of his neck, clenching softly. "He is, too," she said. "But he has something very interesting to tell you, once we get out of here."

Shoving past Don, Bill ran a thumb down Fiona's cheek, notched with faint cuts. "What happened to you out there?"

"Nothing bad," she said, the lie clear in her face.

"Oh, come on." Bill said.

"I'll tell you later. It's a long story." With her free hand, Fiona gripped his thumb and squeezed it twice before letting go. "We got a car down the road a bit. Driver's waiting. Don's plane is at the airport. We can't go direct from the States, because of the whole embargo thing, but I was thinking we'd go to Mexico City, catch a commercial flight from there."

"Where are we going?" Bill asked.

"New York. Belly of the beast, if you want to get dramatic about it."

"You're kidding."

"Nope." Fiona released Don's neck. "There's a real money-making opportunity, so long as our little buddy here isn't messing with us."

Don's left eye twitched. "Hey, I get well off this, too."

There's no interest like self-interest, Bill thought. "We should move. We're being hunted," he said. "Two hitters."

"Man and a woman?" Fiona asked.

"Yeah."

"Big guy, small lady, real whitebread-looking?"

"Exactly the same, yeah."

"Dressed kinda like tourists?"

"How do you know this?"

Fiona pointed behind him. "Because they're right there."

Bill spun around. No more than thirty feet away, from the direction of La Cabaña, the couple marched toward them in lockstep. The man's right hand jammed deep in the pocket of his khakis, the woman's hidden in the folds of her bright skirt. In the fading light, the bottomless depths of their sunglasses made their faces look like skulls.

Pushing up his left sleeve, Bill retrieved the long shard of mirror glass held in place by the strap of his watch, its ragged edges sheathed in a shred of Che t-shirt. The cloth doubled as a handle, so he could clutch the improvised blade in his right hand.

The couple stopped fifteen feet away, close enough for Bill to judge the expensive cuts of the his-and-hers outfits. The man was massive, his neck (partially covered by a loose red kerchief) linebacker-thick, his linen shirt straining against slabs of muscle. Beside him, the woman looked as small and sharp as a bone scalpel.

"Hi, Barbara," Fiona said.

The woman's head tilted slightly. She removed her hands from her pockets and brought them together, knotting her fingers into a ball. Bill noticed her silver watch had a thin band and a chunky face, too large for her wrist.

"You know them?" Bill asked.

"Yeah, these bland motherfuckers are Barbara and Ken. Good friends of The Dean," Fiona said, raising her voice. "Right there is fine, thanks."

Ken smiled. "Long time no see, Fiona."

"Believe it or not," Fiona said. "But you're the second guy to say that to me this week. And the first guy's dead, so don't press your luck. We're leaving now."

His shard of glass pressed against his hip, Bill retreated until he stood alongside Fiona, who placed her hand between Don's shoulder-blades. Don seemed in shock, his face pale, his breathing shallow.

Moving in perfect sync, Barbara and Ken stepped forward. It reminded Bill of wolves in nature documentaries, how they worried their prey to death from a distance.

Bill and Fiona retreated, pulling Don by his shirt.

Barbara and Ken mirrored their movement.

Bill heard the low murmur of rubber on gravel. A horn tooted. He risked turning his head. The sight of the white Peugeot, two police officers in the front, dumped a quart of adrenaline into his blood. It took every ounce of his self-composure to keep his feet rooted to the ground.

"This is either really good," Fiona said, "or really, really bad."

The cop car eased to a stop. The police inside took their sweet time climbing out, the one in the passenger seat pausing to adjust his belt before closing the door behind him. Neither appeared too concerned about the situation. They probably assumed everyone here was a tourist.

Fiona offered the cops a wide smile and burbled something in Spanish, too fast for Bill to catch. The cop from the driver's seat smiled and said something back. Barbara and Ken stood still, their hands in their pockets. Bill studied the sidearms in the officers' holsters. How quickly could they draw down on a threat?

The cop from the passenger's side, the one not talking to Fiona, glanced at Bill's waist and startled.

Bill looked down at the shard of glass in his hand.

Oops.

The cop yelled to his partner, his hand darting for his pistol. On reflex, Bill dropped the shard and raised his hands, part of him praying that Fiona had a weapon and could drop these fools, another part hoping they could still talk their way out of this.

The other cop trotted around the front of the Peugeot, his pistol drawn and aimed down. He was clearly following procedure, flanking the group from another angle. It was a smart move, except it brought him too close to Barbara and Ken.

As the cop passed the couple, focused on Bill, his pistol drifting upwards, Barbara's right hand moved over her left wrist. There was a faint click, and the cop swiveled in her direction. Too late. Barbara's hands darted around his head, and a thin line appeared across his throat.

A wire.

She was garroting him with a wire hidden in the watch.

Grunting loud, Barbara rammed a knee into the small of the cop's back, driving him to the ground. A sheet of red ran down his throat and soaked the gray collar of his uniform.

Moving fast for a man of such enormous size, Ken scooped low to retrieve the dying cop's pistol.

The cop's partner fired three times, the bullets zipping over Ken to spark off some priceless Revolutionary hardware. The lead missed Barbara by inches, and yet she seemed as unconcerned as if a few insects had buzzed past her head. She had her left forearm behind the dying cop's head, pressing his face into the gravel as she pulled the wire taut with her right hand. The cop's legs spasmed.

Fiona hurled her duffel underhand at the cop firing his pistol. The bag smashed his elbow as he pulled the trigger a fourth time, sending the bullet on a downward trajectory that, as luck had it, ended at Ken's right wrist.

Ken grunted and dropped his new pistol, his other hand rising to clutch his wound.

Before the cop could turn on her, Fiona sprinted the ten feet between them, her elbow descending on his surprised face. Bill heard the nose break with a loud crunch. The cop gurgled and fell, Fiona wrestling his sidearm from his grip. She had mistimed knocking him cold—if she had waited another half-second, he might have plugged both Ken and Barbara.

"Bill," Fiona said, aiming the pistol at the couple. "Get Don, and get in the cop car. Take the officer, too."

Bill already had a hand on Don's shoulder. "Why?"

"Because they'll kill him if we leave him here."

Ken hooked two fingers into the kerchief around his neck and pulled it loose. Pushing back his red-splattered sleeve, he wrapped the fabric around the wound and cinched it tight. "You know how much this shirt cost?" he asked calmly, unruffled and smooth as a radio announcer reading the weather report.

Barbara unwound her wire from the dead cop's neck and stood, careful to avoid the blood spreading toward her feet. Reaching into the cop's back pocket, she snatched free a handkerchief and used it to clean the dangling wire. The bloodied cloth she let flutter to the ground; pressing a button on the side of the case retracted the wire into the watch.

Bill had seen a lot of dead bodies in his time, some barely recognizable as human thanks to fire or a storm of bullets. He liked to think all that death had driven the squeamishness from him. But watching Ken and Barbara beside the cop's corpse made his skin curdle into gooseflesh.

For years, Bill had regarded Fiona as the epitome of a predator, someone who could pump a bullet into someone's head before heading out to brunch, but even his girlfriend suffered the effects of taking lives. He doubted that Ken and Barbara ever felt anything close to remorse: they treated killing the way someone might sort through bottles of hot sauce at a store.

"Bill," Fiona said. "Get moving."

Bill shoved Don into the backseat of the police car before returning to the unconscious cop on the ground. You had to give Fiona credit: she knew how to use every ounce of her one-hundred-thirty pounds to deliver the hurt to whoever stood in her way. But knocking someone out also turned them into dead weight, and that was a problem for Bill as he strained to load the snoring policeman into the vehicle.

Don squawked, slapping his hands in the air as Bill shoved the cop's body on top of him. Bill smirked back, feeling no amusement whatsoever. None of the numbers looked good: two killers in front of them, maybe a couple minutes at best before someone new appeared on the road.

Tossing their two duffel bags atop the lovebirds in the back, Bill circled to the driver's side. Ducking behind the wheel, he prayed that the cops had left the keys in the ignition.

The ignition was empty.

Bill's heart stopped cold.

When he looked again, a set of shiny keys dangled in the slot.

*Oh, brain, you silly joker! Haha!*

The vehicle was a stick-shift, and that was okay: Bill's mother had taught him how to work one when he was fifteen. Pressing down the clutch and brake, Bill twisted the key, and the motor coughed awake. How long had it been since he'd last seen a manual gearshift? Twenty years?

Standing outside the car, Fiona flicked her pistol at Ken. "Kick his gun over here."

Ken lashed out with his right foot, sending the dead cop's gun skittering beneath the Peugeot. He winked at Fiona, daring her to kneel down and look for it. "We're going to kill you," he announced.

"I don't think so," Fiona replied. From the far side of the harbor—maybe closer—drifted a faint siren. She knew she should put this pair down, but it was one against two, and they both moved like devils: blasting one would give the other an opening to attack.

Gritting her teeth, Fiona climbed into the front passenger seat and shut the door, her arm with the pistol poking out the open window. She aimed at the space between Ken and Barbara, making them guess which one she would shoot first if either made a move. "Reverse," she told Bill. "And hit it."

Bill fumbled with the shifter, which lacked one of those little diagrams on top of the knob that traced the gear layout. On his mother's old car, you threw the stick all the way to the right and up in order to engage the reverse. He did that, hoping it was the right choice, and slowly eased up on the clutch while giving the engine a bit of gas.

The engine thumped, choked, and died.

Fiona glanced at him.

"Stick," Bill said, stomping on the clutch and twisting the ignition.

The engine caught on the second try. It was hard to tell over the growl of pistons, but the sirens in the distance grew louder. Through the windshield, they saw Barbara grin and take a tiny step forward—daring Fiona to pull the trigger.

Bill moved the shifter to the left and up. That was another way to do it, right? On his old car, there was always a deep click as the reverse gear engaged, but he heard nothing. Was he doing it right?

Again he let up on the clutch while pressing down on the gas pedal.

The engine coughed and shuddered silent.

In the backseat, Don moaned in terror.

Bill twisted the key again. "I'll go forward," he said. "They'll get out of the way, dive."

"No," Fiona snapped. "Reverse. Other car's that way."

Barbara turned to Ken and said something. Ken laughed and strolled to his left, toward Bill's side. With every step, he made it harder for Fiona to cover both of them.

The engine grumbled. Bill ran his numb fingers along the shifter, trying to figure out what he might have missed. On the underside of the knob, his thumb skimmed a rubber ring—he lifted it and felt a spring inside the shaft. A distant memory came to him: this was the lift collar, which prevented the driver from accidentally throwing the vehicle into reverse while driving. Sort of like the safety on a gun.

Lifting the collar, he pushed the shifter all the way to the right, and it went further than before. Then he moved it down, just to try something new, and miracle of miracles, that worked, too.

Bill eased the clutch, pushed the gas, and the Peugeot sprang backwards, the motor whining. Their front hood retreated, uncovering the cop's pistol on the gravel. Ken leapt for it, and Fiona opened fire. Puffs of dust exploded around the assassin, forcing him back.

Fiona's pistol snapped open, empty, and she threw the pistol into the grass alongside the road. Barbara and Ken had disappeared, lost in the puzzle of trees and sunset. In his mirrors Bill could see where the road opened onto an intersection, a black Lada parked on the grassy shoulder. For weeks, Bill had joked with Fiona about those Russian vehicles, four-wheeled death traps with ancient engines. *We get into a wreck in those, we'd be dead*, he said. *They might as well make the seat-belts out of piano wire.* That aside, if that cruddy little car could deliver them to the airport alive, Bill would stoop and kiss its dented bumper out of pure gratitude.

"Thought you knew stick," Fiona said.

"Are we not driving?"

"Whatever."

"Hey, I would have knocked this cop out after he shot them, not before."

"I timed wrong. Shut up."

The cop car bumped onto the shoulder beside the Lada, and Bill stood on the brakes. Before they came to a full stop, Fiona had her door open, a fake smile on her face as she waved at the Lada's driver, who looked nonplussed. He was probably thinking about how ten years in a Cuban jail would go.

Bill shoved Don into the Lada's backseat. Those sirens sounded too close for comfort. At least the knocked-out cop was safe. The inside of the Lada smelled of fried food. Fiona in the front seat telling the man to drive, drive, there was a big payment if he delivered them to the airport in record time.

Shoved tight against squirming Don, their duffels under his arm, Bill wondered if he should have shifted the cop car into first gear after all, tried to crush Barbara and Ken like bugs. They won't stop pursuing us, he thought. Not until they're dead, or we are.

# 10

**THE PILOT CLICKED** on the intercom to announce they had left Cuban airspace.

Flying in a private jet made Bill's nethers tingle. Despite his love of luxury, he had never risen higher than first class on a domestic flight, where the seats were plush but you often had to share a row with a businessman who loved talking about widget manufacturing protocols. After unclipping his seatbelt, he took a few silent victory laps around the cabin, running his hands over the leather and wood, marveling at the collection of snacks and drinks in the galley.

In her own seat, Fiona clutched the armrests so hard her fingers threatened to punch through the expensive leather. When Bill placed a hand on her shoulder, she brushed it away.

"Jeez," he said. "Sorry."

"You sorry about before?"

He crouched in front of her, close enough to kiss. "I'll spend less."

She leaned forward, her lips brushing past his before arriving at his ear. "You'll listen," she whispered. "That's it. All I want. Got it?"

Bill kissed her on the neck and sprung back, as joyful as a kid sprung from detention. Stretching out his arms to touch the gleaming white walls, he sang: *"All I want is you."*

Relaxing her grip on the armrests, Fiona grinned. "You want this jet, too."

"You got that right," Bill replied, retrieving a bottle of whiskey from the liquor cabinet, along with three glasses. The elaborate calligraphy on the bottle's label looked Japanese, and the liquid inside smelled top-shelf. "Started from the bottom, now we're here."

"Enjoy it now, because we're in the cheapest possible seats on the way to the States." Fiona turned to Don, who had spent takeoff brooding in a seat on the far end of the cabin. "You want to tell Bill what you told me?"

"First things first," Bill said. "What happened to you in Nicaragua?"

"Remember Crew Cut?" Fiona made fists in case her hands started shaking again. Her arms flared in pain, every nerve a needle in her muscles. Screw aspirin: she needed some of that whiskey. No, actually, a lot of that whiskey.

"He showed up?"

"He did." Unclenching her fists, Fiona nodded at Don. "Because this chump called him."

"And here I was," Bill said, pouring himself a glass of whiskey, "thinking Don was a nice guy."

Fiona laughed. "Can I tell him the landmine story?"

Don sighed, his head drooping. "Whatever."

"The first time I go down to Nicaragua," Fiona said, "I drive over to the tobacco fields that supply these guys' factory. And I see this ratty pickup filled with a bunch of drunk guys, driving back and forth over every square inch of the field. Don and his idiot brother are standing on this little hill, watching them do it.

"I park my car and ask them what's going on, and Don said: 'We paid these guys at the bar five bucks apiece to drive around our new field, look for landmines.' Can you believe it? Potentially ending three guys' lives, just because they're too cheap to hire a professional to actually clear mines. How much does your cigar label earn per year, Don? Must be in the millions, right? Why the hell do you even have cash problems?"

"Hey," Don said. "Those guys in the field? They took the money. Free markets."

Fiona grunted. "So I pull out my pistol and fire it in the air until those guys stop driving. Don gets a little peeved over it. His brother's too busy staring at my ass. Anyway, Don phoned up Crew Cut, who is very dead."

Bill waved his glass at Don's wrecked face. "Looks like you got some payback."

"Nah, that wasn't payback," Fiona said. "True payback would be shooting Don in the head and leaving him in a ditch. But he came up with a business opportunity."

"Enough money to buy this plane?" Bill asked. "Because I'm digging this mode of travel. I don't think I can go back to commercial flights, honey, I'm sorry."

"My father owned a bar near Union Square," Don said. "He was a World War II vet, made a lot of money."

"Which bar?" Bill asked, after downing his glass and refilling it. Damn good whiskey. He topped off the other two, handing the slightly fuller one to Fiona before walking the other across the cabin to Don.

"Dusty's. Our old man's last name was Dyzek, but he changed it to Dusty before we were born. I don't know why he chose that name."

"You never asked?"

"Dad's motto is punch first, answer questions later." As much as Don tried to make his shrug look casual, Bill could read the pain in his face. "Anyway, he gave his new name to the bar, too. His father—my grandfather—started the place, but I don't think it really had a name at the start. They probably called it 'The Tavern' or some shit."

Bill handed him the glass. "I think I went there a few times. Looked like nobody had cleaned it in fifty years, right? Cheap drinks, though."

"It wasn't dirty, it was authentic," Don said. "We sold it ten years ago. The rent was too damn high. It's an art gallery now. Story of everything in Manhattan. The cool stuff goes away, gets replaced by overpriced crap."

"This is the part where you tell me what your family's bar has to do with anything," Bill said, bringing his glass to his lips. Empty. That was odd. He had no memory of draining it. He fetched the bottle from the far side of the cabin, ignoring the voice in his head that told him to take it easy on the drinking.

"There's gold under the floorboards. It used to be in a box," Don said. "Dad's the paranoid type, so he bought this enormous safe. It could probably take a nuclear blast and stay shut."

"How did it get there?" Fiona asked. The whiskey warmed her body, driving back the pain. A little.

Don mimed firing a rifle. "Dad found it in Europe, during the War. Never told us where or how. Just in case you haven't picked up on it yet, he isn't exactly the warm and fuzzy type."

"He's still alive?" Bill freshened his whiskey.

"Oh yeah," Don said. "Ninety-two years old and still a bastard. I'm convinced the old man's invincible. Nothing's been able to kill him so far: not cancer, not a couple of heart operations, not falling off his roof when he was fixing it."

Fiona made a speed-it-up motion with her finger. "Why didn't you take the gold when you sold the place?"

"Um, we didn't know it was there." Don spoke slowly, as if explaining something to a child. "Dad never mentioned it. Probably afraid we'd try to steal it. We sold the bar long-distance, from Managua, and when I called him about it, he starts yelling that I'm an idiot, that we lost a whole fortune."

"That's what you get for selling it from underneath your old man," Bill said. "And let me guess: you didn't mention it to the gallery owners or anyone, because you were scared someone else would try and take it from you."

"Yeah. And we were too busy with the cigar business." Don squirmed. "Every week, I search online, looking for articles about someone digging up a ton of gold in an art gallery. Nothing. I guess the current owners didn't rip up the floor."

"And you never tried stealing it before now?" Fiona asked.

Don smirked. "Never met any thieves."

"Careful," Bill said, waving the bottle, "or you're not getting a refill."

"I'm sorry," Don said, holding out his glass. "I owe Fiona. I'm sorry for what I did. But that's not the only reason. I want a big cut. It's my family's gold."

Erupting in the fakest laughter this side of a used-car dealership, Bill walked over and poured a single amber drop into Don's glass. "How much?"

"Thirty percent," Don said, shaking his glass.

Bill poured another lonely drop. "That's a little rich. Ten percent."

"Twenty percent."

Bill poured a bigger splash of whiskey. "Twelve."

Fiona rolled her eyes. "It might be twelve percent of nothing. Your father wouldn't be the first dude to blow smoke up everybody's asses over how much money he had."

"Dad's not the lying type," Don said. "He's got the key, at his house in Queens. Unless you want to try and hack the safe, or blow it up, whatever, I suggest we head over there when we land. And I'm warning you now: he might look old, but he's vicious as hell."

# 11

**NEW YORK, NEW** York: big city of dreams, the closest thing Bill and Fiona had to a hometown. This shiny marvel of glass and steel, much of its old grit washed away by an endless flood of money, the flop houses and junkie haunts of the Village transformed into condos with doormen and gyms, the dank bars replaced by all-organic eateries, the grimy old buried deep below the ultra-expensive new. If you wanted the underbelly, you needed to dig for it.

Bill, much to his regret, had arrived in New York too late to experience the Bad Old Days, when you could stand on a corner in Times Square and quickly field offers for any number of goods and services, from cheap pistols to a pipe loaded with premium crack. Stand in the same place today, and you would most likely draw someone dressed as a superhero or oversized cartoon, squeaking and stunting for a crisp dollar. In those first days of his long residency, Bill found himself tempted to pickpocket tourists, if only to inject some of the old spirit back into the city. The scattering of police cameras on every corner always made him think better of it.

Nor would he have much opportunity to cause mischief on

this trip: Fiona had him on the tightest of leashes, especially after he told her about abandoning most of her stuff in Havana. From the airport in Newark they had taken a cab to the nearest train station, paid cash for tickets, and crossed under the Hudson on a local. Rising from the maze of train tracks and concrete platforms into the dingy bustle of Penn Station, Bill's pulse accelerated to maniac tempo. This city he loved so much would become a death-trap if they made a single wrong move.

Standing beside him on the escalator, Fiona spied the single drop of sweat trickling down Bill's forehead and prayed that he would keep his cool long enough to complete this mission. Sure, Bill had already survived quite a bit, and yes, he came with his own set of street smarts—but just as metal in a forge begins to warp and bend when you apply too much heat, the past few months had made him more brittle at the edges.

"Where are we going first?" Don asked them.

"Queens," Fiona said. "Taking the subway."

"I haven't called my Dad." Don's nose was healing nicely: aside from the occasional slurred syllable, he sounded almost normal. "He has no idea we're coming, and he really doesn't like surprises."

"We'll deal with it," Bill said. "How bad can he be?"

"You'll see," Don snapped back. "He can kick your ass."

"I'd buy a ticket to that," Fiona muttered.

Bill smirked and adjusted the wrists of his dark blue hoodie. Fiona and Don wore the same sweatshirts, purchased in a seedy kiosk in Jersey. The screaming eagles on their chests made them look like ultra-patriotic monks. It sucked as a disguise, but the hoods might prevent anyone in the station from getting too good a look at their faces. Bill and Fiona knew The Dean had a few men lurking around Midtown.

The bags over their shoulders held clothes and Fiona's cash and not much else. When Fiona thought about gold, she pictured enormous piles of gleaming coins, like something out of a pirate fantasy. It was enough to propel her aching, bruised body down the ramp to the subway. If we survive this, she told herself, we're going to spend some of that treasure on a five-star hotel room. And once we settle in, I'm going to fill the tub with ice and soak in it for a month. I'll prevent hypothermia by hooking my veins to an IV bag full of top-shelf vodka. I deserve nothing less.

The subway rumbled them across Manhattan and the East River in twenty minutes, the tracks rising into Long Island City, its skyline jagged with new high-rises. Bill held a palm to his mouth, stifling a yawn: the overnight flight from Mexico City to Jersey, crammed in steerage with dozens of sunburned tourists, had left him feeling drained as a vampire's victim. At least customs had swept them through without so much as a second glance, despite their bruises and last-minute plane tickets.

They left the train at the Court Square station and walked down the iron stairway to the street, lined on either side with elegant brownstones and tall, arching trees. The street was empty except for a couple of teenagers on the corner, staring at a video on a phone.

"Swanky neighborhood," Bill said, nodding appreciatively. "You know, for all the time I lived in New York, I don't think I ever made it to Long Island City. No, wait, isn't there that restaurant…"

"M. Wells," Fiona said. "Couple blocks north."

"Waffles with caviar on them." Bill smiled. "Good cocktails. Your Dad must have done well for himself, Don."

Don shook his head. "My father bought his place when it was a normal neighborhood. We weren't special. But he held on all this time, God bless him, so I guess that makes him a millionaire on paper."

The brownstones stood three stories tall, fronted with elegantly curved windows and doors. They walked midway down the block, stopping in front of a house that stood out like a dead tooth in a row of pearly whites: the windows soaped with dirt and covered with cardboard, the stoop crumbling, the gutters crumpled. A sun-faded sign tacked to the front door announced: 'COME BACK WITH A WARRANT.'

"If this neighborhood ever had, you know, one of those

contests for the best-looking house?" Bill said. "This house would lose every single time."

Don sighed. "My father sort of stopped giving a shit."

Fiona squinted at the sign. "He hasn't lost his sense of humor, though."

"No, he's serious," Don said. "I heard he gets noise complaints all the time. I keep in touch with the neighbors, just in case anything happens. Can we get this over with?"

Don climbed the stairs first, followed by Bill, then Fiona with her hands in her pockets. When they reached the top, Don took a deep breath, held it, and knocked on the door. No response. He pressed an ear to the rough wood and shook his head. "Don't hear anything," he said.

Bill gripped the brass knob and twisted hard. "Maybe it's unlocked…"

Don raised a hand. "Don't—"

A small hole appeared in the door to the left of Bill's head, accompanied by a muffled thump. Bill stumbled backward, swiping at flecks of wood and paint in his eyes, and almost tumbled over the railing before Fiona grabbed his collar and yanked him toward her. Their dropped bags flopped down the steps. All three crouched as two more holes popped beside the first, raining blue and green paint-chips on the stone.

"Dad," Don called. "Dad, stop!"

From the other side of the door, they heard a voice rough as ball bearings in a blender. "Son, is that you?"

"Yes," Don smiled. "Yes, it's me."

Another hole punched through the wood, the bullet missing Don by an inch as he flopped facedown on the stoop.

"I get you, you little prick?" asked the voice.

"Yeah, he's dead," Fiona called, winking at Don.

A long pause. "Who are you?"

"His probation officer," Fiona said. "He was coming to say how sorry he was."

"Yeah, he's sorry now," the voice retorted. "I'm sorry for the shooting, but you know my sons left me to die in here? Those ungrateful bastards."

"I'm sorry, sir," Fiona said, easing upright as quietly as she could. "I'm not police. Can you open the door so we can talk about this?"

"Say you're not police."

"I'm not police." Fiona glanced across the street, curious if the bullets had smashed any windows. No faces visible, no screams or sirens. God bless a neighborhood where everyone had an office job during the day.

"Say it again," the voice asked.

Bill twirled a finger beside his temple.

"I'm not police," Fiona said, gesturing for Bill to move back from the door.

A heavy bolt thumped, and the door cracked open. Fiona raised her foot and drove it into the metal plate beneath the knob, snapping the door wide. In the shadowy foyer sat an ancient man in a wheelchair, a thick red blanket draped over his legs. He wore a threadbare gray t-shirt that displayed his wrinkled biceps. In his left hand he held a small silver pistol.

Before he could pull the trigger again, Fiona darted forward and nipped the scorching-hot weapon from his gnarled fingers. "Trespassing," he said, leveling his faded blue eyes at cowering Don and Bill.

"That cop thing is bullshit, by the way," Fiona said, moving past him to check the hallway beyond. "Undercover cops, they don't have to tell you the truth if you ask three times. Figured you'd know that, since you're older than dirt." Rows of cardboard boxes lined the wall to her right. To her left, a pair of glass doors opened onto a darkened living room. She tossed the pistol atop the highest stack of boxes, well out of reach of someone in a wheelchair.

"My name's James Dusty," the man said. "I apologize for my weak sons. I can't explain it, my sperm is strong."

"Thanks, Dad," Don said, grimacing as he stood and dusted

himself off. Beside him, Bill unzipped his hoodie, offering a lovely view of his sweat-stained shirt beneath.

"I'm Fiona," she said. "That sweaty guy is Bill, my boyfriend. We're very pleased to meet you. We have a lot to discuss."

"You got a fine ass," James said, wheeling his chair down the hallway after her. "Maybe we could talk about that."

He is a senior citizen, a voice in her head reminded her. Do not inflict pain upon an old guy, even if he did try to shoot you. He's a veteran, like your father.

*Screw it, I've had too long a week to act nice.*

"I'd grab your cock and rip it off," she said, spinning on him, "but I didn't bring any tweezers. So why don't you cut the shit and tell me about the gold?"

# 12

**THE KITCHEN STANK** of burnt beans and grease. James ground his wheels over the stacks of takeout menus, used styrofoam cartons, and newspapers that covered the scratched linoleum. He parked himself at the round table at the far end of the room, and gestured for the rest of them to sit. Fiona evaluated the chairs piled high with mail and opted to lean against the ancient sink. Bill, always mindful of stains, placed their bags in the hall and stood in the kitchen doorway, careful not to touch anything.

Don ignored the mess. Clearing a chair of junk, he plopped down, exhaling loudly. "Like what you've done with the place," he told his father.

"You're talking pretty brave for someone I almost plugged," James said. "You wet yourself when that bullet shot past, boy?"

Don gestured toward his pants. "Dry as a bone. Do better next time."

"Gentlemen," Fiona said. "If we could stop the pissing match for just a moment, I'll break down the situation for you, because I don't think we have a lot of time. James, the bar you used to own, it has gold underneath the floor, right?"

"This dimwit tell you everything?" James asked, baring his

yellow teeth at his son. "He had the balls—the absolute balls—to call up and say he'd sold it because he needed the money for his precious cigar factory. That place was mine, you little shit. I kept it running, just so you and your tubby-ass brother could take it from me."

"You hadn't been there in a decade," Don said, his jaw tight.

"I love family harmony," Bill said, edging away from the wall as a massive cockroach scuttled past. "Reminds me so much of my own home growing up."

Fiona shot him a look: cool it.

"What's your interest?" James asked Fiona.

"Your son almost got me killed. He offered me a cut of the gold as a make-good," Fiona said. "I took him up on it."

"He offered it to you?" The old man laughed until he began to cough, his thin frame shuddering. When he recovered, he cleared his throat and rasped: "He offered it? That gold is mine."

"Maybe you can spend it on a cleaning lady," Don said, kicking at a pile of yellowed tabloids near his foot.

"We can negotiate," Fiona said. "I'm open."

"It's my gold," James said. "All of it."

"And you're not getting an ounce unless someone digs it up," Fiona said. "Think it over."

James turned his head to the window, as if the rusty fridge and thick weeds in the yard could give him insight into this conundrum. "Fine," he said. "Eighty-twenty."

Fiona laughed. "Your son wanted a cut, too."

Don nodded furiously. "Fifteen percent."

"You're not dealing with this little pissant," James said, thumping a fist lightly against the side of his wheelchair. "You're dealing with me. I scalped and shot a lot of Nazi bastards for that gold, which entitles me to eighty fucking percent. And if you have a problem with that, I will get out of this wheelchair, so help me God, and boot your fine head through that fucking wall. I don't care that you're a woman."

Fiona laughed and turned to Bill. "I like him."

Bill shrugged. Standing in this hoarder's abode, with its weird smells and tight spaces, made him nervous. He wanted out of here. Sooner or later—probably on the sooner side, knowing his luck this week—word would trickle back to the Rockaway Mob that its favorite fugitives had returned to the Big Apple, and a lot of scary people would pour onto the streets after them.

Fiona swiveled back to James. "Fifty-fifty, because we have to go dig it up. And like I said, there's no digging it up without us. I checked online when we were coming here, the gallery's closed today. We go in this evening, it gives us a lot of hours to work the problem."

James shrugged. "Not like I can spend that much money in the time I got left," he said. "Probably can't get laid without my ticker blowing up. So, sure, fifty percent."

Fiona clapped her hands. "That safe got a key or a combination?"

James nodded at the sideboard, where a small ceramic bowl sat precariously on a tower of past-due notices. "Key's in there," he said. "On the keychain. The old-looking one with the wolf's head."

Fiona found it. "You have my word on fifty percent," she said.

"We'll see," James said. "You're just some chick who bangs in here, says everything's all good." He jutted his chin at Bill. "Your boy-toy here stays behind, until you come back."

No can do," Bill said. "I'm the one who knows locks."

"Then the woman stays," James said. "I don't give a crap. I wasn't born yesterday, sonny. How much of an idiot do you have to be to call yourself an expert in turning a key?"

"Don't answer that," Fiona said, tossing a wink in Bill's direction. "Okay, we have an agreement. But if anything happens to him while I'm gone, all deals are off, okay?"

"Don't I get a say?" Bill asked, spinning to survey the mountains of trash, the scurrying critters, the sink piled with plates and scorched pans. "Every minute I stay here, I feel like my risk of catching Ebola goes up."

"Aw, it's okay," Fiona said. "His gun's on those boxes in the hallway, if you get nervous."

"How are you going to carry all that gold?" Don asked. "Or break through the floor?"

James shrugged. "Listen, girl, my boy here is the biggest idiot alive, but he still got a point. When I bought the safe, I buried it in the northeast corner of the room… you can tell directions, right?"

"Don't try me," Fiona snapped.

James held up his hands in mock surrender. "Apologies. Go to the northeast corner. It's ten feet along the north wall, ten feet south. Break through the floorboards, it should be right there. Got no idea why they haven't found that gold yet. My guess is they never tried putting in new flooring when they made their pussy little gallery. Got that?"

"Distressed flooring is in," Bill said. The idea of spending a few hours in this house did not sit well with him, pistol or no.

"Don't you fret," Fiona said. "I have this criminal thing down cold." On her way out the doorway, she slipped a hand into Bill's hip pocket, giving his thigh a friendly squeeze before extracting the phone he brought from Cuba. "I'm going to borrow this."

"Stay safe," he said, touching her wrist.

"You watch yourself," she replied.

"Is that a request, or a threat?"

"Bit of both." Fiona smiled and turned for the door.

The next time she saw Bill, his face would be nearly as battered as hers.

# 13

**FIONA SENT A** few texts from Bill's phone as the subway carried her one stop to Queensboro Plaza. When she was a kid, this area had been little more than a grime-smeared ramp to the Queensboro Bridge, lined with strip clubs and fast-food joints and an Army recruitment center. Now it hosted the corporate headquarters of a major airline, a youth hostel gleaming with blue lights, and a row of restaurants that charged thirty bucks for a burrito or a burger.

But the grit was still there, if you knew where to look.

Walking up a quiet side-street that angled away from the Plaza was like rewinding a couple decades back in time. She passed boarded-up storefronts, a small bodega with a torn awning, an empty lot piled high with wet gravel and shredded tires. A sign on the lot's chain-link fence proclaimed this block was the future site of Scion Condominiums, "A Wonderful Place to Live!"

At the end of this throwback street squatted a concrete warehouse, windowless and unmarked. Fiona slipped through a gap in the fence that separated the loading dock from the street, waving at a pleasant-looking boy in a black wool suit who emerged silently from the building's shadow.

The boy escorted her inside, down a narrow corridor lit by a line of bare bulbs. They crammed into an ancient elevator with an accordion door, which groaned and wheezed its way up five floors.

The car stopped with a disconcerting thump, and they entered another infinite hallway. The boy led her to a steel door, this one blackened by fire. Fiona took a deep breath, smelling incense and fried chicken.

The boy knocked, the door booming loud under his knuckles.

"Come," said a voice from inside.

They entered a life-size jewel-box, every inch a study in elegance. Thick Persian rugs covered the floors, and the walls gleamed with mirrors and daguerreotypes in ornate frames. Thick velvet drapes covered the windows. At the far end of the space, behind an enormous wooden desk, sat a figure who looked more wolf than man: his gray sideburns thick and tangled, his nose a narrow ramp supporting a pair of round sunglasses with gold rims. This was Simon Genka, a man with his fingers in a little bit of everything.

Back when Fiona did dirty deeds for the Rockaway Mob and The Dean, Simon had ensured she had the best tools, albeit for a premium price. Like many people raised in the world's roughest backwaters, Simon had a taste for expensive fabrics and timepieces, something that Fiona also recognized in Bill.

"It's been a long time," Simon said, gesturing to a baroque chair with gold armrests on the far side of the desk. "I won't ask how you're doing. Only idiots ask that question. I can tell by your face. Ouch. What can I do for you?"

If you believed the stories, Simon had once drunk the blood of a dead rival out of the man's leather boot. You could dismiss half the tales you heard on the street, but the stoniness of Simon's eyes always made Fiona believe that one. Good thing he nearly always wore sunglasses; the smoked lenses made it a little easier to talk to him.

"Equipment," Fiona said.

"For protection?" Simon leaned over the silver tray on his left, where a teapot steamed alongside two cups and ceramic bowls filled with sugar cubes. "Child, with all due apologies, because I know you're a tough lady, but a pistol isn't enough for you. Not now, not with your kind of enemies. I can, however, make arrangements for your safety. For a price."

"A pistol will actually do me a lot of good," Fiona said, holding up the fingers for two sugars while Simon poured tea. "Plus something a little heavier."

Simon passed her a cup. "Taking the war to some old friends?"

"No. Different show. One night only. Then I'm back out."

Simon nodded. "Then I am at your service."

"I appreciate it." She took a sip of the sweet brew, letting the silence stretch out before asking: "You hear anything from The Dean?"

"He's still angry, of course." Simon's lips jerked an inch or two: his version of a smile. "In the past few months, he's probably earned several times over what your boyfriend stole from him. Doesn't matter. With a man like that, it's always the principle. You want a meet? See if he'll listen to reason?"

"No." Fiona's teacup trembled slightly in her hand. "Just hoping to avoid him until our work is complete."

Simon cocked his head. "I was joking about a meet."

"I'm running on zero sleep. Makes me sensitive."

"I see. Your hand is shaking. That's unlike you."

She clenched her hand until the trembling stopped. "Comes with the territory."

Simon shrugged. "This work, your special one-night appearance, as you call it: there's money involved, I assume?"

"You assume correct."

"Then I want a cut, when you return the equipment. Consider it a finder's fee."

I hope there's a metric shit-ton of gold under those floorboards, Fiona thought. Otherwise once everyone takes their slice, we're leaving New York with a grand total of twenty bucks. But what choice do I have? "Sure thing," she said. "And one other item, on top of everything else: I'll need a van, clean as possible. It'll get returned, no damage. You still doing vehicles?"

Simon raised a hand, snapped his fingers. The well-dressed boy slipped into view beside the desk. "He'll sort you out," Simon said. "However your score turns out, my compensation will be generous, understand? Tell Ivan what you need."

After Fiona recited her list, and the boy returned to the shadows, she took another sip of tea and settled back. From the inner pocket of his pinstripe jacket, Simon extracted a pack of cigarettes and held it up. Fiona shook her head, noting the Chinese script on the label. Simon, one of the richest men she knew, smoked the same cheap brand he used to buy as a small-time hustler in Flushing.

"Have we reached the psychoanalysis portion of our program?" she asked. The only thing Simon loved more than selling goods to criminals was picking at their brains, as curious as a watchmaker with a new timepiece.

Simon tugged free a coffin-nail with his teeth and lit it with a gold lighter. Taking a few puffs, he leaned back and studied the smoke-ghosts rolling into the dimness above. "Criminals are stupid," he said.

"Tell me about it."

"Real morons. That's why they commit crimes. It's not like they can hold down a real job."

"Preaching to the choir, buddy."

"That's why you fascinate me," Simon said, blasting smoke through his nostrils like a dragon. "Not in a sexual way, of course. But you're bright. You could've done anything else, gone legit, made a fortune."

"I hate cubicles," Fiona said.

"Good a reason as any." Simon squinted through the carcinogen haze. "You haven't killed Bill yet?"

"Nope. Although he's been pissing me off lately."

"I don't blame you. What Bill did was insane, stealing money from The Dean like that." Simon's eyebrows arched. "I was surprised when you backed his play instead of putting a bullet in his head."

Fiona shrugged.

"When I was your age, I hated it when older men tried offering me advice. So I feel a little odd doing the same to you, but here it goes: no matter how much you love Bill, no matter how much you think he loves you, you'll need to get rid of him sooner or later." Simon raised a hand in the air, as if anticipating her protests. "I know what you're going to say: love conquers all. And it might, for normal people. But we are not normal people. Rain dogs like us, we worship one God, and that's survival."

"What the hell is a rain dog?"

"Term from an old album. It means the criminals, the down-and-outers…"

"I get it. I wasn't going to say love conquers all."

Simon blew a smoke-ring. "Of course, that would have been boring."

"I was going to say: John Wayne and Jimmy Stewart."

"Two great actors."

"Guess which one was the war hero in real life."

Simon thought about it. "John Wayne."

"Why?"

"Because he was John Wayne."

"You're wrong."

"Jimmy Stewart? No, he was a weakling. A sap."

"*Au contraire, mon frere.* He was the highest-ranked actor in the U.S. military, ever. Flew combat missions over Germany, bombed a couple of U-boat docks, delivered the pain." Fiona's hand imitated a bomber flying through the air. "Not only that, he volunteered for it. He figured that, because his granddaddies were in the Civil War, and his daddy fought in World War I, that meant he needed to do his duty, Hollywood star or no."

"How do you know so much about this?"

"When I got shot—the second time—I spent four weeks in bed. Watched a lot of documentaries. Anyway, you know what John Wayne did during World War II?"

186

"Nothing?"

"You guessed right. John Wayne stayed home. Blamed it on the studio not wanting to lose one of their biggest stars. Toured some bases and hospitals, but he didn't exactly fight to get to the front."

"That's sad." Simon shook his head slowly. "John Wayne was a huge patriot."

"Sure, later in life. Maybe out of guilt, if you want to play armchair psychiatrist."

Simon took a final puff of his cigarette and stubbed it out in the ashtray beside his elbow. "What's this got to do with Bill?"

"Bill is Jimmy Stewart. He doesn't look like much, and he's a little too obsessed with fashion and luxury and all that crap, but he's a survivor." It was Fiona's turn to smile. "The way he dresses, it's like a suit of armor against the world. His way of keeping the mess, the chaos back. You know what that's like."

"He's still not much of a fighter."

"No, he's not. But if that was any sort of qualification, there are a dozen guys I'd have married by now. There's more to life than fighting. Bill gets that. He's the one who keeps me from getting too blood-simple."

Simon's face glowed red as he lit a fresh cigarette. "You know The Dean's sent people after you."

"I know," Fiona said. "Barbara and Ken, can you believe it? We ran into them in Havana yesterday."

"I'm surprised you're still alive."

"Cops showed up."

"Then you were lucky. I met them once, when I was in the market for good freelancers. Remember what I usually ask killers?"

"Why they do it?"

"Yes. Barbara looks at me like I'm stupid and says, 'The money.' I just looked at her, and she added, 'I need a new pair of boobs.' Ken volunteered that he wanted a new Porsche and a time-share. Most criminals, even if they really have no morals, they like to pretend that they do."

"Not those two."

"No. They're creatures of pure desire. No morals, no ethics, no mercy. Amazing that they found each other. Reminds me of you and Bill, actually."

Fiona chuckled. "Screw you, Simon."

"No, no, not the 'no morals' part." Simon bowed his head, letting the confusion pass, before resuming: "People like Ken and Barbara, they're meant to be lone wolves, and yet they found each other somehow. That's how they're like you and Bill."

"That's very romantic of you, Simon. You sure you're not softening in your old age?"

"Never."

Fiona set down her tea. "I shot a man in Oklahoma."

"Correction: you shot several men in Oklahoma."

"You know the one I mean. That assassin The Dean sent. The crazy one. Only he wasn't attacking me, he was trying to help." She felt a tingling in her hands, like a live wire beneath the flesh. "It bothers me."

"Don't be so hard on yourself," Simon said. "With the crazy ones, who knows what they'll do. You can't take chances."

The voltage in her hands increased, the muscles beginning to twitch. "I shot someone else, yesterday, but I almost couldn't."

"That guilt, I've always called that the Slaughterhouse Blues. Gets us all, sometimes. I used to have nightmares, back when I still slept."

"I can't imagine you sleeping."

"Never for long, or deeply. Ken and Barbara, they don't get the Slaughterhouse Blues. Remember that if you see them again. It might stop your hands from shaking."

"Aw, you care."

Blasting smoke out his nose, Simon shook his head. "Child, I just want my cut. You bring me back something good, you hear? I have expenses."

As Fiona stood to leave, Simon rose from his chair and executed a neat little bow. She had a better view of his jacket, and what she had assumed was pinstriping. In place of solid stripes, the tailor had sewn lines of a succinct phrase in tiny type: FUCK YOU. You can take the hustler off the street, but you can't take the street out of the hustler.

# 14

**AFTER FIONA LEFT,** Bill retrieved the pistol from atop the boxes in the hallway and returned to the kitchen, where he leaned against the cleanest-looking wall. No way in hell will I open that fridge, he thought. No matter how hungry I am. The fungus inside has probably built a complex civilization, complete with nuclear weapons.

James squinted at Bill. "Gimme my gun," he said.

Bill shook his head.

James gripped the handles of his wheelchair. "Don't fuck with me, son. I will come over there and take it from you."

"Not if I tip a chair in your way."

"C'mon, Dad," Don said. "Just chill."

"When my father was sick, I took care of him." James jabbed a gnarled finger at his son. "To the bitter fucking end, no matter how much it cost me. It was the least I could do. I'm sorry I raised a piece of shit who couldn't do the same. Where's your brother?"

Don took a deep breath, held it, exhaled loudly. "Nicaragua."

"Is he still a fat fuck?"

Bill's stomach growled. "Speaking of fat," he said, "I want takeout. Anyone want in on that?"

"Good Chinese place a couple blocks away," James said, nodding at the phone attached to the wall near Bill's head. "Number's written there."

"Should you be eating that?" Don asked. "Too much sodium?"

"During the War, we had C-rations," James said. "It tasted like cold rat assholes. Don't tell me what I can put in my body. I'm your fucking father."

With a theatrical shrug, Bill picked up the cracked handset and dialed the digits scrawled in faint pencil on the paint beside it. The voice that answered, over a cacophonous din of crashing pots, told him it would take ten minutes to deliver an order of sesame chicken and some wonton, okay? Yes, that was very okay. Fat and salt was exactly what the doctor ordered.

Hanging up, Bill turned to James, who had steepled his hands beneath his chin, looking almost professorial as he studied his son. Don fixated on the table as if the world's most fascinating object had suddenly appeared there.

"Where'd you find that gold, anyway?" Bill asked.

"Told you, during the War," said James, ever the conversationalist.

"I picked up on that part," Bill smirked. "But what actually happened? We got nothing going on right now, man. You might as well tell me a good story."

James cleared a gallon of phlegm from his throat. "My unit was in Germany," he said. "We raided a house occupied by a group of Nazi officers. Bad men, the kind who had overseen the camps. Upstairs we found some bags filled with gold teeth, gold coins, bits of jewelry. I remember how heavy those bags were. My memory's been going the past couple years, but what sticks with me is how much muscle it took to drag all of it down the stairs."

Bill shivered. "You brought the teeth back?"

James chuckled. "And not just those from the house. Yanked a few out of some German mouths. My family's Polish, it was payback. My buddies who worked supply, they snuck the loads back into the States. We melted everything down. You know how much they paid us in the Army? Nothing. That gold was fair salary for getting my ass shot at."

"Why not bury it here?" The backyard looked plenty soft for digging, once you cleared away the heaps of mushy cardboard and the rusty hulks of refrigerators past. Plus the tall brick walls blocked any snooping neighbors.

"Always felt funny about having it too close, like someone might try to rob me. And I really did think we'd always own the bar," James said, glaring evil at Don. "Guess I was wrong on that front, thanks to this pissant over here."

Don tapped the table. "What happened to those officers?"

"The ones we took the gold from?" James snarled. "We dragged them outside and shot them all in the backs of their blonde Nazi heads, pop-pop-pop. I know I've done a lot of bad in my life, but I can go to my grave knowing I did that little bit of good."

There was a knock on the front door.

"Food's here," Don said, standing up.

Bill glanced at the clock on the wall. "Bit early, huh?"

"Like my Dad said, the restaurant's close." Shoving past Bill, Don walked into the hallway. "I know I didn't ask for anything, but you better believe I'm going to steal a bit of whatever you ordered."

Bill flexed his grip on the pistol. His palms suddenly wet. "Hold up, man."

James sensed Bill's tone. His wrinkled hands slipped beneath the thick red blanket covering his legs.

Don was halfway down the hallway, one hand fishing in his jeans pocket for his wallet, when the front door slammed inward. Ken stood in the doorway, so tall he blocked the sun.

What happened next, Bill had to admit, was impressive. Despite his busted leg, Don dove to his right with the panicked speed of a rabbit on quality meth, crashing through the glass doors that separated the hallway from the living room. Through the wall, Bill heard Don's body thumping and crashing over boxes and furniture.

Ken locked on Bill. Whereas in Havana the assassin had rocked tropical-appropriate khakis and a straw hat, now he opted for hitman chic: a black suit with a dark gray shirt and a black tie. It made him look like a used-car salesman who lifted weights on the weekends. There's nothing worse than a serial killer with poor taste and a credit card.

Bill raised the pistol and squeezed the trigger, Ken in his gunsight ducking outside, disappearing behind the doorframe. Bill's shot rocketed down the hallway and across the street, sparking off the brownstone opposite.

"What's happening?" James yelled.

"Bad people," Bill said, retreating into the kitchen. The pistol threatened to slip from his sweaty fingers. His breath too fast and tight.

"Got one in the yard, too," James said.

*Time to get your shit together.* Bill glanced over his shoulder in time to see, through the dirty window, a dim white shape drop over the brick wall. "Her name is Barbara. She's a killer," Bill said, attention shifting to the silver .22 automatic in the old man's lap. "Wait, where the hell did you get that?"

"Your girlie-girl wasn't going to reach in my pants," James cackled. "Perfect place to hold a weapon. She couldn't handle *these* goods."

A thump from the hallway. Bill took a deep breath, grit his jaw, and swiveled, catching a black flicker as Ken disappeared through the splintered doors to the living room. Too late to shoot. A window shattered, followed by rapid footsteps, and Don wobbled into view on the stoop, shaking bits of glass and wood out of his hair.

Bill gestured for Don to come down the hallway. Don flashed him the finger and disappeared down the stairs to the street.

So much for family loyalty.

Bill knew the dining room behind him was piled high with crap, and that a tall bookshelf and several crushed boxes barricaded the door at its far end. That door had two deadbolts. If it led outside, all that weight and steel might prevent Barbara from entering, unless she scaled to the second floor. Who knew what crazy acrobatic skills she had?

Better to handle Ken first, then deal with his nutso girlfriend.

"Old-timer," Ken's voice drifted from the living room. "You got a gun?"

"I do," James called out. "Locked and loaded."

"Then how about you aim it at Bill there, and let us take him off your hands."

James cocked his head. "And you'll let me live?"

Bill offered him a look that said: Really, man? Really?

"Yes. It's okay, you don't really have a choice," Ken said. "You're surrounded."

From the dining room came the faint creak of a doorknob twisting, the thump of wood straining against a lock.

"We got gold," James said.

Sweat trickled down the back of Bill's neck. If I fire through the walls and run, he thought, can I keep Leon's head down long enough to make the door? Your chances are roughly one in three million. You're basically dealing with the Terminator, remember.

"So you've got gold." Ken said. "Ever think of spending it on a little upkeep?"

"It's from teeth," James said, as if that explained everything.

A long silence from Ken, followed by: "Huh?"

Screw it, I'm not going to die listening to this crap. Bill leveled the pistol and tried to pinpoint Ken by his voice. Just inside the glass doors, to the left. Get some oxygen in your lungs and hold it. You can do this.

Pulse thundering in his ears, Bill glanced at James, who had swiveled his wheelchair to face the wall between the kitchen and living room. The old man had his dinky .22 aimed at the cracking paint, ready to back Bill's play. Maybe he wasn't such a bad dude after all.

Bill nodded.

With his free hand, James offered him a middle finger.

Like father, like son.

Bill pulled the trigger. What was left of the glass doors spat wood and slapped inward.

James fired his weapon in sync. The .22 made a dull snap, and bits of plaster burst from the kitchen wall. Bill doubted the lead punched through. Even so, Ken would hear two guns and hopefully keep his head down.

*Move, move, move.*

His feet were already in motion, carrying him through the gunsmoke haze, over bits of paper and glass, the front doorway a bright dream in what suddenly seemed like an impossibly far distance. As he rushed past the doors to the living room, he pivoted and squeezed off four more wild shots, the muzzle-flashes illuminating couches with torn-out stuffing, a broken table, tangled mounds of clothes—but no Ken.

Bill barely had time to consider this mystery before his momentum carried him out the front door and onto the stoop, into cleansing sunlight and New York City air that had never smelled so fine. A savage joy took hold of him, the same kind he imagined Fiona felt at times like this. I'm going to make it out alive, he thought—right before a fist rocketed into his jaw and the world cut to black.

# 15

**THE PISTOL BARREL** was a cold circle against the base of Bill's skull. Face-down in the back of what looked like a very expensive Tesla, Bill felt his stomach clench. His bladder, achingly full, threatened to let go and soak his pants, along with the premium leather seats.

"What did the old man mean about the gold?" Ken asked, grinding the barrel harder into Bill's head.

The funny thing was, Bill felt pretty good about his performance back at the house. Showed a little initiative. Did something in a gunfight other than blunder around like a big idiot. Fiona would have been proud.

With a theatrical sigh, Ken placed his knee onto Bill's lower back and applied every ounce of his two-hundred-plus pounds. Bill pictured his bladder as a water balloon slowly squashed by a rolling tire. "What did he mean?" Ken asked again.

"Is this a rental?" Bill grunted. "Because I'm about to piss myself."

Ken climbed off and yanked Bill out the Tesla's open door in one easy move. They stood in the shadow of a low drawbridge that Bill immediately recognized as the Pulaski, which joined Long Island City with the old Brooklyn neighborhood of Greenpoint. Below the bridge flowed the toxic green waters of the Newtown Creek, which stank like a dead man's fart. Bill scanned the nearby warehouses, the empty parking-lots lined with chain-link fences, and saw nobody. Maybe that was best.

"What are you waiting for?" Barbara asked, leaning against the Tesla's hood.

Wrinkling his nose, Bill unzipped his fly and proceeded to water the pavement between his feet. His bladder deflating felt like pure bliss. "Near Union Square," he said. "But I'm not saying anything more until we make some sort of deal."

Barbara snorted laughter. "Yeah, right."

Bill turned to her, zipping his fly. "Did you kill the old man?"

Barbara wore black leggings and a loose white top, along with her silver watch. "That geezer?" she said. "He opened his window, started firing at me in the yard. Then he shot at Ken. We left. We weren't, like, paid to deal with him, you know?"

"I like how you got slapped back by a guy pushing a hundred," Bill said. "Makes me feel all kinds of warm inside."

Ken shoved the pistol into his waistband and walked over. For the first time Bill noticed the extra padding beneath Ken's right sleeve, where Fiona's bullet had hit him. You're hurt, he thought. Excellent. We can work with that.

His right arm was injured, but Ken's left hand was like a bulldozer claw covered in warm flesh, exerting terrible pressure on the back of Bill's neck. "We like gold. We have stocks to buy, a timeshare to fund, some furniture we need to have—"

"Dream sofa in linen," Barbara said. "Non-toxic padding. Very important."

"We like gold so much," Ken continued, "that if we get our hands on some, we might even forget about Fiona." He smiled without joy. "What do you say?"

"Cut the shit. I know you're going to kill us."

Ken shrugged. "We just want cold, hard cash, okay? If we make more from gold than your contract, we might overlook the contract."

"You wouldn't. You don't want the Mob on you."

"Think of it this way," Barbara said, her voice sharpening. "You take us where we need to go, you might get a chance to warn Fiona. You die here, you don't get the chance to complicate things."

That makes no sense, Bill thought. No assassin opens up to chance like that. But maybe that's it. Maybe they're too confident. Or totally insane. Either way, what choice do you have?

"A gallery on University," Bill said. "It's in a safe. And I don't have a key."

Barbara and Ken exchanged a whole conversation in a look. "Get in the front seat," Ken said, shoving Bill toward the car.

Bill did as ordered, while Ken climbed behind the wheel. Barbara slid into the back. Neither bothered to cuff or zip-tie Bill's wrists together.

Ken fastened his seatbelt and tapped the dashboard screen to life with his right hand, wincing slightly as he did so. When a search box appeared, he typed 'Union Square' on the virtual keyboard, and a map popped into view, with a little arrow directing them to the Midtown Tunnel.

"Swanky," Bill said. "How much this cost?"

Ken glanced at Barbara in the rearview mirror. "Borrowed it."

"Okay, but how much does it cost?" When Ken remained stony-faced, Bill smirked and said: "C'mon, man, don't tell me you don't know the prices of things. You're like me: buy the best, cry once." That was flattery; there was nothing unique about the way they dressed. If Bill had to guess, they bought and wore whatever appeared on the covers of the fashion catalogs that hit their doorstep. It was their camouflage.

Ken's stoniness cracked. "Good phrase."

"My Mom taught it to me," Bill said. "And it's true. So come on: how much do you think this car costs? I mean, I'm not an expert, but it looks like it has all the options."

"Low six figures," Ken said, swinging the vehicle in a wide arc. "I want one, but I'm concerned about driving long distances, you know, with a lack of chargers at rest stops. And when you charge up, it takes an hour or something."

"I read they're putting more chargers up."

"Yeah, but that restricts you to certain routes," Barbara piped up. "And we go on little roads a lot, you know. The woods. Part of the job."

"I'm sure," Bill said mildly. The Tesla bumped onto a service road, passing the loading docks of a fortune-cookie factory and a brewery. Ken took a left at the next intersection, onto a broader avenue. No workers, smokers, or joggers on the sidewalk—not that any of them could have helped. Bill knew the exit to the tunnel was coming up, and that a cop car or two usually lurked around there.

As Ken maneuvered the Tesla onto the onramp, he tapped a small lever behind the steering wheel. An upbeat chime sounded, and Ken placed his hands in his lap. "Autopilot," he said. "Welcome to the future."

It took every ounce of Bill's self-control to not squeal as the Tesla merged into a lane. The wheel twisted on its own. Bill gripped his seatbelt, half-expecting the onboard computer to merrily plow them into the car ahead. Instead it braked, matching the speed of traffic heading into the tunnel.

"Let's get some music in here," Ken said, tapping the dashboard. The amplified voice of Chris Martin burst through the speakers, accompanied by a rising organ.

"Please, God, no," Bill said. "Pull my fingernails out, rip out my nuts, but please, no Coldplay."

"Make fun of Coldplay," Barbara said, so close her breath tingled the back of his neck, "and we'll kill you slow."

"Our favorite band," Ken announced, smiling as he cranked the volume.

"I liked them better when they were called U2," Bill said, doing his best to look for cops at the tunnel entrance without moving his head or eyes. He might have been a fugitive from the law, but the prospect of handcuffs and a cell seemed more appealing at the moment than ending up in a ditch with a bullet in his head. "By the way, I have a question."

"Shoot," Barbara said.

"In Havana," he asked. "How'd you find me?"

Barbara laughed. "Those guys you ripped off in the Dominican Republic? Only too happy to give us the laptop they gave you. I know you think you wiped everything on it, but we got enough about your new identities, your cards, everything."

Bill snorted. "Aw, heck."

The tunnel blotted out the sun, a shadow dropping over Ken's face as he smiled. "In Havana, when you tried giving us the slip, we wanted you gone," he said. "Figured out which room you were staying in, put a couple of trackers in your stuff. You were smart enough to dump the clothes, but you weren't going to give up a bag that nice. Trust us, we know."

Barbara touched Bill's ear with a cold finger. "After you left Havana, we called The Dean," she said. "Described the guy you were with. He said it was Don, that he had a father in New York. We took a guess that you'd come here. Risky, but it worked out."

"God, I love this song," Ken said, tapping the music louder and louder. "Third time we saw them in concert, they did this ten-minute version, and it was *amazing*."

"Let me guess," Bill said. "You love Michael Bolton, too? Your playlist have any Kenny G?"

Barbara hit him on the side of the head, softly, and Bill did his best not to flinch. He had spent the trip down the tunnel with his left hand on his right shoulder, thumb hooked into the collar of his shirt, in case she tried to loop that evil bit of wire around his neck. Then again, if he had to spend another thirty minutes listening to this soaring crap, he might ask her to garrote him as a mercy.

A milky glow seeped into the tunnel ahead. The Tesla surfaced into the concrete maze of Midtown. While the autopilot would never beat out a human cab driver for daredevil sangfroid, it managed to avoid other cars as they took a left onto Park Avenue.

Bill gazed out the window at the crowds of pedestrians, the hundreds of harried and tense faces. He envied their everyday problems. "How do you do it?" he asked.

"Do what?" Ken said. Mercy of mercies, he turned the Coldplay down to a murmur.

"Keep your relationship going," Bill said. "You know, with everything."

"You really have to listen," Barbara said. "Oprah always had good advice about that. It's about balance, you know, and giving and receiving. Not just working *hard* on the relationship, but working *smart*."

"Every time we have a teachable moment," Ken said, his eyes finding Barbara in the rearview mirror, "we really sit down and discuss it, you know? And when we're dealing with pressures at work, we make sure to voice those issues, rather than let things build up inside."

"And you have to speak with love in mind," Barbara said. "Are you having communication issues at home?"

"It's been a little tense," Bill admitted.

"Comes down to finding the Zen in the relationship," Ken said. "What the address of this gallery?"

"University and Twelfth." The actual address was two blocks further south.

"Flank." Ken placed his hands on the wheel, and the autopilot chimed. The Tesla whispered to the curb.

"See you in a bit," Barbara said, blowing him an air kiss, and exited onto the street.

As they rejoined the flow of traffic, Ken tapped the autopilot again. The Tesla mingled with a school of yellow taxis swimming downtown. Reaching beneath his shirt, Ken drew his pistol and placed it against his thigh, beneath the level of the window.

Bill's heartbeat accelerated to running pace. "Seems like you two have it together," he said.

Ken shrugged. "All about the listening, man."

A taxi veered into their lane, and the Tesla responded by

slamming the brakes. The momentum jolted Ken forward, his grip loose on the pistol.

Bill lashed out with his right fist, aiming for Ken's neck. The assassin might have packed a couple hundred pounds of muscle and bone beneath his tailored suit, but his throat was still a delicate bundle of nerves and vessels.

Bill's knuckles slammed into Ken's windpipe. Ken gagged and dropped the pistol. Bill punched him in the face as hard as he could, slamming Ken's skull against the headrest, before diving for the weapon. His hand brushed the checkered grip when he spied a blur of movement at the edge of his vision—Ken lunging to headbutt him.

With an audible click, Ken's seat-belt locked, pinning his shoulders back, his forehead stopping six inches from Bill's temple.

Bill had a hand flattened on the pistol when Ken stabbed an arm down, slipping a finger onto the trigger. In the tight confines of the car, the gunshot was apocalyptic, world-ending. The bullet plowed into the dashboard to the right of the steering wheel, leaving a smoking hole. Recoil jolted the barrel upwards. Ken's finger twitched again, and a second round vaporized the driver's side window in a chunky spray of safety glass.

Even seven-point-five grams of lead traveling faster than the speed of sound through luxury circuits failed to stop Chris Martin serenading their bloody fight. The hot pistol tumbled from their grip, disappearing beneath the pedals. Shifting tactics, Bill drove his shoulder into Ken's torso, hoping to drive the air out of his lungs. It felt like tackling a refrigerator.

Seemingly unfazed by Bill's attempt to play linebacker, Ken wrapped his left hand around Bill's throat. Bill responded by slamming his fists into the bandage on Ken's right arm, hoping to bring the pain.

No luck. Those massive fingers applied industrial pressure directly to Bill's trachea. The world trembled and darkened at the edges. His lungs burning, Bill placed his palms against Ken's chest and pushed as hard as he could. Ken's thumbs eased a bit, affording Bill the faintest sip of oxygen. Then Bill's hands slipped and Ken bulled forward again, to tighten his grip.

Instead of trying to meet Ken on his own terms, Bill planted his right foot against the dashboard and shoved backward with his remaining strength. That worked: he tore free of that iron grip hard enough to slam against his passenger door. Ken's face twisted with rage, his hands slapping the air.

*Attack, baby,* Fiona urged in his head. Bill took his foot off the dashboard and slammed it into Ken's chest as hard as he could.

In an ordinary fight, a super-killer like Ken would have blocked a move like that easily, and probably snapped Bill's ankle in the bargain. Weakened by pain and that blow to the throat, Ken could only grunt as his body thumped against the driver's door, pinned by Bill's expensive shoe and locked knee.

The Tesla, its robot brain unconcerned by the battle rocking its front seats, continued down Park Avenue at a stately pace. Bill had read enough magazine stories about these cars to know that touching the steering wheel or tapping the pedals would shift the steering back to human control, yet that blue autopilot icon glowed on the dashboard screen. Bill wondered if the first bullet had damaged the electronics.

Ken took a deep breath and tried to shove Bill's leg aside, so Bill rammed his other foot into Ken's chest. Both legs straight, knees locked, Bill braced his shoulders against his door and rose off the seats, seeking maximum leverage. His muscles screamed for mercy.

Ken, failing to budge Bill's locked legs, reached into the footwell. The pistol. If Bill dropped his legs to scramble for it, a freed Ken could do any number of horrible things. If he stayed in place, Ken's long arms would reach the weapon anyway, and then—game over.

No way am I dying to this awful music, Bill thought.

Park Avenue heading south into Union Square had two lanes, plus a far-right one for parking. The Tesla had chosen the middle lane, clear of traffic for the next few blocks. To their left, a pair of white box trucks trundled along, brake lights flaring as they approached the intersection.

Ken's hand rose, the pistol in his grip.

Bill's feet slid a few inches down Ken's sternum. Muscles quaking, Bill extended his legs. Ken had size, but Bill had enough leverage to push the upper half of Ken's body through the shattered driver's window. The rear truck's bumper passed the Tesla. As Chris Martin worked a high note, Ken's head connected with two tons of metal at thirty miles an hour.

That song about peace and harmony climaxed with a meaty crunch.

The pistol clattered out of sight.

Bill drew his aching legs back, relieved when Ken's body remained jammed in place. The prospect of a headless corpse flopping back into the driver's seat, neck painting the cabin with blood, was more than his nerves could take.

The Tesla's sensors, recognizing a red light ahead, braked the car. Bill exhaled loudly and closed his eyes.

Someone screamed, high and shrill.

Bill's eyes snapped open. The windshield framed a family in the crosswalk: a hipster father with a blonde goatee, gripping the handles of a tri-wheeled baby carriage, beside his tattooed wife toting two bags of groceries. The sight of a gore-splattered Tesla seemed to disturb them. The father shrieked again as he pushed the baby carriage for the curb, followed by his gibbering wife.

Stunned by the noise, Bill waved back. Freakout aside, the family did have a point: a car with a headless corpse, idling at one of the city's poshest intersections, was liable to start attracting attention. Especially with cheerful music blaring out its shattered window.

Unbuckling his seat belt, Bill shoved the pistol into his waistband and draped his shirt over the handle. He stepped into the street, closing the Tesla's door behind him. A dozen taxi drivers regarded him with studied coolness. Bill figured a few had come from war-torn countries where the burning of your village is just another Tuesday; on that scale, decapitation via luxury car barely rated a yawn.

The traffic light flicked green, and the Tesla hummed away, bearing headless Ken into the distance. Bill assumed the vehicle would follow whatever route Ken had pre-programmed, and park itself once it reached the final destination. Welcome to the future, filled with dead men at the wheel.

A few pedestrians stopped to snap photos of the passing Tesla with their phones. Ignoring them, Bill adjusted his lapels and walked in the opposite direction.

# 16

**A LONG TIME** ago, Dusty's had dominated a corner a few blocks south of Union Square. Bill remembered it from his early days in the city: a place so old-school it still had an ornate wooden bar, a potbelly stove in one corner, and sooty light-bulbs older than most of the clientele. It attracted a peculiar combination of drinkers: hipster kids on a misguided quest for authenticity, businessmen looking to murder their livers in a hole convenient to their office, and old-timers clinging to a last bit of old New York like shipwrecked sailors clinging to flotsam.

That was all gone now. In its place stood a gleaming cube of steel and smoked glass. The front door, distinguishable from the rest of the translucent front only by the most discrete of handles, had the word 'GALLERY' etched on it, with the open days and hours beneath.

Bill tried the handle. The posted hours said the place was closed, but what if someone was working alone, or expecting a special customer? The door was locked. He ran a thumb over the deadbolt below the handle—possible to pick, if he had the tools. Where was Fiona?

As if summoned, she stepped from between two parked cars and asked: "What happened to you?"

"Ken and Barbara," he said, as she ran a hand down his face, pausing at the scratches on his cheeks.

Fiona glanced around. "Where?"

"Barbara might be close. As for Ken, let's just say he got ahead of himself."

Fiona squinted at him. "What?"

"He tried to be head and shoulders above the rest."

"Start making sense, dear."

"He got his head knocked off by a truck."

Fiona paused. "So he's dead."

"Oh, I hope so."

"You know, you can come out and say it, instead of trying to be James Bond with the puns." She laughed, her palm on his chin. "You're so ridiculous."

"Barbara got out of the car before Ken and I started fighting. She's headed in this direction."

"Then we better move fast," she said, nodding toward a battered white van parked midway down the block. "I got a van."

"How are we getting inside?"

Reaching into her pocket, she said: "Got tools."

"A rock?"

"Ha, you're funny." She drew a small device that looked like a steel cutout of a pistol, with a long needle for a barrel. Its handle reminded Bill of a miniature caulking-gun.

"Believe it or not," he said, "I've never seen a snap gun before."

"My lockpicking skills have gone to crap," Fiona said, adjusting the brass thumb-wheel on the back of the device. "Not that I was ever great with a rake, anyway." Handing the snap gun to Bill, she dug into her pocket again and extracted a small metal pick, which she slipped into the deadbolt and twisted until the tension felt right.

Bill returned the snap gun. She slid its tip into the keyway, above the pick, and pulled the trigger—snap, snap, snap.

The deadbolt pins popped. She twisted the pick, and the lock popped open.

Gripping the door-handle, Bill asked: "What if there's an alarm?"

"Of course there's an alarm, doofus," Fiona said. "It's already taken care of."

With a final glance at the empty street, Bill pulled the door open. He bowed theatrically, ushering Fiona inside. She smiled and tipped an imaginary hat as she entered the lobby, and Bill's heart leapt. They were getting through this. Everything would be okay.

The lobby was paneled with blonde wood, the reception desk a glass surfboard balanced on a narrow aluminum curve. Bill spied a small white panel embedded in the wall, its lights blinking green, and tensed for a siren.

"Hello?" Fiona called, peeking through the wide doorway that led to the gallery's first room. "I think we're alone."

"How'd you disable it?" Bill asked, locking the door behind them.

"I bet the alarm would be wireless," she said. "It's all the rage these days. No wires, minimal installation, you can even use a remote control to disable it without a code. Simon gave me a gizmo that mimics that remote. I used it before we picked the lock."

"How is Simon these days?"

"Still scary as shit. But he sends his love."

"That's a relief. I'd hate to get on his bad side."

"He's the least of our problems." Fiona ducked into that first room, trailed by Bill. It was the scene of a stop-motion car bombing: chunks of white sedans dangled from the ceiling on nearly invisible wires; blinking fluorescent tubes pierced the wreckage at odd angles, representing physics, pressure, fire. According to the text printed on the wall beside the doorway, the artist, Chun Li, had always been obsessed with the illusion of order in a chaotic world.

They kept walking. At the entrance to the next room hung a

small drawing, four inches by five, in a thick white plastic frame. The artist had executed his work with chalk, pencil, and a few ounces of his own blood. The subject was a nude woman on her hands and knees, with what looked like an automobile driveshaft jutting out her mouth.

"Matthew Barney rip-off," Bill said. "But good lines. What do you think, honey?"

Fiona sucked air through her teeth and entered the third room, where black-and-white prints of cow carcasses lined the walls, sharing space with gluey collages of religious icons and porno. In the center of the space, the *pièce de résistance*: an actual human brain in a jar, in a red leather wing chair, facing an old-style television looping a six-second clip of Jerry Seinfeld laughing.

"I hate all of it," Fiona said.

"Hate's a strong word."

"Oh, you like it?"

Bill smiled, showing some teeth. "I'm sure it'd fit right into the living room. Like, Hannibal Lecter's."

The fourth room was the largest yet, lit from above by harsh white light. Behind a glass wall to their right, arrow-pierced tigers snarled at them, frozen in the act of leaping, their heavily muscled legs twisted in death. To their left, an unmarked white door: the back office, hopefully. Bill made a beeline for it, while Fiona behind him kept a slower pace, frowning at the dead predators.

As Bill reached for the doorknob, they heard a loud click, followed by a booming voice:

*"The lion…"*

They spun, startled, ready for the attack.

Behind the tigers, a widescreen flickered with images of the African veldt: lions stalking through the brown grass, sedate rhinos bathing in mud. A nature documentary, another part of the exhibition. The narrator was cultured, British, amused by the hunt.

*"…stalks the plains in search of whatever it can find…"*

Fiona pointed above their heads. "Motion sensor," she said. "It must click on whenever anyone enters the room."

"Any way to shut it off?"

Fiona spread her arms and spun. "You see any buttons around here, hotshot? Maybe behind that door."

Maybe some relationship counseling wouldn't hurt, Bill thought as he opened the white door. In the gloom beyond: wide desks, tall leather chairs, a window that offered a stunning view of a brick wall. The window was open an inch. "We could have just come…"

A fist rocketed out of the darkness, colliding with his nose.

Bill stumbled, face crackling with pain. A pale flash. On instinct his arms rose to protect his face. A glimpse of Barbara, her hand a bright blur. His jaw exploded, and his knees turned to gelatin. He toppled, flashing on the dead cop on the road in Havana. What the hell did she hit me with? What a stupid—

Barbara's shirt exploded and she fell backward.

"Bill?" Fiona called out. The pistol in her hand smoking. Bill was facedown, not bleeding but not moving. She wanted more than anything to kneel and place her hand on his back and feel him breathing, sense the blood thudding through his veins, but the bitch beside him was twitching, still alive, too close at this range for a clean shot with her shaking hands.

Barbara ran her hands over her torn shirt. Mushroomed bits of metal rained to the floor. "Kevlar," she wheezed, tapping the heavy vest beneath the cloth. "Prepared."

"Get up," Fiona said. "Interlace your hands behind your head and move to the left." Not that she had any intention of letting this psycho live. She just wanted a clean shot.

As Barbara followed orders, Bill's hand scratched the polished gallery floor. His fingers skimmed his jaw. The pain was immediate, a gasoline fire beneath his teeth. Beside his arm, a compact stun-gun in silver, the kind that fit in the palm of your hand. Nothing like a couple thousand volts to make you feel like crap. "Barb," he rasped.

Barbara met his eyes, her face pinched into a bloodless mask of fury.

"I don't know if you know this," he said. "But Ken really lost his head."

And he grinned.

Barbara kicked him in the face, hard, and Bill flopped backwards.

"That wasn't nice," Fiona said.

"I should have brought my real gun," Barbara said, "and not that little toy. But people can't answer questions when they're dead."

"You're a straight-up psycho, aren't you?" Fiona replied, circling so that Barbara would step away from Bill. Instead the woman held her ground, arms raised away from her body.

"In the car, he said you were having problems," Barbara said. "Do you love him?"

"Talked to a mutual friend," Fiona said, sighting the pistol between her eyes. "Told me you got a boob job with blood money. Doesn't look like it, sweetie. Your chest looks as flat as Ken's pulse-rate."

"I'm going to kill you," Barbara said, and took two steps the left.

Perfect.

Time to end this.

"You'll try, bitch," Fiona said, her finger already tightening on the trigger—but that damn shakiness took hold, her finger loose and weak even as every nerve in her head screamed fire, fire, fire.

Quicker than quick, Barbara darted across the empty space and slammed a fist into Fiona's face. Another into her ribs. Bone cracking in both places. Fiona's hand snapped open, her pistol clattering away, and suddenly she didn't care. The pain deep, blinding—she crumpled to her knees, choking for air—

Barbara tried driving a knee into Fiona's nose. Fiona raised a hand to block it, the impact shaking her arm. With her other hand, she popped the blade from her belt buckle. Barbara spied the steel a microsecond before Fiona swung, leapt back.

Standing on the balls of her feet, Fiona slipped the weapon between the second and third knuckles of her right hand. Forced herself to take a deep breath with burning lungs, to tighten the quaking muscles in her arms. *Please don't shake*, she tried to tell her body. *Please, we need to live.*

"You arrogant fuck," Barbara eyed the pistol on the floor. "You're not half as good as they said you were."

With her free hand, Fiona made a come-hither gesture. "Come on."

If Barbara leapt for the pistol, she would turn her back on Fiona. They both knew it. Barbara tore off her shirt, revealing her pockmarked black vest and a t-shirt beneath; she wrapped the shredded cloth loosely around her right forearm, to blunt Fiona's blade.

"You're boring me," Fiona said.

Barbara charged, and Fiona raised her knife, expecting the trick, the feint. Barbara shoved her wrapped forearm in Fiona's face, hiding her movement as her other hand went for the knife. After she grabbed the wrist of Fiona's knife-hand, Barbara would shove a knee into Fiona's stomach. Fiona would have done exactly the same thing.

Instead of slashing blindly, Fiona sidestepped and grabbed Barbara's wrist, and pushed. Barbara slammed face-first into the wall. Fiona dropped her knife, gripped all that shiny hair, and smashed Barbara's head into the floor, into the wall, smashed until everything was a red mess, smashed until her forearms were covered with tabs of skin and white bits of bone.

Afterwards Fiona lay there for a minute, struggling for breath as her adrenaline turned weak and sour. Her nose throbbed, warm wetness trickling out. That's what you get for your stupid hands shaking. Talk all you want about being a badass: in the end you're just another fuck-up. *Oh, is Fiona's poor little nose bleeding?* Good. Let it bleed. You earned that. You earned everything you got.

On the far wall of the gallery, the documentary about life in Africa kicked back to life, the sonorous tones of the narrator rumbling over Fiona's gasping form. "In the wilderness," he informed the room, "the battle for survival is often quick and merciless, and the only reward is the victor gets to fight another day…"

"No shit, buddy," Fiona called out. "Tell me something I don't know."

Spitting a mouthful of blood, she rose to her knees.

"The hyena," the narrator continued, "is a master at this sort of survival."

Slapping a red hand against the wall, Fiona struggled to her feet, her chest burning. There was always the danger that a broken rib could slice through an organ, or peel open an artery. She would have to risk it: she had promises to keep, and miles to go before she could head to the emergency room.

"I am a master at survival," she hissed through gritted teeth, driving her foot into Barbara's belly for old times' sake. The body skidded a few inches, barely worth the bolt of pain that shot up Fiona's body.

"The hyena will use whatever cover it can take to approach its prey," the narrator boomed.

"Smart animal," Fiona said, and began the long odyssey over to Bill. It felt as if someone had filled her stomach with gasoline and struck a match, but her legs and arms still worked just fine, thank you very much. She knelt and touched Bill's neck, and his eyes fluttered open.

"Barbara," he murmured.

"Splattered."

"That's what they get for Coldplay."

"Don't get you, hon." Patting him on the top of the head, Fiona stood and hobbled for the office, leaving Bill to roll onto his stomach and shove himself upright.

With the lights on, the office was a standard-issue space, startling only in its blandness after the weird sights in the gallery. The furniture and light fixtures were gleaming plastic and chrome, but the brick walls and gray floorboards seemed untouched from the bar days. As she paced the floor, Fiona saw some of Barbara's blood drying on her shirt. She felt no guilt. Barbara had once been meat that could think. Now she was just meat. Meanwhile Fiona had to find this loot and get out of here.

When she believed she had the right spot, she took a deep breath and held it, willing as much of the pain away as possible. She slipped her knife between the floorboards and levered until one popped loose with a loud crack and faint puff of dust. Bill knelt beside her to yank the adjacent ones loose. They found dirty insulation, tangles of dust and litter, the translucent curves of mouse bones. Bill swept those away to expose the rusty angle of the safe.

The front of the safe featured gold trim and the word 'NICHOLL' in fine script, along with a keyhole. Massive hinges held the double doors in place. Bill brushed the dirt away from the lock.

"Here's the key," Fiona said, handing it over.

Bill tried to slip the key into the slot. "It doesn't fit." He glanced at her, eyebrow raised, and she made a show of raising a hand to slap him. Even that gesture sent a sharp bolt of pain up her arm.

"Think the old man was trying to screw us?" Bill asked.

Fiona shook her head. "Nah. He probably just forgot which key. Hold on, Simon gave me something for this, but it's in the van." Fiona stood and hobbled out of the room. Bill heard the front door of the gallery open, close, open again. She reappeared with a shrink-wrapped block of gray putty. A stamped label on the front said 'SEMTEX.' Taped to it, a bundle of black and red wires.

Bill took the bundle of plastic explosive from her, turning it in his hands. "You scamp, this is cheating."

"Lighten up," Fiona said, bending to brush more dust from the hinges. "It'll be fun."

# 17

**BACK AT THE** house, James clapped his wrinkled hands and laughed at the sight of the bag plopped in the kitchen doorway. The cops had left long ago, but a few strands of police tape still fluttered loosely in the front hallway. Raindrops spattered the dusty kitchen window. All you need is a hundred-year flood, Bill thought, and that glass might actually get clean.

Fiona knelt and unzipped the bag. "Heavy as hell," she said. "Good thing we had a vehicle."

"Got no idea what I'm going to do with it," James said. "But probably safer in my yard than underneath some pansy's gallery, am I right?"

"Yeah, galleries are dangerous," Fiona said. Cupping a gnarled lump of gold in her hands, she limped over to the kitchen table. Don shoved a stack of stained takeout menus aside so she could place the treasure in front of James, whose purple lips split into a wide yellow grin.

"You know, when we went in and shot all those Nazi bastards, we weren't looking to get rich," James said. "But considering how much killing we had to do, I figure nobody would begrudge us taking a little something-something."

"No doubt," Bill said, turning to Fiona. "So what now?"

"We take our share," Fiona said, nodding to the bag on the floor, "and leave. You cool with that? You better be, because that's the deal."

"Maybe with all that money," Don said, "you can hire a nurse or something."

James froze. His grin faded. "Excuse me, boy?"

"I have to go back south." Don shoved his chair back. "We got a factory to run, remember? And now we have a real shot at being profitable again, thanks to my cut of this."

"You're leaving me?" James's lips quavered. His hand retreated beneath his blanket.

"Sorry," Don said, not sounding sorry at all.

The rain drummed hard on the window, churning the dirt into brown streaks. The yard beyond dissolved to gray. Bill was suddenly aware of how every heartbeat made his sore muscles ache and twinge. We need to get out of here, he thought. A half-hour to the airport, and a couple of hours to someplace new. We can take another chance at living, instead of just existing.

"When your grandfather was sick, I took care of him every day," James said. "I went through some miserable shit, because I believed in duty." He jabbed a gnarled finger at Bill and Fiona. "These two, they came back with my gold. Didn't have to, but they did. You could learn something from them."

"Not so sure about that," Bill said, and Fiona elbowed him in the ribs.

"If you didn't want to be alone in your old age, maybe you shouldn't have been such a hardass," Don said. "I want my cut. I have a plane to catch."

A silver flash as James's arm swooped in a tight arc that ended with Don's hand, outstretched on the table. A long blade buried between Don's second and third knuckles, Don screaming shrill as a fire alarm as James roared with youthful vigor: *There's your cut, you little shit!*

# OKLAHOMA (AGAIN)

# 1

**DEATH SUCKS.**

But it's probably a whole lot better than waking up in an Oklahoma hospital room, plugged into a dozen beeping machines, while a red-cheeked FBI agent screams in your face. Insult to my (serious) injury, it felt like a sadist of a nurse had shoved something very wide and long up my back exit.

The agent wore a black windbreaker with 'FBI' in giant yellow letters on the right breast and sleeve. He was bald and short, and thick in that way of bald, short men who think that regularly pumping three hundred pounds of iron to the point of aneurism is the best way to compensate for being bald and short. He was so angry that I could barely discern what he was actually saying through his clenched jaw, or maybe that was the morphine flowing into my veins from the jumbo IV bag hanging beside the bed.

"And after you tell us about the barn," the agent hissed, bending so close I could smell the gas-station burrito on his breath, "you're going to tell us where your little asshole friends went, you understand, you piece of shit?"

I swallowed. It took a Herculean amount of energy to open my mouth. "FBI," I said.

"FBI." The agent nodded vigorously. "That's right, fuckface. And now you need to get seriously scared, because if you don't answer my questions, you're going in a hole for the next fifty years, I swear on all that's…"

"Female Body Inspector," I said, and grinned.

The agent jerked back. "Excuse me?"

Laughter would have hurt my busted ribs too much, so I made do with a loud snort. "Funny Business Incorporated," I tried.

A vein in the agent's temple twitched in a way that reminded me of The Dean. "You… don't you…"

"Fun Beyond Imagination," I tried. Not exactly my best effort, but then again, considering everything I'd gone through in the past day, I figured I would cut the comedy-producing part of my brain a little slack.

"I…" The agent's stubby finger jabbed in my face, but some of the fight seemed to have drained from him. "Okay, cut the crap. What's your name? Who do you work for?"

"Food Borne Illness."

Instead of yelling, he glanced out the window that framed the corridor. Someone must have been out there, gesturing, because he raised his eyebrows and nodded. Swiveling back to me, he said, "I'm going to get a cup of coffee. And when I get back, you better give me some damn answers, you understand?"

"Fat Boys of Illinois."

"Fuck you," he said, and stomped out.

I was alone. Excellent. The hospital room was drab and small, with a dead television bolted into a high corner. Tilting my head a few degrees to the left gave me a better view of the windows that presumably opened onto the outside world, but the curtains were drawn. Tilting to the right, I could see a sliver of the corridor through the interior window. Either the FBI agent had left, or he was standing a bit too far to the right, in the blind spot created by the edge of my pillow.

I sensed that my next movement would spark a lot of pain,

so I shifted my gaze forward again, taking a few deep breaths to prepare myself. That's when I saw the FBI's version of an insult: There was no clock on the wall beside the television, although there was a lighter circle on the paint where one had hung recently. They must have taken it down in a pathetic attempt to mess with my mind. They couldn't even do sadism right.

Now came the hard part. Taking a deep breath and holding it, I tilted my head downward for a better look at my body, sparking an agony in my spine so intense it pierced the morphine's warm, happy cloud. My wounds were hidden beneath the hospital gown, but my stomach and chest burned in harsh lines where the surgeons had cut to save my life. I could wiggle my toes, a heartening sign that the bullet had missed all my vertebrae. I tried to think through the opiate brain-fog, to recall those final moments in front of the burning barn…

Fiona.

She'd been the only one positioned during the gunfight to put that bullet in my back.

That little minx.

I didn't blame her at all. I know that sounds strange, especially after I saved her and her hustler boyfriend, but we all worked a peculiar business. Someone who saves you today could very easily shoot you over a failed deal tomorrow. That lack of sentimentality is something that precious few people can handle well.

I needed to escape from this hospital, pronto, and not just because the FBI would stuff me under the jail once they found out I held the world record for killing the most people with common household tools. Once The Dean heard I was alive, he would send lots of men to finish me off. Those big, scary specimens of ill-developed manhood would work out all of their daddy issues on me with a couple of chains and a power saw, after which they would cut off my head, stuff it in a box of dry ice, and bring it back to New York for preservation and display. Spending my afterlife as a juicy paperweight on The Dean's desk wasn't the most appealing idea, to put it mildly.

During my self-examination, I'd noted that either the FBI or the cops had handcuffed me to the bedrails. Both wrists, because you can never be too careful with a bedridden gunshot victim. Combined with my wounds—and not to mention the enormous *whatever* jammed up my chocolate starfish—that was a real problem.

Good thing I was a lunatic. We have all kinds of useful knowledge for causing trouble.

# 2

**BRACING MYSELF, I** bent forward again to peer into the corridor. Moving just a few inches felt as if someone had filled my torso with gasoline and struck a match. I would have screamed if the morphine hadn't taken the edge off.

I assumed it was night, because the hospital floor beyond my room lacked the usual bustle of doctors and patients. A lone nurse hunched at her station, her face tilted toward a bright screen as she made notes in a folder. An officer sat beside the door to my room, the tilt of his head suggesting he was awake but barely, his hands folded in his lap. The FBI agent had disappeared. Maybe he had headed to the cafeteria for a cup of substandard coffee, or to the bathroom in order to conduct an aerial strike on Porcelainistan.

As I flopped back in bed, a traitorous part of my brain whispered that prison wasn't so bad, at least you got three meals a day and books and an hour to run around the yard. Not that I would live to see any of that, if I let them book me into the system.

I rocked my left arm back and forth until the tube feeding drugs into my bloodstream swung close to my jaw. I snatched it between my front teeth, then bent my head back until the needle in my arm pulled free. Ow. A faint rill of donated blood trickled down my skin to stain the sheets. Leaning forward, trying not to whine in pain, I twisted my head until the loose tube flopped against the bedrail, the red-flecked needle close enough to my right hand.

Twisting my wrist, I gripped the needle between my thumb and forefinger. Jabbing its tip into the handcuff lock, I did my best to bend the thin metal without breaking it. A hard-enough task when sober, much less with a pharmacy's worth of drugs in my system, but I managed. With the needle now curved at the right angle, I wiggled it deeper into the handcuff's cheap mechanism until the loop popped open, freeing my wrist.

After cracking the handcuff on my other wrist—easy enough, with one hand free—I braced my hands against the bedrails, pivoted my body, swung my legs over the edge of the bed, and stood. Saying it hurt would be like describing a tsunami as a wave: technically true, sure, but nowhere close to capturing the scale. I ground my tongue into my teeth to stop from screaming. The true extent of my wounds was a mystery to me, although I suspected a single punch to my abdomen would burst me like an overfilled water balloon.

If that wasn't bad enough, the hospital gown, which opened in the back, left my pasty ass flapping in the breeze. And I'd forgotten about the tube slipped deep in my chili hole, which slithered free, my sphincter spasming with a once-in-a-lifetime mixture of needling discomfort and almost orgasmic relief.

The pain I could barrel through, but my ability to work—that worried me a good deal. Perhaps the surgeons had replaced my leg-bones with chopsticks, and my leg-muscles with bags of gelatin. It was the only way to explain how my legs felt utterly weak and unable to support my weight. *It's a cognitive illusion*, I told myself. *On a big-picture level, you are totally fine. Totally!*

I believed that enough to lurch toward the door. The next step was pretty simple: Succeed or die. Easing the door-handle down as smoothly as I could, I cracked the door open. The cop was right in front of me, in his plastic seat. Despite my quiet, he must have heard the faint click of door-lock against jamb, because he started to move. But I already had a hand on his holster, freeing the pistol there.

"Hey," he started to say, but I had the pistol's barrel jammed into the back of his neck. I felt a momentary flush of pride: You could pump me full of lead, cut me open, sew me back up, and then flood of body with drugs—but I still had my reflexes.

"Hey yourself," I said, and grit my teeth, willing myself to keep standing as my knees wobbled. Just as I feared total collapse, though, my brainstem came through with a nice dose of adrenaline that made me stand a little straighter.

"You got to get back inside," the cop said, as if I was a naughty kid who'd escaped his room.

"Don't think so, Dad," I said. "Stand up."

He did, swallowing hard as he did so, and I felt a little weird about that 'Dad' wisecrack. He was no more than twenty-two, his cheeks covered with faded blots of acne. His eyes rolled from side to side, trying to lock on me, but I made a point of standing directly behind him.

"What now?" he asked.

I scanned the empty corridor. "Where's your partner?"

"What?"

"The guy you're on shift with."

He shook his head. "Had to leave."

I would choose to believe that for the moment. "Where's that FBI guy?"

"He had to leave, too." Another swallow. "Somebody called something in. Something big."

What was bigger than me wiping out most of this county's police force, along with its corrupt sheriff and probably a few townies? Suddenly I understood how Elvis must have felt when he heard about the Beatles for the first time, overshadowed by something far bigger. I was tempted to ask about the nature of the emergency, but my soul would have been crushed if he'd said my infamy was eclipsed by a shootout at the local meth lab.

"Elevators," I said, glancing over his shoulder at the nurses' station, whose lone occupant was still focused on her computer. "Move. Now."

I slapped a hand on his shoulder before he started off, but he only needed to take a step before I realized this wasn't going to work: He was too big, too fast, and I was too weak. Digging my nails into his uniform, I said, "Stop."

He obeyed.

"Nurse," I called, raising my voice to a damaged warble.

She looked up from her computer, her eyes widening.

"It's okay," I told her. "I need you to bring some epinephrine, right now." My adrenaline was doing its best, but I needed a real rush, the kind that came out of a biomedical lab in a little glass container.

"But." Her mouth flopped open, closed, opened again. "I'd need to call a doctor…"

I jammed the pistol harder into the kid's neck. "Pretty please," I said, "and thank you."

"It's okay, miss," the cop told her. "Just do it, please."

The nurse stood, her wheeled chair rattling back, and scampered away, hopefully in the direction of a drug fridge. "Okay," I told the cop. "Meanwhile, we're heading for the elevators. And you go slow, understand?"

He nodded. "Whatever you say."

As we inched down the corridor, I felt my bladder tremble and release, the warmth running down my leg and dribbling on the floor. Between that and my ass exposed for all to see, the embarrassment was becoming worse than the pain. I had never been the most elegant person, but even a broken-down schlub like me has some standards. We arrived at the elevators as the nurse appeared in the hallway ahead of us, carrying a syringe on a tray.

"If that's not epinephrine," I told her, "the cop dies."

"I get that," she said, taking the syringe in one shaking hand as she tucked the tray into her armpit with the other.

"Good," I said. "Then inject it. Give me a meg."

"Excuse me?"

"Milligram."

"That's not how we say it." She frowned. "It's just 'milligram.'"

"I don't need a semantics lesson," I said. "I just need that shit in my veins, understand?"

"Okay, okay." Up close, I noted she was quite pretty, in an Italian Renaissance sort of way. Reminded me a bit of my ex-wife, who would probably pop a bottle of fine champagne and crank the Aretha Franklin if she heard I'd met a grisly end.

I stuck out my free arm, ready for the stick. "No tricks," I said.

"No tricks." Despite her nervousness, she was a wizard with the needle, sliding it under my skin so smoothly I barely felt the prick. As she pressed the plunger home, she offered me a little smile that threatened to crack my heart in two.

"Do this cop a favor: Don't call for help for ten minutes, or he's dead," I said, as she removed the needle. "And I'm sorry for this, by the way."

"You should be." That smile widened a bit.

Damn, maybe I still had the old mojo.

The cop grunted, and I snapped back to reality. "Hit the down button," I told him, pressing the pistol harder into the base of his skull, and he obeyed. The doors opened immediately. As we walked onto the car, I offered the nurse a cheery salute.

"You'll never make it out," the cop told me once the doors closed again. "If there are no cops in the lobby, the hospital staff will still see you, call it in. You won't get three miles."

"First floor, please," I said. My arm was tingling, but nothing I expected from a shot of epinephrine—a racing heart, torrential sweats—seemed to hit. Had the nurse injected me with saline? Was she really willing to put a cop's life at risk like that?

"Tell me," the cop said, hitting the button for the first floor. "You actually kill all those people on that farm?"

I jabbed two fingers into my neck, feeling my pulse nice and steady when it should have been jackhammering like an over-caffeinated porn star. What the hell?

"They say you were wearing, um, an Elvis outfit," the cop continued, seemingly undeterred by my silence. "That true?"

"Where's my stuff?" I asked.

"I don't know, evidence bag somewhere?"

Damn, I missed that white jumpsuit, although I suppose the blood and bullet-holes had ruined it for good. As the display overhead blinked toward the first floor, I told him to hit the emergency stop.

The cop smacked that bright red button, and the elevator wheezed to a halt.

"Take off your clothes," I said. My arm tingled harder now. Saline wouldn't have produced this kind of reaction. I wondered if the nurse had injected me with poison. She had a steely glint to her eye, despite her fear. A stunningly high percentage of serial killers probably enter the nursing profession. Imagine my luck if I'd stumbled upon Oklahoma's gender-flipped version of Ted Bundy.

Before my brain could spiral any further down that worrying hole, the cop whined, "Do I have to?"

"Clothes. Off. Now." When the cop hit the stop button, it must have done something to the current flowing through the fluorescents overhead, because the light had… changed. A little more bluish. It contrasted nicely with the green of the cop's eyes as he tilted his head, trying to get a better look at me.

"Uh, why?" he asked.

"Because I'm leaving here dressed as you, idiot."

He stripped, taking his time unbuttoning his shirt. He tossed it aside, kicked off his shoes, then dropped his trousers and stepped out of them. He wore boxer shorts with little hearts on them.

"It's date night or something?" I asked him.

He flushed. "Actually, yes. My wife…"

"I don't want your life story, jackass. Kick your clothes behind you. Then kneel down." The world wavered, and I took a deep breath. If that nurse had tried to off me, couldn't she have injected me with something that stopped my heart instantly? Was that too much to ask?

"You won't kill me," he said as he knelt.

I debated whether to try and pistol-whip him into unconsciousness. Unlike the movies, where smacking someone on the head with a heavy object will send them easily into slumber, a couple of swings with a piece of metal was just as likely to kill as knock your target out. And that's if he didn't fight back, and I was in no shape for a brawl in tight quarters.

Instead, I plucked the handcuffs from his pile of clothing. "Put your left hand on that rail," I told him, meaning the one that ran along the elevator car's walls at waist weight. He did as ordered, and I cuffed him to the far side of the support, limiting his movement to the front half of the car if he tried something stupid.

He was restrained and facing away from me, so I felt comfortable enough to set the gun on the floor behind me. With both hands free, I stepped into his trousers and pulled them up to my waist. The cop's belt held a keyring loaded with about five pounds worth of keys, a small flashlight, and a few extra clips for the pistol, but only an empty nylon holster where a pepper-spray canister would have slotted.

In his pockets, I found a phone, wallet and a relatively clean handkerchief, which I stuffed into the cop's mouth over his slobbery protests. "What did Cinderella do when she got to the ball?" I asked. "She gagged."

The cop failed to laugh. Maybe he was too clean-cut to get the joke. Stepping behind him again, I stripped off my hospital gown, examining my damage in the elevator's terrible light.

Oh damn, Fiona. You messed me up good.

My torso was a mess of bandages and tape. Gritting my teeth, I peeled back the edge of the dressing directly below my sternum, revealing a surgical slice crosshatched with stitches. Huge chance of infection. I would need a doctor at some point.

Buttoning the cop's tunic over the mess, I stepped into one of his shoes, as if I could slide into it like a slipper, but the cop's feet were at least three sizes smaller than mine. I'd made a lot of messy escapes in my time, but never barefoot. I loved always playing the game of life on the maximum difficulty setting.

"Here we go," I said, releasing the emergency stop button. With a mechanical grunt, the elevator renewed its descent. First floor. Ding. I hoped nobody was waiting to get on.

The doors slid open, revealing an empty hallway. Finally, a bit of luck. Before I stepped out, I hit the button for the basement, then offered the cop my middle finger as the doors slid closed again.

Hoping that nobody noticed my bare feet, I followed the hallway signs that directed me to the lobby. I swiped the cop's phone to life, just to verify that it was locked with a password, before dumping it into a trashcan. If I kept it, they could track me down in minutes. Maybe it was my blood pressure, but the fluorescents seemed to waver, the walls shimmering liquidly.

*Hey, buddy!*

I almost fired the pistol into the ceiling. What the hell? Who was speaking? Spinning around made me dizzy, and only by slapping a hand against the nearest wall did I avoid toppling to my knees.

*Whoa, there, partner! You don't want to topple on your ass, do you?*

A bright splotch in the corner of my eye. I turned to find myself face-to-face with a pink teddy bear, no bigger than the palm of my hand, floating in midair. I almost screamed.

The bear winked, speaking directly into my head: *Don't want to lose your shit, either.*

"The fuck are you?" I blurted.

*Your imaginary friend*, the bear said. Its voice was surprisingly deep, like a Nixon-era lounge singer with a three-pack-a-day habit. *Let's get the fuck out of dodge, what do you say?*

# 3

**AS I HOPED,** the lobby was empty of law enforcement. Whatever the nature of that emergency the cop mentioned, it must have been huge. But the patients and relatives in their rows of plastic chairs glanced at me with curiosity as I walked past, and I knew some of them would remember me if questioned.

In the parking lot, I found three empty cruisers, and I had to try the cop's keys on two of them before I found the right one. First things first: I checked for coffee, soda or fast food in the cupholders and front console. Nothing, not even a stick of gum. By this point, I felt so weak and hungry, I could have torn the head off a live bat with my teeth, just for the calories.

*Get moving, slowpoke*, the bear snapped, buzzing past my left ear like a fuzzy insect.

"You're not real," I told it. "Whatever that nurse gave me, it's a hallucinogen. You're just a figment. Which is good, because if you were real…"

The bear snarled: *Yeah? What would you do, tough guy?*

I mimed snatching the creature out of the air and eating it.

The bear chuckled. *Yeah? You'd be shitting pink fur for a week. Now drive, drive, drive!*

I twisted the engine alive and hit the gas, the pedal bracingly cool on my bare foot. Oklahoma wasn't friendly territory, and I needed to leave it as speedily as I could. Once out of the hospital's parking lot, I activated the siren. The bear squealed as we hit a hundred miles an hour on the open highway.

I inventoried the rest of the cruiser. The shotgun clipped to the dash could come in useful. I tapped buttons on the dashboard computer until it snapped to life, but it was locked with a password. I flicked on the radio beside it, the speakers crackling with cops murmuring in code. After a minute of listening, I couldn't figure out the nature of that mysterious emergency that demanded both the local law and the FBI, but at least nobody was screaming about an escapee from the hospital, either.

*I want waffles*, my imaginary friend snapped. *And bacon.*

"I want to live past the next twenty minutes." I had no idea what cities I was near, but the highway signs suggested I was headed east, and that was okay. The state line was my friend.

*Only carbohydrates and fried fats can fend off your encroaching feelings of death.*

"Can't you be a comforting hallucination?"

Floating over the dashboard, the bear whirled around faster and faster, dissolving into a pink blur. *Sure! Sing the bear song with me! Bear! Bear! Bear! Bear! Be—*

"Actually, shut up." I slammed a hand against the steering wheel, then winced at the bolt of pain that shot up my arm. "Just please, for the love of everything holy, shut the hell up."

The bear, still spinning, fell mercifully quiet. A sign snapped past: Truck stop, ten miles. That gave me a better idea than trying to bum-rush the state line with army of uniforms on my tail.

Eight minutes later, I pulled off the highway. The truck stop was a massive complex, glowing bright as a starship in the Midwestern night. A dozen 18-wheelers lined up behind the main building, and another twenty cars in the parking lot beyond the gas pumps and car wash. I pulled the cruiser into the darkest spot in the lot. Before I shut off the engine, I spent another few moments listening to the radio, still emitting a constant stream of cops spewing codes and curses.

At least if they caught up to me, I wouldn't be arrested. The cop soul can't forgive humiliation. They'd kill me on sight rather than risk me describing how I made one of them strip in an elevator.

I popped the trunk and climbed out of the vehicle, leaving it unlocked and the keys in the ignition. I hoped that the trunk would offer an extra pair of shoes or boots in roughly my size, but instead I found a box of latex gloves, a first aid kit, rolls of yellow and blue police tape, road flares, a short shovel, a speed gun, and a black nylon windbreaker. I slipped on the windbreaker, then raided the first aid kit of its aspirin and bandages, which I stuffed into my pockets.

With great reluctance, I decided to leave the shotgun in the cruiser. A weapon like that would draw far too much attention, even in a state where people loved their guns. The pavement cold on my bare feet, I walked across the parking lot, the bear buzzing around my head. That traitorous nurse's drug must have been wearing off, because the little creature was a little translucent, the parking lot's powerful lights shining through that pink fur like stars.

*Pancakes! Bacon! DOOM!*

"Shoes first," I said. "Then food." My stride was a mess, my arches cramping on the cold pavement. For the first time since escaping the hospital, I allowed myself to focus on the pain, and found to my great relief that it had subsided a bit. I wouldn't do a high-wire routine for Cirque du Soleil anytime soon, but I thought I could engage in most of my usual shenanigans if I had to.

The bear pouted. *Get over yourself. You're a mess.*

"Now you sound like my ex-wife."

*You never gave her enough credit, you know. She was just trying to help you be better.*

"Too late for that."

*And you think that one little thing you did back there, helping*

*Bill and Fiona escape, you think that redeems you? That you rediscovered the power of love, and that somehow made everything A-OK?* The bear giggled. *It did not. Becoming a better person takes more than one solitary act, shit-heel.*

I ripped open the truck stop's front door, and the bear smacked into the moving glass, flattening instantly into a bright pink mess. The sight made me laugh, drawing an odd look from trucker exiting through a door marked 'Showers.' Ignoring him, I circled the place for what I needed.

The truck stop was clean, bright, and jammed with people, despite the late hour. One section held two fast-food restaurants, serving burgers and fried chicken, and despite my hunger I avoided them in favor of the adjoining convenience store, which featured bins of clothing in addition to the typical shelves of junk food and drinks. Although I had a vague idea of shoplifting pants and a hat, I dropped it when I saw the security cameras overhead.

Those showers might offer some opportunities. As I drifted in that direction, I realized that my cop uniform was drawing some side-eye from the locals. Couldn't be helped. I pushed open the door and found myself in an empty lounge with beaten-up couches, a vending machine, and a television baring a Jason Statham action movie at top volume. The doorway beyond led to a long corridor of doors, each with a large red number on them. The doors faced a wall of lockers where you could presumably park your stuff while you rinsed off. It smelled faintly of chlorine and soap.

At the far end of that corridor stood a huge man in an oil-stained pair of coveralls, his face flushed and slick with sweat. He gripped a young woman by the elbow. She was no more than sixteen years old, in a pair of loose jeans and a tight blue t-shirt with a cartoon on the front. She was bent over, her eyes wide with terror, her mouth twisted in pain.

From that point onward, my night went from merely terrifying to downright weird.

# 4

**"OFFICER," THE MAN** said, as the teenager continued to struggle in his grip.

I stepped forward, deciding to play the role assigned by my disguise. "Miss, are you okay?" I asked, trying to inject as much authority into my voice as possible.

The teenager's mouth opened but nothing came out. The man adjusted his hold on her elbow, grinding her bones together. "She's fine," he said. "Just a little sick, is all."

Every fiber of my being told me to turn around and walk away. Stopping to play white knight would burn precious time, wrecking any options I might have left. But as I stood there, my knees quaking, my breath rushing up my lungs a little too fast, I had a thought that was impossible to flush: The guy's clothes would fit me, down to his shoes.

"I was asking her," I said, itemizing my weapons. Although the pistol on my belt would make quick work of this guy, a gunshot would set off chaos outside. Which left me with exactly jack-squat aside from my fists and feet.

*You're so weak!* The bear was back, self-inflating to full roundness. *And you're in so much pain!*

The girl stared at me with a combination of terror and hope, her lips trembling.

"I said she was fine," the man grunted. "I'm her father."

"Yeah, I noted the resemblance," I said, deadpan, as my hand fell to my pistol. When in doubt, go for intimidation. "How about you move away from her?"

The man dropped the girl's elbow and stepped left.

"Come here," I told her.

Wiping her elbow, she lurched toward me.

"And you," I told the man. "You're going to strip right down."

The man squinted. "Excuse me?"

"Your clothes," I said. "Get naked, now."

"Wait." His voice rose. "What kind of fucked-up shit is this?"

Maybe I should have asked him to get on his stomach, first, and interlace his hands behind his head. Sue me, I'm improvising here. Popping the strap on my holster, I said, "Sir, I'm going to ask you to calm down."

"You're no cop." He advanced on me, his hands balling into fists. "You're not even wearing shoes. What're you, some kind of pervert?"

"Yeah, you're one to talk."

He accelerated, his sneakers squeaking on the tiled floor. So much for the intimidating power of a gun. It also told me everything I needed to know about this specimen of humanity. He clearly felt he had nothing to lose, which meant he was engaged in lots of nasty stuff.

The bear clapped its paws together: *Oh, you're unbelievably hosed now, buddy, you're so very hosed...*

"Tell me something I didn't know," I muttered out of the corner of my mouth.

The girl, pressed against one of the shower doors, gave me a confused look. It's nothing, I wanted to tell her, just talking to my imaginary friend. But her kidnapper was only fifteen feet away and approaching at a high rate of speed despite his bulk, and I needed to figure out how to keep my skull intact.

In my weakened state, I lacked the strength or reflexes to

pummel, choke, or flip my attacker. Instead I waited until he was almost on top of me, and then I simply stepped aside, jabbing out a foot in his path as I did so. He tripped, squawking as he flew forward and impacted with the tiled wall face-first. Boom.

As tactics go, it's a classic.

The bear roared: *Olé!*

"Oh shit!" the girl called.

"Shut up and get that door behind you," I said. When she opened the stall, I gripped the man's collar and dragged him inside, my stitched wounds sizzling with agony. It was a good thing that my Three Stooges routine had worked on this guy, because I would have lost a drawn-out fight.

The stall featured a sink, toilet, and, beyond a smoked-glass divider, a shower positioned over a drain. A plastic tray by the sink featured tiny shampoo and conditioner bottles, along with a stack of soaps. It was quite elegant by truck-stop standards.

The girl, having followed me into the stall, slammed and locked the door without my prompting. The man groaned, bracing his forearms on the tile as he tried to sit up, and I drew the pistol and slammed the slide into his jaw until he flopped down again, not knocked out but stunned into submission. Holstering the pistol, I grabbed his shoes and yanked them off, and then— bracing myself for what was surely a nightmare of untended body hair and worse odor—I unzipped his coveralls and pulled them down.

Her voice stunningly calm, the girl asked, "Who are you?"

*Tell her you're her fairy godfather!*

"I'm nobody," I said. "Who are you?"

"Well, I'm nobody, too." She sounded like she was smiling, but I couldn't risk a look over my shoulder, because I was sliding the coveralls over the dude's waist and didn't want to accidentally touch his sicko junk. That was an amateur mistake. I barely felt her hand at my waist before she had my pistol drawn and aimed.

"You idiot," I told her as I pivoted on my heel, trying to move as slowly as possible. "I'm here to help you."

"Yeah? Why?" The pistol was aimed at a point between me

and the big pervert. Under normal circumstances, I was probably fast enough to snatch it away before her finger tightened on the trigger, but I wasn't having my best night.

On the other hand, I had zilch to lose by telling her the truth. "Because I need his clothes and car. You're free to go and do whatever. I just ask that you don't turn me in."

"Why? Is there a reward for you?"

"No. At least, I hope not. That would make things so much harder."

"Okay." Whether or not she believed me, at least she lowered the pistol.

"I'm going to change into this guy's nasty-ass coveralls and shoes, okay?" I held them up. "That means, unless you turn away, you're seeing me in underwear."

"Seen worse." Her lips jittered. "I was traveling with this fucker for two days. You want to kill him, I won't mind."

"Whatever he did to you, I'm sorry." I crab-walked away from her until my back hit the opposite wall, then stood. I shed the cop uniform and slipped on the coveralls, which smelled like farts and fried food. I stuck my hands into the deep pockets, careful of a blade or needle, finding only a car key and a moist wad of five- and ten-dollar bills. "Where's his driver's license? His phone?"

"In the car, I think."

I slipped on the pervert's boots, which were a little small in the toes but otherwise fine. Retrieving the cop trousers and belt, I dumped the flashlight, aspirin, bandages, and extra clips in the coverall's pockets, along with the fifty dollars in cash from the cop's wallet. The cop had two credit cards, almost certainly deactivated already, but I kept the metal one in case I needed a hard edge.

"What kind of car is it?" I asked, not liking how all that gear made my waist look lumpy. "Color? Make? Any engine issues?"

"It's an old red Ford sedan," she said. "It's crappy and it smells, but it seemed to run fine. What happened to you? You're all bandaged up."

"Shaving accident. Give me the gun back?" I stuck out my hand.

She shook her head, adjusting so the weapon pointed at the back of the stunned man's skull. "What if I do it?"

"You'll blow out our eardrums for starters," I said. "And then, when the cops get here, they'll arrest you for murder."

*And blow your head off on sight, good buddy!*

"Yes, that, too," I told the bear.

The girl blinked. "What?"

"Nothing," I said. "You're meeting me at a very confused time in my life. I'm not going to hurt you. Just give me the gun."

"No."

"Okay. Then stand aside so I can leave."

"What about him?"

I shrugged. "What about him? I'm assuming he gave you a ride, right, in exchange for terrible things? I didn't say you shouldn't kill him—just don't use the gun, it makes too much noise." Sticking out my thumbs, I added: "You want to do it right, you dig your thumbs into either side of his neck, choke off the arteries. Stay that way for four minutes, until brain death."

"Who *are* you?"

"Like I said, I'm nobody. And I really need to get going, so stand aside."

"Fine. But I'm keeping the gun. I got a lot of miles to go." She nodded toward the pervert. "And I keep running into assholes like this."

"Fine. Just move, okay?"

She pressed herself against the wall beside the sink so I could pass. Poking my head out the door, I noted the corridor was clear. Turning back to her, I again mimed shoving my thumbs deep into an invisible carotid artery, but when she offered only a blank stare in return, I left.

After my strange encounter in the bathroom, returning to the truck stop's lobby felt like a whole new world. I stopped by the fast-food emporium, where I purchased two double-cheese burgers, a bulging bag of fries, and a jumbo cup of soda. My arms loaded with enough fats and carbohydrates to give an elephant a heart attack, I headed to the parking lot, wondering if the girl would kill her kidnapper. On one level, the death of yet another pervert made no difference to me. But when you murder someone, it takes a piece of you away, and a girl that young deserved to grow up whole.

I should have done it myself. Saved her the moral conundrum. But I was tired of killing, too.

*Better fill that hollowness with junk food!*

"Shut up," I said to the bear, who was trying to balance (however precariously) on my left shoulder. "Shouldn't you have faded away by now?"

*Hey, I like it here! Isn't that the car?* A tiny pink finger jabbed toward a blood-red sedan parked beyond the gas pumps.

"Yes, it is," I said. "Now go away. I need to think."

The bear snapped from existence, and I shifted the food to my left arm so I could fish out the keys with my right. I was about to unlock the vehicle when I heard footsteps behind me, and I spun to find the girl sprinting across the lot, waving her arms. She stopped ten feet away, bent over, and took a deep breath.

"My name's Lola. Can I get a ride?" she asked.

# 5

**AS EXPECTED, THE** inside of the pervert's car was a hoarder's paradise, packed with boxes, wrappers, papers, and assorted junk. It also stank like a dead dog wearing a dirty diaper. At least the front seats weren't completely buried. My stomach flipped at the idea of driving such a shit-heap, but it wasn't like I had time to steal another vehicle, did I?

"If you want a ride," I told Lola, who plopped on the hood, "you have to give me the gun. No argument. I'm serious."

"Fine." She drew the gun from her waistband and held it out to me, grip-first. "I didn't use it to kill that guy, if you're wondering."

"So you killed him."

"Yeah," she said, shrugging, but her eyes flicked away from me, toward the truck stop's front door.

"You strangled him," I said.

"Yeah."

I calculated times in my head. "How long you keep your hands in position?"

"I counted to two hundred, okay? I checked his pulse. Nothing."

That didn't mean much. "Okay," I said, placing the fast-food bags on the Ford's hood so I could take the pistol from her clammy hands and slip it into the left pocket of the coveralls. Steeling myself in case I touched something truly unpleasant—finding the mummified corpse of Jimmy Hoffa wouldn't be a stretch in a mess this epic—I began to shovel out the car, dumping double-handfuls of junk on the pavement.

Lola sorted through one of the fast-food bags and popped a fry in her mouth. "Don't toss out the green backpack in the front seat," she said. "That's mine. What's your name, by the way?"

"It doesn't matter. Better if you don't know, in fact."

"Well, what do I call you?"

I thought about it as I pried a broken umbrella from the mess, depositing it on the growing pile of debris. Finally, I said: "Elvis."

"What, like that old singer? You want to choose a name that's not ancient?"

I pointed at her. "Watch it. Elvis was a golden god."

She giggled. "Just fucking with you."

I had cleared out enough clutter to give us more breathing room in the front. "I can't believe you rode around in this for days."

"Well, when the guy who owns it threatens to kill you if you say anything, you get used to it really quickly."

"I'm sorry about that." I slipped behind the steering wheel, adjusting the seat so I could reach the pedals. The pervert had been a massive dude. In the door pocket, I found a crowbar, perfectly positioned if you wanted to whack a couple of hitchhikers without too much fuss. No visible weapons on the passenger side. If Lola decided to turn traitorous on me, the best she could do for a club was a stack of moist newspapers. "Get in," I told her, buckling my seatbelt.

She did, tossing the bags of fast food onto the pile of paper and crushed soda cans that covered the center console. She kept her green backpack in her lap. The engine roared to life at the first key-twist. No warning lights on the dashboard, a full tank of gas, no weird rattling—none of that made up for the stink, but it was a good start. The vehicle accelerated smoothly as I angled it toward the lane that connected the parking lot to the highway.

A few minutes later, cruising east down the six-lane, I told her, "Buckle your seatbelt."

"The fuck, you're not my daddy."

"You're right, I bet your daddy wouldn't care if you wore a seatbelt or not. Buckle it or I'm booting you out."

"Fuck you."

There was no conviction in her voice. I slowed to forty miles an hour, aiming for the shoulder as I did so, and no sooner had my front wheels rumbled on gravel when she reached over, pulled the seatbelt loose, and buckled in.

"That was still mean," she said, settling back in her seat.

"Just looking out for your safety. Unlike your daddy."

She sighed. "Come on, man. I just killed someone, okay? Give me a fucking break."

"You wipe your fingerprints?"

"Of course," she said with no hesitation. "In fact, I turned the shower on before I left. Then locked the door from the inside."

The shadows made it difficult to read her face. There was every possibility she was a young sociopath. Lord knew enough of them stalked the highways and byways of America. She could be telling the truth, though. Take it from me, not everyone freaks out when committing murder for the first time.

"You can have one of those burgers if you want," I said.

"Nah, I'm vegetarian. I'll stick to fries, if you don't mind."

"Then give me a burger. I'm starving."

She dug through the bag and handed over a cheeseburger, which I devoured in two bites. My stomach spasmed as the chewed meat plopped in it, like a kid flinching at a fake punch, but once it realized the nutritional bounty, it clamored for more. My stitches itched, which I chose to take as a sign of healing as opposed to infection.

"Why were you dressed as a cop?" Lola asked.

"Don't you want to listen to the radio or something?" Without waiting for her to answer, I turned it on and spun the dial to a news channel. I doubted that the cops would announce much about my escape, but if they did, I hoped a detail or two about their pursuit would slip through.

"No, I want to talk to you." She smiled, although I noted she had her back pressed to the passenger door, her feet angled to lash out if I tried anything funny. As I watched her, I tried to remember how I'd felt after my first kill. Lots of adrenaline and fear and… excitement, I guess, although that also makes me sound a bit too much like Charles Manson. The regret came later. I hoped she felt regret, the crushing kind that left you never wanting to do something again, because the alternative led nowhere good.

"The cop uniform? It was just some stuff I picked up," I said. Technically not a lie. "I've been traveling a lot. Like you."

"You're a hitchhiker?"

"No, I'm… I guess you could say I'm a wanderer. I drift."

"Drift toward where?"

"East Coast, at the moment. Once I'm there, I'll decide." The newscaster, as expected, babbled about the shootout on the sheriff's property. He seemed very excited to detail all the goods and guns found in the smoldering wreckage of the barn.

Lola didn't seem to care about the radio. "Well, that's a problem," she said, "because I'm headed for the West Coast."

"Really? What's there?"

"Los Angeles."

"Oh God."

"What?"

"Do you want to act or something?"

"God, no. What do I look like, a complete fucking idiot?" She laughed. "No, I want to be a screenwriter. Then a director, eventually."

"How dumb was the blonde actress?"

"I don't know, how dumb?"

"She fucked the screenwriter."

"Wow, that was just... tasteless."

"True, it was funnier in my head. Why a screenwriter?"

"I like movies, I guess."

"As good a reason as any."

"What did you do, before you decided to walk the Earth?"

"I was a cleaner." That also wasn't a lie, technically.

"Thankless job."

"Tell me about it. You got parents? Family? Anyone to go back to?"

"My parents are religious wackos. Family doesn't give a shit if I live or die. I graduated high school, but I got no money for college. You know what finally got me kicked out of the house?" She unzipped her backpack, and I tensed, half-expecting her to pull a knife or a can of mace. Except the pervert would have stripped her of weapons a long time ago, right?

"What?" I asked.

From the backpack's big pouch she pulled a dogeared copy of Anaïs Nin's erotica. "This. Can you believe it? They take one look at this shit, call it the work of the devil, and give me the boot. And those fuckers can barely read." She snorted. "Yes, I'm a total cliché, too."

"I always liked Henry Miller better."

Her eyes widened. "Sacrilege. She made Henry Miller."

"Sorry to disappoint you, I have bad taste." I took a deep sniff. As our food cooled, the faint aroma of deep-fried grease started to lose out to the Ford's overwhelming funk. I zipped down the window a few inches, enjoying the wind roaring past my ears. The mile-markers snapping past made me think about the miles we'd put between us and the truck stop made me think about the mysterious emergency that had pulled the cops and FBI away from the hospital, kicking off my escape.

Amidst one of the strangest weeks in a strange life, that event was a little too odd for my blood. I needed to find out more. I needed to access my email and texts.

"You got a phone?" I asked her.

"Sure." She tapped the glove compartment. "He threw it in there. It's locked."

"No offense, but why'd you get into this car, anyway? That guy didn't exactly come off as George Clooney."

"Because right before that, I was hitching with this truck driver who was worse. He kept saying, 'Ass or grass, nobody rides free, and you don't got no weed.' Then he'd laugh. If I'd stayed in that truck another twenty minutes, I would've ended up in a ditch with a garbage bag over my head." A long, shuddering sigh. "So, I jumped out at a gas station and ran. When this guy stopped for me, it was late, and he kept swearing over and over that he was okay, that his car was messy but that wasn't a sin."

"Then what happened?"

"What do you think? He switched personalities like," she snapped her fingers, "that. Suddenly he's scarier than the guy I just escaped from. I was frozen. And he didn't sleep at all, never took his attention off me. Then he started saying truly scary stuff. That he'd stolen this car a year ago and nobody had caught him yet, because he was blessed by the devil. If you hadn't come along, who knows what sick shit he would have done to me in that shower."

"Well, I'm glad I came along."

"I am, too, Elvis." She wiped her left eye and smiled. The tear could have been an act, but something told me it was genuine.

Reaching into the door pocket, I handed her the crowbar. "Get that glove compartment open."

She inserted the chisel edge into the lid's top edge and levered it downward, rising from her seat as she did so. It didn't take much force to pop the compartment open, unleashing a small flood of phones, every model and shape and color from the past ten years.

"Take your pick," I said, and laughed, although I felt a growing disquiet. What kind of person stuffed a glove compartment full of phones, especially ones that looked totally new?

Sometimes it takes a killer to recognize a killer. And my killer's instinct told me that, out of all the truck stops and vehicles in the great state of Oklahoma, I had somehow found my way to stealing a serial killer's car. In the back seat, those piles of discarded clothes and toys and tools might have belonged to victims, turning it into what prosecutors liked to call a treasure trove of evidence—and that's before you considered whatever might lay in the trunk. Did I want to bet there was a corpse or two shoved atop the spare tire?

The cops would love to pin at least some of the crimes committed in this rolling junkyard on me, whether or not they let me live. Hell, they'd probably charge Lola with a couple of murders just for fun. Nothing would ever link back to that dead pervert, if he'd told her the truth about stealing the car.

How much worse could my luck get?

The universe must have decided to show me, because at that moment a van slammed into the sedan's trunk, sending us spinning down the highway in a spray of glass and metal.

**6**

**I STEERED INTO** the spin. The impact unleashed a storm of debris inside the car, pelting me with stinking clothes and bits of paper and soft, mushy stuff that I hoped was nothing more than old food. Lola screamed, her hands slammed against the sides of her head, her shoes drumming an idiot beat on the floor of the footwell. Bet you're glad you're wearing a seatbelt, I wanted to yell at her, but I was too busy pumping the brakes until we skidded onto the shoulder.

The van rocketed past us, its hood crimped, its brake lights flashing red. It was old and battered, with a logo on its passenger door that announced, in faded balloon letters, 'AL'S PARTY SUPPLIES' beneath a graphic of a jaunty birthday cake.

I shook the junk from my shoulders and drew my pistol from the coverall's pocket. Maybe this was just an accident, but I wasn't still upright and breathing after all these years because I believed in random mishaps. Al Capone might have said that once is chance, twice is coincidence, and thrice is enemy action, but if you want to stay alive and out of jail, you need to walk around believing that all first contact is hostile until proven otherwise—especially if they're promising you party supplies.

The van stopped in the middle of the highway, its tailpipe farting white clouds. I had no time to stick around and exchange insurance information. With the pistol in my lap, I eased on the gas pedal, disliking how the engine wheezed and the frame rattled. As we came alongside the van, I glanced at the driver.

It was the pervert.

The dim light from his dashboard reflected off his pale shoulders, suggesting that he had never replaced the coveralls after picking himself off the shower-stall floor. The blotches around his neck might have been blood, bruises, or shadows. His pupils reflected his headlights—two glowing points of light in the near-darkness, focused on me.

"You didn't kill him, did you?" I asked Lola.

She shook her head, tears on her cheeks. "I just…"

"It's okay," I said, meaning it. As much as I didn't need yet another turd in the proverbial punch bowl of my life, especially one driving a scary van, I was glad she hadn't killed someone.

"I mean, I hit him, I hoped he'd stay out longer. I couldn't do it. I couldn't."

"It's okay," I said, pressing the gas pedal down a little more. The engine bucked and snarled. The speedometer stuck at thirty miles an hour. In the rearview mirror, I had a better view of the van's smashed-up front, oozing steam and fluids. Had the impact totaled his vehicle? I hoped so. Then again, precious little had gone right tonight.

As if summoned by my thoughts, the van rolled forward. The pervert's gaze locked on mine in the rearview. How had he tracked us down? Did he just luck out in choosing the right highway?

Maybe. Or else there was a GPS tracker of some sort in the Ford. You couldn't put anything past a maniac.

The van gained speed, its headlights blinding. Lola groaned beside me, clutching her backpack to her chest. If he smashed into us again, he might knock us off the road, roll the Ford, kill us both.

"Take the wheel," I told her.

Her lower lip trembling, Lola gripped the wheel with one hand.

"Keep it straight," I said, and zipped down the driver's side window. When I tried to twist around in my seat, my wounds screeched bloody murder, wrecking my concentration. Instead, I sat back and extended my right arm across my chest, my right hand with the pistol poking out the window. The firearm pointing at the pursuing van, I knew that the recoil was liable to break my bent wrist, but I didn't have much of a choice. Referencing my side mirror to better angle my barrel, I fired.

The pistol kicked in my hand, almost slipping from my grip, the snap and burn in my wrist not nearly as bad as I feared. In the side mirror, the van's windshield shimmered as the bullet punched through it, leaving a darker hole the size of my fist just to the left of the pervert's head.

The pervert never flinched.

"You get him?" Lola called.

"No." I aimed again, and this time the pervert took evasive action, the van swerving to the left with a cinematic screech of rubber. I leaned out of the window a bit more, hoping that he would swoop back into his old lane. He was too smart for that— the van now worried our right flank, where I couldn't hit him unless I wanted to try and shoot through the back window.

"You want to trade seats?" Lola asked, realizing the problem. "I can drive."

"No." Dropping the pistol onto the seat between my legs—too late, I realized the barrel was still hot enough to sizzle my nuts like eggs on a skillet—I took the wheel from her and steered to the left, trying to put an extra lane between us and the van. The speedometer needle, trembling at the edge of forty-five miles an hour, refused to climb any higher.

"Give me the gun," Lola said. "I'll take a shot." Before I could stop her, she snatched up the gun and turned to her window, zipping it down. The pervert, sick but not stupid, anticipated that another gunshot was coming. Stepping on the brakes, he dropped back fifty yards before shifting into our lane. He knew that the one safe spot was directly behind us.

On the horizon, blue and red lights flickered. Maybe ten miles away, given how flat everything was around here. "Roadblock?" Lola yelped.

"That's right," I said. "This gets better and better."

# 7

**SHOULD I TAKE** the next exit? A one-lane offramp was nothing but a kill box with that van looming behind me. I could try jumping the median onto the opposite lanes, pull a U-turn, and evacuate the area with due haste, but even if this broke-ass vehicle survived off-roading the median's grassy ditch, I faced the same set of problems: If the pervert didn't get me, the cops could chase me down in a minute or two.

Running the roadblock offered some twisted appeal. Who wouldn't want to go out like Clyde Barrow, grinning into the barrels of your firing squad as you charge forward into eternal glory? Only I didn't want Lola to die in a hail of gunfire, not after she'd survived this psycho and the various indignities of the road.

"What would Elvis do?" I asked.

"Why me?" Lola murmured under her breath, her head in her hands.

Despite our damage, we approached the roadblock at a respectable rate of speed, close enough to see the individual cops silhouetted by their cruisers' flashing lights. Most of them crouched behind hoods and trunks. I guessed we had a hundred yards before we hit a spike strip.

The pervert's headlights flared in the rearview mirror, his engine roaring. He meant to ram us. I waited until his front bumper almost kissed our rear, then steered hard to the left.

I hoped he would overshoot us, but I timed it wrong. Instead, his van ground against the side of the Ford, crumpling metal and glass. The wheel turned traitorous in my hands, burning my palms as it tried to slither to the left and right. As I wrestled with it, I risked looking to my left. Through the milky crush of my window, I locked eyes with the pervert. He seemed totally calm, as if he was watching a dull educational clip on YouTube instead of trying to kill two people within sight of a police roadblock.

Lola screamed: *"I can get him—"*

She held the pistol in her shaking grip. I didn't have time to warn her about the dangers of firing a weapon a foot from another person's head before she yanked the trigger. The gunshot was a railroad spike punching into my already-injured eardrums, and I screamed. At least, I thought I screamed. I could feel my throat vibrating, but my personal soundtrack had dissolved into a high-pitched whine.

The pervert's passenger window shattered. I couldn't see if our attacker was wounded, but the van shot ahead of us, weaving into our lane as it did so. The roadblock was too close, cops scrambling for cover. Whether or not they had thrown out a spike strip, they would open fire in another moment or two.

Then I had an idea.

The worst idea ever.

"Duck," I told Lola—or I hoped I said that, at least.

She scooted down in her seat, dropping the pistol into the footwell as she did so.

I stomped on the gas. Faint wisps of white smoke trickled from the edges of the hood, as all of my engine gauges redlined. The Ford bucked forward, crunching into the van's rear. Better yet, our front bumper locked onto the van's trailer hitch.

The pervert tried to steer to the right, and I matched him. He veered left, and I matched that, too. His brake lights flaring as he tried to slow down, and I stood in my seat, doing my best to smash the gas pedal through the floor. My hearing was returning, the idiot buzz of my damaged eardrums replaced by the equally disconcerting sounds of the Ford's engine whining in terminal distress. The smoke boiling from beneath our hood turned black, and the smell of scorching metal seeped through the air vents. Lola slammed the vents closed with the palm of her hand.

"Hold on," I said.

The pervert accelerated. Maybe he thought that, by doing so, he could break the trailer hitch free of our bumper. Or maybe he realized that, with the roadblock ahead, this was the end of the line for him, too. Whatever his reasoning, he was doing exactly what I wanted.

Flames licked from beneath our hood, bubbling the paint. Lola moaned in fear as smoke pumped through the closed vents. The white flanks of police cruisers bright in our combined head-lights, a garbled wail that might have been a startled command-er's voice through a bullhorn, a loud pop that was either a cop firing at us or another engine part cooking off, and I threw my arms in front of my face as the pervert's van smashed into the roadblock at seventy miles an hour, pulling us along for the ride.

As I'd so fervently hoped, the van hit the cruisers in the right spot, knocking two of them aside. I lowered my arms as we shot through the roadblock, sliding down in my seat in case the cops behind us opened fire. The Ford's windshield a mess of shattered glass and leaping flames, the smoke stinging my eyes, I stomped on the brake pedal with both feet while twisting the wheel to the right, hoping we wouldn't flip.

With a screech, the Ford's bumper tore loose of the trailer hitch. A chunk of the van's frame came with it, the van's rear smashing into the pavement in a storm of bright sparks. Suddenly freed, the Ford hurtled onto the shoulder as I fought for control, my forearms aching for mercy. Through the flames I glimpsed an access road leading to an industrial complex, large white buildings lit by strings of yellow lights. I steered for it as best I could, not bothering to track the pervert's wrecked van behind me, or the cops still in pursuit.

**8**

**WE WERE SCREWED,** but maybe a fraction less screwed than before. The road swooped toward a gate with a wooden barrier arm. I plowed through it, my eyes stinging from the smoke, not caring what happened to the Ford so long as it kept rolling forward and didn't explode. I steered around the first large building and slammed to a stop behind it.

"Get out," I told Lola.

Shoveling an armful of phones from the floor into her backpack, she kicked open her door and scrambled clear, leaving the pistol in the footwell. I grabbed the weapon as I scrambled across the seats behind her, my torso a thunderstorm of reawakened pain, my lungs burning, my head spinning from what I hoped was only mild oxygen deprivation. If I fainted now, I was probably done for, because no way could a little wisp like Lola drag my fat ass to safety before I cooked like a pork chop.

Instead of springing from the car with foxlike agility, I flopped onto the pavement, scrambling away from the flames on my hands and knees until I found the strength to stand. Lola had moved twenty yards away from the car, spinning in circles as she yelled, "The hell are we?"

Spinning with her, I spotted grain silos looming against the stars like missiles, an empty railroad siding, a line of box trucks parked against the side of a massive warehouse. I was no farmer, but I bet this was a processing center for grain or crops of some sort. Nobody in sight, no roaring engines or shouts to stop, likely meant no night shift. If we were lucky, whoever owned this place was too cheap to pay for more than a guard or two.

Taking Lola's hand, I guided us deeper into the complex, away from our burning vehicle. The fire had crept from the hood to the Ford's interior, where it feasted merrily on the heaps of paper and other junk. I hoped it would consume the gas tank next, resulting in a massive fireball that might keep the cops and fire department occupied long enough for us to escape the area.

We needed another vehicle. Tucked in the warehouse's shadow, I angled us toward the box trucks. No, bad idea. The cops would roar down that access road within the next minute, and whether or not they paused to observe the Ford's fiery death, it would be impossible for them to miss a truck backing out of its slot. But what choice did we have?

Speaking of the cops, where were they? I turned back. The pervert's van was a burning star atop the highway's black rise. A string of police lights approached it, sirens wailing. From the blaze, a white flare arched into the night, followed a moment later by an echoing boom.

I grinned at Lola. "This might be good."

"What do you—" she said, but her expression snapped from annoyance to wonder at what happened next.

The sky above the highway split apart, sliced by bright red and yellow and blue sparklers that flared high into the atmosphere before fading away. Each arching brightness accompanied by a loud boom that rolled across the plains, humming the ground beneath our feet. The sign on the side of that van, advertising party supplies, hadn't been kidding: It evidently held enough fireworks to power a dozen Fourth of July celebrations.

Against that shimmering backdrop, I spied a stooped lump that must have been the pervert, lurching away from the colorful bonfire as fast as he could. At this point, I didn't care what he told them once they slammed him to the pavement and put him in cuffs, so long as his struggles bought us enough time to get away.

The police cruisers screeched to a stop, doors opening to disgorge screaming cops, their weapons raised. A rapid series of pops, almost lost in the gunpowder thunder of fireworks, and the pervert lurched and fell face-forward.

Well, I guessed the Oklahoma police weren't taking prisoners tonight. Totally fine with me.

"Let's move," I said, guiding Lola further into the shadows. In the middle of the complex, beside a smaller warehouse, we found an old pickup truck with a corncob logo on the door. I imagined this was a vehicle that people used to drive around such a huge property instead of walking. The interior was filthy, with stacks of old invoices on the seats, but it seemed practically spotless after the rolling disaster of the pervert's car. I found the keys tucked beneath the driver's floormat.

The engine purred smoothly to life. There was a quarter-tank of gas. Keeping the headlights off, I sped us away from the chaos.

# 9

**I DECIDED TO** resume my original plan of heading for the state line. Beside me, Lola settled back in her seat, her hands shaking on her thighs.

"Deep breaths," I told her. "Count them. Focusing on your breathing solves, like, ninety-nine percent of life's problems."

"Yeah? That work for you?" She tried breathing deep, holding it, although her fingers shook harder.

"It does, actually."

"How would you know? What have you been through, Elvis?"

I swallowed. After everything we'd endured in the past hour, I felt I could tell a version of the truth without her trying to bail out of the car at eighty miles an hour. "I used to kill people for a living."

"You're shitting me."

"I shit you not."

"That doesn't surprise me at all."

"Don't worry, they all had it coming."

"Like an assassin? That's fucked up."

"Sure. I don't disagree. But it's also one of those jobs where, once you're in it, it's sort of hard to get out, you know? You can't exactly quit."

"You worked for someone?"

"Yeah, a really bad man."

She relaxed a little. "I always knew you were something. The way you took that asshole down at the truck stop. The way you drove."

"That's right. I'm something."

"Now that you've told me, do you have to kill me?"

I shook my head. "I'm done with that life. Besides, I generally don't kill folks for free."

"Well, I guess that makes you different from the guy who kidnapped me."

"That, and I don't smell like a pigpen."

"Which I appreciate. Are you all fucked up inside?"

"You mean in my head?" I laughed. "Oh yeah. I'm a total mess. Divorced, overweight, and now with some fresh holes in me. But you know what? I'm still alive. Which means I have the chance to change."

"That's a pretty chipper way of looking at things." She studied my face. "I'm not sure I totally believe you. Tell me something only an assassin would know."

"No."

"Why not?"

"Because it doesn't matter."

"You're no fun."

"That's right. I'm the least-fun person you're going to meet tonight, and that's probably for the best, wouldn't you say?"

"So what now?"

"We drive. I think about what to do. If you want out, I'll drop you somewhere safe."

"No, this is fine. Think the cops will come after us?"

"I think they'll be tied up back there for a long time."

"Good." Unzipping her backpack, she extracted her phone and turned it on, flicking through brightly colored apps. That gave me an idea.

"You took a bunch of phones, right?" I asked.

"Yeah, but I bet they're all out of juice. Plus, they probably have passwords." She held up her device. "You want to use mine? I trust you."

"Thanks. I just want to check my email." Placing the device on the steering wheel so I could watch the screen and the road at the same time, I opened the browser, typed in the address of my mail service, and inputted my username and password. As I expected, my inbox was clogged with the usual newsletters and spam, except for the top item, which came from a sender I didn't recognize.

The subject line said: "You're welcome."

I tapped it open. No text in the body of the email, only a phone number that I memorized before deleting the email, signing out of the service, and handing the phone back.

"I have a weird question," Lola asked as she opened her apps again.

"What's that?"

"If I write about this, like for a screenplay, are you cool with that?"

"Sure. Just take as much artistic license with the details as humanly possible. Make me dashingly handsome, whatever."

She laughed. "You got it."

A part of me already knew who left that message. As much as I enjoyed Lola's company, I needed to leave her somewhere safe before I pulled her any deeper into what promised to become yet more weirdness. "Here, let me have your phone again," I said.

"Why?"

"I'm giving you a present." Tapping open her notepad app, I inputted a username and password, along with a web address. "This is a bank. Not one you've ever heard of. Call it a… private one." I handed the phone back. "Don't share that around."

Her eyes were wary. "What am I doing with it?"

"Whatever you want. There's enough to buy a house."

"Like, a Beverly Hills house?"

"Probably not. More like a Long Beach house. Or a Santa

Monica house, away from the water. Just don't spend it all in one place, okay?"

"Does it come with a debit card? Anything like that?"

"No. If you need folding money, there's an option on the website. Type in how much you want, plus your address, and they send a courier with the cash. But it's more for electronic transfers, big sums."

"Why?"

"Why what?"

"You know why what. Why me?"

"Because like I said, I'm done with that life. And it's blood money. Untraceable, don't worry."

"I don't know what to say."

"Don't say anything, just spend it well." A highway sign flashed by, indicating the next town was ten miles ahead. "I'm going to stop at this place, and you're going to take this car. It seems run well. Get to Los Angeles. Do the screenwriter thing."

"And you don't want anything."

"Not a thing."

"You're a weird dude."

"Guilty."

"I don't mean that in a bad way. Not at all."

"Then I'll take it."

"And you're a good guy, too, I hasten to add."

"Well, there are a couple hundred people who'd disagree with you on that one. Along with every cop in Oklahoma."

# 10

**I HAD HER** drop me off in front of a big box store on the very edge of town. There was no tearful goodbye, no promises to call or text me from Los Angeles. If anything, she was still stunned from the night's events, and who could blame her? I gave her shoulder an affectionate squeeze before exiting the truck. I did my best to smile warmly as she shifted into gear and drove away.

In my old life, most of my goodbyes were marked by copious amounts of bloodshed. By that metric, Lola's departure was a pretty happy one. Once her headlights disappeared down the street, I turned on my heel and walked into the store, which was probably the only thing open in this shit-speck of a town at this hour. No greeter at the sliding doors, only three tired teenagers working the registers.

In the electronics aisle, I found a prepaid phone with an astounding number of minutes. On my way to the registers, I swung past the snacks aisle and loaded up on chips and soda. My night wasn't over yet.

Back in the parking lot, I freed the phone from its packaging and powered it up. Punched in the phone number from that mysterious email. It rang twice before a deep voice answered: "Took you long enough."

"Look, I was busy." I paused to tear open a bag of potato chips and munch a handful of salty carbohydrates. "What big emergency did you use to pull all those cops from the hospital?"

Laughter like a distant truck struggling up a steep grade. "That's your first question?"

"It's been bothering me all night."

"Emergency notice went out. Wanted terrorist spotted at Tulsa airport. You know how it goes."

"I can't complain. It worked."

"What's your second question?"

"Why'd you break me loose?"

"We need you to take out your former boss."

"What's in it for me?"

"All kinds of cool shit. What you want? A new identity? A house in the tropics?"

"How about a new Elvis jumpsuit?"

"Excuse me?"

"Never mind. Sure, I'm interested. I guess I better finish off The Dean before he finishes me, right?"

"That's the spirit. How soon can you get back to New York?"

I sighed. "Give me a week."

"Okay. Once you're back, give me another call."

The phone clicked dead. Talk about blasts from the past. I finished the bag of chips as I studied the parking lot's blacktop wasteland, debating whether I should actually follow through on my promise to head back to New York City. As much as part of me wanted to run as fast as possible in the opposite direction—a powerless cabin in the wilds of New Zealand seemed like an enticing option—I knew that I was already mired in a new, terrible situation. It was bad enough that The Dean wanted to wire my nuts to a car battery. Now I was on the hook with one of the scariest bureaucrats ever to crawl from the gray bowels of the Deep State.

The fatty, salty snacks made my bruised guts burn. How much

damage can a body take? Does it all depend on how badly the mind wants to live?

"What do you think?" I asked my pink bear friend, but he seemed to have disappeared along with the drugs in my bloodstream. That was something of a mercy, at least. I wasn't a good person, but I was trying. Lola had proven that.

# ACT III

---

# MAIN BAD GUY

# 1

**FIONA HAD BEEN** an honor student throughout school, a pigtailed brown-noser who aced every test and kept her hand raised in class until it went numb. "I want to win everything," she always told her classmates, an attitude that would serve her well in adulthood—especially when she had to walk into rooms full of men with guns.

Under different circumstances, she might have become a neurosurgeon or a business executive. Instead, she met August Leadbetter, the self-styled Che Guevara of her eighth-grade class, and the best kisser in her life until she met Bill. (Every school has a few of those revolutionaries, to balance out the brown-nosers.)

August liked to leap on his desk and yell punk lyrics in class.

August stood on the roof of his mother's house on humid summer afternoons and tossed water balloons at the open sunroofs of passing cars, hoping to send a soaked and panicked driver off the road.

August also pushed little red pills. And Fiona was the experimental type, if you pressured her hard enough.

"Oh, come on," August said one afternoon, unzipping his

pin-studded backpack to reveal his stash, most of it stolen from his mom's medicine cabinet. "It'll be fun. The world goes into slow motion. It's the only way to survive math class."

They stood behind the equipment shed at the far end of the football field, safe from prying eyes. Fiona extended a hand, fear prickling her belly—or maybe it was excitement. The pill in her palm seemed very large. She asked: "What if I overdose?"

"You only overdose if you mix drugs," August shot back. "Come on, it'll relax you. Exams are making you all stressed out."

Figuring you only live once (*carpe diem*, as her Latin teacher always said), Fiona popped that little bundle of chemicals in her mouth and swallowed, her throat clicking…

…and felt rain on her face.

The smell of the ocean filled her skull.

Opened her eyes—had she closed them?

She saw gray sky, black pines. She lay on something rough and cold. A dim roar filled her ears: the blood in her veins, amplified to superhuman decibels by whatever the fuck August had given her. No, wrong: the sound came from outside of her. Holy crap, she thought. Where am I?

She turned her head and saw a maroon station wagon barreling toward her.

Her confused brain burned two precious seconds wondering if the car was an illusion (the "drug talking," as the characters in novels always put it) and she was "tripping out" or whatever. Her hammering heart said no, she was a real person on a real road with a real mom-mobile about to squish her flat.

She thrashed, and her body flopped across the yellow line as the honking station wagon screeched to a stop three feet away. The driver's door opened, and a middle-aged lady with a pinched face burst out. Through the windshield Fiona saw a young kid staring at her slack-jawed, shocked. You and me both, she wanted to tell him. You and me both.

When she got back, she planned on murdering August in as painful a way as possible. Dunking him in a piranha tank seemed like just the thing. Or skewering him with a red-hot poker.

The lady yelled: "Are you okay?"

Fiona opened her mouth to speak and emitted only the softest of gurgles.

"Oh my God," the lady continued. "Are you on drugs?"

Fiona grunted like a bullfrog. Her legs and arms refused to peel from the pavement, no matter how hard she tensed her muscles. The lady hovered over her, and Fiona's roving eyes settled on something that sent a shivery bolt of fear through her gut: the station wagon's license plate.

It read: Delaware.

And Fiona had popped that pill in the great state of New Jersey.

Fear dumped enough adrenaline into her bloodstream to reactivate her knees. She stood on quaking legs, brushing away the lady's hand. Another car hummed to a stop behind the station wagon. Fiona could see something bulky on its roof, like a ski rack.

No, those were bubble lights, because it was a friggin' police car.

Well, today was going nowhere but up.

"This girl's on drugs," the lady yelled at the bored cop with a porn-star moustache who climbed out of the cruiser, his hand on his service pistol. As he hip-strutted toward them, Fiona pictured her parents' faces hard with disappointment, the school principal wagging a finger in her face, her science-club friends whispering behind her back. No top school would accept a girl with an arrest record. And getting a good job? Forget about it.

August had set her whole life on fire.

"What's your name, girl?" the cop asked, halting five feet away.

Keep up the zombie act, Fiona told herself. Make them think you're not a threat. Letting her chin droop to her collar, she shuffled a few steps to the left, trying to clear a little space between her and the adults.

"Kids these days," the lady continued. "I mean, it's not like we didn't have controlled substances in our day, officer, but from what I hear they're getting into now…"

The cop swiveled toward Mom of the Year, to better absorb

her nuanced assessment of the nation's drug problem, and Fiona saw her chance. She sprinted for the cruiser, the cop shouting at her to stop, reaching for her—too late. She slammed the door and locked it before he could grab the handle. The keys were in the ignition, thank God.

As the cop pulled his baton from his belt, readying to smash the window, Fiona keyed the engine to life and pushed the column-shift and hit the gas, barreling down the road in reverse. The cop's baton smacked the hood as she passed. She giggled. It was like something out of a movie.

Now to deal with the problem at hand: escaping. She was tall for her age and had no problem seeing through the windshield. Her lifetime experience behind the wheel amounted to driving a pickup on the backroads of her cousin's farm, but she had watched enough action movies over the years to absorb how stuntmen executed a turnaround at speed, and it seemed simple enough. A hundred yards down the road, she stood on the brakes and spun the wheel, the view out the windows blurring, the cruiser tilting hard as it skidded onto the shoulder. Her heart froze. You've lost it, you idiot. You're going to crash.

But the cruiser bounced back to pavement, facing in the right direction. In the rearview mirror, the shrinking cop yelled into the radio on his shoulder, no doubt calling backup. Beside him, Mother of the Year clutched her jaw, swaying from foot to foot.

At least he didn't shoot at me, Fiona thought. The only thing worse than getting kicked out of school for drugs is a bullet to the head.

She accelerated to ninety, trying to put as much distance as possible between her and... what? They would scramble a fleet of cop cars to hunt her down, from all directions. Helicopters overhead, armed with snipers and spotlights, as the radio waves crackled with her name and description. So long as she stayed in this vehicle, nowhere was safe. You need a big parking lot. Like a mall or something. Dump the vehicle, call your father, and hide. At least you feel fine. Imagine if that pill had messed up your ability to walk.

Even as her brain puzzled over logistics, she found herself laughing uncontrollably. This was *fun.*

Three miles later, the road widened into four lanes, and the forest on either side of the road gave way to endless concrete: a sea of parking lots around the glittering island of a mega-mall. Some Dark God was protecting her. She steered the cruiser into the first open space she saw, locked it, and ran toward the mall, avoiding the front doors in favor of the loading docks in the rear.

Her joy at finding an ancient payphone on the mall's third floor curdled when she tapped her hip and realized, for the first time since waking up on the road, that her cute Paul Frank monkey wallet was missing. Had that little shit August taken it?

Across from the payphone was an Irish pub, packed with hungry shoppers. Through the windows, she saw a family stand to leave, the father dropping a few bills and quarters in tip money on the table. Guilt squeezed her throat as she entered the pub and scooped up the change, ducking out the door before a waiter noticed. How long until the cops swept through the mall, on the hunt for a teenage carjacker?

"Get in the ladies' room," her father told her over the phone, once she explained everything that had happened. "In a stall. Wait. Don't leave for anybody or anything. I'll get there in exactly three hours from this moment, after it's dark. What's the back of the mall like?"

She wiped a tear from her cheek. "Like you'd expect. There's like the place where trucks come in, some dumpsters, stuff like that."

"I'll be by the dumpsters. You know the car."

"Okay, Daddy. I'm so sorry."

"Don't be sorry. Just get through it."

Her father was waiting where he promised. He still had his work beard, which made him look a bit like a young Fidel Castro. I guess it helps him blend in, Fiona thought. Wherever he's been going lately, it gives him a serious suntan. His sleeves had slid away from his wrists, revealing small cuts and a few nasty bruises.

When she slid into the front seat, he jabbed a thumb over his shoulder. She opened the rear door, and he said: "No. The trunk."

"Okay, okay," she said. "I'm sorry about what happened, but that's a pretty messed-up punishment."

"How else am I getting you past any cops?" he said.

But there were no checkpoints. Cocooned in the warm darkness of the trunk, Fiona contemplated her wild day. Sure, it was a rush to score a hundred-ten on a test (she always went for the extra credit) or show off her math skills in front of the class, but that was nothing compared to the high-octane thrill of ripping off a police cruiser and taking it on a high-speed chase. The fear just added to the excitement. For the first time in her life, she wondered: who am I really?

Once they crossed into New Jersey, her father pulled the car onto the side of the road and let her out so she could ride in front. They sat in silence for the next fifty miles, Fiona chewing her nails and doing her best not stare at her father too closely.

After what seemed like an eternity, he asked: "So what happened?"

"A boy at school gave me a pill. I'm sorry I took it. I was stupid."

"You were curious." He smiled. "It's one of the best things about you. But you can't take a teenage boy at his word."

"I'm sorry."

"And I'm sure you'll never do it again. Did the cops identify you?"

She shook her head. "I didn't tell them my name. Didn't tell them anything."

"Good. And I bet they'll want to cover all this up. It doesn't reflect well on a department when a kid steals an officer's car. I'll make some calls, see if anyone's making an issue of it. If they are, well, someone down the line probably owes me a favor."

"Thank you." Relief swept through her like a warm wave. She added the mileage from the highway signs and figured her body had traveled some hundred-fifty miles south while her mind orbited Mars. At least she had done it (somehow) in a single afternoon; she could plead illness at school tomorrow. Her mother, working yet another epic shift at the hospital, would have no idea what happened, provided her father kept his mouth shut.

Fiona suspected he would. Her father never liked starting drama, and things had been powder-keg tense for a long time between her parents.

Her father's next question snapped her back to reality: "What was the boy's name?"

"August."

"What are you going to do to August?"

She lashed out a foot. "Hit him in the balls."

Her father shook his head. "No, sweetie, that's not good enough. You need to punch him in the face, not just once but repeatedly. You need to break his nose. Understand?"

"I don't want to hurt him for life. Or disfigure him."

"You're such a kind soul, hon." He squeezed her shoulder. "But if you break his nose, you're doing him a favor. For the rest of his life, every time he looks in the mirror, he'll remember what happened. The consequences of doing bad. So maybe the next time he wants to push drugs on someone, he'll think better of it."

It made sense. August might have killed her with that pill. If he did the same thing to someone else, and they died, how could she live with herself?

"In fact, when we get home, I have a gift for you." Her father smiled. "Something that might help you out with your friend."

The gift was a pair of brass knuckles. Her father taught her how to hit with the added weight on her hand, using one of his worn-out punching bags in the garage. He demonstrated proper technique with his own steel knuckle-dusters, which had a little spike on the pinkie edge ("It's for opening beer bottles," he joked). They had a weekend of real father-daughter bonding before he had to leave again.

The next time August saw her behind the shed, between fourth period and lunch, his eyes sparkled with relief. "Thank God," he cried, arms spreading wide for the hug. "I don't know why the hell you wandered off like that..."

She hit him hard in the face, twisting her hips like her father taught her. The brass knuckles crunched the delicate bones around his nose, and blood flew. She let him fall to his knees without punching him again; her father might have advocated crippling someone who crossed you, but Fiona figured she would show August a little mercy. After all, he had given her the most exciting afternoon of her teenage life.

"Why did you do that?" August blubbered through his bloody hands. "You're nice."

"You have no idea who I am," Fiona said, wiping the brass knuckles on her jeans. She didn't know who she was, either; not really. But she intended to find out.

# 2

**THEY WERE HALFWAY** to the airport when the big black car tried to kill them.

Out of the corner of her eye, Fiona saw it swerving across three lanes of highway, its fender aimed at their cab's rear panel. Classic pursuit intervention technique, beloved by cops the world over. No time to scream. She had her seatbelt buckled, as she always did in cars. She grabbed Bill by the shoulder, pulling him toward her, her arms cradling his neck and head.

Their cabbie never saw it coming. He was too busy talking about making a fortune in real estate, through some scheme involving credit cards and home equity loans. Fiona loved how everyone in New York had a hustle. The cabbie's last words ("I'm paying the mortgage, *double-time*, okay?") were interrupted by the mighty crunch of steel on steel, and his head smacked the scratched plastic partition between the front and back seats, painting it red, as the cab flipped onto its side.

Bill's heavy body crashed into Fiona, blasting the air out her lungs. Her face pressed against the cracked window, gravel on the far side—they had stopped on the shoulder. She smelled gas and scorched rubber, felt a slick warmth on her back. She was cut, but how bad?

"Haven't we suffered *enough*?" Bill braced his feet against the partition, levering his body away from her.

Wincing at the ache in her ribs, Fiona unbuckled her seatbelt and twisted around until her legs were under her, feet flat on the window. She stood, pressed tight against Bill, their heads a few inches below the door that had become their ceiling. She reached behind her back and felt the source of the blood trickling into her waistband: a clean laceration to the right of her spine, long but not deep. Her shirt would staunch the bleeding until she could slap a bandage on it. Hopefully.

Stuffing a hand through the broken cash hole in the partition, Bill stabbed two fingers into the driver's bloody neck. "I think this dude died, dear."

"Losing half your skull tends to do that." Fiona drew her pistol and checked that the safety was on. "Cover your eyes."

Bill did as he was told. Gritting her teeth, Fiona reversed the pistol in her grip and smashed it against the window one, two, three times until it shattered into a gummy mess, each blow sending fresh pain down her arm. Using the pistol-barrel as a rake, she swept the broken glass from the window-frame, then poked her head into the open air. Nobody took a shot at her. Traffic along the highway had already slowed, dozens of faces gawping at her through windshields.

The black car was nowhere in sight.

That was weird. What kind of professional didn't confirm the kill?

"Get the bag," she said, pushing through the window. Her every joint and tendon begged for mercy: too many weeks on the road, too many fights, too many tumbles and punches and falls. The cab rocked under her weight, threatening to tip over. She stood, arms out, surfing it as she sought a good place to jump.

"Ma'am, yes, ma'am," Bill shouted, and their bag sailed out the window. Because it was filled with lumps of gold, it flew only a few feet before thudding onto the white strip that separated the shoulder from the roadway. Fiona leapt after it, ears pricked for sirens.

It took Bill a little more effort to squeeze free of the cab. He jumped and stumbled hard, hands flailing for balance. Fiona already had the bag looped over her shoulder, its strap biting into her bruised flesh. She needed to call their contact at the airport, the man who would have changed their gold into cash for a hefty premium. Plans had changed. The new plan was hiding out and staying alive.

Dragging Bill upright, she led him toward the small thicket of elms beyond the shoulder. Her body felt like a crumpled soda can, everything bent and broken, her pulse too loud in her ears. How much longer could they go before she collapsed?

"I'm done with this shit," she told Bill as they ran. "We need out of this life."

# 3

**THE DEAN WAS** pissed.

Or pissing, if you wanted to get technical about it.

"You might think this is barbaric," he said, unzipping his fly. "But trust me, the desecration is appropriate to the situation."

Having justified his actions to God and man, The Dean unleashed a spray on the thick Persian rug, swirling his hips as if trying to scrawl his signature in urine. He whistled a song through clenched teeth, tuneless and off-key. His dark-suited men, lining the walls on either side of him, struggled heroically not to laugh.

At the enormous desk behind The Dean, Simon also fought to keep his expression neutral. His round sunglasses helped, but it was hard to keep his lips from peeling into a snarl. He busied himself with lighting a cigarette, telling himself: Best to let this *pizda*◻ get it out of his system. I can always have a rug cleaned, and a war is something I don't need right now.

The Dean shook out his last drops, zipped up his fly, and swiveled on his heel. His eyes blazed with fury. From the jacket of his herringbone suit he drew a thin cigar, bit the tip, and spat a wet nub of tobacco at the silver bowl on a nearby table. "Now," he said, patting his pockets for a lighter or matches. "Where was I?"

"You were blaming me for Fiona and Bill," Simon said.

"Yes, and you didn't seem to be *empathizing* properly, so I made an example of your rug." The Dean, finding no fire for his cigar, snapped his fingers for Simon's gold lighter on the desk. "Fiona comes to the city, asks for your help, and you not only give it to her, but you neglect to tell me?"

"I don't work for you." Simon blew a smoke ring, making no move to hand over the lighter. "You and I are business partners, out of convenience. And your conflicts are not mine."

"That's what you think." The Dean took the seat across from Simon. "Speaking honestly, when Bill first stole that money from me, and Fiona joined him, I pictured it as a small issue. Just send men with guns."

"A straightforward solution. How many has she killed?" Simon asked.

"Enough to give me heartburn." The Dean began to reach for Simon's lighter, and stopped. It was clear from his expression that he wanted Simon to hand it over, to complete this little power game. When Simon crossed his arms and leaned back, smoke trickling from the corner of his mouth, The Dean's cheeks reddened.

"It's not easy replacing men with guns," The Dean continued, adjusting his collar. "Not like you can go online and just order more, two-day shipping, satisfaction guaranteed. And now Fiona and Bill are back in the city, merrily wrecking things left and right, which just draws attention to us. You included."

"I am not concerned," Simon said. "What bothers me is, how you discovered she came to me."

"We have eyes everywhere. Who crashed a car into her cab?"

"Excuse me?"

"Someone rammed her taxi off the highway. Not long ago. We have the video. Security camera on a building nearby." The Dean frowned. "Fiona and Bill ran off. They're hurt, albeit not badly enough for my tastes."

Simon shook his head, wondering (not for the first time) what kind of man used words like 'albeit' in everyday speech. "Fiona and Bill make enemies like a dog picks up fleas."

"Well, it wasn't my men who crashed into her." The Dean, rather than suffer the indignity of begging for a light, chomped the unlit cigar. "So, who the hell did?"

Simon shrugged.

"Our purchased cop, he said the cab was on an airport run. They're trying to get out of town." The Dean laughed. "We have people at every airport, and Penn and Grand Central, and as many subways as we can cover. We will expose those cockroaches to the light, given enough time. Keep that in mind if she reaches out to you again."

"I'll remember my rug," Simon said. "Hundred dollars per square foot."

"As if you didn't have the funds to repair it." The Dean pointed the cigar at the lacquered woods and gold-leaf highlights of Simon's office, the antique furniture, the ornate paintings hanging on the walls. "Fiona appears, you tell me. No equivocations, no prevarication. Understood?"

Simon stubbed out his cigarette in the ashtray by his elbow and lit a fresh one. His next smoke ring drifted into The Dean's face. "I understand perfectly," he said, stuffing the lighter in his pocket.

The Dean's cheeks colored heart-attack purple. "Fine," he hissed through a tight throat. Slipping his unsmoked cigar into his vest, he stood and marched for the door, his men falling into line behind him. "Otherwise, this all ends in tears for you."

# 4

**WALKER SPENT A** few days in a trailer-park motel on the rim of Hudson Bay, seventy loonies a week for a double-wide at the very edge of the property where the mud and gravel gave way to pine woods filled with trash. The sun never set. It was a white-hot lance that pierced through the frayed curtains at all hours, keeping him awake despite the beer and pills, and after two miserable days he took refuge in the windowless bathroom, finally dozing in the shower stall atop a sheet.

On the third bright night he walked into the trailer near the front gate that served as an office, on the hunt for aluminum foil to cover his windows. The old lady behind the desk ignored him, her faded blue eyes locked on the small television in the far corner. The screen trembled with images of fire, dead bodies under white sheets, an Elvis costume riddled with holes. The footage cut to a mugshot of a suspect: a young woman with raven-dark hair, smirking for the camera. Then another police-precinct portrait: a handsome man with a heavy jaw and black hair streaked with gray, his face beginning to soften with age.

He knew the couple. Without a word he dropped into the plastic seat beside the door, and the old lady silently poured him a juice-glass full of whiskey from her stash beneath the register. They sat and drank and watched as the newscaster described a trail of murder and thievery from Oklahoma to Nicaragua to New York City.

Once they finished the bottle he returned to his trailer and shrugged on his canvas jacket over his frayed t-shirt and pocketed his last two hundred loonies in cash. He had no passport, no driver's license, no phone, no cards. The old lady offered a limp wave when he opened her door just long enough to toss the keys on her desk.

A single call to the States would have summoned someone to retrieve him. Instead he walked down the two-lane that led from the trailer park to the logging town at the bottom of the valley, his steel-toed boots clicking on the pavement. The inside of his head felt bruised and his stomach boiled with acid, but every breath filled him with new life.

The town had one convenience store, where he bought a bus ticket to Montreal and waited the ninety minutes until it arrived on the bench outside, sipping a jumbo cup of black coffee. Nobody spoke to him. His white beard was a grimy thicket and his eyes were hard. He kept imagining people blown to black clouds, all their flesh and dreams drifting from a gunmetal sky.

In Montreal the bus dropped him on Rue Saint-Denis, beside a strip of upscale bars and a cat café. This far south, at this time of year, the sun set after nine, darkness comforting him like a warm blanket as he stood on the sidewalk rotating his neck, popping his joints, bending to touch his toes. He played an invisible piano to loosen his hands. His time up north had helped clean his blood and clear his head, but he worried about his reflexes, his gift for shifting a mark's attention.

He also needed a place to lay low, and something to eat. From his previous stay in the city he knew there was a sculpture garden at the bottom of Saint-Denis where the junkies had a sleeping-bag colony. A couple decades ago he might have taken that option, fought for a strip of cardboard beneath an overhang. Now he needed to renew his strength for the days ahead and that meant a clean bed, a door with locks, new clothes, and a shower hot enough to boil away the dirt crusting his skin.

His first stop was the loudest watering hole he could find, a sweaty box stuffed with screaming college kids. Dark, no security cameras, a bored lump of a bouncer more interested in chatting up underage girls than watching the door. Perfect. He made one pass, departing through the back ten minutes later with a pair of stolen wallets in his pockets, fat with bills and credit cards, and a shiny phone swiped from a coat. So far, so good.

The phone's SIM card he dumped in the alley. At an all-night market he used one of the credit cards to purchase a razor, a pair of steel barber scissors, athletic tape, a prepaid SIM, and a handful of gift cards. He remembered his nephew telling him about the orange pills that everyone in his unit popped to stay awake on night missions in Iraq, their blood humming electric as they swept villages and kicked down doors. He wished for a handful of those bright little babies, which were probably a lot cleaner than the pills he had swallowed in Vietnam, but caffeine and sugar would have to do.

Next door to the market, a fast-food joint served poutine to a crowd of happy drunks. He locked himself in one of its two bathrooms and hacked off the beard and shaved the stubble, ignoring the fists banging on the metal door. After he finished, he slipped the barber scissors down his sleeve, hidden by his jacket and held in place by his watchband, retrievable in an instant. He popped the prepaid SIM card into the stolen phone, slipped the tape and gift cards into his jacket pockets, and dumped everything else in the trash, along with the credit card he used at the market.

Exiting the bathroom, he waited his turn at the counter and ordered a jumbo coffee, plus an extra-large basket of fries and cheese curds. Despite the crowd he found an open stool beside the window, with a good angle on the street. Chewing and sipping, he wondered about his next move. How long since you really hustled at street level? Nine, ten years? I don't know the new traps. The ways they can sniff you out. How fast they can nail you. It's so tempting to not cross the border. But family is family.

A whiff of perfume like wet candy, the fission of someone invading his airspace. Turning his head, he found himself nearly nose-to-nose with a girl in fishnet stockings and black-rimmed glasses. "Hey, old guy," she said. "What's your name?"

He tilted away from her, curious about the chemical making her pupils vibrate at such a high frequency. "Walker," he said.

"Walker, you leaving anytime soon? Because we'd like your seat." She nodded toward a strapping young man standing a few feet away, his arms slabbed with muscle, a poutine basket in each hand.

"I'm not done yet," Walker said, lifting his half-empty coffee.

The girl was having none of it. Placing her open purse on the counter beside his gravy-spattered basket, she said: "That's okay. We can just share your space. Right, Rog?"

Rog seemed unsure. He locked eyes with Walker and took a step sideways, mumbling about finding another seat.

Walker shrugged and shifted his gaze to the window. A soft man in a good suit leaned against a streetlamp, bent at the waist, and vomited a greenish muck on the sidewalk. The crowd moaned and laughed at the spectacle. The suited man straightened, spat, and commenced a zombie-like shuffle down the street. It gave Walker an idea.

A fist poked his ribs. The girl punching him, not hard enough to hurt. A violation nonetheless. Walker stood and she hit him again, in the sternum this time, biting her lip with the effort. "Time to go," she said. "Get your ancient ass out of here."

No point in trying to reason with this surly space alien. Instead Walker lifted his coffee cup and upended it into the girl's purse, filling it to the brim.

"Now I'm through," he said.

The girl screamed and shoved past him, fishing her phone and keys from the drenched ruin. The restaurant frozen silent, thirty pairs of eyes memorizing his face, his clothes, the way he moved. There I go again, Walker mused. Too impulsive for my own good. Heading for the door, he jabbed a finger in Rog's stunned face. "Trade up," he told the kid.

Outside again, a little anxious about cops, he followed the suited man around the far corner. Down a residential street of quiet houses, lit dimly. Walker slipped close, the acid stink of vomit and cheap beer making his nostrils flare, and executed his gentlest sleeper hold. The man grunted, hands thrashing against Walker's forearms like anxious birds, before slumping into unconsciousness.

Walker dragged the wheezing body into a nearby alley and propped it against a wall. Rifling through the suit pockets, he found a key-fob. He walked down the street, pressing the button on the fob until a late-model Audi honked in response.

In the trunk he found a dark blue suit in a bag, roughly his size, and a striped button-down shirt. A road-kit with a flashlight and some flares. So far, so good.

The Audi's booming engine carried him back down Rue Saint-Denis and over the river and onto the highways ringing the city. On the satellite radio he found a channel playing heavy metal, not something he usually liked, but it would serve as a little aural caffeine for the trip. He gave up on the idea of a soft bed in Canada. Better at this point to keep moving south. Turning on his new phone, he dialed a number he knew by heart.

# 5

**I WAS BACK** in the motherland, baby, well-healed if not well-heeled. Whoever told you that Times Square had outlived its glory days, that it's become nothing more than a corporate playground filled with chain restaurants and cartoon characters, well, let's just say they never walked its western edge far enough to find the smeared-glass doorway of Pruitt's Costume Emporium, where all your dreams can come true for a low-low price.

The Emporium featured everything you needed for a kickass Friday night, from nunchucks to colorful bongs to a galaxy of dildos with sci-fi names—The Inner Limits, Logan's Gun, The Pool Boy—but none of those interested me. I practically skipped to the back, which offered an array of costumes, and I didn't give a second glance to all the boas and sequins and furs. No, I knew what I wanted, and I found it on a glittering gold hangar, the Emporium's terrible fluorescents gleaming off its white hide.

Fifteen minutes later I exited onto the bustle of Eighth Avenue, where I immediately proceeded to do a very New York thing: Slipping out of my dirty sneakers, I dropped my jeans right on the sidewalk, exposing my boxers for all to see. Then I stripped off my shirt, flinging it to the homeless dude crouched a few feet away; he caught it in one hand, gave it a deep sniff, and offered me an enthusiastic thumbs-up. As the stream of suits diverted to avoid me, I pulled on the spangly jumpsuit, slipped on the rhinestone-studded sunglasses I'd purchased along with it, and executed my best Elvis Presley split.

The homeless dude applauded.

"Thank ya," I said, stepping back into my shoes. "Thank ya very much."

Believe me, it was hell returning to the city. I knew The Dean had men at the Port Authority and Penn Station, along with the airports. And the longer I lurked the streets, the higher the likelihood that word would trickle back to him that his favorite assassin was still alive and ready to party. I figured that dressing like this was the best way to avoid detection—everyone does their best to avoid eye contact with a lunatic.

Added bonus: The slick jumpsuit against my cool skin felt very nice indeed.

Objectives met, I exited Times Square as fast as I could, because the last thing I wanted was a brawl with one of the Elvis impersonators accosting tourists for spare change. There's nobody quite as fast and vicious as a street performer who thinks you're standing between them and seventy-five cents. I ducked into the subway and rode it to the furthest reaches of Queens, the train rising from the dark onto the elevated track and brightest sunlight, graveyards and blocks of small houses blurring past, the smell of the sea growing stronger as the doors opened at each station.

I'd spent the past several days popping steroids and vitamins, supplemented by all the greasy protein I could stand. I was the new best friend of every roach-coach proprietor between Hudson Yards and Union Square. Healing-wise, it wasn't quite as effective as a couple of weeks laid up, but I was feeling a lot nimbler than during that night in Oklahoma when I woke up in the hospital bed. My subway car emptied out by the time we reached the shore, and I spent a little time stretching in the aisle, practicing my best dance moves. Limbering up for the big show.

The Rockaways was a peculiar split of sand. At one end, public-housing towers shared avenues with cute beach rentals. At the other, in the enclaves of Breezy Point, rows of small houses lined the beach, filled with retired firemen and other city workers. During World War II, the federal government had built gun emplacements at Fort Tilden, now a sandy and overgrown patch of land at the Rockaways' very tip—a good place for a secret meeting, as I had learned on more than one occasion. Hurricane Sandy had filled basements with oceanwater, torn up the boardwalk, and wrecked lives, and yet the place had come back stronger than before.

I stopped at a fruit stand outside the subway station at Beach 90th and bought the smallest banana on offer. Slipping it into my pocket, I headed over to the Sea Shack, a seafood restaurant on Rockaway Beach Boulevard, squeezed between a taco joint and a laundry. The Rockaway Mob had once ordered Bill to do his business out of here, until something freaked him out and sent him on the run. The Dean still had an interest in the place, because selling fried calamari and oysters to legions of sunburned beach visitors (cash only) is a great way to launder your illegal gains. I recognized Bill's replacement, sitting at a corner table with a cup of coffee in front of her: Five-foot-seven of chopped-blonde badass, her thin arms tattooed with elaborate black whorls, her feet propped on the seat across from her. Almost falling asleep in the warm sea breeze drifting through the door.

"Hello, Aurora," I said, standing to her left.

She looked up, and it took her a few moments to recognize my face behind the sunglasses. When she did, her right hand lunged for her hip, but I was faster. I gripped her right wrist and slammed it into the table hard enough to make her empty coffee cup topple over.

The restaurant was sparsely populated, but the crash made everyone stop and look. I stared at Aurora, my eyebrows raised, until she announced: "Everything is fine."

People resumed their eating, giving us a nervous side-eye as they did so.

"You gonna be good?" I asked her. "Or are we gonna have a problem?"

She shook her head. "No problem."

"Good." I released her arm.

"We heard you were dead," she said, rubbing her wrist.

"I was. It's very invigorating. I highly recommend it."

"Why are you here?"

I smirked at her. "You know."

"I don't, I swear."

"Basement."

"Oh, come on, man." With deliberate slowness, she returned her coffee cup to the saucer. "You know, if I do that, what will happen to me. The Dean will rip my head clean off."

"And if you don't do it, it'll be me ripping your head off. You can tell yourself that you never had a choice."

Her jaw flexed. I could sense her feeling a little brave, so I shoved a hand into my pocket and gripped the banana so it poked against the fabric like a gun barrel. "This is a .45," I said. "First shot's in your knee."

She sighed and shoved her chair back. "I like my knees."

I kept ten feet behind her as we exited through the kitchen, wary of her grabbing a knife or a hot pan and swiping it at me. I knew Aurora was a survivor. She reminded me of an older version of Lola, who I hoped had made it to Los Angeles, the land of sunshine and enchantment.

At the far end of the kitchen, we entered a narrow hallway. Aurora opened an unmarked door and flicked on the light, revealing a set of stone steps slicing deep into the earth. It had flooded during the hurricane, I remembered, destroying a couple kilos of product that The Dean had secured down there. Someone had died for that.

"Move slow," I told her.

Nodding, she descended the stairs, her fingers skimming the rough walls. At the bottom, she flicked on another light. We stood in a basement lined with wooden and cardboard boxes of all shapes and sizes, stacked beneath plastic bags filled with junk.

"We're a little slow at the moment," she said. "You want some blue suede shoes to go along with that nutso outfit of yours? The benefit of offering 'protection' to all those shitty secondhand stores is they pay you in goods nobody actually wants."

"Knock it off," I said. "Where's the real shit?"

"No coke right now, no heroin, nothing," she said, sounding nervous enough for me to believe her. "Things have been chaotic. The Dean's got issues with the guys up north, plus the Rough Riders have been giving them hell…"

"The Rough Riders? Those cowboy cosplay losers?"

"Yeah, but they know how to shoot, and they want their territory back."

"Interesting."

"Why?"

"Never mind. What you got for me?"

"There's some guns just in. They're clean, never used, numbers filed off. That cool with you?"

I sighed. "Show me."

With the edge of her foot, she shoved a three-foot-long cardboard box into the middle of the room. As she bent to tear away the tape over the lid, I gave the room a closer inspection. There was a workbench to my left, loaded with the tools and bits you needed to keep kitchen machines in shape. I pocketed a screwdriver.

Opening the lid, Aurora tilted the box so I could see the two pump-action 12-gauges and a .45 automatic inside, along with a scattering of ammunition. She asked: "This work for you?"

"That's it?"

"Like I said, we're light this week."

"I guess beggars can't be choosers." I retrieved a half-used roll of duct tape from the workbench and held it up. "Go over to that wall with the pipes, put your hands around the biggest one. I'm gonna tape you up."

"Punch me in the face while you're at it," she said, walking over to the pipes. "Left side, ideally. Try not to crack one of my damn teeth."

"Kinky."

"You don't get it. Maybe if I look like I put up a fight, they'll let me live."

"Don't worry about it, fair lady," I said as I taped her up. "If everything goes right, The Dean will be dead before he knows you sold him out." Finished, I stepped back, admiring my handiwork. "Oh yeah, one last thing." I slipped the banana out of my pocket and set it on the concrete floor. "Just in case you get hungry."

Aurora spat curses as I tore open loot bags and boxes. I found a bright red gym bag that would hold the stubbier of the two shotguns. The pistol went into my pocket. Armed, I retreated up the stairs, not bothering to say goodbye as she offered to rip out my lungs and use them for bagpipes. I debated turning off the lights behind me, but I was trying to be nicer these days.

# 6

**THE DOGS IN** the kennels snarled and barked. The one closest to Fiona, a gray pit bull with one eye and a scarred flank, jabbed its nose between the wires of its cage. She offered the animal a fist to lick, and it calmed down.

"After we're done, I need you out of here," Trevor said, snapping on a pair of surgical gloves. The smudges under his eyes suggested the tail end of a long shift. He was a vet trying to work his way from under nine years of school debt, which always made him more than happy to help Fiona—for a price.

"Understood," she said, peeling off her bloody shirt. Bill, standing behind her, slipped a playful finger under the elastic band of her sports bra. She slapped his hand away. "Just wait until your shirt's off," she told him. "We'll get a poke at those man-boobs."

"I'm serious," Trevor said, plucking alcohol wipes from the container beside the sink. "I got guys coming in and out of here all the time, needing help. One of them sees you, I have a real problem."

"You won't tell anyone we were here," Fiona said, her tone flat.

"It'll just make things rougher for you. Someone might do some Reservoir Dogs shit."

"I'm just trying to keep the bailiff away from the door." Stepping close enough to see the bruises and cuts marking Fiona's torso, Trevor whistled softly. "They really did a number on you, didn't they?"

"You should have seen the other lady," Bill said, extending his hand to the gray pit bull, which bared its fangs and growled.

"If you have some super-glue," Fiona said, "I can take care of my smaller cuts. But my ribs are really busted up from a fight, and I have a bigger cut on my back that feels like it's about to rip open again. Just patch me up best you can."

"This is really going to cost you." Trevor opened drawers beneath the table where Fiona sat, retrieving packs of bandages, a pre-loaded skin-stapler, tweezers, and a bottle of hydrogen peroxide. "The Dean, the Rockaway Mob put a huge price on your head, plus the cops want you, and who knows who else? It's a lot of heat."

Fiona unzipped the bag beside her and pulled out a small lump of gold, placing it on the table beside her hip. "This should cover it," she said. "It's more than The Dean pays people for information. Don't ask where I got it."

Trevor squinted at the precious metal. "What are those white flecks?"

"Bits of Nazi teeth," Bill said. "Let your imagination fill in the rest."

"Not the weirdest coin I've been paid in, believe me," Trevor said, unfurling the stethoscope around his neck and placing its disk against Fiona's back. After listening to her breathing, he probed her bruised ribs with the tips of his fingers. "This hurts a lot, right?"

Fiona bit her lip, hissing: "No, feels wonderful."

"Good news is, doesn't feel like anything's broken," Trevor said. "But you need to heal. How many days can you rest?"

"How about none?" Fiona said. "None sounds about right."

Trevor swabbed the cuts on her back with alcohol wipes.

"I'm serious. Fortunately for you, it doesn't seem like anything's infected, but the longer you keep moving, the more you'll wear down. If you don't choose to rest, your body will make you rest."

"We'll figure something out," Bill said, patrolling the edges of the examination room. He peeked into the empty hallway and the reception area beyond. Trevor's veterinary practice was a small one, squeezed between a liquor store and a Tibetan restaurant, and supposedly there were no more appointments today. The front door was locked. So why did Bill suddenly feel so paranoid?

"I heard you fled down to South America," Trevor said, slipping bandages over Fiona's smaller wounds.

"Who told you that?" Fiona asked.

Trevor shrugged. "Every desperado coming in here to get patched up. You're legends. Said you caused some chaos in Oklahoma, too. Killed some cops?"

"Bill let himself get seduced by some little slattern outside of Tulsa," Fiona said. "The town bartender, of all people. Her cannibal relatives would have buried him in the chicken coop if I hadn't shown up."

"Hey," Bill said. "That lady drugged me. I was helpless."

"A likely story." Fiona grinned at him. "Then we went south for a little while. Not all the way to South America, but pretty close. We're back because we needed money, and someone had a gig for us."

"That's where the gold comes from, I assume." Trevor picked up the stapler. "That bigger cut in your lower back, it's clotted up, but that won't hold. I'm going to staple it, okay?"

"What's one more scar?" Fiona said, biting her lip. "Do it."

Bracing his free hand against her spine, Trevor pressed the stapler to her flesh and snapped seven staples across the wound, closing it tight. Then he applied alcohol and a fresh bandage. "Reminds me of school," he said, with a slight smile.

"I remember your hands always shook when you patched me up," she said. "They're steady now."

"Well, I was a dumb kid back in the day." He slid his hand up her back. "In more ways than one."

Fiona glanced at Bill in the doorway, his attention still focused on the reception area. She flicked her head at Trevor, not unkind. He nodded and removed his hand, snapping his gloves into the trash as he moved to the sink. He asked: "What's your plan?"

"Better you don't know," she said. "Just in case."

Trevor shrugged, scrubbed his fingers, and slipped on new gloves. "Yeah, just in case someone threatens to pull my tongue out. Bill, you ready? Let me examine those bruises."

Bill's cheekbones had swollen so much, he feared looking at himself in the mirror. He felt an absurd jealousy for action-movie heroes who could emerge from a pummeling with only a photogenic cut or two on their brow. In real life, skin behaved like ripe fruit when you hit it.

"I'm okay," Bill said, glancing at Fiona. "Nothing that won't heal."

Fiona rolled her eyes. "Give it up, tough guy. I didn't mean the man-boob comment."

"These are pecs," Bill said, slapping his chest. "Nothing but muscle here." With that, he stepped toward the exam table, which might have saved his life.

A metal flower popped open on the doorjamb, near where he had stood before. A loud crack echoed through the reception area.

Fiona hit the floor, pulling Trevor with her. Bill joined them, landing beside a hot lump of metal: a spent bullet, big. The dogs howled in fear.

Fiona's hand tightened on Trevor's collar until it cut into his throat. "Did you tell anyone?"

Trevor shook his head and moaned. "I've been in your sight the whole time."

The dogs paced and howled, saliva dripping from their jaws. The gray pitbull threw itself against the cage door, desperate to break free. Crawling on elbows and knees, Bill peeked into the reception area: still empty. A cracked hole dead-center in the smoked glass of the front door.

"Bill?" Fiona asked. "Who's coming in?"

Still on his stomach, Bill edged into the hallway until he could see through the wide window to the left of the door. The sidewalk was empty, and so was the street beyond. "Nobody," he said.

Fiona groaned. "What the hell?"

"I bet it's our buddy from the highway," Bill said. "Messing with us."

"The back door, it's past the other exam room," Trevor offered.

"We can take a hint, dear." Fiona released his collar. "But before we go, I'm helping myself to some of your doggie painkillers, okay? And your phone. And a t-shirt that's not covered in my blood."

# 7

**SULLY WAS A** second-generation pot farmer who dressed the part: faded denim jacket over a black hoodie, hiking boots clotted with drying soil, work-pants with big pockets. His blonde moustache, carefully waxed into whorls, gave his face a whimsical air, but Walker knew him as one of the hardest men between Burlington and Boston, which was saying something. The remains of more than a few enemies had fertilized Sully's secret fields over the years.

For this late-night meeting with Walker, Sully had selected a cozy flatbread restaurant at the end of Burlington's St. Paul Street, by the water. They sat in a dim booth beneath an antique poster for tractor parts, Sully with a micro-brew in front of him, Walker nursing a cup of black coffee. Walker wore the suit and shirt from the Audi's trunk, the pants a little short but otherwise a perfect fit.

Sully drained his beer, spotting his elaborate moustache with foam. "Didn't expect you this soon," he said.

"Got business south," Walker said, trying to leave it at that.

"Don't get me wrong, it's always good seeing a friendly face, even one as ugly as yours," Sully said, not laughing. "But in my line of work, I don't like unexpected things."

"We're not in business together," Walker said. "You're just holding my stuff, remember?"

"Oh, yeah. For no money."

Walker smiled without warmth. "Good thing we're friends."

"I know I owed you a favor, but after this, we're settled, okay? You talk to your other old friends lately?"

"Which old friends?"

Sully shrugged. "Fed friends?"

"No," Walker said. "They're unpleasant people. You got what's mine?"

Sully studied him, still holding his empty beer glass, until Walker snapped his fingers twice.

"Chill out," Sully said, eyebrows raised.

"I am chill."

"No, chill people aren't rude. When you're in the weed business, you know tension in all its varieties. If the Feds talked to me, I'd be tense, too."

"I think your weed's making you paranoid." Walker leaned close, squinting. "You know I stopped working for them years ago. I got sick of their business."

"But they still call you from time to time, right?"

"What's up with you?"

"Couple of my guys just got snatched up. Merchandise disappeared. Then you come around. It's been an odd week. You said you came from Montreal?"

"That's what I told you." Walker slapped the table.

"What'd I say? Chill. We're just talking. Border's locked down. How'd you get over?"

"Walked."

"You didn't bribe nobody?"

"Didn't see anybody."

"Walked through the woods?"

"You see my shoes?" Walker had parked the Audi on the shoulder of a gravel road two miles from the border, used the flashlight from the trunk to guide his way into the United States. His feet sinking ankle-deep in mud, mosquitos dive-bombing his neck, the bagged suit on his arm snagging on branches. The fantasy of a cool bed and a hot shower powering him through the dark.

Sully craned his neck so he could see beneath the table. "Better get those polished up."

Walker shrugged. A few miles south of the border, he had slipped onto a farm near the road and stolen a mountain bike from an unlocked barn, leaving a wad of loonies and one of the gift cards behind. The less Sully knew about his choices in trans-portation, the better.

"Anyway, I'm impressed." Sully leaned forward, close enough for Walker to smell prime weed seeping from the man's pores. "I tried the same thing once, just to see what would happen. I picked this big stretch of forest north of here, nobody around for miles. Or so I imagined. I park the car and hike until the map on my phone tells me I'm on the Canadian side, then I turn around and come back. Thirty seconds after I cross over, these bor-der-patrol dudes show up on ATVs, yelling that I'm in the States. I was like, 'I realize that, gentlemen.' They would've thrown my ass in jail if I hadn't started waving my driver's license and saying I'd gotten lost, it was all a mistake, sorry."

"How do you think they found you?"

"Who knows? Drones, heat sensors, whatever. There's no more privacy in the world."

Walker made a big show of keeping his hands flat on the table, bracketing his coffee cup. Trying to project an aura of zero threat. "Cool story, brother. Listen, I just want my stuff."

"You'll get what's yours. Why all the nervousness? You're fan-cy-free on U.S. soil. Where you staying tonight?"

"Just a house. Not far from here. And not for long."

"You should have a beer. Coffee wires you up."

"Got miles to go before I sleep."

"Couple lines of poetry will definitely get you right laid around these parts. The grad students pop right open for a gangster who knows his verse. One of the better perks of living in Vermont. If you talked to the Feds, it's okay. Doesn't mean anything."

"How many times I got to tell you?"

Sully stroked his moustache. "That wasn't a 'no.'"

Walker pulled up his shirt, revealing a pale torso etched with scars. "You see a wire? I'm not a snitch."

"Listen now, I'm not implying anything." Sully raised his hands in mock surrender.

"Why don't you chill out?" Walker tucked his shirt back in. As he shifted his left wrist, the scissors pressed cool and sharp against his skin. At the table to their right sat Sully's usual security, a pair of hefty types in unassuming fleece and jeans, an untouched fennel-sausage flatbread between them. Too much weight for Walker to handle, hidden knife or no.

"I am sub-zero," Sully said. "If you want your stuff, sure, I got it right here." Reaching slowly into his unzipped hoodie, he retrieved the slim manila envelope that Walker had given him earlier that year, passed it under the table.

"Thanks," Walker said, tucking the envelope into his jacket pocket.

"Can I ask you something?"

"Yes."

"What's your business south?"

"Family." With a wink, Walker drained his coffee cup and stood. The normalcy of this place—the tables packed with university types, the bustling waitstaff, the blazing clay oven—made him tense, his nerves crackling. Or maybe it was the caffeine he kept mainlining. Or maybe it was the knowledge that, once he left here, paranoid Sully would almost certainly try to kill him. Why had he trusted his stuff to this whackjob?

Headed out the restaurant's front door, Walker glanced over his shoulder and saw Sully's grim men already out of their seats, their hands in their pockets. On the sidewalk he hooked left, around the corner that led to the parking lot.

Sully always spent top dollar on the best muscle, ex-military types who would sweep the zone quick and careful, giving

Walker precious few chances for an ambush. Not that he had any intention of committing suicide by taking them on, but their caution might buy him a little more time to escape.

A pair of lamps bolted to the restaurant's roof cast a pale glow over five rows of parked cars. Nobody in sight. With just a few seconds before the muscle rounded the corner, Walker settled on a late-model BMW in the middle of the nearest row. He slammed his elbow into the driver's side window until it crunched into a milky cataract. The car's alarm blared, head-lights flashing in panic.

He ducked and ran to the far end of the row, stopping beside a battered blue SUV with a fading 'Feel the Bern' sticker on the back window. Pressing his palms against the rear bumper, he bounced until the alarm kicked off, joining the BMW in wail-ing chorus.

Stooped low, breathing hard, he retreated to the fifth row, where the light and pavement ended in shadowy trees. Dropping to his hands and knees beside a truck, cheek almost pressed against the cold gravel, he spied two pairs of hiking boots swiv-eling on the far side of the BMW. If they saw him now, they would kill him, alarms or no.

The restaurant's rear door crashed open, ejecting a swarm of line cooks in splattered whites. Flashing their onion-flecked knives, they howled in Spanish at Sully's men, who raised their hands and retreated the way they had come.

Walker had already ducked into the woods, angling for the dirt path that led to the lake, and the large pine where he had propped his bike. As he stepped through the underbrush, the envelope in his jacket pocket tapped gently against his ribs. A car key, a padlock key, a driver's license under yet another name, a clean credit card with a ten-thousand-dollar limit: he hoped that Sully had left it all alone.

*I was an idiot to trust him,* Walker cursed as he pulled the bike free of the branches. *A guy so paranoid, he proba-bly thinks an FBI midget is snorkeling in his toilet-tank. Just*

because an associate buries some bodies for you over the years
doesn't make him your lifelong buddy. You're slipping, old man.
You're slipping.

# 8

**THE REAR OF** Trevor's clinic opened onto a narrow alley with high brick walls. Fiona crouched in the doorway, her eyes locked on the opening to the street. In her experience, you put a bullet through someone's front door if you wanted to flush them out the back, into an ambush. But if the shooter was the same person who smashed into their cab on the highway, they were displaying a stunning lack of follow-through.

"Maybe we have a secret crush," Bill said, "and they're showing it in a really odd way."

"Hey, there's nothing odd about it." Fiona paused to draw her pistol, keeping it pressed tight against her leg. "There's nothing more romantic than a car crash."

"You scare me sometimes, dear. Especially with that shirt."

On their way out the door, Trevor had tossed Fiona an old t-shirt from a drawer, light blue with the words 'YOU CAN'T BUY LOVE, BUT YOU CAN ADOPT IT' on the front in comic sans. The back featured a black paw-print with the name of a local pet-adoption agency beneath. Hey, at least it was clean. Reaching back to squeeze Bill's knee, Fiona said: "At least it doesn't read, 'I'm with stupid.'"

"You're a laugh riot." Bill sighed. "Seriously, who'd we piss off this time?"

"Zero idea," she said. "And that's what freaks me out. I like to know who's shooting at me."

"Let me have Trevor's phone?"

"In my back pocket."

Bill gave her a friendly pinch as he extracted the device. While he tapped and swiped the screen, she could hear Trevor trying to quiet down the barking dogs. She felt a little guilty about barging in on him, sure, but what were ex-boyfriends for?

At least Trevor had done a fine job of patching her up. Three doggie painkillers dampened her sharper pains to dull aches, and the staples in her back pinched only a little when she straightened her spine. "You better not be checking your email," Fiona said.

"Just updating my Facebook status," he chuckled. "I'm writing, 'Back in New York, hunted by my old boss, anyone want to hang?' Seemed like the right time for it."

"Stop."

"I'm looking up that luxury condo over on Vernon," Bill said. "Remember all the news about it? The neighbors were protesting? I think construction got shut down while they paid off whoever needs paying off."

"Why don't we just steal a car? Get out of the city?"

"With everyone right on our ass? And if we get clear, what's next? Find some small town and hide out? I'm done with small towns." Bill flipped the phone so she could see the screen, and the image of an iron finger extending into a blue sky: a half-constructed high rise, its massive girders draped with orange mesh like a Christo art installation. "Name me another big place on this side of the river that's empty like this. We can rest, make some calls, whatever."

Fiona chewed the inside of her cheek. "I bet there's a guard on-site," she said. "Someone to stop people from coming in and ripping the wiring out of the walls."

"We sneak past him, take a high floor," Bill said. "Easy to

defend, nobody around, no cops. Trust me, where else we going to find that in New York City?"

Fiona took the phone back, flicked open a map. "We'll walk there. Subway's too much of a box for me."

"Sure, that's fine." Bill hefted the bag, its gold softly clinking. "This is real light."

"Think of it as a really good workout."

At the mouth of the alley they stopped again so Fiona could peer around the corner. The sidewalk in front of Trevor's door was still empty—not unusual for a side-street in Queens in the late afternoon, but it made Fiona wonder if any bystanders had heard the shot and taken cover. Or called the police.

Heart pounding, she gestured for Bill to follow her, then walked south, toward the water. It was a bit of a hike to Vernon Boulevard, if they stuck to residential streets. Bill was in full paranoid mode, eyes flicking to every window and passing car, which made her feel safe enough to dial Simon from Trevor's phone. Her other hand stayed in her pocket, on her pistol.

That familiar growl answered on the fourth ring. "Yes?"

"It's me," she said. "Fiona."

Her phone beeped, the call dropping. Fiona pulled it away from her face, confused, and saw four bars of signal. Had Simon hung up on her?

"What happened?" Bill asked.

"I don't know," Fiona said. "If he doesn't want to talk to me…"

"Bad sign. Hold on a second." Raising a finger for her to wait, Bill disappeared inside a small convenience store on the corner, reappearing a minute later with two baseball caps and two pairs of sunglasses. "Look at these badass accessories. We're masters of disguise now."

Fiona mimed sticking two fingers down her throat. "Could you have picked any team other than the frigging Mets?"

"I just grabbed the first ones I saw." Bill grinned. "I swear, I didn't deliberately pick a team you hated with a fiery passion."

"Piss-poor disguise, anyway," Fiona said, slipping on the

sunglasses and tucking her hair beneath the cap. "Any cop will see right through this."

Before Bill could respond, Fiona's phone buzzed, flashing an unknown number. She answered, hoping it wasn't one of Trevor's idiot friends. "Yeah?"

When Simon spoke, she heard a crowd murmuring behind him, punctuated by a honking horn. He sounded irate, his accent thicker than usual: "Are you a child?"

"Okay, I'm sorry for calling you direct," she said. "My back's in a corner."

"So is mine," he said. "I am on a burner, on the street, surrounded by the cowards and ingrates who make up the public. That is to say, I have a mole in my crew, reporting to The Dean. You didn't make it to the airport."

"That's right. Someone hit us on the highway."

"You know who?"

"No idea."

"It wasn't The Dean. He knew about the crash, thanks to a security camera. How many police are on his payroll, you think?"

"Not as many as he would like, fortunately. You tell him I was meeting your gold guy at the airport?"

"No, and he has people at the airports, so your attacker may have done you a favor." A click, a loud exhale as Simon lit a cigarette. "You still owe me some money."

"Sure, I got it right here," she said. "It was a good little score."

Next to her, Bill offered an arched eyebrow.

"A good little score, but not a stealthy one." Simon chuckled. "You are all over the news, dear. Every channel, plus whatever the Internet does. The thing with the Tesla was particularly colorful. I am old enough to remember when a decapitation in Manhattan was not a newsworthy event."

"We'll pay you more if you help us."

Simon coughed, and Fiona pictured him blasting plumes of smoke out his nostrils. "As much as I would like to, my dear, I am in the bind. The Dean is watching everything. You're the bit of meat stuck in his tooth, irritating him to rage. He will spare no expense to put your head in a cardboard box on his desk."

"Well, he hasn't succeeded so far. If you can't help us, how are you getting your money?"

Simon fell silent long enough for Fiona to wonder if she had gone too far, dangling a threat like that. Through the line she heard a kid hollering, and the rumble of a truck. When Simon spoke again, his voice was gentle, the words paced. "I've always cared about you, Fiona. Not like a father, because you already have one of those. But because you're a different cut of criminal. Smarter, efficient. You wouldn't deny me what's mine."

"You're right," she said. "I wouldn't. Just make sure none of your people help The Dean, please?"

"I have no intention of allowing any of my people to assist that intellectual." Simon spat the last word. "I'll kill him at the first right opportunity. Now stay alive until you can pay me." With that last bit of encouragement, he hung up.

Slipping her phone back into her pocket, Fiona told Bill: "Went fine. Couldn't you tell?"

"Absolutely."

Heading south, Fiona found her thoughts drifting to Trevor. Not the worst relationship: he had been kind, funny, not terrible in the sack. They had rented an apartment together off-campus, their only tension stemming from Fiona's refusal to tell him how she paid her share of the rent. One night, four glasses of wine gave Trevor courage enough to stammer: *You're not doing sex work, are you?* Rather than take offense, she had laughed and kissed him on the forehead and said: *Of course not, silly.* She neglected to mention how she was making a thousand dollars a week as a courier, transporting packages between an ever-changing cast of Shady Dudes.

Things had come to a head when a skinny freak kicked open the front door of their apartment, intent on finding where Fiona had delivered a particular package. She had no idea, of course— if you wanted to survive the courier business, you never asked the clients their business. As the freak charged into their living room, Fiona plucked a hardcover copy of "Moby Dick" from the nearest bookshelf and hurled it at his skull hard enough to leave a dent; as he writhed on the floor, screeching and muttering, she had fetched a long knife from the kitchen and slammed it through his palm, pinning him to the hardwood. In all the excitement, she forgot that Trevor was in the apartment, studying for an organic chemistry exam.

Long story short, Trevor was a little nonplussed to find out her real occupation. And to be fair, maybe she should have trusted him with that information before some Martian crashed into their humble abode, looking for blood. When they broke up, Fiona felt something like relief—no more hiding her true nature from anyone. That's what she loved so much about Bill: not only had he accepted everything about her, but, as the past few weeks had demonstrated, he could deal with any sort of weirdness.

It took them another half-house to reach the construction site. A high wall of blue-painted plywood marked the perimeter. They walked around it until they reached a chain-link gate on tracks, wide enough to accommodate trucks. On the far side of the gate, beside a gravel roadway leading into the site, stood a double-wide trailer with barred windows and a small wooden porch.

Fiona placed a hand on the edge of the gate, testing its push along the track, when the trailer door opened and a guard sauntered onto the porch. He was portly, with a gray moustache that made him look like a cartoon walrus. Less comical was the pistol dangling from a holster on his hip.

Fiona ducked away from the gate, pulling Bill with her. "What kind of rent-a-cop packs a gun with real bullets?" Bill hissed in her ear.

"One who really doesn't want anyone getting in." As much as Fiona wanted to pull out the phone and search for another hiding spot in the city, a little voice in her head—her personal devil—suggested this situation was worth exploring further. A guard needed a gun to protect something valuable, no?

Bill, her other devil, grinned as he picked up her frequency. "Might as well hide out in a place with our own guard."

"That's right," she said. "It's not like we can get in more trouble than we already are."

How wrong she was.

# 9

**THE DEAN'S NEW** lieutenant, Rex, must have possessed some kind of death wish, because he arrived at the Pot O' Gold, the bar that doubled as The Dean's office, in a bright red Ferrari.

It had already been a long afternoon at Long Island City's most legally suspect drinking establishment. In the kitchen, two of The Dean's men scrubbed the tiles with bleach while a third one rolled up a bloody tarp. In the bathroom, a fourth goon used tweezers to pry bits of bone out of the graffiti-scarred wall.

The Dean, atop his usual stool, devoured a steak. Murder always made him hungry, and why not? He was a lion, the unstoppable ruler of this particular veld. Claudius, his bodyguard behind the bar, seemed a little pale after the afternoon's work, and that was okay: sometimes you needed to show these young punks what you were capable of.

He was sawing off a fresh chunk of beef when the gleaming super-car pulled to the curb outside, framed by the front window. When The Dean spied the driver, he slammed his knife into the steak and stood, adjusting the lapels of his suit jacket. Without a word, he extended his hand to Claudius, who retrieved a long steel pipe from its special shelf and placed it gently in The Dean's palm.

Rex entered the bar, the bell over the door ringing merrily. The sight of The Dean, armed, brought him to a startled halt. "Boss?" he asked.

"That," The Dean said, jabbing the pipe at the Ferrari, "is a very ostentatious vehicle."

"Oh, I didn't buy it," Rex said. "I won it at poker."

"Do you know what 'ostentatious' means?" The pipe squeaked as The Dean tightened his grip on it.

Rex locked eyes with Claudius, making a silent plea for help. Claudius shook his head slightly. "I don't," he said, shoulders tensing.

"It means flashy," The Dean said, striding toward him. "It means flamboyant and gaudy. It means something that people notice. It means something that a *cop* might notice, and ask questions, given how it's parked outside a *known criminal establishment*. You get the idea?"

Rex cringed, his hands rising to his face, but The Dean brushed past him and out the door, marching down the sidewalk toward the Ferrari. It was a sunny day, the street dotted with hipsters on the way to lunch at the ridiculously overpriced diner beside the Pot O' Gold. The kids veered wide to avoid him, although it was an open question whether they did so because he held the pipe like a club, or because he had launched into a loud rant about the lack of subtlety in modern culture.

"Better go out there," Claudius told Rex.

"Why?" Rex whined.

"Because otherwise he'll come back inside and crush your skull. It was a long morning."

Rex glanced toward the kitchen, where two men shoved the gore-speckled tarp into a trash bag. "Who was it this time?"

"Pop, finally. Plus his main nurse. Got a little rough." Claudius jutted his chin at the window. "You better get out there. Now."

Rex stepped outside just as The Dean lifted the pipe and

brought it down with surgical precision on the left headlight, shattering it. Nodding at the result, The Dean adjusted his grip and smashed the right headlight before moving to the side mirrors. Rex had witnessed his share of rage and destruction, but this was something different: The Dean was cool, methodical, really taking his time and adjusting his angle before every swing.

Across the street, a gaggle of hipsters raised their phones to film the Ferrari's death. The Dean offered them a two-finger salute before driving the pipe into the windshield. The glass splintered around the impact, leaving a hole.

Rex swallowed and shuffled his feet. "You know, I could just… return it?"

"You'll do no such thing, my boy." The Dean swept the pipe along the windshield frame, clearing out the glass. "That's not enough of a lesson here."

"I'm sorry about all this?"

"You phrasing that as an interrogative, as opposed to a declarative, is the rancid cherry atop this particular shit sundae." The Dean drove the pipe into the hood, denting it. "Of course, while failing to keep a low profile is your fault, I am also a little emotional after the action of the past few hours, to put it mildly. Do you realize it's all my firm now?"

Rex, who had no idea what 'interrogative' meant, said: "What can I do to fix this?"

Gritting his teeth, The Dean white-knuckled the pipe. Instead of swinging away, he forced himself to take a deep breath and set the weapon against the Ferrari. Snapping a handkerchief from his pocket, he wiped his hands. "Fix this? You can't. But if you want to live out the week, you'll help find Bill and Fiona. They're so close I can smell them. Their spoor is failed dreams and all-American grasping."

"Everyone's on it," Rex said, locking eyes with the hipsters across the street, who lowered their phones and slunk away. The Dean could talk all he wanted about "low profile," but his one-man demolition derby might have made him a YouTube star by the end of the day. And what if one of those kids called the police?

A solid whack to the front passenger door separated the panel and sent it clattering to the sidewalk. The Dean paused, his shoulders slumping. "We need to solve Bill and Fiona quickly. Our friend in the north will figure out that we're responsible for his men disappearing, and then we'll have yet another war to wage."

Rex had no idea what The Dean was talking about, but 'our friend in the north' sounded pretty medieval. "And it's delivery day," he said, thinking: Maybe I can sell the car parts for scrap. Someone out there could use a supercharged engine, right?

"Yes, yes, yes, and a security change." Tossing the pipe into the gutter, The Dean unscrewed the Ferrari's gas cap. He stuffed his handkerchief partway into the filler pipe. "We're about to make the world's most expensive Molotov cocktail," he announced, patting his pockets.

As he shifted from foot to foot, Rex wondered if a flaming bit of cloth could actually ignite the gas tank. He opened his mouth, closed it, then opened it again. The Dean's search had turned frantic, his hands darting into every pocket of his suit.

Rex's tongue felt too dry and thick. He had to swallow twice before he could speak. "Sir, I, uh…"

The Dean stopped patting and spun around. His eyes reminded Rex of distant planets seen through a telescope: distant and choked with ice, indifferent to life. "What?"

"What about, um, the low profile?"

The Dean's gaze cracked. Adjusting his lapels, he strode for the bar, his shoes crunching on glass and metal bits on the sidewalk. "You're right, an explosion is a little *gaudy*," he said as he passed Rex. "Just get it out of my sight."

Despite all that damage to the bodywork, the Ferrari started with a magnificent roar when Rex twisted the key. He drove three blocks before remembering the handkerchief still deep in the filler pipe, its end fluttering in the breeze. His foot fluttered on the brake before returning to the gas. Yes, the prospect of spending even another few seconds within a hundred yards of The Dean seemed less appealing than the possibility of exploding into meaty scraps. He shifted into a higher gear and ran the light.

10

**FOR A BUNCH** of guys who liked to wear cowboy outfits and ride horses down streets like it was the Spanish-American War all over again, the Rough Riders did a good job of hiding. That was partially my fault. I had killed a few of them over the past year, on orders of The Dean.

Before I could start playing detective, I needed to make a call. Fortunately, the Rockaways offered a one-of-a-kind historical artifact: a pay phone bolted to the side of a bodega on the corner of Rockaway Beach Boulevard and Beach 97th. The ocean air had rusted its chrome, and the plastic handset was chipped and scarred, but it worked. I pumped four quarters into the slot and dialed a number.

That booming voice answered: "Yeah?"

"It's me, back from the wilds of Oklahoma."

"Good. I was wondering if you'd made it. How's the hunting?"

"I've almost started," I said, adjusting the gym bag on my shoulder. "Got any intel for me?"

He laughed. "Oh, I've got some intel, all right. Bill and Fiona are back in town."

I almost dropped the phone. "What?"

"They were just in a big car accident. Trying to flee, I assume. If The Dean doesn't know about it yet, he will soon."

"I don't get it."

"It's so simple. Find Bill and Fiona, and The Dean will be right along directly."

"No, I get that part. Why did they come back?"

"Oh, probably the usual bullshit. Money, or to settle a grudge. From what I've been reading, they strike me as more style than brains."

"Fiona's smart."

"Yeah, she's got a real smart mouth from the looks of her."

I felt a perverse urge to defend the woman who'd blasted my insides to bits. "She was smart enough to get the drop on me."

"No comment. Anyway, that's all I have for you."

"You're a huge help, Dash. A huge help."

"Don't you ever speak my name on an open line."

"Relax, it's a pay phone. Remember, you owe me big." Without bothering to say goodbye, I hung up and walked the three blocks to the beach. I had a lot to do, but I also needed some time to think.

The concrete boardwalk was empty except for a few bicyclists. Taking a seat on a bench, I let the sun sparkling off the waves lull me into a trance. I had given Bill and Fiona the opportunity for a whole new life, paid with my blood. They could have gone anywhere, and yet they decided to reenter the belly of the beast. Why? No matter what Dash thought of their intelligence, they were too smart to take on the Dean by themselves. They must have come back for something else.

I could only hope they survived again. I still bore Fiona no ill will for shooting me, and I'd meant everything I told her and Bill about the power of love. A life of hatred and gunfire had no worth. But if that was true, why was I back here? Why hadn't I ridden with Lola all the way to the West Coast, started fresh?

Old habits die hard, I guess. Speaking of old habits, Dash would become a problem at some point if I didn't come through with The Dean on a slab. I had done a freelance job for him a long time ago, in Osaka, in exchange for an unconscionable amount of taxpayer dollars. The first and last time I ever dipped my wick into that Black Ops stuff.

The waves weren't calming me anymore.

Hoisting my shotgun bag, I headed inland. I needed to find those cowboys.

# 11

**ON THE FAR** side of the construction site from the gate, Fiona noticed two boards peeling away from the fence, with enough gap for someone to slip through. Beyond the fence was a field of waist-high weeds, dotted with giant piles of sand. A gray hose snaked around a tall stack of softly rotting lumber, leaking water into a set of bulldozer tracks. Above them rose twenty floors of luxury condo in mid-construction, a maze of concrete and steel frames and wooden planks, the north side plated with windows. The sun glinted off the bright red cage of a construction elevator bolted to an exterior track.

Bill craned his head, using a hand to shield his eyes. "I wonder if that elevator has power."

"We're taking the stairs." Fiona slapped his chest. "It'll be quieter, unless you start panting."

"Don't make fun of my hatred of exercise."

"My turn to take the bag." Fiona eased the sweaty strap off his shoulder and slung it across her chest. The weight of the gold guaranteed her a miserable time up those stairs, but Bill needed a break. His shirt was wet with sweat, his neck red.

Bill kissed her on the forehead and crossed the field toward the condo, weaving around small piles of gravel and rusting rebar. The builders had abandoned this place in a hurry, but not before curtaining the outside of the first floor with orange construction mesh. They pushed through the mesh, into a raw concrete atrium that would someday house an elegant lobby, if work on the place ever started again.

At the far end of the space, beyond the concrete column that encased the empty elevator shaft, they found a stairwell. Bill stepped into the bottom of the well and squinted into the dizzying heights, a puzzle of sunlight and steel extending into infinity. His stomach did a slow somersault.

Placing a hand on his arm, Fiona whispered: "Did you hear something?"

Bill listened, catching the faint rustle of mesh in the wind, a rhythmic clanking that might have been a loose piece of metal somewhere. "Nothing weird."

Fiona drew her pistol. "I'll lead."

They ascended, pausing every other flight to listen. By the tenth floor, Fiona needed to set down the bag and rub her aching shoulder, which was becoming the least of her problems: The cut on her back itched, her ribs throbbed with renewed pain, and her left calf had a nasty twinge that threatened to leave her limping. Her demon laughed at her: You're getting weaker, you loser. You can't. You're not tough enough.

After a few rounds of this mental pummeling, her inner cornerman whispered that a little slowness was okay this week. You survived two car crashes and a couple of beatings, okay? You're human. Now wipe your eyes and get back to it.

As she boxed with her demons, Bill ducked through the fire door. He found a maze of drywall that would someday become apartments, the floors stacked high with marble counters and fixtures draped in dusty plastic. He clicked his tongue until Fiona poked her head through the doorway.

"Remind you of someplace?" Bill asked, throwing his arms wide.

Fiona almost said something sarcastic, before she took

another look at the half-completed walls, the angles of the windows, the painted splotches that marked the edges of future rooms. "Actually, yes. Five years ago?"

"Never forget a floorplan, do you?"

"Not when it's part of a job, no." Fiona dropped the bag on a stack of marble. "But this isn't the same place, obviously."

"Maybe the same developer. You know, they're putting up so many of these luxury buildings around here, they probably just use the same plans every time." Bill pointed at the other end of the floor, hidden behind huge bags of plaster and boxes of tools. "Want to see if they have that special something?"

"If they do, might make a good hiding place."

There were no walls or windows on that part of the floor, only a long drop to the weeds below. Bill pointed at the concrete between their feet, dotted and dashed with neon-red paint. "Doesn't seem like they've built it yet, but there are the marks."

"They might have built one on another floor," Fiona said. "Way things are going these days, every rich person wants one."

"Shall we try the penthouse?"

"Might as well. I know you're loving the exercise."

When they reached the top floor (Bill breathing hard through his nose, his feet heavy on the stairs; the bag-strap cutting a fiery line into Fiona's shoulder), the stairs ended in yet another fire door. Fiona pressed an ear to it, listening, before turning the knob and pulling it open a few inches. She paused in the gap.

"We okay?" Bill whispered.

Fiona opened the door wider and stepped through, Bill on her heels. They emerged into a concrete space, empty and featureless except for thick pillars every thirty feet or so. To their left, dusty windows broke the sun into flickering light-ghosts. To their right, the wind rustled across clear plastic sheeting stretched floor to ceiling. Through the plastic: blazing lights, a dark flicker, a flash of blue.

Someone was up here.

Neat as a dance partner, she gripped Bill by the elbow and swept them behind a pillar, hoping nobody on the other side of the plastic saw them silhouetted against the windows. Beneath the wind she heard—or thought she heard—the faint gurgling of water, a footstep.

What the hell was this?

A clank and rumble from the far side of the floor: the construction elevator climbing the building. Maybe headed up here.

*You know what this is.*

"You have to be kidding me," Bill said, putting the pieces together.

"Leaving now," Fiona replied, ducking low as she scuttled for the door, Bill her shadow. The pillars offered a little bit of cover. Reaching the door, she tried to open it as quietly as possible, wincing as the hinges squeaked. Seven or eight minutes to reach the first floor, she figured, and another couple of minutes to sneak off the lot—

From below came a chorus of footfalls on the stairs.

It sounded like a big crowd.

Headed this way.

They retreated through the door and Fiona had the pistol leveled as she sought hiding spots, doorways, another stairwell leading down, anything. Somewhere to their right, the unseen elevator screeched to a halt, followed by the metallic slap of its door sliding back. How long until the crowd below reached their level? If there was another set of stairs up here, they could reach the ground that way—

The nearby plastic peeled along a seam, and a man in a white jumpsuit stepped through. A burst of humid air swept through his long black hair. Something about his angular face reminded Fiona of a crow. Beyond his shoulder, as the plastic flapped back into place, Fiona glimpsed what looked like a forest sprouting from the concrete, bathed in the light of a hundred violent suns.

Crow Man regarded them with pale eyes absent of fear or surprise. "You're not the delivery guys," he said.

# 12

**THE PADLOCK KEY** opened a self-storage unit on the north side of Burlington. Walker flicked on the light before lowering the roll-up door behind him. The bicycle he left outside, propped against a light-pole; it was time to upgrade. The overhead bulbs made the dark green Aston Martin DB Mark III gleam like a sculpture. From the trunk he removed a leather shoulder-bag stuffed with bound stacks of twenty-dollar bills, three full magazines of 9mm ammunition, a pistol and holster, and a phone.

The unit also featured a battered gym locker in the corner, a refugee from the enormous junk-pile beside the storage facility's main gate. Walker opened it to reveal a light gray suit, tailored impeccably to his hundred-seventy pounds. He shed his borrowed two-piece, keeping the shirt, and buttoned himself into his bespoke, instantly feeling more complete. Keeping on his stained socks, he traded his mud-splattered boots for the pair of custom-made leather shoes tucked into the bottom of the locker.

The car offered a reassuring purr, eager to escape the tight confines of the unit. He drove out the main gate of the storage facility, bumping onto the two-lane that would take him to his temporary crash-pad a few miles south. He felt more relaxed with the pistol tucked beneath his armpit, not to mention the bag of cash in the footwell of the passenger seat.

On the console between the seats, his phone rang. He read the number before hitting the speaker button. Asked, in his most relentlessly cheerful voice: "How you doing, Sully?"

"I don't get you, man."

"I didn't realize you had this number."

"This is your old number, man."

"I actually gave it to you? I really am slipping."

"Why'd you run out like that?"

"Aren't you worried the cops are listening to us right now? I mean, since for no reason you think I'm some sort of snitch?"

Sully sighed. "Let's meet up. It's a tense time, you're going through a lot. Happens to all of us. I don't want this to wreck all the history we got together."

"We just chat, have a beer?"

"Exactly."

Go screw," Walker said, and disconnected the call.

Ten minutes from home he stopped at a gas station. After filling the Aston Martin's tank, he headed inside and bought a jumbo-sized travel mug (in a nuclear shade of orange) along with a small package of instant coffee. The stuff tasted like used motoroil, in his opinion, but he could use the chemicals for the drive to New York in the morning. "You're welcome, sir," said the kid behind the counter, after ringing up the gas and the purchases.

Walker smiled back. Nothing like a little respect to brighten your day. It made him miss the military, where everyone snapped you a salute when you entered a room. Only he had really screwed that career, hadn't he? That, and everything else in his life.

With a wink, Walker left the kid three twenties in the take-a-penny tray beside the register. Unlocking the car, he scanned the midnight road before climbing in. Beyond the station's island of antiseptic light lay an almost velvety darkness. His lizard brain sensed something out there, despite the lack of movement.

For the rest of the drive, he kept glancing in the rearview

mirror every few seconds, and made some extra turns that took him in a long arc through quiet subdivisions.

Home for the moment was a ranch-style house tucked behind a tall hedge, at the end of a cul-de-sac. In the backyard, a creek ran through a deep cut in the earth, fast and rough with summer rainwater. To Walker, it made a nice little moat. The house featured a wraparound front porch, three bedrooms, one and a half baths, a finished basement with racks of tools, a large and gleaming kitchen, a living room with thick carpeting in a spectacularly ugly shade of orange, and a line of bullet-holes in the hallway wall.

In the basement, someone had driven a sledgehammer through the drywall in three spots, dusting the rug white.

In a corner of the master bedroom, a dried brown stain ruined the obnoxious yellow wallpaper.

Yellow crime-scene tape still webbed the back door.

Walker had found the place the previous night, a few hours after crossing the border. Cruising the roads on his new bicycle, he had spied a long piece of yellow tape limp on the gravel driveway, alongside a latex glove wrinkled and pale as a beached jellyfish: signs of a recent cop gathering. The street dark and quiet at that late hour. The front door unlocked.

The crime (whatever its nature) had occurred some time ago. The blood in the master bedroom was dried to a hard crust, the kitchen counters dusty, the packaged food in the fridge well past its expiration dates. The upstairs closets featured men's and women's clothing, the former in sizes too small for his needs. Under different circumstances, Walker might have felt the faint sadness that sometimes comes when standing in an abandoned space. But the prospect of hot running water and a real mattress overrode any melancholy.

Now, having dodged Sully and retrieved his property, it was time at last for a good scrubbing. After parking the Aston Martin in the backyard, he went inside and locked the doors and drew a bath, placing the phone and pistol on the tile beside the tub.

He preferred showers, but feared the hiss of falling water would disguise a breaking window, a furtive step on the stairway.

Before bed, Walker took two thin-stemmed wine-glasses from the kitchen and two hardcover books from the shelf in the living room and propped the books against the front and back doors with a glass balanced atop each. From the recycling bin underneath the sink he fished an armful of empty tin cans and walked through the house placing them on the closed windows, beside the locks. He even did the ones in the basement, barely large enough for a child to crawl through.

He kept the door of the master bedroom open, to better hear any glass breaking or tin toppling, and lay in the tub after padding its bottom with a pair of thick blankets. He placed the pistol on the tile again, within easy reach.

He had always slept lightly. Any sound could snap him from the deepest dreams.

The night stayed silent.

In the gray hour before dawn he opened his eyes and believed for a freezing second that his daughter was sitting on the toilet with a rifle, watching him, until he blinked and her familiar face dissolved into the play of light and shadow on the bathroom wall. He climbed out of the tub, shaking the blood back into his knees and hands, just as glass shattered downstairs.

Walker slipped on his shoes and suit in record time. Chambered a pistol round as he left the bedroom. The upstairs hallway hazy with smoke. He crouched at the head of the stairs, weapon aimed at the sliver of front door visible through the banisters. The polished floorboards at the foot of the stairs flickered orange with reflected flame.

A window broke in the living room, the tin can toppling from its perch beside the lock. A wine bottle rolled toward the kitchen doorway, trailing a stream of orange flame. Sully must have found him somehow. He had taken care to cover his tracks, but Burlington is a small place.

Walker crept to the ground floor, heat baking his skin, coughing on the gray smoke clouding the light. The top half of the front door was pebbled glass with clear edges. Keeping low, he peeked through the bottom rim and saw one of Sully's men standing next to a black pickup truck parked in the driveway, dressed in a black windbreaker and a bullet-resistant vest, a lit Molotov cocktail in his hand.

Walker turned and scrambled for the rear of the house. The kitchen was already ablaze. The back door cracked open, framing Sully's second bodyguard behind the Aston Martin. The man had a rifle cradled in his arms, his expression patient as a deer hunter in a blind.

The front-door window shattered, along with the bottle hurled through it. The curtains framing the door dissolved in flame, the paint bubbling and peeling. Walker's body kicked into emergency mode, sweat soaking his shirt and suit, his hands slippery on the gun. He opened the door that led to the basement. Fast down the stairs. Smoke seeping through the cracks in the ceiling, like gray fingers reaching for him.

Too late he remembered the shoulder-bag still in the upstairs bedroom, with the money in it. At least he had his wallet and keys and phone in his pants pockets.

Jamming the pistol into his waistband, he threw the latch on one of the small windows that opened onto the crawl-space beneath the porch, slamming it open with the heel of his hand. Stuck an arm through the gap and tried to slither through. His body jammed at the shoulder. Smoke raked his nostrils, trickling his throat. No good, man. You're trapped.

He relaxed and let his body drop back into the basement. Fumbled through the nearest rack of tools for anything that might help, his shaking fingers spilling coffee cans full of nails and screws on the floor. Warm metal slapped his forearm. A pry-bar on a hook. Yes.

He swung the bar at the window-frame, the bent claw biting into the wood, and pulled as hard as he could. The house dying around him, crackling and roaring as flame filled its rooms. A smoke detector shrieked once and fell silent. He braced a foot against the basement wall and strained on the bar, regretting every missed gym session and extra glass of whiskey.

The window-frame tore free of the wall, spraying him with glass and wood. Walker dropped the pry-bar and hoisted himself through the rough opening, wide enough this time for his shoulders to fit through, his suit tearing on the brick. Wriggling for daylight, his back scraping the underside of the porch, the pistol held in front of him.

Wooden latticework sealed off the crawl-space from the lawn. Through its diamond-shaped holes, Walker spied Sully's man still beside the truck, gaze focused on the second-story windows. Walker aimed the pistol and fired four times, the bodyguard collapsing as bullets bit into his legs. The fifth shot went through the top of his head.

When the other man rounded the corner of the house, Walker shot him in the ankle and, as he fell, the neck. After shoving his way through the latticework, he ransacked the bodies for anything of use, which came to eighty-three dollars, another phone, and a rifle and pistol. Straining to hear sirens over the crackle of burning wood, he jogged for the backyard, bracing himself for the worst. Nobody had touched the Aston Martin, thankfully.

As Walker accelerated out of the backyard and down the driveway, flames punched out the first-floor windows: red hands waving him a cheerful goodbye. He felt jubilant, like he always did after firefights. Nothing like dodging bullets to make you feel more alive.

For added laughs, he dialed Sully, waiting until the highway sign welcoming him to the great state of New York disappeared in his rearview mirror.

"You're dead," Sully said.

"You know, for a guy who grows weed and talks a lot of I Ching bullshit about rolling with the punches, you sure don't stay relaxed when things don't go your way."

Sully laughed like a buzzsaw choking on a thick piece of wood. "You think I won't find you? You know how easy it was to find you before?"

"How'd you do it?"

"Like I'd tell you. You're real lucky you left me with a mess to clean up here. It'll take a little time before I can focus on you. But don't you fret, I'm coming for your ass real soon."

"I guess the friendship is over, huh?" Walker said.

Before Sully could reply, Walker disconnected the call. His mirth had cooled, leaving him with a roiling gut. His hands stank of smoke.

# 13

**FIONA AIMED HER** pistol between Crow Man's eyes. "That's right," she said. "We're not the delivery folks."

Ninety-nine times out of a hundred, pointing a weapon in someone's face made them flinch. Crow Man was a very special case. He smiled and nodded, biting his lower lip, as if Fiona had presented him with a tantalizing dessert. "Inevitable," he said. "I told him this would happen."

"Bill," Fiona said through gritted teeth, "will you please check this gentleman for weapons?"

"I'm not armed," Crow Man said, as Bill circled toward him. "Well, armed in the sense that I have arms, with hands and fingers and all that, but I don't have any weapons. I'm a pacifist. Too many guns in the world."

"Don't disagree with you there, buddy," Fiona said, stepping closer. "But raise your arms—your real arms, with the fingers on the end—so we can get on with this."

While Crow Man followed orders, Bill dropped his duffel bag on the concrete, stooped, and patted down the man's ankles, thighs, waist, shoulders, feeling nothing but taut muscle under the jumpsuit. The guy stank of weed. Or maybe that was the smell wafting through the split plastic behind them.

"He's clean," Bill said, stepping away to retrieve his bag.

"I'm guilty, is what I am." Arms still raised, Crow Man locked gazes with Bill. "Ever wonder if today is your last day?"

"Only every morning." With a grunt, Bill lifted the bag onto his shoulder, which felt raw after their cross-borough run. Maybe a puff or two of this strange dude's weed would sort him out, after they reached some kind of safety.

Fiona heard the footsteps in the stairwell, louder, hammering, like the sound of her doom rushing down. Or maybe it was her heart slamming against her ribs. "Spare me the existential navel-gazing," she said, waving her pistol at the shimmering lab behind him. "Let's go in there."

"The grand tour," Crow Man said, leading them through the plastic sheeting. "I'm the chief horticulturalist of this particular institution. Also the chemist."

Fiona counted twenty, twenty-five, thirty long rows of marijuana in huge pots, the stems held upright by twine webs, bathed by hot lights overhead. Between the lights, silver ventilation tubes hummed. Across a narrow aisle from the plants, on wooden tables that ran the length of the floor, she saw cardboard boxes piled high with plastic bags full of weed; and below the tables, plastic drums and tool boxes on rolling pallets.

"Biggest bloom room I've ever seen," Bill muttered.

"Thank you," Crow Man said. "If you want to sample anything, feel free. I'm always in a hospitable mood when someone has a pistol to my head."

Over the thump of machinery and the hiss of mechanical air, Fiona caught faint voices. The people from the elevator. Crap. "Tell me who they are," she said.

Crow Man shrugged. "The real delivery people, probably."

"And who's on the stairs?" Bill asked.

"New security." Crow Man tapped his temple. "Wrong hour for you to show up. Shift change and delivery? Glory, glory, glory, paranoia."

Fiona directed them into the nearest row, the plants tall enough to hide them if they crouched a bit. "Whose place is this?"

"Rockaway," Crow Man said. "New venture, big money. Yes, weed's legal in New York. But up here, we spray down the crop with a very special preparation of my unique design."

Bill giggled. It was an ugly sound, muffled by the knuckle in his mouth. Fiona punched him in the shoulder, her usual move when he did something antisocial, but her own lips were pulling back, her throat hitching with laughter.

Crow Man's face twitched with confusion.

"The Good Lord himself," Bill informed him, "has taken a personal interest in screwing up our lives."

"We're overdue for payback," Fiona added. "Too much killing. Too much bullshit. Too many parking tickets."

Beyond the plastic sheeting, the door clanged open, followed by the rapid drumbeat of boots. Someone yelled a greeting.

"Anyway, we need your panic room," Bill hissed in Crow Man's ear.

"There's a lot of panic in here," Crow Man agreed, nodding.

"Where is it?" Wrapping a hand around the back of Crow Man's neck, Bill squeezed hard.

"Safe room, separate room, locked room," Fiona murmured, scrambling for synonyms as she adjusted her sweaty grip on the pistol.

Crow Man's eyes widened, and he jabbed a finger to their left. "Oh, yes. The most special room. My place of worship. Down there."

Bill followed that finger through shifting leaves, spying a flash of metal. No way to see more from this angle. He wondered if it was really a door. If the panic room had a working lock and finished walls. Add to that Crow Man's mention of "place of worship," and Bill had no doubt that some spectacular weirdness awaited them in there. But it's not like we have a choice. Either we go for it, or these men kill us.

"No time like the present," Fiona said, and stood, her pistol dug into Crow Man's neck hard enough to make him wince.

As she shuffled her hostage into the aisle, a half-dozen men appeared at the far end: big muscles, bad tattoos, shaved heads, body armor. High-priced merc security, the kind that Rockaway hired for top dollar, but nobody she recognized. At least she wouldn't have to kill anyone she knew, if it came to that. She was tired of murdering folks, whether or not they deserved death.

The men yelled in unison and reached for their weapons. Fiona twisted her body behind Crow Man, trying to give them as small a target as possible, and tugged on his collar. Crow Man took a hesitant step backward, then another.

Bill stepped behind Fiona, hoping that Crow Man provided enough cover for the two of them—and at that most excellent moment, he heard a faint sound that sent an iron spike of pure terror through his heart: the faint purr of fabric ripping. The gold clanked as it shifted, and he glanced down as the bottom of the bag split open an inch.

Fiona bumped into him. "Better move," she hissed through her teeth.

"Bag's ripping," Bill said, trying to adjust his grip so his hand covered the growing hole.

Fiona pushed into him again, harder, as he looped his arms around the bag, cradling it like a baby. That would hold for a few more minutes or until their gruesome deaths, whichever came first.

Bill retreated for the panic room, Fiona almost on top of him, Crow Man shuffling with his hands up. The stark light twisted and lengthened their shadows into a monstrous centipede.

"This will go better if you stop," said one of the mercs, cocking his head. They were too close, a few of them drifting into the weed aisles.

Fiona snorted loud enough to hear over the hum of equipment.

Bill's fingers ached, the gold digging into his palms. The bag was still coming apart, strand by strand, but the door to the panic room was only a few feet away, close enough to see that it lacked knobs or keyholes. Hopefully it'll open if I push, Bill thought. If it doesn't, we're pinned.

"Good day to die," Crow Man said, loud and cheerful.

They reached the door. Sweating, half-expecting a bullet to crash into his chest at any moment, Bill pressed a hand against the cold steel and pushed. It refused to budge, and his stomach flipped. Was it locked?

He shoved harder, and the door hummed open, on springs, revealing a room lit pale by fluorescent tubes. Stacks of cardboard boxes lined the steel walls, along with shrink-wrapped bales of cash. He stepped inside and saw a giant red button beside the door, with the words 'PRESS TO LOCK' on the wall above it in big red type.

In the doorway, Fiona planted a hard boot in Crow Man's back, sending him sprawling into the aisle. She ducked into the panic room, and Bill hit the button. The door wheezed shut, blocking the sight of more men charging through the weed forest. With a roar of relief, Bill dropped the ruined duffel bag on the floor, and it tore open, scattering rough gold chunks across the featureless concrete floor.

The door's heavy bolts slammed home. Fiona looked at Bill, jabbed a thumb at the cash. "How much you think is in here?"

"Enough to buy a small country," Bill said.

"If only we could see The Dean's face when he hears about this. His head will explode." Chuckling, Fiona pulled out her phone. No signal. The universe obviously wanted them to play this game on the Nightmare Difficulty setting.

Leaning against the wall, forcing herself to take measured breaths, Fiona cycled through her memory. Had she seen a keypad outside the door? She didn't think so. Maybe this model only locked when someone inside hit that button. The big dudes outside could take a cutting torch to the door, or explosives, but it might take hours for them to get in here. Maybe days, if they were lucky.

"Gonna take inventory," she said.

"If there's some aspirin," Bill said, wincing as he rotated his shoulder, "I could use, like, ten. Along with a big shot of vodka."

"You and me both, love." She started at the far end of the room, where three small propane tanks on a rolling pallet, alongside four full water-cooler jugs, but no stove or water-cooler. The pallet pinned a single-gear bicycle with a heavy red frame to the wall. The bicycle had a fat pair of training wheels bolted to its rear frame.

Fiona opened a long metal box beside the door and found two fire extinguishers, a box of flares, a fire-retardant blanket, duct tape, two gas masks, and a small medical kit. So at least they had some safety supplies, but what she really wanted for Christmas was a metric shit-ton of ammunition. What kind of self-respecting drug lab didn't have an armory of some sort?

At least the medical kit had ibuprofen in little packets. She dry-swallowed five pills before tossing three packets to Bill, who was standing in the center of the space, pointing at the ceiling. "There's a vent," he said. "Too small to crawl through, though, unless I lost, like, a hundred and forty pounds."

"There's also a tragic lack of secret hatches in the floor," Fiona replied, stomping on the concrete before resuming her search. Another metal box, in the opposite corner, looked enticingly like a gun locker. Opening it shattered her hopes: instead of weapons, she found a plastic doll of a woman, nude and life-size and disturbingly pink.

"I wouldn't touch that," Bill said. "Not unless you want a juicy case of syphilis."

"I can scrub my skin with bleach," Fiona said, slamming the lid shut. "But there's no bleach that can clean the memory of that from my head."

"Hey, check this out." Bill tilted an open cardboard box so she could see a collection of wigs, fake jewelry, and women's clothing. Using two fingers, he pulled up the leg of a light blue pantsuit. "What's he doing, dressing it up like Hillary Clinton?"

"I like to think I'm open about folks' sex lives. Live and let live," Fiona said. "But then I see something like this, and I'm all like, 'Kill it with fire.'"

"When I was a kid, we broke into this old dude's house down the road, found a sex doll in the garage," Bill giggled. "The sick bastard had put a rubber Ronald Reagan mask over the head. It was a female doll, by the way."

"Who didn't want to bang the Gipper?" Wiping her hands on her jeans, Fiona shifted to the boxes beside the doll locker, which held more energy bars in weirder flavors (she dared not taste *Pink-Bubble-Crunch!*) along with neon-colored energy drinks. In the last box, she found cardboard cartons with black cobras winding above militaristic script: fireworks.

"Because when I'm running a top-secret drug lab," Bill said, when she held up a box, "I like to unwind after a long day by shooting off loud, colorful fireworks on top of a building that everyone can see for miles around. That's not conspicuous at all."

No ammunition! Anger roared through Fiona, hot and electric, and she kicked a stack of boxes away from the wall beside the door—revealing an intercom with three buttons and a small screen embedded above a speaker.

At least this was something she could use. Pressing the red button made the screen snap to life, revealing a line of men standing in front of the door, pistols and rifles raised as if they expected Bill and Fiona to merrily waltz out. Idiots. Based on the angle, the camera was embedded in the top of the doorway.

Bill peeled open the energy bar. "Want to hear the good news?" he asked.

Taking a seat on a million dollars in twenties, Fiona popped the magazine from her pistol and did a shell count, shucking the brass into her lap: a ritual that always soothed her. "Sure."

"We wanted a secure place to lie low." Bill took a bite, chewing hard, and spread his arms wide. "Hey, mission accomplished."

# 14

**I'M NOT THE** best detective, I'm the first to admit. It took me the rest of the day to track down the Rough Riders' hideout, and my methods mostly involved walking into bars and asking people. It was a wonder that someone from the Rockaway Mob didn't get word and track me down, but as I eventually learned, they were dealing with much larger issues by that evening.

As dusk settled, I found myself on Dumont Avenue where it smacked into Ruby Street, and the low houses gave way to vacant lots overgrown with vines and piles of rusted junk. This was The Hole, and I knew it well. I made my way down Ruby, careful to sidestep the deeper puddles, pausing at the gaps in the sagging chain-link fences to examine the aging double-wides and RVs mired in weeds and mud.

How many bodies had I planted back here over the years? Three or four, at least. The Hole had a long, inglorious reputation as a mob burial ground. Nobody cared what happened here. It was as close to the Wild West as you could get in a teeming metropolis.

In my left hand, I carried a milk jug filled with a pinkish liquid. I'd duct-taped a black plastic square with a digital display to the front of the jug, and a set of white and red wires ran from it to the jug's mouth, which I'd also taped over. The wires ran under the tape, the stripped ends dangling in the liquid inside.

In my right hand, I held a plastic handle with a big red button on top. When I found the right lot, I placed my thumb on the button and walked in. The building I approached was made from three construction trailers, bolted together into a U with the open end facing the street. In the makeshift courtyard between the trailers, gray boards and nylon fabric formed a rough covering. In the shadows beneath, two men sat at a picnic bench.

They rose as I approached, stepping from beneath the overhang into the setting sun. Both were dressed in jeans and loose denim shirts, with white cowboy hats perched high on their foreheads.

"Greetings, gentlemen," I said, stopping five yards away from them. "Lovely evening, no?"

"Gonna rain later," said the one to my left, who rocked a resplendent gray moustache that would have done an Old West gunslinger mighty proud. His left hand had slipped behind his back, where no doubt he kept a firearm. I hoped it was an old-timey six-shooter with a pearl handle.

"State your business," said the one to my right, whose facial hair had been pruned into an extravagant set of muttonchops.

"I'm here to see the man." I still had the gym bag slung over my shoulder, heavy with the stubby shotgun and the .45, but neither would do me much good. I'd known that before walking in here, of course, which is why I'd opted for Plan Bomb.

"What man?" Muttonchops said.

I cocked my head as if to say: Do I need to utter the words?

"What's that in your hand?" Moustache asked.

"This?" I lifted the jug. "Oh, this is a gallon of high explosive wired to the dead man's switch in my right hand. This is to keep everything nice and calm. Peace through security and all that."

They retreated a few steps. "Wait," Moustache said, squinting at me. "You're that guy."

I cocked a hip. "I am indeed that guy, yessir."

"What the hell's with that costume?"

"Only expressing my individuality," I said, shifting foot to foot in a half-assed karate move, just like the King himself.

Now Muttonchops recognized me, too. "You got some balls, showing up here."

"Look," I said. "I'm sorry I've killed some of you guys. It was just business. I'm here to make amends, but that means I got to see the man."

"Not with that explosive, you're not," Muttonchops said.

"I'll make it worth his while," I offered.

A new voice from the shadows of the overhang: "How's that?"

"I'm offering victory," I told the darkness.

The gloom parted like a curtain, and Howard, the leader of the Rough Riders, stepped into the lot. He was a thick slab of beef in a white shirt with rhinestone buttons, his leg muscles barely contained within dusty jeans, his feet sheathed in shiny black cowboy boots. In contrast to Muttonchops and Moustache, he wore a gray ten-gallon hat. His left hand rested on a silver .45 in a leather hip holster.

Despite his hilarious idea of casual dress, Howard was someone you messed with at your peril. The Rough Riders ran a protection racket around these parts, and they were more than willing to ride down a varmint in the middle of the street at high noon, if it came to that. Some of them were former cops, which is why the NYPD let them get away with recreating Deadwood.

Howard moved in front of his men. "Give me one good reason not to kill you right now and bury you out back."

"Because if my hand slips off this neat little switch," I said, holding up my right hand, "we're all on a first-class trip to Mars."

"Yeah? That a real bomb?"

"You remember Frank Jenkins?"

"Big Bone Frank? Yeah."

"I'm the guy who wired up that obnoxious pink Cadillac of his, so yeah, I know my way about explosives." I tensed my thumb. "Want to find out?"

He sighed. "Just tell us what you want, you crazy idiot."

"I want to give you everything. The Rockaway Mob's every stash and safe house that I know of. I'm ready to sing, baby."

"Let's say you're not full of bullshit. What you want in return?"

I thought about it. Really thought about it. Nothing clarifies your thinking like a man ready to quick-draw on you. And then it came to me, a perfect diamond of an idea, dropped right into my hands by a benevolent God.

"Absolutely nothing," I said.

Howard's lips twisted in confusion. "The fuck?"

"I'm out of this life. But my retirement's short-lived as long as The Dean's alive. So someone needs to kill him before he can kill me."

"It's like that."

"It's like that. How well you know Long Island City?"

"Okay, I guess."

"The Dean's there most days. At the Pot O' Gold. A real craphole, but there's only two doors to cover in and out. You want where those Rockaway pricks store their goods, they got one place in Jackson Heights, another in downtown Brooklyn. Heavy security, but nothing that strapping lads like you can't handle." I rattled off the addresses for both those places, hoping that their memorization skills were better than their fashion sense.

Once I finished speaking, Howard nodded once. "If you're lying to us…"

"Yeah, yeah, you'll do something outlandish like tie my limbs to four horses, draw and quarter me. Like I said, I'm out. Have a nice day."

Without waiting for a reply, I turned and left, swinging the jug at my hip. I hoped that Howard took me at my word, because there was no way I could tackle The Dean and all of his men with a sunny smile and a couple of firearms. At least if the Rough Riders wiped them out, Dash would be satisfied enough to leave me alone.

When I reached Linden Boulevard, I stripped away the car radio I'd taped to the front of the jug, along with the wiring, and helped myself to a sip of watery Kool-Aid. As fake bombs went, it was pretty delicious.

# 15

**TWO HUNDRED MILES** from Brooklyn, Walker made a point of keeping under the speed limit, praying that no cop would pull him over to admire the car. His identification would check out, but the ripped suit and the smell of smoke might raise some questions. The pistol was tucked under the driver's seat, the rifle stashed in the trunk, and Walker had no intention of causing trouble until he crossed the East River.

In New Jersey, he noted more police presence: helicopters overhead, cruisers howling down the left lane every few minutes. Raindrops spattered the windshield, blurring the slowing traffic. An electronic road sign flashed dire warnings about weather and delays. Trapped behind a truck, Walker sighed and flicked on the radio. The newscaster babbled about explosive vests and fundamentalism. A guest interrupted to wonder if the country was in trouble. When is the country not in trouble, Walker almost shouted back.

The storm passed as soon as he crossed the Brooklyn Bridge. Entering the borough of his birth felt as warm and welcoming as slipping back into that bespoke suit after all his time up north. The stately apartment buildings shaded with a couple decades' worth of car exhaust and industrial soot, the dingy pagodas with barred windows, the hip eateries where bright white light reflected off blonde wood—he loved every inch of it. The sight of a crushed beer-can on the rain-slick sidewalk brought back memories of his teenage years in Bushwick, and the summer parties where he would crouch in a cool corner with a moisture-beaded bottle of beer, listening to tattooed gargoyles discuss the finer points of music and heroin: His years before the military, and all the messiness after.

When Walker turned onto Metropolitan Avenue and Driggs, he opened the glove compartment and removed a slim plastic fob, pressed a button. Down the block, at the base of a steel building as angular as a knife, a garage door rose. He maneuvered into a concrete cube lined with other luxury vehicles, backing into his designated space with inches to spare on either side. The Aston Martin was not a vehicle you parked on the street, no matter how gentrified this neighborhood had become in the past decade.

An elevator took him to the third floor, where he unlocked the blank metal door that led to his condo. After throwing the four deadbolts, he shed his shoes on a small rug in the entranceway and padded into his place for the first time in many months.

The interior of his apartment was a spread from an upscale furniture catalogue, spare and pale, with some whimsical touches. The Buddha in the living room, smiling from a deep shelf built into the wall. The framed, yellowing Wanted poster for John Dillinger in the hallway leading to the bathroom. Walker liked to think this place had the most character of any unit in the building, although he knew that particular bar was not hard to clear. His neighbors on all sides were finance bros, the kind who decorated mostly with empty bottles of vodka and pizza boxes.

Every surface had a fine coating of dust. Walker never employed a cleaning service. It would take an hour to wipe everything down, once he completed some pressing tasks. He peeled off his ruined suit and folded it neatly before depositing it, with a sigh, atop a pile of faded and torn clothing in the hallway closet. It always hurt to lose a good two-piece, although he had seven more in the bedroom.

After disposing of his ripped ensemble, he showered and dressed in a pair of designer jeans and a plain white t-shirt before heading into the kitchen, where he ground a few ounces of the ultra-caffeinated coffee he liked.

While he waited for the coffee to steep in the French press, he walked into the tiny office off the kitchen and spun the dial on the Döttling faux-antique safe beside the desk. The heavy door opened to reveal a wood-lined tray honeycombed with five circular holes, each filled with an expensive watch that glittered under the safe's dim light. The deep drawer beneath the tray held a few stacks of cash, three passports, a handful of phones, and an old (and much beloved) pair of brass knuckles.

Back in the living room, he sank into the oversized leather chair beside the window, sipping his giant mug of coffee. Despite the shower, he could still smell the smoke on his skin. He made a phone call. The man on the other side suggested meeting at Walker's favorite bar, which was no surprise.

With an hour to burn, he flicked on the television. More death and destruction, on every channel. He raised the remote, about to turn it off, when the image cut to a Tesla parked in Union Square, its windshield spattered red, a pixelated mess hanging out the open driver's window. An unusual murder in Manhattan, a voice droned. Another cut, to a familiar mugshot of the prime suspect, handsome and heavy-jawed.

Walker settled back in his chair, smiling. That was Fiona's boyfriend for you: too flashy for his own good, without much to back it up. At least that confirmed his earlier guess, that the two of them had headed back to New York. You still got your hunting instincts, old man.

It also ratcheted up the urgency of his mission. Fifty minutes later, he headed four blocks east—and found his favorite bar erased.

How many nights had he spent at a back table in that pleasant stinkhole, smoking small Cuban cigars in defiance of the city's health laws, as he downed pint after pint? But during his time in Canada, someone had purchased the Dog and *gentrified* it into a monstrosity.

The new owners had painted the walls sky-blue and hung velvet paintings of bulldogs every few feet. They had replaced the tables with long picnic tables designed to foster love and community. The speakers overhead blared a pop song that sounded like a castrato trapped in a video arcade.

As he ordered a microbrew at the bar, Walker felt like he was attending a wake for someone that nobody in the room had liked. Bearded kids kept their heads down, dour and silent as they tapped away at their phones. He remembered how, in the nights following the collapse of the Twin Towers, people had crowded the bars, went home with strangers, knocked on their neighbors' doors for the first time: anxious for any sort of connection, to feel united with the living. Most of the people in this bar had been small children at the turn of the century, and grew up with the omnipresent fear of the hijacked airplane, the backpack stuffed with explosives left under a bus seat. They were too frightened by existence to do anything other than stare at little screens.

His contact, sitting at the picnic table closest to the rear wall, blended into these fancy environs as well as a hyena in a nursery. The cheery lights glinted off the man's bald head, well-hatched with deep scars. The music seemed to ratchet something in his body inch by painful inch, his hands gripping his full pint glass harder and harder.

"Dash. Long time no see," Walker said, taking a seat where he could see the bar and front door. Two old warriors perched beside one another, drawing anxious side-glances from the kids.

Dash's eyes widened in fake surprise. "I'm amazed, man," he said. "I've never seen a ghost before."

Walker shrugged. "Told you I retired."

"Yes, you did," Dash said. "But you wouldn't believe the rumors. For months everybody was convinced someone had finally double-tapped you, tossed the body in the water. When you didn't wash up, they said someone buried you in a foundation somewhere."

"People love to chat, don't they?"

"Anyway, so now you're back." Dash flashed his teeth. "And I bet it's because of your dear daughter."

Walker shrugged. "She's been a busy girl."

"You approve of her lifestyle?"

"No, but she's going to do what she wants. At least she's really good at what she does, even if it isn't very nice."

"Well, she's been doing unkind things for a pretty nasty crew. We're talking the sort of guys who'd sell their mothers into sexual slavery for a buck ninety-five."

"Charming." Walker leaned close. "You'll watch how you talk about my kid."

Dash raised his hands, palms out. "No offense. I know what it's like, not being around a lot for my daughter. I feel guilty, too."

"Now you're just poking me."

"Can't resist. You're too serious."

"I know I could've been around more for her," Walker said, refusing to let it go. "But I had a job to do. As did you. I've tried to have a normal relationship with her. I'm still trying. Don't mention it again, or I'll tell people that you're speaking to me. That's a potential career-ender for you."

Dash winked. "Or a career-maker."

Walker took a sip of beer. "Color me intrigued."

"Things haven't changed since you were shooting folks in the head for Uncle Sam. The FBI is almost totally focused on stopping terrorism. We're also tasked with pushing back against the cartels, along with our good friends at the DEA. Which doesn't leave a lot of budget or manpower for anything else."

"That's why you pay contractors like me."

"And quite handsomely, I might add. You made what, a thousand dollars a day in Iraq?"

"Hazard pay," Walker said, neglecting to mention the real

payday that had taken place in Baghdad, near the end of his last contract. Some off-the-books work with a few trusted friends, working off a tip yanked out of a former Republican Guard colonel (along with most of the man's teeth). Why deal with red tape and taxes when you can walk away with millions of Saddam's bunker dollars?

"More than I've ever seen in my paycheck. I should have gone freelance, instead of carrying a badge." Dash leaned back. "The guys your daughter works for, the Rockaway Mob, they're small fry compared to the other groups on our list, but they're a rough crew. Twenty, thirty years ago, we'd have a task force dedicated to bringing them down. These days, we can't spare the agents."

"I get the idea," Walker said. "And I think I know where you're going with this."

"Let's say—speaking hypothetically—that a real hero destroyed the Rockaway Mob. Dismantled their operations, made their people disappear for good. If something like that occurred, the FBI would certainly owe that person a big favor."

"Speaking hypothetically, what kind of favor?"

"In this hypothetical world, there's only so much the FBI could do on a local level. That being said, I think the FBI could persuade the NYPD and the DA to stop caring about the hero's daughter. I imagine they'd appreciate the Rockaway Mob going bye-bye. It's in their backyard, after all."

"What about the daughter's loser boyfriend?"

"Are we talking about dropping all charges for him, or making sure nobody finds the body?"

Walker made a three-act play of puzzling it over. "Dropping all charges, I guess. Unless he opens his smart mouth at the wrong moment."

"I'm sure something could be arranged."

"Whatever the deal, this hero would need it in writing. Signed, sealed, delivered."

"We might not have time for lawyers." Dash checked his watch, a battered warhorse that Walker remembered from their days in the field together. "But you have my word—and you know my word is good—that we'll work this out for you. The question is, are we good?"

"What kind of timetable are we talking? I'm on a tight schedule."

"Soon as possible. Oh yeah, there's another player, as well. This psycho lunatic who also used to freelance for us on occasion. I'll be honest with you: I turned to him first. But he's such a loose cannon, I don't know if he'll actually come through. You're much more reliable."

"You always were a big fan of double-booking."

"It's called being thorough. So, with all that in mind, we good?"

Walker downed his beer. "We're good. You have eyes on my kid?"

"Queens, last I heard, which was a couple hours ago. This new system we have, facial recognition and geolocation, ultra-fast, it's really something to see. Rang cherries on some security-cam footage, she and her boyfriend running across a street. Since then, nothing." Dash slapped the table and stood to leave. "I'll email the intel I got. Same address?"

"Yeah." Walker stood.

"You good on equipment? I have a connection, lend you some heavy-gauge stuff."

Walker thought about the foldaway panel in the rear of his closet, and the things in the hideaway behind it. "I always bring my own tools."

Dash grinned. "I'd expect nothing less."

Walker drained his beer, offered Dash a quick salute, and marched for the exit. The lighting, the music, the hipsters seemed to grate on him more with each passing step. By the time he reached the door, his jaw was clenched tight, his hands in loose fists. It took every ounce of his considerable self-control to not slam a boot through the door, or snatch a random glass off the bar and send it through the window with its idiotic puppy stencil.

Back on the street, he filled his lungs with cool night air and held it. The rage had nothing to do with those angel-headed hipsters, of course. It was all about Fiona. He was going to take all that rage and use it to rip apart everyone threatening her. And if Bill didn't survive—well, Walker always told Fiona that she should trade up.

His phone rang.

# 16

**A BIG BLACK** car angled for the gleaming bull's eye of the Holland Tunnel. In the front passenger seat, Sully took an epic hit of his most powerful weed before passing the joint to his three men squeezed in the back. The driver squinted through the smoggy windshield, unfamiliar with the terrain. It was a big risk, smoking up as they neared one of the most-surveilled places on the East Coast, but Sully liked how the danger amped him up.

Besides, if a cop pulled them over, the weed might end up the least of their problems. In the trunk, nestled beneath a geologic layer of dirty clothes, Sully had tucked five automatic rifles—one for each man in the car. It was a lot of firepower for a straight-forward job, but Sully believed that, when it came to Walker, overkill was a virtue.

# 17

**THE CONSTRUCTION ELEVATOR** was little more than a cage with a control box and a sliding door. As it ascended, the wind whistled through its steel grating, a mournful sound interrupted every few seconds by The Dean cracking his knuckles. The popping bones made the men around him twitch as one. Through the grating, they had a sweeping view of the Queens waterfront, the glass skyscrapers glittering in the dusk.

It never ends, The Dean mused. You can kill your rivals. You can kill your business partners. You can kill your head of security. But the problems never stop cropping up, because criminality attracts morons who literally can't function in normal society. Which makes it similar to academia, when you really think about it. Why did I bother leaving the university?

The Dean turned to Rex and asked: "What else was in there?"

"Some money," Rex muttered.

The Dean balled his hands into fists. "I need grand totals, boy. It was delivery day, after all."

Rex swallowed hard. "Five million, I think?"

The men behind The Dean stepped back until their spines flattened against the grating. They were hulking as football players, and tough, but none wanted to deal with The Dean throwing fists in an enclosed space. They considered their take-home pay generous enough to deal with their employer's eccentricities.

But this time, The Dean surprised them. Instead of trying to slam Rex's head into the wall, he closed his eyes and rotated his neck until the joint popped. "Seems high," he said, so quietly it was almost lost in the grinding of the elevator's gears.

"Our friends up north paid some tribute. We were using this place as the waypoint. Figured it'd be okay with the added security."

"Yes, if any of you knuckle-draggers were halfway competent," The Dean said. "Honestly, this all comes down to killing two people. Is that really too much to ask?"

Before anyone could reply, the elevator thumped to a halt, and the door rattled back to reveal pure chaos. Someone had torn down part of the plastic wall that shielded the weed forest from the elements, the precious plants rustling in the high-altitude breeze. Mercs in body armor stood among the rows of plants, their pistols aimed at the steel door of the panic room.

As The Dean strode into the forest, Crow Man scuttled beside him. "Thank you for swinging by," he said, as if The Dean was there for a quick drink and a chat.

The Dean had no use for small talk. Jutting his chin at the steel door, he said: "Is there a keypad?"

"No. Just one button, on the inside. Doesn't lock unless you hit it. They hit it." Crow Man punched air as he danced from foot to foot, clearly agitated.

The Dean pointed at the tables to their left, and the tool boxes beneath. "How long to cut through it? I trust you have something suitable down there?"

Crow Man snorted laughter. "It's two feet of steel. You got a nuke in your back pocket?"

"An answer, please."

Crow Man punched air again. "I don't know, a day or two? If they don't shoot back, or try anything tricky?"

They arrived at the door, and The Dean craned his head, examining the seamless steel. "Can we cut off their oxygen?"

"Again, I don't know. I think there's a vent somewhere." Crow Man waved a finger at the ceiling. "Like, on the roof. But what if we cut off their air, and they don't come out? It's not just the money in there. They got my favorite toys, too."

The Dean shuddered to think what might serve as the favorite toys of Crow Man, who once snorted so much bad meth he tried to build a time machine from a tape recorder and a car battery. The guy might have been a stellar chemist and a better botanist, but sane he was not.

"Then we can cut through it at our leisure." The Dean sneered at the door. "When last I checked, I owned this building."

"We got a time limit on that money, chief," Crow Man said. "Folks expecting delivery real soon."

"Ah, yes. Right." The Dean cracked his knuckles again. "Any way to communicate in?"

Crow Man nodded. "They have an intercom. It's got a camera, too."

They heard a soft click, barely audible over the gurgle of the ventilation system, followed by a thunderous voice: *"Is that my good buddy?"*

The Dean startled. "Bill?"

*"It is!"* Biblical Bill boomed from a speaker in the ceiling. *"Hey, honey, look at the screen! It's that dimwit who used to pay us!"*

The Dean, his cheeks reddening, ran his hands over the door-frame until he found the black dot of a miniature camera lens. "Come out of there, you little shit," he hissed into it. "Or we'll only make it that much more unpleasant when we get inside."

*"Um, let me think about that."* A click, and a long pause.

The Dean froze.

Another click. *"After a lengthy period of careful deliberation, we've decided to decline your offer. Fuck off and die."*

The Dean stepped back, struggling against the smile tugging

the edges of his lips. Despite his rage, he felt almost giddy. When was the last time he'd faced an interesting opponent?

"Dear boy," The Dean said, removing his suit jacket and draping it carefully on the nearest table. "We find ourselves at a bit of an impasse here. The unstoppable force—that's me—has encountered an immovable object. That's the room you're in."

Click. *"Wait, let me guess: you're going to try and bore us out of here."*

"Oh, it's going to be more kinetic than that, don't worry." The Dean rolled up his sleeves. "By the way, a hearty hello to Fiona. We have unfinished business, dear."

*"That's right,"* Fiona laughed. *"My boot hasn't finished up your ass yet."*

The Dean's memories drifted to destroying the Ferrari that afternoon. How its sleek metal had crumpled as easily as paper under his confident blows. It was a real thrill, ruining something beautiful. Like Fiona's face.

*"Near as I can count,"* Fiona continued, *"there's maybe four million dollars in here."* The amplified sound of shredding, loud as a fender-bender. *"Whoops, there goes a hundred bucks. How much of this can we rip up before you get in here?"*

From his hip pocket, The Dean drew a small tan bag, made of wrinkled material. He shook it so they could hear the coins jangling inside. "Bill," he said. "You remember Pop, correct? Such a terrifying individual, his bedridden state didn't stop people from shitting themselves in his presence. You could say he had real big balls."

Crow Man cocked an eyebrow, as if to say: This is too crazy, even for me.

The Dean shook his change purse. "Turns out, his balls weren't all that impressive. I can barely fit three quarters in here." Returning it to his pocket, he shot his cuffs and smiled.

*"If you do try to get in,"* Fiona added, *"there's a couple of propane tanks in the corner here. We might die, but we'll make a real bonfire on our way out, understand?"*

"Perfectly." The Dean spun on his heel and paced down the

nearest marijuana row, the leaves brushing his shoulders. The merc in his path stepped aside, and The Dean paused. Something clipped to the man's vest interested him a good deal. In fact, it presented an elegant solution to this siege.

# 18



**WATCHING THE DEAN** pace on the tiny video screen, Bill offered a hearty thumbs-up. "As much as I hate this guy, he did the world a favor by taking out Pop. That dude always freaked me out. Not to the point where I shit myself, I hasten to add."

Fiona tore open an energy bar and wolfed it down. It tasted like crap, but she wanted the calories and sugar. As her adrenaline faded, her pains returned with fangs. Her back muscles twinged around the staples, her bruises throbbed, and her left eyelid had decided this was the perfect time to start twitching. "What are they doing?"

"The Dean's lecturing everyone, as usual." Bill wiped the sweat from his forehead. "It's getting hotter. Is there a fan or something in here?"

"Probably not installed yet," Fiona said, waving her hand below the ceiling vent. "You want some water?"

"I'm okay." Stacking two bundles of money into a soft stool, Bill sat with his back against the wall. "Want a quickie?"

Fiona grinned. "Maybe when we're not surrounded by an army of gunmen."

"Oh, come on. You mean the prospect of being shot to death isn't a turn-on?"

Digging into the box beside her, Fiona held up two more energy bars. "You want chocolate or vanilla? Better get some food in you. Could be a long night."

"Chocolate." He tore the wrapping off the bar and chewed. It tasted like flavored drywall, but better than nothing. He pined for a shot of espresso, and maybe a shortbread cookie to go with it. Heck, why not fantasize about sitting outside a Barcelona cafe, watching the crowds walk through the heat and sunlight?

"Can I ask you something? It's something that's been in my head for weeks, but I haven't..."

Fiona rolled her eyes. "Spit it out, sweetie. No time like the present."

Bill took his time chewing the last of his energy bar. "If we make it out of here, what are we going to do? We can't run forever."

"Our retirement plans hinge entirely on neutralizing every fucker out there," Fiona said. "If we figure that out, we can do anything we want. Where do you want to go?"

"Spain?"

"Sure." Fiona slapped a stack of money. "With this sort of cash, we'd live like royalty."

"Where you want to live?"

"Montreal, maybe. I went there once, for work, remember? Cool place. We could learn French, pretend we're hipsters, listen to Leonard Cohen in bars."

"Too cold in the winter."

Fiona smiled. "The tropics didn't work out too well for us."

"My big lesson from that: No matter what, we gotta stick together. My brains, your brawn." Bill held up his hands, palms out, as if she might smack him. "Just kidding. You know I can take care of myself. Everything that's happened to us over the past couple days? I think I'm getting more of a taste for the rough stuff."

"Well, don't get too used to it. I'm trying to cut back. Wherever we go next, I don't want to hurt people anymore, okay?" Fiona lifted her pistol and ejected the magazine. "I'm forever done with this bullet shit. It's blades to ploughshares."

"If we don't kill anything other than beers for the rest of our natural lives, I'm fine with that," Bill said. "Whatever works. I love you."

"I love you, too." She snapped home the magazine. "The only moment I ever wavered, it was in Oklahoma, when I wondered if you'd actually dumped me. That night I caught up with you, I was angry as hell."

"When I left New York, I was worried that if you knew anything, if I'd told you anything, that The Dean would have killed you to get to me."

"And you were probably right. Remember how my father used to vanish?" Her hands waved like birds. "Just pick up and go, no word, and reappear six months later, sometimes with a new wound or a tattoo or whatever? I think that warped something in my head. I can't let someone leave without them telling me why."

Bill tensed as he thought about Fiona's father: wiry and tough, with eyes like chips of stone and a shoulder-heavy walk that broadcast he was always ready for violence. "Where's your Dad right now? If he's close. Maybe he can help."

Fiona laughed. "Yeah, and after he killed everyone threatening us, he'd probably take a few potshots at you, just for old times' sake."

Bill remembered how the last family meeting ended. So did his left knee, which sparkled with phantom pain. "I don't get why he doesn't like me. I always tried to be nice to him."

"Yeah, and you both love the same pretentious suits and cars and stuff." Reaching over, Fiona patted his hand. "I've tried telling him that you're a sweet guy, but he doesn't buy it."

Bill took her hand and held it. "Maybe it's because you said I'm sweet."

"I don't understand."

"Your Dad is the ultimate hard-ass. He probably wants you to have a boyfriend who can kill four people with a teacup."

"Next time you see him, tell him you decapitated that dude with a Tesla. He'll be real impressed."

"That was out of character for me."

"You killed that sheriff in the farmhouse."

"Well, you massacred all his deputies. Along with that Elvis guy."

Fiona winced. "I feel bad about that. About Elvis, at least."

Bill chose his words carefully. "You can't predict what people will do. You were just trying to protect us."

She sighed. "I hope so."

On the intercom screen, The Dean waved a hand at two of his men, who disappeared into the weed forest. Something was afoot.

"I was serious about calling your Dad," Bill said.

"Why?"

"Because he can kill four people with a pencil. Besides, it's better than just sitting here, waiting for them to cut their way in."

Fiona shook her head. "There are other people we can try. Simon, maybe. He likes money. He hates The Dean."

Bill read her face. "You're scared."

"A little bit, yeah. I haven't called my Dad for help since I was a teenager. It makes me uncomfortable."

"You know what else will make you uncomfortable?"

"Those guys outside shooting us full of holes?"

"That's right. Calling him, it's a fantastic idea, if I do say so myself."

Fiona stood and tossed a block of money into the center of the room. She repeated that process with another million dollars, and then another, until she had a platform of cash roughly four feet high. "Don't get full of yourself or anything," she said, stepping onto it. "I once found you dangling from a gantry by your ankles."

Bill snorted. "That little bartender knocked me out."

"A likely story." Fishing a coin from her pocket, Fiona loosened the two screws holding the ceiling vent in place. After handing the vent to Bill, she pulled out her phone and extended it into the shaft as far as her arm could reach, the lit screen tilted toward her. If the phone was outside the panic room's concrete shell, it might catch a bit of signal…

*Please give me some good luck today.*

The phone flashed one bar. She almost yelped with joy.

"It work?" Bill asked, his voice rising with hope.

"Maybe," she said, dialing a number she knew by heart. It rang, and she tapped the speaker button. Come on, she thought. For the first time in years, I need you, so pick up, pick up, pick up—

A click, followed by a voice deep and rumbling as a rock-slide. "Yeah?"

Relief washed through her, so heady she laughed. "Dad?"

"Kiddo?"

"Yeah," she said. "Hey, listen, where are you?"

"If you're still in New York, closer than you think," he said. "Bill with you?"

"Hey, Walker," Bill called out. "How's it going?"

"Fine, Bill. Kiddo, let's get to it. You're in trouble. I saw on the news."

"We're in a panic room," Fiona said. "My former boss is out-side. They can't get in, but we can't stay here forever."

"The Rockaway Mob?"

"Yeah. The Dean, plus most of his guys, I'm betting. I'm sorry, this is humiliating."

"Actually, it's good news for me. I'll explain more later. What's the address?"

She rattled it off. "It's a building under construction. Top floor. I'm warning you, there are a lot of men here."

"The more the merrier." Walker chuckled. "You armed?"

"Yeah, with barely a pop gun."

"Still better than no gun. Hold tight, I'm on my way."

"Why are you here?"

"What?"

"In the city?"

"I just said: I saw you on the news. Figured you needed the

help. Plus, it gave me an excuse to leave Canada. It's boring up there, and not always in a good way."

"Well, we're glad you're here."

"So am I, sweetie. How's your battery life?"

"Twenty percent."

"Then turn it off. Call me back in forty-five minutes. Got it?"

"Got it."

"See you soon."

Withdrawing her hand from the shaft, Fiona powered the phone down. She debated whether to reattach the vent. No, she would just need to unscrew it again. Besides, maybe leaving it open would drain off some of this sticky heat.

Bill held out a hand, escorting her from atop the money pile. "That was lucky," he said.

"Oh yeah. It'd been awhile."

"When we were down in Cuba, you didn't try ringing him up?"

Fiona slipped the weapon into her waistband. "Truthfully, I did. Once. He didn't pick up. He gets weird sometimes, disappears to this place in northern Quebec. It's like a retreat for old spies, someplace they can hang out and drink, fight over who set up the most coups or whatever."

"Maybe we should have run there."

"No chance. Very exclusive. You need at least four former dictators in your phone contacts to get in. I'm kidding, but sort of not."

"And your Dad hates me, so there's that."

"You're just not his type, but that's okay." Fiona kissed him on the cheek. "What matters is, you're my type."

Bill kissed her forehead before turning to the intercom screen. The Dean stood in the middle of the floor, his hands on his hips, chin upturned, dramatically lit by grow-lights. He looked like a bronze statue to assholedom, something you'd set up in a park for the dogs to piss on. What was he waiting for?

Something rattled in the ceiling. Fiona stepped away from the vent, her hand skimming her pistol-grip. Her nostrils flared, scenting vomit. No, it was a different smell: acrid, almost like a burning. She knew it well, and adrenaline spiked her blood. As Bill retreated against the wall, she grabbed one of the water-cooler jugs and dragged into the center of the room. Her fingers tore at the thick plastic covering the neck, not finding a grip, slipping. The rattling overhead louder now, the smell beginning to sting her eyes.

"We can toss it out," Bill said, reaching for the red button.

"No," she snapped, her fingernails biting into the plastic, peeling it away.

The tear gas grenade dropped through the open vent, trailing a glossy stream of smoke.

Fiona snatched it in midair. The metal hot, burning her fingers, as she stuffed it down the neck of the jug. It splashed into the water, and she lifted her leg and slammed her heel over the opening. Her eyes throbbing now, tears frying her cheeks, her throat shut tight. Panic clawing in her skull, yelling at her to run, scream, cry.

"Oh shit," Bill said, coughing and sneezing as he lifted another jug away from the wall.

Water will deactivate the tear gas, she wanted to say, only her throat refused to open. She forced herself to take a slow breath, ignoring how it made her chest burn.

Then another inhale.

Then another.

*You're okay. You'll make it.*

Bill had the plastic torn off the second jug, and she bent forward so he could pour water over her face, the blessed coolness sweeping away the snot and tears and drool.

"Oh baby, that was the coolest thing," Bill murmured.

She stuck her hands beneath the waterfall pouring from her head, to wash the gas particles away. From the way her fingers ached, the grenade had left burns. Her breaths came a little easier now, but she knew from past experience her lungs would burn for hours. Just another injury for the ledger. At least her vision had cleared to a crimson murk.

Beneath her heel, the grenade had turned the water milky.

"Tape," she croaked, pointing to the metal box, and Bill scrambled for it. A minute later, they had the top of the jug mummified with duct tape, and she could step away. She plucked an energy drink from the stash and drained it, hating the taste but loving how it soothed her throat.

"Where'd you learn to do that?" Bill asked, awed.

"Tulsa," she said. Dispatched by The Dean to solve a problem with a rival, Fiona had found herself in the middle of a riot sparked by a police shooting. From the roof of a burnt-out store, she had watched as protesters dragged plastic water-barrels to the front line and dunked every incoming tear-gas canister.

She said: "How do I look? Fantastic?"

They regarded each other. Fiona with her red eyes and swollen cheeks, her skin stippled with cuts, her body crooked from aches and pains. Bill with his bruised face and bloody knuckles, his front teeth loose, his collar crusted with snot and tears. There was no doubt in Fiona's mind that they shared enough contusions, small fractures, and low-grade organ damage to make a medical billing clerk salivate.

"If we have to go to the ER," Bill said, "we're going to win Patients of the Week."

"At least we have the cash to pay for it." Tossing the empty energy-drink bottle into the corner, she opened a second one and chugged it. Her feet splashed in an inch of water as she walked over to the intercom and hit the button.

*"Missed us, fuckers,"* she boomed into the weed forest, and had the immense pleasure of watching The Dean shake his fists.

The vent must connect to the roof, where The Dean had sent at least one of his men. She bet they wouldn't drop down a fragmentation grenade, but they might try another round of tear gas or pepper spray if the siege dragged on too long. We need to go on offense, Fiona thought, before they hit us again.

"I have a good idea for getting us out of here," she told Bill, pulling out her phone. "But I'm warning you now, it's also pretty damn weird."

# 19

**WALKER ROLLED OUT** a blanket on the gravel rooftop and knelt down, pulling the rifle-parts from his bag. He fumbled a little when assembling the weapon. He estimated the range at one-fifty yards, light wind. Through the scope he saw people silhouetted against the plastic sheeting that stretched around the inner perimeter of the tower floor, their shapes bulky and spiked in ways that suggested body armor, armaments, serious firepower. Frantic movement, a hoarse shout lost in the wind moaning off the river.

What had Fiona told him once about her employers? They shot first, asked questions last. Fierce types. That was okay, actually. Aggression could be turned against itself, like a rabid dog chewing its own legs.

On the walk from his apartment to the rooftop Walker had stopped in a fast-food place on Vernon to purchase a large soda with fries. To an outsider it might have seemed callous, stopping for snacks while his child sat in a panic room surrounded by armed men, but he trusted Fiona to keep everything locked down until he assessed the situation. If he wanted to stay useful, he needed the calories.

The lights reflecting off the sheeting blocked his view of the interior. He needed to wait for his moment. Flat on his stomach, eye to the scope, he tried to settle into the blanket as best he could, gravel biting his elbows and knees through the thin fabric. When was the last time he had fired this rifle at a human being? Managua?

In addition to the long-gun, he had a pistol with a silencer in the rifle bag, and enough ammunition to last him all night, if things came to that. As much as he had enjoyed his little self-imposed exile up north, the ritual of assembling his armory had activated a deep and pleasurable circuit in his head. He imagined that a chef preparing for a long dinner shift, or a monk squaring away the temple for morning services, felt much the same way.

On the gravel beside him, his phone rang. He tapped the screen without shifting his eye from the scope, expecting to hear Fiona. But the voice that filled his earbud was unwelcome.

"Hey," Sully said. "We're in the city, thought we'd swing by, have a chat."

"You know the first rule of threatening people, Sully?" Walker helped himself to a fry.

Sully snarled: "You're always saying I'm threat—"

"The first rule is, you don't do it," Walker said, talking over him. "If you're going to do someone harm, you don't warn them first. I used to think you were such a smart guy, when you're really just another punk. What do you want?"

"Just a talk, dude. We can work things out."

Walker shifted his gaze to the phone, extended a finger to end the call. Stopped. "You know what? I'll take you up on that."

"Okay?" Sully sounded surprised. "Where you at?"

Walker gave him the address and hung up. That paranoid bastard would expect some sort of trap, of course, but that was okay. A long time ago, in the jungle, Walker had learned to treat confusion as one of his best friends.

Another five minutes passed. His phone buzzed. Fiona had always been a very punctual girl. "Hey," he said, his finger skimming the rifle's trigger.

"You in position?" All business, that one. Just like her old man.

"Got overwatch, sweetie. What's your play?"

"Loud. Soon as you see anything, if you could start killing everyone in sight, that'd be a big help, okay?"

"Okay. There's something going on in there. Lots of guys running around. I can't quite tell what they're doing, but probably nothing good." For the first time, he wondered how much cover the edge of the roof would provide if these guys shot back at him.

"Just be ready," she said, and clicked off.

On the street below, a black sedan with a smashed front fender cruised at walking pace. Walker shifted and tracked it with the rifle, but the angle made it impossible to see the driver. The sedan squealed to a stop in front of the construction site. From his elevated position, Walker could see the double-wide trailer behind the site's front gate, and the guard who stepped onto its small porch with a submachine gun in his hand.

The driver must have spied the guard through the gate, because the sedan roared forward, its tires leaving faint drifts of smoke. Walker heard its engine echoing off the buildings as it disappeared into the neighborhood. The guard shrugged and headed back inside.

So that was interesting. Who was this other player?

# 20

**FIONA REGRETTED HANGING** up so fast. Given everything that might happen in the next few minutes, a part of her wondered if she should have offered more of a goodbye, something heartfelt, in case something happened. But that had never been her relationship with her father: they never had to say the words. They just knew.

It wasn't quite time for fireworks yet. Sitting back, popping bullets from her magazine into her lap, Fiona remembered the heist, five years before, that had put her in a panic room almost exactly like this one. The big difference: instead of sex dolls and energy bars, that room had held a Modigliani painting, along with some mighty fine watches and dusty Civil War antiques. The Dean had wanted the painting ("Not that I particularly like Modigliani, that bohemian caricature," he had told her, "but an asset is an asset..."), so Fiona had broken in, tied up the owner in the kitchen, and snatched the painting.

In short, a perfect job: fast, efficient, painless for everyone except the insurance company. On the way out of the panic room, she had grabbed a timepiece from the shelf: the Piaget Altiplano that still sat on Bill's wrist, thin and precise and beautiful. Almost as good as a wedding ring, as far as she was concerned. Emphasis on *almost*.

"Speaking hypothetically," Bill said behind her, "if I unleashed an enormous fart, do you think it would linger in here?"

Love is a weird thing, Fiona thought. An evolutionary trait, maybe, guaranteeing that we don't kill our mates before we have a chance to reproduce.

"It's not going to matter," she said.

"Why?" Bill asked, looking concerned.

"Because we're leaving." Standing, Fiona slammed the magazine into the pistol and walked over to the bicycle beside the pallet. She pushed it free and stood on the pedals, bouncing to test the wheels. It would roll, and that was all that mattered.

"Hold off, Sundance. We have a problem," Bill said, pointing at the intercom screen, which framed The Dean standing in the open space between the weed forest and the panic room. The Dean gestured at a figure kneeling on the concrete before him. Despite the screen's low resolution, Fiona could see the figure's fine suit shredded, his hair a messy tangle, his face black with injury.

"Oh, Simon," Fiona sighed, climbing off the bicycle. Her stomach felt like an elevator car with the cables cut, plunging for the basement.

The Dean tapped his ear, indicating they should listen in.

Bill swiveled past her to hit the intercom button.

"I'm going to deny my usual impulse to speak at length," The Dean said, "and just put it like this: either you come out, or I'm going to exsanguinate dear Simon here."

Bill released the button. "What's that mean?"

"They're going to kill him," Fiona said, and bit her lower lip.

"I got that part. What's 'exsanguinate' mean?"

It was so tempting to hit Bill, until Fiona remembered that he had met Simon a grand total of twice, for no more than fifteen minutes total. There was no way that Bill would ever understand Simon's grand bullshit sessions, and how she could sit with a barely repressed grin as he tried to pick apart her brain, lighting a fresh cigarette every few questions. Bill never had good mentors.

"It means you bleed out," Fiona said, and took a deep breath. She was sick of killing, sure, but she was going to make an exception for The Dean. In fact, choking him out would put a nice little cap on her murder career.

"What do we do?" Bill squeezed her shoulder.

Pushing Bill's hand away, Fiona pressed the intercom button and held it. *"Simon,"* her voice boomed across the floor. *"Don't give that prissy intellectual any satisfaction, okay?"*

Simon turned his battered face to the ceiling. They had taken his signature sunglasses. The graininess of the intercom screen made it hard to see, but he may have winked. Fiona would have expected nothing less.

The Dean snapped his fingers, and one of the mercs walked over with a wicked blade, offered handle-first.

21

**WALKER'S EAR BUZZED,** and he answered: "Yeah."

"Do it," Fiona said, sounding tense.

Walker tucked into the rifle, eye slotted to the scope. "What am I firing at?" Shadows jumped and merged behind the plastic. "I can't see shit."

"Doesn't matter," she said, and through his earpiece Walker could hear a faint crackling. "Just need the noise. Now. Please."

Walker's finger tightened on the trigger. He found a halfway suitable target—a dark splotch that looked like a giant with a machete—and took a deep breath. Held it. Exhaled, and pulled.

# 22

**THE DEAN'S FINGERS** had barely touched the handle of the merc's offered blade when the merc's head exploded, ruining The Dean's suit.

The other mercs, acting on instinct, dove for the concrete, their weapons already unslung. One spied the hole in the plastic that marked the trajectory of Walker's bullet, and fired off a burst that converted a thousand dollars' worth of prime weed into a spray of leaves, stems and dirt.

That was all it took: everyone else with a weapon pulled its trigger, unleashing a storm of lead that shredded the plastic sheeting. Bullets sparked off concrete and steel, echoing into the night.

The Dean wiped a moist sleeve across his face, clearing his eyes, and looked around for Simon. That damn philistine had scrambled off somewhere, probably cowering behind a pillar while The Dean's men decided to wreck this entire harvest.

Retrieving the blade from the floor, The Dean stalked after his prey—but only made it three feet before the panic room door slid open, revealing something that left him, the most prolix of men, utterly speechless for the first time in his life.

# 23

**BILL KNEW HOW** plans could implode.

Years ago, as a favor he quickly regretted, Bill had offered to stage-manage the robbery of a bank vault loaded with a hundred million dollars in precious diamonds. It was a little heavier than his usual scams, but The Dean had faith in Bill's abilities to wrangle a group of psychotic idiots. The vault was protected by the latest in technology: thermal and light sensors, as well as a set of large magnetic plates around the three-foot-thick door. If anyone tried to enter the vault without inputting a twelve-digit code into the keypad, the opening door would break the magnetic field produced by the plates, summoning every cop for two hundred miles around.

Bill found three men with the know-how for the job: an old-school Lock Picker who could, with the aid of his trusty stethoscope and a few other tools, suss out the combination of the vault lock; a punky Kid with some experience in alarms and traps; and a Lunatic who could handle the magnetic plates. Bill's internal warning system, usually so fine-tuned, should have blared when the Lunatic raised his bandaged hands and announced that he had embedded magnets under the skin of his palms, the better to sense the magnetic fields. The rhythms of the galaxy, the man called it. Whatever.

The night of the robbery, things commenced smoothly. Bill sat in a car parked across the street from the bank, the police scanner on the dashboard blissfully silent, sipping the world's worst cup of takeout coffee. From the phone on the seat beside him came the Lock Picker's voice, narrating their progress. With his tingling hands, the Lunatic had duct-taped custom magnets to each of the magnetic plates, keeping the field intact. The Lock Picker had cracked the combination, and the Kid was using hairspray and towels to disable the sensors inside the dark vault.

Even as he mainlined caffeine, Bill felt his body begin to relax. In addition to the diamonds, the lockboxes in the vault supposedly held all manner of ledgers, illicit photos, and blackmail material—more than enough to fuel Bill's projects for the next year or two.

Over the phone, someone began screaming.

Bill shot upright, lukewarm coffee drenching his designer jeans. Over a loud boom, he heard the Lunatic shriek about the rhythms and power of the universe, and he knew the job had gone totally to shit. Bill slapped the glove compartment until it popped open, revealing a small pistol he always tucked there just in case. Then he was out of the car, running toward the bank just as the Kid and the Lock Picker burst through the front doors, bags over their shoulders, their faces hard with panic. They barely made the sidewalk before the bank exploded with harsh light and alarms, loud enough to pulverize Bill's eardrums into a quaking mess.

They dove into the car, Bill fumbling for the ignition as the Lock Picker screamed something about the Lunatic knocking the magnets free and retreating into the vault, ready to meet God. Maybe all those magnets under his skin had screwed with his nerves, but whatever the case, the entire operation was toast. Bill hit the gas and headed for the Queens-Midtown Tunnel, praying that The Dean wouldn't kill any of them for screwing this up.

The police arrested the Lunatic, who confessed only to

wanting to touch the face of the Almighty. Less than five hours later, someone drove a pencil through his neck in a holding cell. And the next morning, The Dean assigned Bill to the Sea Shack, that little restaurant on the rougher end of Rockaway Beach, where he could run his blissfully lower-key scams in peace.

So Bill could tell you all about things going haywire.

Like Fiona's plan, for instance.

How the hell had he agreed to *this* insanity?

The answer was obvious: They had no choice.

# 24

**AS SOON AS** Fiona ended the call with her father, she smacked the big red button that opened the panic room. The door groaned inward, plowing a small wave of murky water over their feet. A bullet sparked off the steel frame and angled into the room, exploding into a box of energy bars, and Bill ducked with a yelp. Fiona dug her heels into the wet concrete, gripped the bike seat, and pushed with all her might.

That exertion made every muscle in her back scream bloody murder, her knees quake, her head throb—but it was all worth it when the bike hissed out of the panic room, gaining a bit of speed on the slight downslope, the sex doll in the saddle already spurting black smoke from its eyes and mouth. By the time it reached the weed forest, the flares and fireworks that Fiona had stuffed into its unmentionables had begun to cook off, red and yellow sparks vomiting from its mouth. Its prim blue pantsuit burst into flames.

The Dean, along with every merc, turned their collective head to watch the abomination cycle past, bubbling and popping.

Fiona leveled her pistol, ready to use this precious instant of distraction to take out as many of these bastards as possible.

That was all according to plan.

What happened next, though, was decidedly not.

The bicycle veered into the line of chemical barrels lining one side of the floor. Bill grabbed Fiona's shoulder and yanked her to the floor as the world flashed white. A storm of flaming weed scraps burst through the gap in the door, sprinkling their backs, as the water around them frothed from the shockwave. Bill's ears popped.

The exterior camera had miraculously survived the explosion. On the intercom screen, Bill saw the bicycle and its plastic rider dissolve into a pillar of flame, screamers and streamers and dazzlers rocketing through space, as the flickering figures of the surviving mercs tried to take cover.

"Think you used enough dynamite there, Butch?" Bill yelled.

"Shut up and get your bag," Fiona hissed. In between wiring up the doll and talking with her father, she had mummified the wrecked duffel bag with the entire roll of duct tape, hopefully making it strong enough to hold all the paper money and gold they had stuffed inside it.

Gritting his teeth, Bill lifted the bag onto his shoulder, and Fiona slid through the doorway into the smoky chaos beyond. The floor was a disaster, coated with dirt and ash and leaves and sliding wet bits. The plastic sheeting torn to shreds. A merc stood to her left, raising a pistol, but before Fiona could squeeze off a shot the right side of his chest exploded, filling the air with pink mist, and he fell.

His tumbling form revealed another merc, who varied from all the other dead and dying men on the floor only by the red bandana wrapped around the lower part of his face. This one managed to lift his AR-15 maybe a foot before the top of his head vaporized.

Fiona was sensing a pattern here.

"Thanks, Dad," she muttered, switching her pistol for the rifle, crouching a moment so she could check the magazine. Fully loaded. Rising, she swept the zone, low and cautious. She passed the doll, reduced to a sludge of bubbling plastic and blackened cardboard atop a pair of pockmarked legs, the bicycle twisted into a black pretzel.

The far end of the floor was a wall of fire, crisping plants, melting plastic, feeding on the scattered bodies. The heat needled her skin. She swept from pillar to pillar, hoping that her father could see well enough through the smoke to cover her back from his faraway perch. Where were Simon and The Dean?

Over the crackle of flames, she heard rumbling machinery. Of course. Moving faster, she angled toward the construction elevator, her traitorous throat itching as she inhaled lungfuls of aerosolized weed, mercs, and plastic. She coughed into an upraised elbow, hoping the sound was lost in the chaos, and approached the edge of the floor. Through the flickering smog she glimpsed the unmistakable figure of The Dean, his arm tight around Simon's neck as he limped toward the open elevator door.

Edging behind the nearest pillar, she called out: "Stop."

The Dean spun, digging a small silver automatic into Simon's chest, near the heart. Simon's cheeks were marked with a dozen rough cuts, his eyes swollen, his hair a gray tangle—but when he saw Fiona, he offered a wolf's smile.

Fiona squinted, judging angles. On a good day, with no injuries, she might have tried to hit the small sliver of The Dean's face she could see over Simon's shoulder. But the rifle trembled in her grip, the iron sights wavering, her eyes watering. Could her Dad see them? Probably not—he would have risked the shot.

"Let him go," Fiona said.

"And then what, you'll let me go?" The Dean laughed. "Not bloody likely, dear."

Fiona sensed Bill limping behind her, and twitched her head to the right: circle around me. He entered her peripheral vision, hunched beneath the weight of the money bag, aiming a pistol with stiff arms. She really would have to teach him proper stance someday.

"A steady return," The Dean said, and took another step backward, pulling Simon with him. "And you had to ruin it."

"Say what?" Fiona took a step forward, mirroring his movement.

"We had a simple goal, my associates and I." Another step. "Provide a steady return for our investors. Profit by any means possible. No different from your typical corporate board, understand?"

"Regular companies don't use bullets," Bill offered.

"Their loss." The Dean's eyes darted between Bill and Fiona, judging which might fire first. "A gun really speeds up negotiations."

Simon sighed and rolled his eyes.

"You should have left us alone," Bill said. "The money I stole from you, kicking this whole thing off, you wouldn't have missed it."

"It wasn't about the money, you ignoramus," The Dean sputtered. "It was about the *principle*."

Simon sighed louder. "Blah, blah, blah," he said, and, quick as a viper, reached up and grabbed the barrel of The Dean's pistol. The Dean pulled the trigger on reflex, but Simon already had the firearm angled up. The bullet plowed through The Dean's head, coating the walls of the construction elevator with all his esoteric knowledge. No great loss.

# 25

**THE POT O' GOLD** had survived New York at its worst. The old timers—what few old timers still lived in Long Island City—could tell you stories of its first owner, Ant Canterino, standing in the front door with a shotgun to fend looters off during the Nixon years. Back then, as the rest of the city decayed around it, the bar stood out as a dot of grimy light in a dying neighborhood.

Fifty years later, things got even worse, because the yuppies moved in. They built glass towers along the waterfront a few blocks away, and the seedy bars and dusty storefronts along Vernon Boulevard gave way to ultra-expensive gastropubs and sushi restaurants. Canterino was long dead by then, and its new owners couldn't keep making their rent payments, so they made a bad deal with The Dean. Don't blame them; it was either that or close the bar, which would have been transformed into a Starbucks clone within a year.

The Dean, whatever his faults, managed to keep the creditors and developers at bay, even if it meant throwing a particularly unctuous (in his words) real-estate bro off the roof of a nearby condo, which attracted far more media attention than he was used to. He also let the regulars keep drinking at the bar, with one unwritten rule: If anyone got out of line, he would settle things with a bat. That might sound harsh, but Canterino would have approved.

But the Pot O' Gold couldn't survive the Rough Riders.

Howard decided that they would wait until midnight, and then ride their horses all the way from The Hole to Long Island City. It was a whimsical move, possibly stupid, but he was feeling big on ceremony at the moment. He and the nineteen men who accompanied him kept their guns hidden beneath their jackets, at least, and they stuck to side-streets rather than the boulevards. Hipsters took photos with their camera phones as the posse passed, and that was okay—Howard felt that the NYPD would turn a blind eye to what they were about to do.

A block away from the Pot O' Gold, they encountered a lone sentry on a street corner, dressed like most of The Dean's men in a black suit, and dispatched by a single silenced shot that echoed off the elevated tracks above. They now had an angle on the bar itself, seemingly empty of life.

"The hell?" Howard said.

"We don't got to go in the place," Moustache said. "Just light it up."

Howard, always suspicious of a trap, dismounted and tethered his horse to a bus stop. He approached the bar from an angle, cautious. The windows were dark, the interior illuminated only by the reddish light from the exit signs.

Maybe it wasn't a trap, he thought. Maybe it was a gift.

He turned to Muttonchops. "You got the stuff?"

Muttonchops grinned, reaching into his saddlebag for the Molotov cocktail wrapped in layers of cloth. "Oh, hell yeah."

"Well, let's get a move on. We got other stops tonight."

# 26

**"WELL, THAT WAS** friggin' impressive," Fiona said, as they stood over the dead body of The Dean, which had toppled into the elevator doorway. The Dean's final expression was a snarl of extreme disgust.

"You have catlike reflexes, Simon." Bill stuffed his pistol into his waistband and bent to loot The Dean's pockets. "If you were ever part of a ping-pong league, you'd dominate. You should totally think about it."

Simon turned to Fiona. "Does he ever shut up?"

Fiona laughed. "No. And that's what I love about him."

From The Dean's inner pocket, Bill extracted an unsmoked cigar, examining its label in the firelight. "Cuban. Looking forward to smoking this."

Simon snapped his fingers. "That's mine. For reasons it would take too long to explain. Give it here."

With a theatrical frown, Bill handed the cigar over, and Simon slipped it into his mouth. "Fiona, you owe me some money," he said, as he pulled a gold lighter from his wrecked suit. "How much is in Bill's bag?"

"Maybe a million in currency," Fiona said. "And a lot of gold chunks."

Simon lit the tip of the cigar and puffed a velvety cloud. "I will take some of those chunks and leave you the rest. You are getting a significant discount, for saving my life, and for helping me take care of our friend here. He killed most of my men, but I have enough left to rebuild."

"Done," Fiona said, shooting Bill a warning glance before he could protest.

Shifting the cigar into the corner of his mouth, Simon walked over to the bag, which Bill had dropped at the foot of the closest pillar, and unzipped it. After a bit of rummaging, he returned with two lumps of gold in his right hand, the tendons in his forearm straining with the weight. "Quite the balls," he announced.

"That's what she said," Bill offered.

"I am going to take this car down, alone," Simon said, kicking The Dean's ribs until the body flopped into the elevator. "The Dean and I have a bit of business to conduct. A little bit of *quid pro quo* for my rug. Do not ask."

"I'll see you around," Fiona said.

Simon hit a button, and the grating rattled shut. "Always up for a chat," he called, unzipping his fly with his free hand as the elevator rumbled out of sight.

"I don't want to know what he's going to do," Bill said, hefting the duffel. "Shall we take the stairs down? I don't really want to wait for the elevator to come back up, considering the whole building's burning."

"Good idea," she said, pulling out her phone and dialing.

Walker picked up on the first ring. "How's it going, you crazy kids?"

"We're coming down." She slung the rifle onto her back. "The Dean's dead."

"Make it snappy," Walker said, all business. "I'm heading down to the street."

"On the way." As they trotted for the stairs on the far side of the floor, they passed the charred remains of Crow Man, an oversized joint still clutched in his blackened hand. She plucked the joint free, slipped it in her mouth, and bent her head to the oily flames snaking up a nearby pillar.

"Really?" Bill asked. "Really?"

Sweaty Fiona inhaled deep, held it, and blew a smoke ring. "It's been a long day."

Shaking his head, Bill resumed his zombie-like shuffle for the stairwell. Fiona took another puff before returning the joint to Crow Man's crisped grasp. It seemed like an appropriate gesture. There was too much adrenaline in her blood for the weed to mellow her out, but she hoped the chemicals would ease the pain in her joints until they could reach a real doctor.

Bill was waiting at the exit door, his back to her. She tapped him on the shoulder: "Come on, move."

"Can't," he said, and when she peeked around him, she saw the reason why: on the lower flight stood a young woman in an oversized nylon jacket. Her hair was tied back in a tight blonde ponytail, her face a bloodless mask in the dimness of the stairwell. She pointed a pistol at them, her hand steady.

Bill said: "Hello, Casey."

# 27

**THE PISTOL IN** Casey's hand trembled a little. It might have been a trick of the firelight behind them, but Fiona swore she saw a tear glinting on the woman's cheek. Fiona's hand skimmed the rifle-strap across her shoulders, but Bill was blocking any shot she could take. Damn.

"Back up," Fiona whispered in Bill's ear, thinking: I guess Dad left his sniper post a little too early. Would've been great to have him send a high-velocity round through this bitch's ear.

As they retreated through the doorway, Bill tossed the duffel bag aside. "Throw your guns, too." Casey said, waving the pistol. With two fingers, Fiona lifted the strap from her shoulder and lowered her rifle to the floor. Moving in slow motion, Bill reached into his waistband, lifted out his pistol by the grip, and tossed it away.

The flames had reached the nearest row of weed plants, which popped and sizzled alight, the heat baking the back of Fiona's neck. The sight of the burning forest made Casey hesitate in the doorway. "The hell is this place?"

"Belonged to our old boss," Bill said.

Casey wiped the sweat from her forehead. "Same guys you were running from?"

"Yeah," Fiona said, pulling Bill after her. If they retreated, gave this girl a little space, they might have more options. "Why are you here?"

Casey's lips wavered, along with her gun-hand. "Why do you think?"

"We killed your family?" Bill offered.

"Yes," Casey said. "It took me so long to find you…"

"You hit us in the car. On the highway." Fiona circled wide, away from the fires, tugging Bill. They could hear, over the rumble of the dying building, the first sirens.

"Yes. I took a shot at you, too," Casey said. "At the vet?"

Fiona remembered crashing through the front door of that Oklahoma farmhouse and finding Casey on the couch, a girl crushed under the weight of her family history. The girl who fled into the night, rather than fight and kill with the rest of her clan. "You're a good tracker," Fiona said. "I admire that."

"Stop moving," Casey said, raising the gun an inch.

Fiona took another step back, and stopped. They were five feet from the edge of the building, the wind snapping at her hair. A storm of orange sparks drifted past, flickering, gone. She gripped a handful of Bill's shirt and tugged to the right, slightly, positioning him.

"Casey," Bill said. "Can you tell my girlfriend here that we didn't do anything in that bar? That you just knocked me out?"

"Hush," Fiona whispered in his ear.

The barrel of the pistol loomed as large as a highway tunnel as Casey came closer, her eyes unleashing the full waterworks, tears dripping off her chin. "I know my people did you wrong," she sniffed. "I do. But blood is blood."

"I'm sorry we killed them," Fiona said. "I'd like to think they understood."

"Okay then." Casey nodded, and her finger drifted over the safety and hammer of the pistol, making sure everything was set properly. She took a deep breath. "Okay."

Before Casey's finger could find the trigger, Fiona braced her hands against Bill's back and shoved as hard as she could, sending her boyfriend toppling into Casey's knees. Casey fell backward, her pistol clattering away. Squawking Bill scrambled after the weapon, and Fiona leapt over him to grab a handful of Casey's jacket.

Casey thrashed, but Fiona was having none of it tonight. She lifted Casey into the air and spun, Casey's boots scraping the edge of the abyss. Every muscle in Fiona's arms burned like the forest behind them. It would have been so easy to loosen her grip, to let the night have this damaged soul. And yet she held fast.

"I'm sorry," Casey said.

"You're fine," Fiona said through gritted teeth, although nothing about this situation was fine at all. "You still have choices."

"Sure." Casey let her head flop back, scanning the ground so far below.

Fiona's arms quivered as she shifted, dragging Casey a foot to the left. "In this life, there's no safe harbor, okay? Remember that, and you'll be fine. When you wake up, get away from the building."

"When I…" Casey's eyes widened.

"Sorry." Fiona tossed her.

Bill rolled to the edge in time to witness Casey crash through four debris nets bolted to the building exterior—slowing her fall considerably—before she landed on a huge pile of sand beside the lobby doors. "Think she'll ever walk again?" he asked.

"Hey, I was gentle." Fiona returned to the duffel bag. Hopefully they wouldn't need to carry this damn thing much longer. Her AR-15 would be a little too conspicuous once they reached the street, so she took Casey's pistol from Bill and shoved it down the back of her jeans.

"Did you mean what you said?" Bill asked.

"About no safe harbor?" Fiona jutted her chin at the streets far below, frantic with colored lights as an army of fire trucks converged on the building. "There's none for us, if we don't get out of here right now."

# 28

**A BURNING TABLE** smashed into the dumpsters to their right, lighting the way as Fiona and Bill trotted for the rear fence. Neither looked back as the top two floors of the building vaporized in a cloud of fire and dust, and a pillar of fragrant smoke rose into the night sky. Crow Man would have been proud: by morning, half of western Queens had a contact high from his final batch of weed.

On the sidewalk, they headed left, away from the fire-trucks screaming for the construction site's front gate. The first responders from the NYPD would likely arrive in minutes, and if they blocked off the surrounding streets, that would create some real problems. What do you say if a cop sees your clothes splattered with blood, your face covered in ash, and a bag filled with crisp hundred-dollar bills on your back? *Oh yeah, just out for a stroll, officer. By the way, I have a really big gun.*

As they scurried across the intersection, her phone buzzed. Fiona pushed Bill into the cover of a warehouse doorway and answered it.

"Where are you?" Walker asked.

"A block away," she said. "You got a car?"

The brick wall across the street flickered blue and red. A siren chirped, and she heard the growing roar of a powerful engine. The first cop had arrived.

"Yeah," Walker said. "I got a car."

"There's a warehouse to the north of the construction site," Fiona said, trying to press further into the shadows, Bill's breath loud in her other ear. "We're in the doorway, but it's a crappy hiding place."

The police cruiser appeared, slowing at the intersection. Its spotlight played over the road, the fence, the wall to their right. Behind her, Bill rattled the doorknob. "Locked," he whispered.

The spotlight hit the doorway, so bright they had to squint. Fiona readied for the megaphoned voice telling them to step out, place their hands on their heads, get on their knees. She had the pistol, of course, but hated the idea of shooting a cop who wasn't crooked.

"There you are," Walker shouted out the cruiser's open window. "Come on, what are you waiting for?"

"Is that you?" Fiona stepped out of the doorway, raising a hand to shield her eyes. The brightness made it impossible to see the figure behind the wheel.

"No, it's Santa Claus." Walker sounded impatient. "I borrowed a cop car. Come on."

"When I was three, you told me Santa Claus didn't exist," Fiona yelled.

"Just preparing you for the real world, baby. Bill, come on."

Grinning Bill had already trotted past her to open the front passenger door. He stepped aside and bowed, ushering her into the seat. She saw her father behind the wheel, silhouetted by the smoky glow of the burning building, and remembered that long-ago night in Delaware, when he had come to save her at the mall.

"Describe this 'borrow a cop car' thing," she said, ducking into the front seat with the bag in her lap. Bolted to the dashboard was a stack of radios and a computer screen in a thick plastic frame. Between that and the canvas rifle-bag stuffed into her footwell, she found it a tough squeeze.

"Cop car stopped right in front of the building where I was." Walker tapped a command on the keyboard built into the console between their seats, and the screen displayed lines of dispatch codes. "Two officers. I didn't kill them, don't worry. I left them cuffed and gagged."

"Good to see you, sir," Bill said from the backseat. "Can we get out of here?"

"Pretty boy, you look like shit," Walker said, and activated the siren. The cruiser had a real beast of an engine: when he stomped on the gas, it went from zero to light-speed in under three seconds. At the next intersection, he did some fast wheelwork, cornering hard enough to press Fiona against her window.

That would have been the one good thing about becoming a cop, Fiona mused. You could drive like this with impunity, never worrying about someone pulling you over. Back when I was a teenager, and took that officer's car, I should have spent a little more time behind the wheel, squeeze some extra fun out of it. Then again, if I'd done that, they would have arrested me, and my life would have worked out totally different. Maybe in some alternate universe, I'm working in an office somewhere, bored out of my skull.

"You okay?" Walker asked.

"Feeling nostalgic," she said. "Remember that time I ended up in that mall, and you had to come and get me?"

"Sure," he said. "Probably your most idiotic moment as a kid."

Bill stuck his fingers through the grating that separated the seats, skimming the back of her neck. "What happened?" he asked.

"Nothing," Fiona said. "Doesn't matter. You got a new car lined up, Dad?"

"There's always a car lined up, you have the right tools." He peered through the windshield, scanning the street. He seemed distracted.

"We okay?" Fiona asked.

"Should be. I expected someone else to maybe show up, but no sign of them. Probably for the best." He studied her in the light of the dashboard screen. "You look like you could use a doctor."

"Know anyone good? I have a guy, Trevor, but I think this is a little outside his skillset."

"Trevor, your ex?"

"Yes, my ex-boyfriend."

Walker winked. "Oh yeah, he was great. How's he doing?"

In the backseat, Bill leaned back and sighed, loudly enough for Walker to lock eyes with him in the rearview mirror. "How's it going back there, Bill?" Walker asked. "Comfortable? I know it's not your first time in the backseat of a cruiser."

"Nothing like a cop car," Bill said.

"I got a guy," Walker said, turning to Fiona. "Physician at Mount Sinai, runs a private office on the side, let's say. Limited hours. We can head there once we dump the car. You going to make it?"

Fiona nodded. "Yeah. Thank you, by the way. We wouldn't have made it otherwise."

A raindrop spattered the windshield, then another. Fiona's heart leapt. Nothing like a nighttime storm to make you a little more invisible. She was smiling, about to say something in praise of the weather, when the world exploded in shattered glass and screaming metal.

# 29

**TWO CAR ACCIDENTS** in one day?

Seriously, what were the odds?

If you're a fugitive on the run, the chances are probably high, although that failed to comfort Fiona as she ran her hands over her body. No wounds, but her guts felt stuffed with ice, making her shiver. That was shock, her old friend, setting up housekeeping.

The police cruiser had flipped upside down, leaving Walker and Fiona suspended by their seatbelts. The cash bag had tumbled to the ceiling, now the floor, along with Walker's rifle bag. She could turn her head enough to see the backseat. Bill was pressed against the grating, bleeding from the head but still conscious.

"Really?" Bill muttered. "Really?"

"Brace yourself," Walker said, placing his hand on her seatbelt release, so she planted her feet on the dashboard and locked her legs. He hit the button, and she let her body sag to the ceiling. As she did, her left side crackled with fresh pain. From her new angle, she could see headlights reflecting through the shattered glass of the passenger windows.

"Who," she said, helping Walker unlock his seatbelt.

Walker's slow somersault ended with them shoulder-to-shoulder. He squinted at the other car. "Friends of mine," he said, turning to yank his door handle. The driver's side door squeaked halfway open before slamming into a parked car. Walker scrambled out, keeping low.

*"Walker,"* someone yelled beyond the headlights. *"We just want to talk."*

Walker rolled his eyes. "Come on, move."

In the backseat, Bill smacked the handles. "I'm stuck in here," he said, voice high with panic.

"Kick, baby," Fiona said, grabbing Walker's rifle bag by the canvas handle and dragging it after her, over the smashed radios and dashboard screen. The pavement was hard on her elbows as she crawled after Walker, toward the rear of the cruiser. Bill slammed both feet into the window a foot from her face, cracking it into a gummy mess, scattering bits of glass over Walker, who held up a hand and snarled.

"Sorry," Bill said.

*"Fine,"* shouted the voice beyond the light, and Fiona, hearing the metallic click of safeties, gripped Bill by the ankles and yanked as hard as her bruised muscles allowed, dragging him over broken glass and the window's crumpled sill into the narrow space between two parked vehicles. Walker behind her, on the sidewalk, crouched behind an ultra-compact Smart coupe that looked barely sturdy enough to resist a spitball, much less the fusillade they knew was coming.

It took only ten seconds for five automatic rifles to exhaust their clips, but the explosions seemed to last forever to Fiona, tangled in the gutter with Bill and the rifle bag. Bits of glass and metal rained on them as bullets shredded the parked cars. A stray shot or twelve hit something inside the cruiser, and the siren shrieked once before falling silent.

"Who are they?" Fiona hissed at Walker, who had drawn a pistol from his jacket.

"Tell you later," Walker said, inching his head to the window of the coupe. The angle of the headlights made it hard to see much, but he picked out Sully's lanky silhouette on the passenger side of the attacking vehicle. Shadows scurried around him, men finding new positions.

Walker poked his pistol onto the window-sill and fired three times at Sully, who disappeared from view. Another flicker, to his left. Walker shifted and fired again, and this time someone screeched like a rabbit caught in a trap.

Between the parked cars, Fiona felt for the pistol in her waistband. It was missing. Had it slipped out? Was it still in the cruiser?

"Walker," Sully called. "Who's that with you? Your kid? How sweet."

Another burst of rifle-fire chewed the edge of the coupe, sending its crumpled rear fender into the gutter. Walker swiveled his head to examine the street. In the chaos and adrenaline of the crash, he had failed to notice the Queensboro Bridge looming in the distance, its steel and stone lit a sickly yellow, shimmery in the soft rain. They were still in that industrial area of chop-shops and boarded-up warehouses that ran like an ancient vein through the shiny new Queens.

Walker edged his head up and fired again, aiming this time at the headlights. One shattered. He ducked as a burst of automatic fire skipped off the coupe's hood.

"That's the best you got?" Sully sounded closer, somewhere to the left.

Fiona dug into Walker's bag, feeling rifle pieces, no time to assemble, damn. The ringing in her ears had quieted enough for her to hear a dull thud.

"Hey, what's this?" Sully asked.

The explosion transformed Sully's big black car into a Detroit-made skyrocket, rising into the rainy sky on a pillar of fire. It managed to ascend twenty feet before jealous gravity brought it crashing back to earth in a storm of sparks and oily smoke. The overturned police cruiser blocked Fiona, Bill, and Walker from the worst of the flames. Raindrops sizzled into steam on hot metal.

Beneath Fiona, Bill was shouting something. She bent her ear close to his mouth, straining to hear him say: "Surprise."

She shouted back: "What?"

Bill held up his left index finger, ringed with a grenade pin. "Got it off a body when I left the panic room. Put it in the money bag."

Kissing him on the cheek, Fiona rose to a crouch. Despite the chemical smoke stinging her eyes, she could pick out one, two, three bodies scattered on the wet road, none moving. If a big car held five people, that meant two others still alive, maybe.

Walker stood, a two-handed grip on his pistol as he side-stepped from behind the coupe. He had never liked explosives. At least with a gun you knew the direction of force. When you blew something up, all sorts of unexpected things could happen. Even so, whatever Bill had done had tied things up quite nicely.

Three dead bodies, and a big chap trying to crawl toward the darkness on the far side of the street, leaving a black smear behind him. Based on that stupendous amount of blood left on the pavement, Walker guessed the guy had a minute or two before he kicked the bucket. Where was Sully?

"Walker," Sully said.

Walker turned and saw Sully on the far side of the pyre, illuminated by flame, his glorious moustache drooping with rainwater. He had a submachine gun in one hand, barrel pointed down. He was trying to pop in a new magazine, but something was wrong with his other hand, his sleeve gleaming bright with blood. Walker noted the bits of window-glass glittering like diamonds in Sully's cheeks and forehead.

"Just wanted a chat," Sully said, and laughed. It sounded bubbly. The magazine dropped from his hand, clattering off his boot. He looked at it and shrugged.

"Yeah, a friendly chat," Walker said, nodding at the dead men with rifles in their hands.

Sully shrugged, his knees wobbling. "I guess you're not a Fe—"

Walker shot Sully clean through the head and tossed the pistol through the window of the burning car. Without pause, he turned on his heel and walked around the cruiser, finding Bill and Fiona on the sidewalk with their bag of money. "You didn't mention you were carrying around explosives," he said to Bill.

"Be prepared." Bill smiled.

Walker pinched Bill's cheek as he took the rifle bag from Fiona. "Well, I'm glad you showed a little initiative," he said. "You can come kill folks with me anytime."

"Can we get out of here?" Fiona groaned.

"So much for bonding." Walker shouldered his rifle bag and started north, toward the bridge, mulling contingencies. Neither cop had gotten a good look at his face when he stole the cruiser. With any luck, the police would take the path of least resistance and pin the theft on Sully.

Bill and Fiona did their best to keep pace with Walker's loping form, but their wounds made it hard to move at anything close to regular speed. If she put her weight on her right leg, Fiona found, she could limp pretty well. She wanted to ask her father about the dead men back there, but he seemed intent on getting as far from the burning car as possible. For Walker, this was just another Tuesday.

# 30

**I WAS WAITING** on the front stoop when my ex-wife slammed through the back door of her new home, an overstuffed garbage bag in one hand. Thursdays at nine; that was her trash day and hour, regular as clockwork for twenty years. I'd spent my entire life trying to be as unpredictable as possible, as a matter of survival, and still managed to marry the equivalent of a Swiss watch. Opposites attract, and all that.

Leonore stopped in her tracks, staring at me with an expression that I wished was wonder, but there was probably a hefty dose of horror in there, too, for good measure. "Surprise," I said, raising my eyebrows. "Happy to see me?"

She dropped the trash bag. Plop. I was sitting on the steps, my hands in my lap, probably dirtying the rear of my wonderful jumpsuit, but presenting no threat whatsoever. My harmlessness must not have sunk in, though, because she retreated for her front door, her hand darting into her jeans. If she called the police, I would have a problem. "Not here to cause trouble," I called. "I just need a minute of your time. One minute, for all our years together."

She stopped. Looked up and down her quiet street. Her

shoulders slumped, and she said: "Fine, okay. But if Scotty comes out, he'll kick your ass."

"Who's Scotty?"

"New boyfriend."

"He live here?"

"No, he's down in Park Slope. But he works at a place in Queensboro Plaza, so he stays here most nights." She descended a few steps toward me, her hands in her pockets. The shadows made it hard to see her face.

"I'm not here long," I said. "I just wanted to stop by."

"You could have knocked."

"Didn't want to cause trouble."

"Well, that's a first. What do you want?"

"Just to say that I'm sorry, not that it matters much. That I'm glad you're finding a new life."

She swallowed, her throat clicking. Shuffling her feet. "Thank you," she said, quietly.

"You're welcome." I stood, brushing the back of the jumpsuit as I did so, hoping it wasn't smeared.

"What's with the outfit? You going to a costume party or something?"

"No. Just drawing some power from the King, you know?"

She shook her head. "No. I don't know."

"I thought I had something to do tonight. Then I thought better of it. Now I'm looking for something new of my own."

Her head dipped to her chest. "Just as long as we're getting confessions out of the way, I want to say: I wished you were dead. I'm sorry for that. You deserve to be happy, even if you've done some bad things."

"No, you didn't."

Her head snapped up, and despite the dimness I could see the old fire in her eyes. "I'm sorry, are you actually telling me how I felt?"

I raised my hands in mock surrender. "No, I'm not. I'm sure you felt that way. What I'm saying is, me being dead wouldn't have been in your best interest. You would have regretted that wish."

"Why is that?"

"Because I'd made arrangements. If I died, a couple of guys were supposed to take my body and throw it in a freezer. They were going to wait until you were in a new relationship, and then they were going to catapult my frozen body right into your bedroom window at midnight."

"What the fuck?"

"I told them to nail an envelope to my chest before they launched me." I was trying hard not to laugh. "Inside the envelope, a piece of paper that said: 'Best wishes on your new endeavors.' It was going to be a cheerful goodbye. I mean, once you cleaned up the mess."

She snorted. "You are so fucking insane it's unbelievable. I can't believe I slept with you, much less married you."

"Hey, it would have been a beautiful gift. Any man who endured all that and still stuck with you? They'd definitely be a keeper."

"You're sick. Fucking sick."

"You know I'm joking. Can you imagine how much money it'd cost to build a full-size catapult? The knuckleheads I tend to run with, do you think they'd actually do what I asked?"

"I'm so regretting so many things right now."

"Oh, come on, baby, you can't say it wasn't fun."

"It wasn't fun all the time."

"It was never boring."

She struggled not to smile. "I'll agree there. It wasn't boring. And it could be fun. At moments. I guess."

"I'll take that." I descended to the sidewalk. "You take care of yourself, you hear? I'll be thinking of you."

"Yeah, you too." She stood on the stoop, watching as I made my way down the block. I glanced back once before I turned the corner, and she was still there. I was sorry our marriage hadn't worked out, but its survival might have been impossible from the start. Creatures like me, I think we're meant to be alone, no matter how deeply we believe in true love. But there's always hope, isn't there?

It was starting to rain, the drops cool and perfect on my skin. I had nowhere to go, so I kept walking west, through the neighborhoods of polite houses and then the looming towers of glass and steel, until I reached the iron juggernaut of the Queensboro Bridge, ascending toward heaven. Faint booms from somewhere south, possibly fireworks, possibly gunfire. It didn't matter—I just wanted to lose myself in the rhythm of walking through the dark, feeling my heartbeat loud in my ears, my breath whistling up my throat.

By the time I reached Manhattan, walking didn't seem like enough of a channel for this newfound feeling of freedom boiling up in me, so I paused on the wet pavement and decided to see if I could really channel the King. His music loud in my soul, I skidded left, then right, before unleashing a stunning series of karate chops. I didn't care about The Dean anymore, or Bill and Fiona, or even death itself. For the first time since I was a kid, I was free.

# 31



**BENEATH THE BRIDGE,** Walker paused beside a boxy car that looked older than Fiona, its white flanks spotted with rust, its backseat stuffed with plastic bags and other trash. Walker lifted the rifle bag and drove it hard into the driver's side window, shattering it, before reaching in and unlocking the doors. "Vintage," he told them. "Just like me."

"Positively ancient," Fiona said, climbing into the back with Bill.

Walker slid into the driver's seat and sorted through the junk in the console. "Hey, it's our lucky night," he said, holding up a screwdriver.

As Walker bent to the ignition, stabbing and prying, Bill asked: "Who were those guys?"

"Old friend," Walker said, fiddling with wires. "Got paranoid, thought I was a Fed. He was the one I was trying to lure into a trap, back at that construction site, but he didn't show in time. Too bad he found us after."

The car sputtered to life, its frame shuddering. Walker flicked on the lights and the windshield wipers. "Where to?"

Where indeed? For the first time in what felt like forever, they had no pursuers. It was an odd sensation, not being hunted. Fiona would need time to get used to it. "Doctor," she said. "Then we're getting out of this damn city, at least for a little while."

Walker nodded, worked the gearshift, and started off. The hit the onramp to the bridge and swept across the East River, toward the bright lights of Manhattan and the darkness of America beyond. The rain came down harder, smearing the world into streaks of color.

Bill leaned into her and asked: "You remember what our friend in Oklahoma told us to do?"

She pressed into him. "Duck or we'll get shot?"

"No, right before the end." His voice lowered. "He said we needed to get married, specifically at a chapel in Vegas."

"You're kidding," she said.

"No, I'm not. You remember." Taking her hand, he slipped the grenade pin over her ring finger.

"Oh shit," Walker groaned, watching them in the rear-view mirror.

"Walker, your opinion is noted," Bill said, staring into Fiona's eyes.

"Okay. I mean, yes. Yes, I will." Fiona wiped at her cheeks. "When we make this legal, which fake identities are we going to use on the marriage certificate?"

"We'll make new ones. Fresh start."

"I'm going to be sick," Walker muttered, but he was smiling.

"Careful," Fiona growled, "or I'm not inviting you."

"Well, I already got your wedding present," Walker said. "Thanks to some work I did earlier, the FBI is already off your ass, along with a big chunk of law enforcement. It's not a totally clean slate, but it's probably as close as you're going to get."

"Daddy, you're the best."

Bill settled back in his seat, musing about clean sheets and healed skin, good suits and Fiona pressed warmly against him in the dark. He squeezed Fiona's hand, hard, and she squeezed back. We're safe, he realized. Maybe I don't deserve it, and maybe it's not for long, but we're safe.

Walker hit the off-ramp. As they swept into Manhattan, Bill glimpsed a figure in gleaming white on the sidewalk. It was a man in a rhinestone Elvis costume, hair swept up in a rockabilly pompadour, boots splashing in the puddles as he boogied his heart out. Elvis saw their car and leapt into a wide stance, one hand above his head, the other pointed at them. Thank ya, the gesture said. Thank ya very much.

# ACKNOWLEDGMENT

**LOVE & BULLETS** wouldn't exist without Ron Earl Phillips, the founder and publisher of Shotgun Honey. Over the past several years, he's published and guided a stunning number of noir and hardboiled writers, and his taste is always impeccable.

As this trilogy shambled to life, it was vastly improved by input by Jen Conley, Angel Luis Colón, Scott Adlerberg, and other great writers whose books you should track down right now. Others whose input and encouragement helped immeasurably included Douglas Sonders, Lucien Sims, Mark Feffer, Ramyar Rastan, Anthony Francavilla, and Rachael Steimnitz. I'm also grateful to Thomas Wörtche, who edited the German version of *Love & Bullets* (which first got me thinking about it as a single volume), and Stefan Lux, who translated it.

Writing is often a lonely profession, and it's the readers who get us through—not just by buying our books, but also by sending us emails, leaving reviews, and generally spreading the word. We're eternally in your debt.

This book is for G., my quarantine warrior.

NK
New York, NY
July 24, 2020

**NICK KOLAKOWSKI IS** the Derringer Award-nominated author of "Maxine Unleashes Doomsday," "Boise Longpig Hunting Club," and "Rattlesnake Rodeo." He lives and writes in New York City. Visit him virtually at nickkolakowski.com.

## Sangre Road

A Moses Kincaid Crime Novel
David Tromblay

April 2021
978-1-64396-191-0

## Houses Burning and Other Ruins

William R. Soldan

Shotgun Honey
May 2021
978-1-64396-115-6

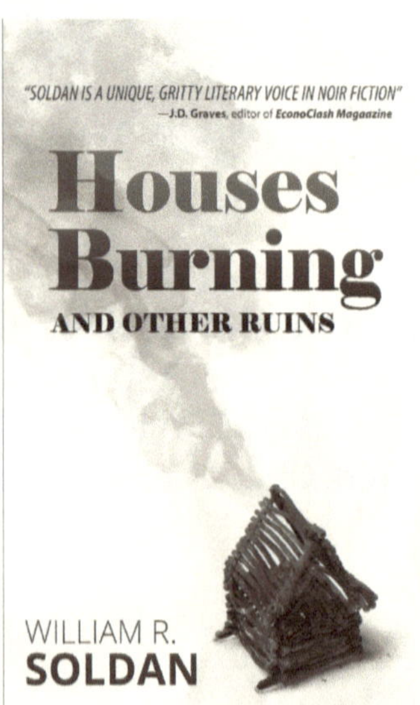


## FIND YOUR NEXT BOOK

shotgunhoneybooks.com